"WE WOULDN'T WANT TO DISAPPOINT THE NEIGHBORS, WOULD WE?" HE ASKED, SMILING DOWN AT HER.

"You wouldn't dare."

Was she issuing a warning? Or a challenge? Alex scooped Kate up in his arms.

"You'd better relax, honey. We don't want the neighbors to talk."

She glared at him. "I'll relax when you put me down."

Alex stepped into the house and kicked the door closed behind him. His shoe caught in the carpeting. They both went down.

Kate's arms were wrapped around his neck, her face inches from his.

Words filled his head. Words like *soft. Warm. Velvety*. Words like *heat*. A rush of fire exploded in his gut.

He allowed himself a small smile. "I'll put you down when I'm good and ready."

Connie Lane

Reinventing Romeo

A Dell Book

Published by
Dell Publishing
a division of
Random House, Inc.
1540 Broadway
New York, New York 10036

This is a work of fiction. Names, characters, places, and incidents either are the product of the author's imagination or are used fictitiously. Any resemblance to actual persons, living or dead, events, or locales is entirely coincidental.

ISBN: 0-440-23593-6

Manufactured in the United States of America

Published simultaneously in Canada

December 2000

10 9 8 7 6 5 4 3 2 1
OPM

To the people and the city of Cleveland.
Thanks for the memories!

Special thanks to the bingo players at
St. John Nepomucene Church,
my polka-loving relatives,
and bowlers everywhere!

1

The last time she had seen Alex Romero, he was wearing nothing but one of those swimsuits that show off way more of a man's body than they cover.

It was blue. A shade darker than the aqua Caribbean where he moved through the waves like a fierce, irresistible Aztec god. Water sparkled off every delicious inch of his tanned body. Sunlight dappled hair the color of Colombian coffee.

The swimsuit was tapered enough to make the most of his broad shoulders. Small enough to show off his washboard abs and rock-hard stomach. Tight enough to ignite any number of fantasies.

Every one of which came back to Kate Ellison in a flash that sent her cheeks flaming and a twin fire sparking through her insides.

This was not the time—or the place—and just to remind herself, she looked around the conference table where she was seated. On her left was a grim-faced man in a pin-striped suit, a man who just happened to be her immediate superior. On her right sat a tight-lipped representative of the New York City Police Department. An attractive middle-aged woman from the mayor's office sat next to him. She was dressed all in red and she didn't bother to introduce herself. She assumed everyone knew who she was.

Two plainclothes detectives sat directly across from Kate, their backs to the breathtaking view outside the floor-to-ceiling windows of the forty-sixth-floor office suite. She'd worked with them for the last nine months—not always amicably. Now they were finally close to blowing the top off a money-laundering scheme the likes of which even this town hadn't seen in years, and the cops made no secret of what they thought of having what they optimistically called "their work" usurped by the FBI.

And then there was Alex Romero.

Kate reined in her wild fantasies. She forced herself to forget the image of Romero in his swimsuit, the one she—and at least a couple million other women—had drooled over when it appeared on the cover of a popular supermarket tabloid under the headline *World's Sexiest Man—Millionaire Playboy Romero Is Jet Set Romeo*.

It took more willpower than she knew she had to convince Kate that a long, heartrending sigh wasn't wise. Or professional. If a picture was worth a thousand words, the real Alex Romero—live, in person, and in an incredible package of poise, polish, and a suit that looked like it cost more than she made in a month—was worth more than any of the photographs of him that regularly graced the fashion magazines, the gossip pages, and the tabloids.

He was a smidgen under six feet tall, with the chiseled features and dark eyes so many women all over the world dreamed about. Though Kate had been introduced to him only a few short minutes earlier, she already knew that he more than lived up to his legend. He was confident. Sophisticated. Aristocratic. Even sexier in person than he was in print.

And a lot more formidable.

He was enough of a tactician to realize the strongest

position in the room was at the head of the table. And conscious enough of the image that had been built around him by an army of corporate spin doctors to keep his trademark bottle of Dom Pérignon '86 iced in a Waterford crystal bucket at his elbow. For those times—the gossipmongers all said—when he had yet another ubiquitous stroke of investment genius, or another corporate triumph, or another female conquest to celebrate.

There was no doubt about it: Alex Romero was the Romeo of the tabloids. He had the patrician good looks of his Cuban ancestors, the razor-sharp mind of a man who'd attended all the best schools, and the breeding that could come only from belonging to the right country clubs.

Right then, he was also in something of a snit.

"You can't possibly know what you're asking." With the slow lift of one eyebrow, Romero let them know exactly what he thought of the plan they'd proposed.

It was not the response Kate was expecting from a man she had assumed would be reasonable, one who was apparently intelligent enough to run a corporation that employed more people than lived in some third-world countries. A little disappointed, she sat up in her seat and watched as Romero rose from his chrome-and-leather chair and leaned forward, his hands flat against the polished marble tabletop. As eminently composed as he was obviously piqued, he flashed a look down the long table. "Are you out of your minds?"

"It's only for four months." Mark Harrison, the special agent in charge of local FBI operations and Kate's boss, was enough of an old warhorse not to be intimidated. Or at least not to show it. He poked one finger at the report on the table in front of him. "We've been through it all before. Our people talked to your people. Your people were supposed to talk to you, and—"

One of Romero's hands went up, stopping Mark midsentence. Romero shot a look toward a bespectacled, balding man who stood behind the massive desk that dominated the far end of the room. Early on in her investigation, Kate had talked to Norbert Fielding. She knew he served as a combination man Friday and confidant to Romero, but the look his boss gave him made her wonder how much longer he'd stay in the inner circle. And out of the unemployment lines.

"My people," Romero said, "were told not to talk to your people." He shifted his gaze back to Mark. "My people were told to tell you we'd see you when the time was right. In court."

Mark could be the very soul of discretion, but apparently, even he found it hard to believe they were meeting a brick wall. "It's not as bad as it sounds," he said in the conciliatory voice his direct reportees hardly ever heard. "Believe me. We've got all the details worked out. If you'd like to look this over . . ." When he offered a slim stack of papers and Romero firmly refused to even glance at it, Mark's cheeks went dusky. "Four months isn't forever. After the trial is over, you can get back to your life."

"Impossible!" Romero's snort of derision could only be described as monumental. "I have business to conduct. Important business. A man of my stature simply can't disappear. Not for four months. Not for four days. A corporation like this doesn't run itself. Not when you've got seventeen different divisions reporting to one office. And to one man." He allowed the barest of smiles to touch his lips. "Me."

Mark didn't smile back. "That's all well and good," he said. "But—"

"There are no buts." Fitfully, Romero undid the button on the jacket of his impeccably tailored navy suit. He paced to the windows and, one arm braced against the glass, leaned forward, his back to the room. Obviously he was used to having the last word in any conversation, and just as obviously he was telling them that the topic was no longer open for discussion.

The two detectives shuffled their feet and the papers on the table in front of them. The man from the police commissioner's office looked up at the ceiling. The woman representing the mayor studied her red nail polish.

"Spoiled son-of-a—" Mark's growl was loud enough for only Kate to hear. She stifled a smile and sat back to watch, more interested now in how the game was being played out than she was fascinated by Alex Romero.

It was funny how quickly reality could chase away fantasies, especially for a woman as down-to-earth as Kate.

No illusions or delusions.

Wasn't that what she always said about herself?

It hadn't taken her long to see through the illusion that was Alex Romero. And as for delusions that his personality might actually match the fantasy lover she'd built in her head?

She smiled again, then erased the expression before Mark could see it and wonder why one of his most dependable special agents was suddenly acting like a lunatic in a situation that was far from funny. Free of Romero's spell, she was able to assess the man objectively for the first time.

She would have had to be completely without imagination not to appreciate the dramatic silhouette he made against the glass. But this time when she let her gaze skim over his shoulders, she noticed not how broad they were, but how stiffly he held them. Mulish to the last. His head was turned for effect, his chin firm and inflexible. Just like his personality.

Kate wondered how long he would stand that way and pretend they didn't exist. But even as soon as the question presented itself, she knew the answer. He would stand there forever if he had to. He would do anything, to anyone, any time, to get what he wanted. And right now, Alex Romero wanted to be left alone.

Surprisingly it was the woman from the mayor's office who had the nerve to break the silence. She cleared her throat, coughed politely. "I suppose, Alex, that you're worried about the meeting of the city business leaders' consortium." It was more of a question than a statement, as if she were testing the waters before she took the chance of dipping a toe into them. "The meeting is scheduled for July and if everything goes as planned, you'd be gone in July." She sighed and drummed her nails against the tabletop. "It would be something of a problem, of course."

"Something of a problem?" Romero's statement was an echo of the woman's, but it contained far more cynicism than Kate imagined the woman ever would have dared. "I've got thirteen hundred invitations out. The most influential journalists . . . the most powerful businessmen . . ." Even a man as articulate as Romero couldn't find the words to voice his outrage. He closed one hand into a fist. "Do you have any idea what you're asking, Sophia? You and the mayor don't honestly think I sit here twiddling my thumbs all day, do you? Tell me you don't really believe that."

The woman folded her hands on the table in front of her. Kate couldn't help but notice they were trembling just a little. "Alex." She aimed a smile at his back, one that wavered just a bit around the edges. "Of course the mayor doesn't think that at all. He's worried about you. As an important member of this community. And as a friend. He told me to assure you that the consortium is in good hands. We've already contacted Bill Gates, and—"

"Gates?"

Kate didn't think Romero's back could get any stiffer. It did.

She didn't think his voice could be any chillier.

But the single word contained all the warmth of an iceberg.

Any other time—in any other circumstances—Kate would have found Romero's whole performance laughable. But there was more at stake here than Romero being upstaged at some event that sounded more like a media circus than a business meeting.

He was messing with the case. *Her* case. And she'd be damned if she'd see it doomed from the start by some pampered Romeo who was more worried about his image than he was about his testimony.

Out of patience, she slapped closed the leather portfolio that sat on the table in front of her and pushed back her chair. It wasn't until she was already on her feet that she even bothered to think about what she was doing, and by that time, it was too late. Every eye in the place was on her—all but Romero's—but right then, he was the least of her problems. Mark Harrison didn't stop her. He must have thought she had a plan.

Now all she had to do was come up with one.

Stalling for time, Kate scraped a hand through her shoulder-length light brown hair. "He's right," she said, with a look toward Romero. Had he bothered to look at the expression on her face, he would have seen that she didn't think he was right at all. "Mr. Romero is absolutely right. He wants to stay in town until July so he can host his important business meeting, who are we to stop him?"

In one quick movement, she reached for her black leather purse, pulled it open, and grabbed for the first folding money she could find. It was a five, and she waved it in the air for everyone to see, then tossed it into the center of the table. "I say we let him continue with business as usual," she suggested to no one in particular. "But I want to be the first one to bet that if he does, he won't be alive in July."

Her statement wasn't as outrageous as it sounded, and they all knew it. Apparently, so did Romero. He turned to face her.

For one split second, she thought he might actually show some emotion. She was wrong. Tightly restrained and totally in control, he skimmed an icy glance from the toes of her functional black pumps, up her sensible gray suit and white oxford-cloth shirt, to the top of her head.

"Who are you?" he asked.

"Special Agent Kate Ellison. FBI." Convinced that

any sign of weakness would be a tactical error, Kate met look for look. "We were introduced. When the meeting started."

Of course Romero remembered. Something told her he never forgot a face. Or a name. Or a woman. He waved away her explanation with one well-shaped hand. "Yes. Yes. I know that. I remember that. What I mean is, who are you? What gives you the right to—"

"This is my case, Mr. Romero." Kate ignored the outraged looks on the faces of the two New York cops. They weren't putting their necks on the line. Not like she was. She'd fight with them later about her choice of words. "I'm the one who's been eating and breathing and sleeping it these past nine months. We've finally got all the evidence we need and we've finally got you, someone with the guts to testify. I don't know about anybody else in this room"—she gave them all a quick look—"but I'm not willing to lose everything I've worked so hard for just because you're too pig-headed to—"

"Special Agent Ellison!"

It was the man from the commissioner's office, and Kate didn't have to look at him to know he was telling her she'd overstepped her boundaries. With an effort that left her knuckles white, she contained her anger and decided on another tack.

"Look . . ." Kate's voice was just about as unsteady as her stomach suddenly felt. She drew in a long breath, hoping to settle them both. "You're a pretty successful businessman, Mr. Romero." It was an understatement, but she didn't give Romero a chance to point that out. "You understand about fighting your way to the top. I've got a secret to share with you. I'm planning on using this case to make a name for myself. I deserve it. I've worked long and hard. I've talked to hundreds of people. I've read thousands of pages of information. I've looked at so many numbers on so many computer screens, my eyes hurt just thinking about it. I'm not going to let you blow it for me by getting yourself gunned down by some two-bit hit man who's being paid to keep you from testifying."

Was it her imagination, or was Romero actually surprised she'd had the nerve to tell him the truth?

Before Kate could find out, the door of the office clicked open and a trim, white-haired woman sailed in.

"I'm sorry to interrupt you, Mr. R." The woman didn't look sorry. She looked like she knew her place in the grand scheme of things, and in the grand scheme of things, her place was obviously as close to the top as it was possible to get. Rank had its privileges here just as it did everywhere else. And one of her privileges was obviously to control her boss's meetings. She was immaculately dressed in a powder blue suit that was simple, yet classic. The impression of understated elegance was reinforced by the single strand of pearls she wore around her neck. In her hands, she carried a stack of newspapers. "You said you wanted to see these no matter when they came in."

She set the papers down on the table and Kate caught a glimpse of glaring headlines. Today, like every day for the past three weeks, the media was in a frenzy over a dissident writer by the name of Ruben Martinez, who was being held under house arrest in his homeland. With a book on the *New York Times* list and a reputation for working for human rights, Martinez and his detention had become something of a crusade. It was no surprise that Romero might want to keep up with the news. Already, a charmed circle of Hollywood's rich, famous, and stylishly social-conscious had traveled to Central America to lead a rally in support of Martinez. No doubt, their names were on Romero's Christmas card list.

The fact that he was more concerned about the flavor-of-the-month social cause than he was about helping them crack an important case didn't surprise Kate in the least. But it did irritate the hell out of her.

"Thank you, Charlotte." Romero gave the front-page

headlines a cursory look. "I'll be done here in another minute or two."

"I hope so." Charlotte headed back toward the outer office. "You've got the bishop at two and the senator at three." She raised snowy eyebrows. "You will be done?"

"Bishop at two. Senator at three." Romero gave his secretary a wink and flashed her one of his trademark smiles, and Kate knew, suddenly and without a scrap of doubt, why so many women fell hopelessly in love with the man. He had a charm so thick, she could feel it in the air. It had apparently wrapped around Charlotte years ago. She simply nodded, content to do whatever her boss asked. Behind her, Kate heard Sophia sigh.

Romero made a great show of looking at his watch. He glanced up, looked surprised to see them all still sitting there, and stepped back, as if to allow them full access to the door.

"Not so fast." Kate wasn't about to be put off so quickly. "We're not done. I told you I'm not willing to lose this case, and I meant it. You've got to listen to us, Mr. Romero. This is for your own protection."

Romero made a noise that might have been a laugh. Or maybe it was a growl of impatience.

"I think," he said, "you're overreacting. I'm surprised an organization that's run as smoothly and efficiently as the local FBI office would tolerate such an overactive imagination in one of its agents." He gave Mark a quick look. It was as friendly as could be, but it left no doubt that if someone didn't shut Kate up, there'd be hell to pay.

Mark took the hint. He reached into his briefcase and pulled out an eight-by-ten glossy. He tipped the photograph forward so Romero could see it.

"Joe Bartone," he explained.

Kate didn't even bother to look at the photo. She'd studied it so many times, she could see it in her sleep. It was a head-and-shoulders shot of a particularly bland-looking man. Ashen hair. Light eyes. A complexion so pale, he looked as if he didn't get out in the daylight nearly often enough. Sophia wasn't familiar with it, of course, and she leaned forward for a better look. Norbert Fielding came around from the other side of the desk and took a look, too. Romero bent forward, studied the photo, then shifted a questioning gaze back to Mark.

"Seen him around?" Mark asked.

"Of course not." Whatever interest Romero may have had in the picture and the question dissolved in a grunt of annoyance. "I'm not in the habit of keeping company with people who are regularly in police lineups. That is where that picture was taken, isn't it?"

Mark nodded. "A couple years ago. Unfortunately. Wish I knew where this guy was."

Apparently Romero was not the type who was content with only part of the story. He pinned Mark with a look, waiting for more.

It was, of course, exactly what Mark wanted.

"Bartone is the most skilled, the most vicious, and the most determined hit man on the East Coast," he said.

"And you're telling me—"

"I'm telling you that you've made some powerful enemies, Mr. Romero. They know you're going to testify against them, and I think they'll do anything they can to stop you."

"Bull!" Romero spun away and stalked over to his desk.

Mark nodded to Kate. He'd given her the rest of the photographs to bring along and, on signal, she retrieved them from her portfolio and took them across the room to Romero.

"We've tried to keep him under surveillance, and we've had some luck," she told him. "Bartone's been seen three times in the last month. And let me remind you, it's been a month since you agreed to testify." She offered the first two pictures to Romero one at a time. "The first time he was spotted, he was near the entrance to the garage of your Manhattan penthouse. The next time, he was on the street just in front of this building. The third time . . ." Before she gave him the final photograph, she looked up, watching to see what Romero's reaction might be. "The third time, he was right there." She pointed at a shadowy spot on the picture, a figure standing in the shade of a giant oak that grew alongside an impressive brick wall and iron gate. "Right outside your Long Island home."

Romero barely looked at the photograph. He turned his attention full on Kate. At close range, his eyes were more intense than ever. They were chocolate brown, flecked with a color like cinnamon. There was a tiny, crescent-shaped scar at the left corner of his mouth and she watched it jump when he gritted his teeth.

When he spoke, his voice was so quiet, she had to strain to hear it. "I'm not the type who runs from trouble, Agent Ellison."

"No." For the first time, she knew they were in agreement. "I don't suppose you are."

"I am the type of man who gets what I want. Every time."

For the briefest of moments, his gaze slid from her face down to where the unbuttoned collar of her shirt bared the hollow at the base of her throat. Kate felt her blood rise in the opposite direction. Heat flooded her chest and raced up her neck and into her cheeks. It was a good thing her skirt was just long enough to cover her knees. Otherwise, he might have seen them knocking.

If it weren't for this case, it was unlikely that Kate Ellison's path and Alex Romero's would ever have crossed. But had they been anywhere socially—some cocktail party or dinner or one of the society fund-raisers he was famous for attending—there would have been no question what he was hinting at.

Somehow Kate managed to find her voice. She forced herself to pretend they were talking only about the fact that he wanted to be left alone until it was time for him to testify. "You can't always get what you want, Mr. Romero."

"But if you try, sometimes . . ." He closed the space between them. Not enough to cause any of those still seated at the conference table to notice. Just enough for Kate to feel as if all the air had been sucked out of the room.

She scrambled to catch her breath and hold on to what was left of her common sense. It wasn't easy. Not when he was in full Romeo mode. She managed a small smile. "What you need, Mr. Romero, is a safe place to lie low and twenty-four-hour security. We've got the perfect place all ready for you. No one will be able to find you. Not even most of the other people in this room."

"You've been watching too many old movies!" With a bark of laughter that didn't contain any amusement, Romero backed away and broke the enchantment that held Kate spellbound. As graceful as an athlete, he moved toward the door, hauling Kate by the arm along with him.

"It's not that I don't appreciate what you're trying to do," he said over his shoulder, effectively ending the meeting. "It's just that I really am a very busy man. You understand, don't you, Ms. Ellison?" He beamed a smile down at her at the same time he snapped open the office door.

Right outside it stood a dark-haired man with a day's growth of beard. He was holding a pizza box. Kate couldn't tell which of them was more surprised, Romero or the pizza delivery guy.

"Sorry." The pizza guy looked from Kate to Romero, and before either one of them could react, he stepped into the office. "Didn't mean to . . . er . . . like, interrupt anything. I was just gonna knock."

"Knock?" Right before the door closed behind the delivery man, Romero looked toward the outer office. "How did you get past Charlotte?"

"Don't know no Charlotte," the man said. "Only know

as how some guy calls and says extra large, double pepperoni, hold the onions. That you?" He felt under the lid of the pizza box, apparently groping for the written order.

It was the *apparently* that made Kate suspicious. That and the fact that pizza delivery guys didn't usually keep their orders in with their pizzas. Alerted by her sudden interest, the man moved quickly. When he pulled his hand out of the box, Kate caught the flash of light against the barrel of an automatic weapon.

After that, instinct took over. And her first instinct was to keep Romero safe.

At the same time she shoved Romero out of the way, Kate called a warning to Mark and tackled the pizza man.

He never got a shot off.

The gun flew in one direction, Kate and the delivery man in the other. By the time she realized they were sprawled on the floor together and she had him in a stranglehold, Mark and the two detectives had things well in hand. They pulled the man away from Kate and had him up against the wall and cuffed before she even had a chance to catch her breath.

Someone offered her a hand up, and Kate automatically accepted it. When she finally scooped her hair out of her eyes and steadied herself on rubbery legs, she was more than a little surprised to find herself face-to-face with Alex Romero.

Romero looked over at Norbert Fielding, who had a phone in his hands, then at the team of company security guards who had apparently come running when Fielding called. When Charlotte came huffing and puffing through the door, he gave her a wink and a thumbs-up. That done, he turned his attention to Kate.

"Thank you," he said, and he was either a remarkable actor or he actually meant it. "I never thought . . . that is, I didn't imagine . . ."

It was as much of an apology as she was likely to get and Kate knew it. She nodded her acceptance and took a step forward. It wasn't until she nearly fell that she realized one of her shoes was missing.

"Careful!" Romero grabbed her arm to brace her. His hand was steady against her sleeve, his grip tight and warm, and Kate wondered if he was trying to reassure her, or calm himself.

"Do you believe me now, Mr. Romero?" she asked.

Romero looked over to where the two detectives were repeating the Miranda warning to the pizza man. "But that wasn't—"

"Bartone? No." Wondering if the rush of adrenaline that was making her heart pump wildly was caused by the attempt on Romero's life or by the fact that he was still holding on to her arm, Kate sucked in a lungful of air. "But you can be sure he was behind it. Which means—"

"He'll try again." Romero didn't sound discouraged or afraid. He accepted the truth with no more than a nod and a grim sort of determination that made his jaw go rigid. An expression she could only describe as outrage flashed across his face. He glanced at Kate out of the corner of his eye. "Looks like you win," he said.

"No." She couldn't quite bring herself to smile. "Looks like you do. The sooner we put some distance between you and New York, the safer you'll be. Don't." She stopped him when he made a move to talk to Norbert Fielding. "I told you. No one needs to know any more about this than they already do."

"Very well." He didn't argue. Funny what a near-death experience could do to some people. It seemed to have knocked some sense into Romero's gorgeous head. "But my papers . . . my clothes . . . How will I—?"

"We've got everything you need, including a new identity for you to use for the next four months. You'll get a full briefing on the way."

"On the way . . . where?" It was clear Romero was the type of man who liked to have all the facts at his fingertips. And just as clear, at least to Kate, that this was not the place to discuss them. Not when the office was swarming with people. Not when she didn't know which of those people she could trust.

"It's a secure place," she told him. "Right about now, I'd say that's all that matters."

Romero didn't look convinced. The fake pizza man was being escorted out into the hallway, and she could tell that the near-death experience was already fading and Romero's protests were about to come back in full force. Before they could, Kate gave Mark Harrison a signal that told him everything was finally under control. Mark hurried over looking more relieved than surprised, and hustled Romero out of the room.

Watching them go, Kate's insides went icy cold, then suddenly hot.

Though witness protection was usually left up to the U.S. Marshals Service, the powers-that-be had decided this was a special case. Alex Romero was a special witness. They'd decided that the FBI should be in on the operation, beginning to end. Thanks to Mark's recommendation, Mark's urgings, Mark's encouragement, and in no little part to Mark's less-than-subtle hints that she'd better not even think about opposing the decision, Kate had been chosen to spend the next four months with Romero at the safe house. It was enough to make any woman weak-kneed.

The next second, Kate thought about the house, and about the identity they had prepared for the Romeo of the tabloids, and she found herself with a grin on her face. She bent to retrieve her shoe, and once she'd slipped it on, she followed Mark and Romero out the door, mumbling under her breath.

"Maybe you can't always get what you want, but you know what, Romeo? This time, you're going to get exactly what you need."

2

"You've got to be kidding."

Alex Romero prided himself in being the kind of man who wasn't easily surprised. Or easily shaken. But this was way too much.

He stopped short on the crumbling sidewalk in front of a two-story house that looked as if it had seen better days, and planted his feet. "There's no way in hell I'm going to—"

"You might want to keep your voice down." At his side, Kate Ellison wound an arm through his and beamed a smile up at him. It was an attractive smile, or at least it might have been if she hadn't been talking through clenched teeth.

"It's been a long twenty-four hours, honey," she said, biting off the last word. She glanced quickly all around. "Why don't we get inside before we discuss this."

"Inside?" Alex took another look at the house. It was beige, or at least it might have been at one time. Years of sun had faded the color to a shade somewhere between atrocious and dreadful. The single picture window at the front of the house was filthy, and what passed for a lawn was spotty and brown, and the chassis of a '79 Nova was propped up on cinder blocks square in the center of it. The entire place—house, yard, and Nova—was coated with a gritty layer of iron-colored dust, the source of which might have been a mystery if not for the view Alex had of the postage-stamp-size backyard. It was surrounded by a drooping wire fence; beyond the fence, down a steep hill and across a convoluted network of railroad tracks, a behemoth of a steel mill belched smoke the same metallic color.

The look of the place was bad enough. The smell was even worse. A rough, chemical taste caught at the back of Alex's throat and his eyes burned.

"I've been more than cooperative," he grumbled, and he knew it was true, even if Special Agent Ellison did made a rude sound at the comment.

"I agreed to the clothes," he growled, glancing down at the ill-fitting, grubby jeans he'd been given back at the FBI office in New York. His T-shirt wasn't much better. It was stretched out of shape at the bottom, longer in front than in back. The shirt advertised some brand of beer Alex had never heard of and probably wouldn't be caught dead drinking if he had.

"I agreed to the glasses." With one hand, he adjusted the dark-rimmed glasses he'd been given. The lenses were clear glass; he didn't need them to see, but the feds had insisted that his face was too famous not to be disguised. Glasses seemed a less offensive choice than the fake mustache they'd actually had the nerve to suggest.

"I even agreed to the haircut." Alex smoothed one hand over his hair. He wasn't sure where the FBI found the barber who'd worked on him, but he would bet a dime to a doughnut the man had never had a pair of scissors in his hands before. His hair had been left too long in front and cut too short in back. It bristled with cowlicks Alex never knew he had.

Sensing his dissatisfaction—or maybe it was just because she knew it would irritate him further—Agent Ellison gave him a pat on the arm and spoke in a voice that reminded him of the patronizing tone used by kindergarten teachers, traffic cops, and doctors right before they said, "Bend over."

"I know. It's been rough. You even lowered yourself to fly all the way to Cleveland coach class."

Finally she was beginning to understand. Alex nodded. "And to drive from the airport in that thing." His upper lip curling, he glanced over his shoulder toward the battered fifteen-year-old station wagon parked near the curb. "I've gone over and above. And I've been damned accommodating."

This time when Kate made a sound of disagreement, he ignored it completely.

"But this . . ." Alex's gaze roamed over the house, the yard, and the '79 Nova. "This is—"

"Home."

Damn her. She was either bound and determined to get his goat or she really meant it. Either way, she sounded way too perky. Almost as perky as she looked.

And she looked pretty damned perky.

While Alex had been busy getting his so-called wardrobe, Special Agent Ellison had gone through some pretty major changes of her own. Back in New York, she looked like the typical career woman: buttoned down, buttoned up. All business, no nonsense.

But with her hair pulled back in a perky ponytail and her body enclosed in lurid green leggings and an oversize if somewhat faded shirt that featured a perky pink unicorn, Kate looked less like an FBI agent than she did a refugee from the nearest thrift store.

Which, of course, was the whole idea.

It had taken a full twenty-four hours, but the reality of the situation finally hit home.

And left Alex feeling worse than ever.

"Four months . . ." A glutton for punishment, he glanced over the scene again, from house to steel mill, from steel mill to car chassis. ". . . of this?"

"I'm afraid so." It must have had something to do with

the training agents got at the FBI Academy. The cold, hard facts didn't seem to bother Kate in the least. She hoisted her huge brown imitation leather purse up on her shoulder and pulled him in the direction of the house. "Home sweet home," she cooed.

"It lacks ambiance."

"Doesn't have air-conditioning, either. But you've got to admit, it's the perfect place to hide out for a couple of months. It's the last place anyone would think of looking for you."

"Thank goodness!" Alex sighed and meant it. He didn't even like to think what the paparazzi would make of this if they caught wind of it. Feeling suddenly self-conscious and more than a little exposed, he headed for the house with Kate at his side.

Before they got that far, a voice drifted to them from across the street.

"Yoo-hoo! Hello!" Alex and Kate turned to find a short, square woman in spandex shorts and a purple tube top hurrying across the blacktopped street. "We've been waiting for you!"

Alex took a quick look around. As far as he could see, there was no *we,* no one but the woman, and had he been feeling more charitable, he might have decided she was the spokesperson—official or otherwise—for the neighborhood. But he was in no mood for charity, no mood to do anything but get inside and not come out again until he could have his life back, and he decided right then and there that the woman was a busybody.

Huffing and puffing, she stopped directly in front of them and gave them the kind of quick but efficient once-over that was mastered only by years of practice. "We saw your furniture delivered earlier in the week," the woman said, wiping a thin ribbon of sweat away from the noticeably darker roots of her golden hair. "We figured you'd be here soon enough. I kept an eye on the moving guys for you. Made sure they were real careful. Had a chance to glance at the packing slips. You must be

Missy." She grabbed Special Agent Ellison's hands in both of hers and pumped them. "And you . . ." The woman was no bigger than five feet tall and she had to back up a bit to take the full measure of Alex.

The moment she did, her eyes widened and her mouth fell open. "Why, if you don't look just like . . ." The light faded as quickly as it came on. The woman snapped her fingers with impatience. "You know, you know that guy I'm talking about." She swung around to Kate, looking for assistance. "You know that guy I mean," she said. "That good-looking one who's always—"

"Must be the light! I mean, just look at the way it's shining off the house today." Apparently as quick with words as she was at disposing of phony pizza delivery men, Kate laughed off the woman's comment at the same time she took her arm and spun her away from Alex, effectively changing the woman's view and the subject. "Andy, my brother, he bought this place a couple months ago and he's renting it to us. You know, when he told me about it, he said it was yellow. Well, it doesn't look yellow to me. Your house . . ." Again, she turned both herself and the woman until they were facing the other side of the street and the house directly across from where they stood. It was garish beyond belief, the color a combination of the rich ochre of Dijon mustard and the brassy tint of a marigold. "Now *there's* a yellow house," Kate said.

The woman beamed with pride. "Earl just finished it. I told him to take it easy on the color, but you know how men can be." She poked a pudgy elbow into Kate's ribs. "My Earl is such a rascal! 'Marge,' he says, 'you want yellow, by golly, you'll get yellow.' " She laughed, uncommonly pleased with the whole thing though Alex could not imagine why. "You'll meet Earl one of these days," Marge informed them.

"I can't wait." Even to his own ears, Alex's voice sounded a little too acid. Fortunately Marge didn't seem to notice. She had already started down the cockeyed walk that led up to the front door. "So I was saying to Earl, I figured you'd be along any day now, what with your furniture and all already here." She stopped at the bottom of the front steps and turned a curious look on Alex. "Where did you say you were from?"

For one uncomfortable moment, a shot of panic streaked through Alex's insides. Though he'd been briefed ad nauseam about how he was supposed to handle the inevitable curious questions, he found himself at a loss for words. He was not the type who routinely told lies, in business or in his personal life, but he was, after all, a successful and wealthy man. He could throw the bull with the best of them.

He was a quick study and an even better improviser. He'd been coached about his new identity by an FBI agent who seemed to take great delight in this sort of role-playing. He knew he was supposed to be Stanley Tomashefski, and over and over again on the flight from New York, he'd drilled himself about the mundane details of Stanley's life: Work history. Education. Family ties.

The story was all there in his head. He just couldn't seem to make it come to his lips.

Denial. That had to be it.

Alex calmed himself with the thought while he stared down into Marge's big brown eyes.

He was in denial. It was the only thing that could possibly explain why he was off his usual game. It was hard enough for him to believe he was in the middle of this ridiculous charade. How could he possibly convince anyone else?

Apparently denial wasn't one of the excuses Special Agent Ellison found acceptable. When it looked as if he wasn't going to answer—as if he didn't remember—she puffed out a breath of annoyance. "Stan and I are just moving down from Erie." She gave him a hard look, one that reminded him they had a story they were supposed to stick to, come hell or high water. "Stan got hurt at the factory. He's on disability. We thought we'd spend a couple months here fixing up the place. Then, if Stan can find work here in Cleveland, we'll buy the house from Andy and stay."

"Oh, that would be so nice! We could use some young blood in the neighborhood." Marge smiled, genuinely pleased. "And you two are just as cute as can be," she purred. "How long you been married?"

Married?

The word echoed through Alex's head and settled in his gut like the remnants of bad lobster thermidor. He'd never even imagined himself a married man. But then, he'd never thought he'd have a room with a view of a steel mill, either.

He came out of his musings to find Kate with her arms folded across her chest and a look in her eyes that told him he'd better get with the program. It wasn't the first time in the last twenty-four hours he'd seen that same look. Twenty-four hours and already he knew the woman could be as stubborn as she was efficient. As efficient as she was attractive.

The thought snuck up and blindsided Alex. It wasn't that he hadn't noticed Kate's obvious attributes: eyes that were more gray than blue, hair that, in this light, was streaked with honey-colored highlights, a body that was compact but well-proportioned. Of course he'd noticed—the moment he met her. But in the last twenty-four hours he'd had plenty to think about. Special Agent Ellison's well-scrubbed good looks had been forced to take a backseat to the more pressing problems of avoiding hit men and walking out on a business empire that depended on him for its very existence.

Then there was the matter of Ruben Martinez.

Alex's mood plummeted. From down-in-the-dumps to somewhere too far below sea level to measure.

He knew none of it was Kate's fault. She was only

doing her job. But he needed someone to blame. For the outfit and the glasses, the haircut and the house. Right about now, Special Agent Ellison was it.

With a lucidity he could attribute only to a combination of stress, shock, and fatigue, and a keen appreciation for the absurdity of the situation, Alex made a decision.

Special Agent Ellison wanted him to play the game?

The least he could do was oblige her.

With a sleek smile and a throaty growl, he sidled up nice and close to Kate and slipped one arm around her waist. She flinched. It was more of a reaction than he'd seen even the day before when the bogus delivery man pulled a gun on them, and heartened by it, Alex flattened his hand against her hip. Just to make things look more genuine, he gave her a little squeeze at the same time he gave Marge a wink.

"We're newlyweds. So you'll understand if we want to spend plenty of time alone."

Marge's face went as red as Kate's went white. She twittered an answer and stepped aside to let them up the stairs. When they got there, Alex watched Kate grope through her purse for the key.

"Newlyweds." Along with a curse, Kate mumbled the word so that Marge couldn't hear. "I don't recall seeing that in our dossiers."

"No," Alex agreed, his voice just as quiet. "But you have to admit, it's a brilliant strategy. If the neighbors wonder why we're not out and about more, we can always tell them we spend most of our days in bed."

"Bed?" The key flipped out of Kate's hand and clattered across the front porch. Numbed—by panic, or by the suggestion, or maybe by a little of both—she stood staring. She recovered in a heartbeat, but what a heartbeat it was! Time enough for Alex to study her slightly parted lips and wonder if they tasted as delicious as they looked. Time to let his gaze slide over to where her cheeks flamed. With a quick intake of breath and a shake that sent her ponytail flying, she jerked back to reality and bent to search for the key.

Alex might have helped if he wasn't suddenly enjoying himself so much. After twenty-four hours of inconvenience, discomfort, and aggravation, it was nice to know that his old charm could still work its magic. Even on Special Agent Ellison.

Kate got on her hands and knees to feel under a rusted porch swing for the key. Watching her nicely rounded backside, a new thought occurred to him. A slow smile tugged the corners of his mouth. The next four months might actually be tolerable. Maybe even a little enjoyable.

This time, it was Alex who was caught in a daydream and Kate who brought him out of it. He heard her give a satisfied *harrumph* and watched her hop to her feet, the key held triumphantly in one hand. She turned the key in the lock.

"You are going to carry her over the threshold, aren't you?" Marge's question was as innocent as could be and about as subtle as a hand grenade. It stopped both Alex and Kate in place.

Before Kate could warn him off, Alex closed the distance between them and smiled down at her. "We wouldn't want to disappoint the neighbors, would we?" he asked.

"You wouldn't dare."

Was she issuing a warning? Or a challenge?

It didn't take long for Alex to decide it really didn't matter. He didn't get where he was in life by playing it safe. Or by ever backing down from a challenge. Without another thought, he scooped Kate up in his arms.

Watching them head into the house, Marge whistled and applauded. "Wait until I tell Earl about this!"

Kate was surprisingly light. And as stiff as a board. "You'd better relax, honey." Alex half-whispered the advice through a smile. "We don't want the neighbors to talk."

Kate glared at him. "I'll relax," she hissed, "when you put me down."

Alex nudged open the door at the same time he nodded his good-bye to Marge. He stepped into the house and kicked the door closed behind him. "I'll put you down—"

Alex's shoe caught against a loose corner of carpeting. He tripped, slipped, and they both nearly went down in a heap.

Kate let out a small squeal of surprise. Alex held on tight to keep from losing his grip.

It was a second or two before he recovered enough to regain his footing; by then, Kate's arms were wrapped around his neck and her face was only inches from his. Even though the drapes on the big front picture window were shut, he could tell her eyes were wide, her pupils deep pools that reflected a face that looked as surprised and as astonished and as intrigued as hers did. Her breathing was in perfect counterpoint to the rough breaths that tore through him. And her body . . .

Alex let his gaze slide down to where Kate's pink unicorn was pressed against his beer logo. Suddenly he wasn't thinking of the unicorn as perky anymore. He was thinking of his new identity and the newlywed game that they were supposed to be playing, and other words filled his head, drowning out *perky* and every other logical thought.

Words like *soft, warm, velvety*. Words like *heat*. And a rush of fire that exploded in his gut.

At the same time he settled Kate closer against him, Alex allowed himself a slow smile. "I'll put you down," he murmured, "when I'm good and ready."

He wasn't exactly sure what happened next. He felt Kate tense. Saw her turn and flip. The next thing he knew, she was on her feet in front of him.

"Cut the crap, Romero." Kate's voice contained as much warmth as the look she shot his way. "I'm not impressed by the Romeo act. As a matter of fact, I think it's only fair to tell you, I didn't want this assignment."

"I can't see why not." Alex took a quick look around. The walls of the room were covered with dark and very fake-looking wood paneling. The floor was carpeted in green shag. There was a cream-colored couch placed predictably against one wall, a nineteen-inch portable TV on a plastic stand directly in front of it. An open doorway on his left showed the kitchen, another ahead of him led to an enclosed porch. Across from him, a low-ceilinged stairway led to the second floor.

He shook his head. "In spite of our accommodations, this must be the cushiest job in the agency. Four months of rest and relaxation. Besides—" He shrugged and maybe he was a glutton for punishment. Or maybe he just never gave up. He offered Kate one of his famous smiles, the kind that was known to melt female hearts at fifty paces. "I'm not a hard guy to get along with. There are plenty of pretty ladies all over the world who'd sell their souls for the chance to play house with me for the summer."

"Please!" Kate turned the word into two syllables. "Let's get something straight, Romero. I didn't graduate at the top of my Academy class so I could baby-sit some pampered playboy. Mark Harrison suggested I take this assignment. Strongly suggested. And when Mark strongly suggests something, those of us who work for him have learned to listen. He thinks it will be good for my career."

"And you don't?"

Her lips pursed, her head tilted to one side, Kate considered the question. "Once Mark explained his position, I saw its merits," she admitted. "But I suppose it's only fair to tell you, it was you or Smokey the Bear."

For a second, Alex wasn't sure he'd heard her correctly. "Did you say—?"

"Smokey the Bear." Kate nodded, and Alex wished the light in the dingy little room was better. He could have sworn she flashed him a tiny, satisfied smile. "Mark's little way of reminding us that no matter how distasteful we find an assignment, there's always something worse." She turned and headed up the stairway.

Alex took a step or two, then decided it probably wasn't wise to follow an annoyed FBI agent up a dark stairway. He got as far as the bottom of the stairs and called up to her. "Smokey the Bear? What does all this have to do with Smokey the Bear?"

For a moment, he thought she wasn't going to answer. He heard footsteps above him as she walked down the hallway, then came back to the landing at the top of the steps. She bent at the waist and looked down at him.

"It's a little-known fact," she said, "that the FBI is in charge of investigating all unauthorized uses of the Smokey the Bear symbol. We open and maintain case files on any individual caught abusing old Smokey."

"Which means?"

She let out a puff of aggravation. "Which means, Mark made me an offer I couldn't refuse. Spend the summer with you, or run down every Smokey case on file."

Before Alex could even process the information, she turned and disappeared down the hallway. A second later, he heard a door close.

Surprised and still stinging from her rejection, Alex glared up the stairs and tossed the first comeback he could think of at the space she'd vacated.

"Oh, yeah?"

The rejoinder was as lame as it sounded, especially from a man who was famous for having a way with words. But by that time, he really didn't care.

Exasperated, Alex raised his voice loud enough to be heard all the way to the second floor. "At least I'm better looking than the bear!"

"Who says?" Kate's voice was muffled by the closed door.

Alex defended himself instinctively. It was ridiculous, of course. They were fighting about nothing. About everything. "I've got better hair!" he yelled, swiping one hand over his head. His shoulders sagged. At least he *had* better hair. Before that excuse for a barber got ahold of him. He gulped down his embarrassment and tried again. "Well, I've got better taste than the bear!"

From upstairs, he heard a door rasp open. The next thing he knew, Kate was at the top of the stairs, looking down her nose at him. "Are you sure?" she asked, each word dripping sarcasm. "Have you looked in a mirror lately? Compared to you, Smokey looks like he just stepped out of *GQ*."

Alex refused to be outdone. He'd never been beaten in business, and he sure wasn't going to be beaten now. Not by Kate Ellison. Or by Smokey the Bear. "*GQ*? Hah! Nobody in *GQ* ever wears such a dopey hat!"

Even from where he stood, he could see Kate's shoulders go rigid. She was as angry as he was, and just as willing to make a mountain out of what had to be the smallest molehill of all time. "Hey, pal, the hat is one of the things the bear has to wear. It's part of his image. And if you mess with his image—"

"Yeah, yeah. I know. The FBI will get me. Big deal."

He wanted to get a rise out of her, and it worked. Kate stomped down the stairs. She stopped on the second step from the bottom so that she was eye to eye with Alex. "You bet it's a big deal," she told him. "If it wasn't for us, you'd have more to worry about than how you measure up to Smokey."

Something told Alex he already did.

Caught unexpectedly by Kate's nearness and the scent of the cheap perfume that was apparently standard issue for her new persona, he allowed himself to glance from her blazing eyes to where her fists were propped against her hips. Her oversize shirt was pressed close to her body, revealing a slim waist and breasts that looked nicely rounded and not too big or too small. By the time he pulled his gaze back up to her cheeks, they were a shade of pink darker than her unicorn.

Alex leaned closer, until his lips were no more than a

heartbeat from hers. "You know what?" he rumbled. "I can be a lot more fun than the bear."

He had to give Kate credit. She didn't back down. And she didn't flinch. She kept her eyes on his and her tongue flickered over her lips. "You know what?" she asked in return. "The bear has more charm."

She was gone in a matter of seconds, and this time when Alex heard the upstairs door slam, he knew it would stay closed for a good, long while.

He spun around and sat on the bottom step, his elbows on his knees and his chin in his hands. It wasn't possible. Any of it. Not only was he confined to this house of horrors for the next four months, but he was being compared to Smokey the Bear.

Compared and found lacking.

Only You Can Prevent Forest Fires!

In spite of himself, Alex couldn't help but think of Smokey's famous line. "Prevent forest fires?" He grumbled his disbelief under his breath. "Not a problem, Smokey, ol' pal. Looks like I can't even strike a spark!"

3

"Rise and shine, Romeo!"

Alex's bedroom door wasn't shut all the way, and when Kate rapped on it, it swung open. She took the opportunity to peek inside. Didn't it figure? He was still sound asleep.

Because he was officially the guest of honor at this little masquerade, Alex had been given the larger of the house's two bedrooms, and since it was the master bedroom Stan and Missy were supposed to share, he'd also ended up with the queen-size bed. In what little morning light crept around the frayed edges of the window shade, Kate saw that he was sleeping on his left side, sprawled against the pillows with the blue-and-green striped sheet draped over his shoulders. One of his arms was tucked under him, the other was flung across the empty spot at his side.

She grumbled under her breath and stretched her neck, working out the kinks that came from sleeping on the lumpy mattress of her twin bed in the room down the hallway. She envied Alex not only his oversize bed but the fact that he'd somehow managed to sleep like a baby. How could he look so peaceful when the reflection staring back at her from the bathroom mirror earlier that morning showed a woman who'd spent the night tossing and turning?

Kate didn't even like to think about it. She didn't want to relive those hours of second-guessing herself.

She'd watched the numbers on her clock radio change hour after hour, and wondered how she'd ever let herself get talked into the assignment. She had punched her pillow and flipped around in bed and told herself this better be good for her career because if it wasn't, she was wasting her time when she could have been back in New York putting the finishing touches on her case. She threw off the blankets, then pulled them back up to her nose and burrowed into her mattress, and she thought about Alex Romero.

Not the playboy-hunk-of-the-tabloids Alex Romero. Or the handsome-face-who-looked-back-at-the-cameras-and-smiled Alex Romero. Or even the business-tycoon-who-directed-each-and-every-move-of-an-international-corporation Alex Romero.

The real Alex Romero. The one who, in the scant time they'd shared, had revealed himself as arrogant, exasperating, disrespectful of even an idol like Smokey, and enough of a Romeo to make the most levelheaded special agent in the entire Justice Department tingle with anticipation every time he so much as looked her way.

That was not a comforting thought, and Kate did her best to ignore it. She lay in bed and reminded herself that the trip from New York had been blessedly uneventful, and the thought was enough to make her finally relax. But the instant she closed her eyes, she saw Alex's face. She remembered the unspoken dare that shone in his eyes when he'd announced they were newlyweds, the one-sided, cocky grin he'd given her when he lifted her into his arms. She thought about the purr of his voice in the half-darkness of the living room: *"I'll put you down when I'm good and ready."*

Even in the glaring light of day, the words shivered

along Kate's spine, just as they'd done the night before. The sensation was somewhere between the hot caress of a lover and the cold certainty that she was in way over her head.

Sometime between when the night-shift whistle blew at the steel mill and the first birds of the morning started to chatter, she'd decided this was one Romeo she'd do best to resist.

"Business, not pleasure." She'd repeated the words so often, they had turned into a kind of mantra. The business was keeping Alex Romero alive. As for the pleasure . . .

Kate sighed.

She'd have to pass on the pleasure. Someday, she supposed she'd look back on it all and wonder what it would have been like. Someday, she supposed, she'd realize she'd passed up the fantasy-come-true opportunity of a lifetime. Someday, when she was free to talk about the case, she'd tell her friends where she'd been all summer, and when that someday came, their jaws would drop, their eyes would pop, and their questions would ring out loud and clear. "You passed up the opportunity to jump into Romeo's bed? Are you crazy?"

Maybe she was. But she wasn't stupid.

Her mind made up, even if her body wasn't convinced. Kate set down the laundry basket she was carrying and knocked on Alex's door again.

When she still didn't get an answer, she took a step inside the room.

Though Alex's room was larger than hers, *large* was a relative word. Kate sidled between the bed and the dresser across from it.

"Hey!" Not willing to get too close or to risk too much contact, she stood as far away from the bed as she could, stretched, and poked Alex's shoulder with one finger. "I said, rise and shine!"

Alex snuffled and mumbled something. He went right on sleeping.

Kate's hesitation dissolved beneath a healthy dose of

aggravation. There was only one window in the room and she went over to it, grabbed the paper shade, tugged, and let go. It snapped up with a puff of dust and a satisfying crack that made Alex bolt up in bed.

"What the hell—"

Kate laughed. With the shade up, sunlight flooded the room. It glanced against the faded blue carpet, brushed the cream-colored walls, and shone full on the spot where the sheet had fallen away to reveal Alex Romero's perfectly muscled, magnificently proportioned, nicely tanned, and very bare chest.

Kate's smile froze. *Business before pleasure,* she reminded herself. Even before the words registered, she felt her glance straying from the surprised, still-half-asleep look on Alex's face to the sprinkling of dark hair on his chest. From there, it traveled to the shoulders that had been made famous in countless tabloid pictures of Alex in swim trunks, Alex in workout clothes, Alex in a hot tub with a supermodel known more for her beauty than for her brains.

Business before pleasure. This time, the words felt less confident and a whole lot less like a good idea, especially when her gaze slid down to where the sheet was tangled around Alex's waist. On this side of the bed, enough of the sheet gaped so that she could see the lean line of his hip, and the solid length of one bare leg.

She'd never even thought he might sleep in the nude.

A wave of embarrassment choked Kate. Her cheeks got hot. So did other parts of her she really didn't want to think about at the moment. Before Alex could notice and realize what she'd seen—and what her reaction had been when she saw it—she sped toward the door. "Come on," she called to him over her shoulder. "We have to get going."

"Going?" Alex sounded sleepy and confused. "Going where?"

Kate didn't answer. She scooped the clothes basket up off the floor and used it as a battering ram to push open the door to her room. She closed the door behind her and leaned back against it, her face fiery, her breaths coming so fast, she felt as if she'd run a mile.

It wasn't until after she heard the bathroom door close and the water running that she dared to move. Swallowing down her embarrassment, she cursed her overactive imagination, and her overcharged libido, and the damned overconfidence that made her think she could march into Romero's bedroom and take charge without a thought for the consequences.

She crossed the room, slammed the laundry basket onto her bed, and bent over the suitcases she'd brought with her from New York. She didn't bother to look through the clothes. Handful after handful, she grabbed whatever was there and tossed it directly into the basket. She'd already emptied one suitcase and had started on the second when her bedroom door swung open.

"Where are we going?"

Kate's fingers tightened around an orange T-shirt she'd just fished from her suitcase. She took a calming breath, willed the redness out of her cheeks, and turned.

Fortunately for both her composure and her resolve, Alex had gotten dressed. Unfortunately for both her composure and her resolve, his choice of clothing left a lot to be desired. Really a lot to be desired.

He was wearing black exercise shorts that didn't cover up very much. They came straight from some secondhand store, just like the rest of their wardrobes. The elastic at the waist was pulled out of shape and the shorts hung low over Alex's hips. His hair was wet and slicked back against his head and that, plus a night's growth of beard, made his face look rawboned and angular. He hadn't bothered with a shirt or shoes and there were drops of water caught in the hair on his chest. They sparkled like diamonds in the morning sunlight.

Damn him, but so did Alex's eyes.

He ventured a couple of steps into the room, and if he felt uncomfortable at all, he sure didn't look it. He glanced around, quickly assessing everything from the single dresser with its drawers standing open to the suitcases on Kate's floor. "Say it ain't so!" Alex held both his hands to his heart. "Missy, my love, you're not walking out on me, are you?"

"Don't be an ass." Kate supposed she should have been grateful he was. It made her remember exactly what they were doing there, or at least what they were supposed to be doing. It also reminded her how much of a pain in the behind Alex Romero could be. With a look that told him exactly that, she dumped everything left in her suitcase directly into the clothes basket. "We're going to the Laundromat."

She hadn't imagined Alex might ever be at a loss for words. Even when the phony pizza guy pulled a gun, he'd never lost his legendary aplomb. Now he stood with his mouth half open and a look in his eyes that told her he thought she was kidding.

There was something about knowing she'd caught him by surprise that bolstered Kate's spirits. She grinned while she poked into the pockets that lined the inside of the suitcase. "I don't know about you," she told him, "but I'm not willing to wear any of this stuff until it's been washed." With two fingers, she lifted a remarkable piece of clothing out of one of the pockets. It was a shirt—or at least Kate guessed that's what it was supposed to be—a shirt made of polyester lace. That was bad enough. The bilious shade of chartreuse was worse. So were the long, tight sleeves and the scooped-out neckline. Whoever had grabbed it off the rack sure didn't know Kate. It was at least two sizes too small.

She held the shirt at arm's length and wrinkled her nose. "No telling where some of this stuff has been. Or who's worn it. Of course, that may not bother you, but I'd feel better if my stuff made the acquaintance of a little detergent and a whole lot of Clorox."

"And then you'll wear it?"

For a second, Kate wondered what he was talking

about. Then she saw his gaze slip from the lace shirt to the front of the pink sweatshirt she was wearing with her jeans. His eyebrows did a slow slide up his forehead. "I gotta admit, Special Agent Ellison, in that lacy shirt, you'd look—"

"Trashy?" There was no use giving him the opportunity to charm her, especially since Kate was afraid one of these times, it might actually work. She stopped him before he had the chance. She tossed the shirt in with her other clothes, zipped her suitcase shut, and slid it under the bed. "Is that what you were going to say?" she asked.

It was apparently enough of a reminder to bring even Alex to his senses. He had the good grace to look flustered. "Trashy? No. I was going to say . . . un-agentlike." He grinned, pleased at his choice of words. "That's what I was going to say."

"Uh-huh." Kate lifted the clothes basket into her arms. "It's up to you," she told him. She didn't have to pretend; she honestly didn't care if he washed his clothes or not. "If you don't think your clothes need to be washed—"

"Well, sure. Sure they need to be." As if working his way through the logic of the plan, Alex nodded. "You can just grab my stuff on your way out, and—"

"Oh, no!" Kate cut him off. "Let's get something straight here, Romeo. We may be playing house this summer, but that doesn't mean I'm willing to act the part of the little woman. I'm not going to pick up after you and I'm sure as hell not going to wash your clothes."

"But—"

"You want 'em washed, you wash 'em. You don't . . ." She shrugged and headed toward the door.

Alex stepped in front of the doorway. She had to give him credit: Even in out-of-shape workout shorts, he looked like the chairman of the board. His eyes glinted with a spark that reminded Kate of sunlight against granite. He crossed his arms over his chest. "I'll just send them out," he said. "There must be a dry cleaner nearby, or a laundry that picks up and delivers."

"On our income?" Kate laughed. "Sorry, that's not part of the deal."

"But a Laundromat?" Alex's lip curled. "I'll pass."

"Can't pass." Right before she got to the door, Kate remembered her carry-on bag. She set down the basket and went back to the bed. She knelt and felt under it and when she found her carry-on, she pulled out the book that was inside and set it on her nightstand. The Bureau had made one concession to her wardrobe—new socks and underwear—and she retrieved the packages, sat on the floor with her back to the bed, and ripped at the corners of the plastic bags with her teeth. She finished tearing them open, pulling out the only things in the world she could say really belonged to her for the next four months: nine pairs of white cotton panties and nine pairs of white cotton socks.

"That's one of the rules. Don't you remember?" she asked Alex. "Whither thou goest, so goest I. And when I goest anywhere, thou has to goest with me. Even when I goest to the Laundromat. I can't take the chance of leaving you alone."

"Chance?" Annoyed and not reluctant to show it, Alex paced from the door to where Kate sat on the floor. It was poor strategy, Kate knew. With Alex standing and her sitting, he was in a much better position of power. She could just stand up, of course, but if she did, she'd be in dangerous proximity of Alex's bare arms, and Alex's bare chest, and the hint of Alex's bare hip that showed above the droopy waistband of the exercise shorts.

She decided to stay put.

"What kind of chance is there that anybody could ever find me in this hellhole?" Alex paced to the door and back again. The floor squeaked with his every step. "You said so yourself, you said that's why this was such a perfect hiding place. No one will ever find me. That's what you said. So go to the Laundromat by yourself and—"

"No can do." One by one, Kate balled up the empty bags and tossed them into the wastepaper basket across the room. She made every shot. When Alex was a safe distance away, she pulled herself to her feet and brushed off the seat of her pants. "As much as I'd like to, I've got clear orders. I go where you go. You go where I go. I can't protect you if I can't see you, and that means I can't let you out of my sight."

"You did last night."

Kate refused to take the bait, or the suggestive little half-smile Alex offered along with it. She returned the smile with one that was tight around the edges. "There's a security system installed, though no one's supposed to know it. Besides, in this room, I'm closer to the stairs. If the bad guys showed up, I'd take care of them before they got as far as your room."

"I'll bet you would."

It was as much of a compliment as she'd ever gotten from him and Kate decided not to argue. She added the socks and underwear to her other clothes and lifted the basket. "Ready?" she asked.

Alex didn't answer. She turned to find him looking at the book he'd picked up from her nightstand. "Ruben Martinez. *Strange Freedoms.* You're reading this?"

Kate wasn't sure why the question put her on the defensive. Maybe it was because she remembered that back in New York, Alex had shown that he was one of the legion of Martinez supporters. Not that Kate didn't think that was a good thing. Martinez was obviously a man of principle who wasn't afraid to put his money where his mouth was when it came to standing up for what he believed. But even before he'd become a cause célèbre, Martinez had been the envy of the intelligentsia and the darling of the social set. Lured by his reputation, not to mention the fact that everyone was talking about him, she'd plunked down her $26.95 at the local Barnes & Noble and plunged into *Strange Freedoms.* Frankly she couldn't understand what all the fuss was about.

"Yes, I'm reading it." Kate tried to sound the way everyone else sounded when they talked about Martinez.

As if his nearly indecipherable prose was the most poetic and the most profound and the greatest thing since sliced bread. "I'm not the type who buys a book just because the author is a celebrity. Martinez happens to be a great man." At least that much was true and Kate wasn't ashamed to admit it. Her next statement wasn't quite as sincere and behind her back, she crossed the fingers of one hand. "Martinez is a brilliant writer."

Alex didn't respond. At least not right away. He looked as if he might. He opened his mouth to say something, then snapped it shut again, and Kate wondered if he was hesitant about saying that he disagreed with her assessment of Martinez—or reluctant to admit that she was right. He didn't bother to enlighten her; he flipped through the book instead.

"He's also something of an intellectual. This is heavy stuff." Alex glanced her way, the gleam of a challenge bright in his eyes. "Do you suppose Missy Tomashefski would read something like this?"

Leave it to Alex to turn even a simple conversation into a chess match. Kate reached over and plucked the book out of his hands. "No one's going to see it, and besides . . ." She held the book protectively to her chest. She wasn't about to admit that she'd left the book in her carry-on bag after a recent weekend trip to Denver. Not anxious to finish it, she'd forgotten all about *Strange Freedoms*. It had ended up in Cleveland as something of an afterthought. "I'm more than halfway through," she said and that wasn't true, either. She'd made it through the first chapter, sure, but after thirty-six grueling pages, she still wasn't sure what the book was about or if she'd bother with the rest of it. "I have to find out what happens. It wouldn't have been fair to leave it behind."

"Something that highbrow isn't exactly in keeping with our characters." Alex nodded, as if confirming something to himself. The hint of a smile touched his mouth. "Why, Special Agent Ellison, you've got a rebellious streak, don't you? No one knows you brought that book with you!"

Kate nearly laughed. Special Agent Kathleen Ellison? Rebellious? The guys at the Academy would be rolling on the floor if they heard that one. If there was one thing Kate wasn't, it was rebellious. She was as by-the-book as any agent she'd ever known and she was damned proud of it. Not that Alex needed to know that, at least not when it meant that by admitting it, she'd also have to admit that she was as shallow as all the other lemmings out there who'd trooped to the bookstore and plunked down their hard-earned cash for a book that really wasn't very good.

"No one knows I brought the book with me," she said, hoping they'd change the subject really soon. She wasn't sure she could keep up the pretense much longer. To get rid of the thought—and the book—she slid open the drawer of the nightstand and dropped *Strange Freedoms* inside. Something told her it would still be there, untouched and unread, when they packed up and headed back to New York. "You going to turn me in?"

He gave her a wink. "You going to make me come to the Laundromat?"

Kate breathed a sigh of relief. Now they were back on solid ground, back in an arena that didn't involve hieroglyphic literature laden with unintelligible imagery or ambiguous messages. She could handle this, and just to prove it, she smiled back at Alex. "Don't forget your glasses."

He gave in with what she suspected was as much good grace as he ever gave in to anything. With a heavy sigh and a grumbled word, he headed toward the door, grabbing the laundry basket as he went. He was already out in the hallway when she heard a long, low whistle.

Too late, Kate realized her mistake. She braced herself for what she knew was coming, swallowed her pride, and followed.

She found Alex standing just outside his bedroom door. The laundry basket was on the floor at his feet. His mouth was open, and his fingers were wrapped around a diaphanous white nightgown.

Even as she watched, he lifted the nightgown in the air so that it hung between them like a gauzy curtain. His gaze roamed to the spaghetti straps and he licked his lips. It moved to the lower-than-low-cut bodice and he swallowed hard. It followed the slit that went all the way from the floor-length hem up to the thigh, and he blinked at Kate through the sheer skirt.

Maybe it was the sheen the fabric gave his face. He looked as if he'd just been sucker-punched.

"You planning something you haven't told me about?"

Kate ignored the heat in her face. "I'm planning on keeping you alive," she told him.

"Not in this thing." Shaking his head, Alex gave Kate a look that caused goose bumps to prickle up and down her arms. "You? In this? My heart would stop for sure."

"Don't tempt me." She snatched the gown out of his grasp and tossed it back into the laundry basket where it came from. It wasn't as easy to toss aside the delicious ideas that popped into her head or the slow burn of awareness that heated her blood. "And don't flatter yourself. I'm not planning to wear it. Ever. It's part of the act. The kind of thing a young wife might have out on the laundry line."

"You brought that along to hang on a laundry line?" As if bracing himself, Alex sucked in a long breath. Shaking his head, he turned around and went into his bedroom. He didn't say a word. At least not to Kate. But before he went inside, she swore she heard him mumble something that sounded an awful lot like, "It's going to be a long summer."

It was going to be one hell of a long summer.

Alex sat on the wooden bench that ran down the center of the Old World Laundry and pushed his glasses up on the bridge of his nose. Directly in front of him, washing machines were lined up against the wall, each one sloshing to its own rhythm. Somehow he'd managed to plunk himself down across from the machine where Kate had deposited her clothes. He watched her perky pink unicorn swim by in tandem with a pair of yellow shorts. They disappeared in a cloud of bubbles, and the white nightgown floated by.

Exactly the way it had been floating through his imagination since he'd found it in the laundry basket.

Well, not exactly, he corrected himself. When he'd imagined the white nightgown, he'd imagined Kate in it. And when he imagined Kate in the white nightgown, he imagined himself helping her out of it, one spaghetti strap at a time.

Uncomfortable with the thought and the pictures it conjured in his head, Alex shifted against the bench and grumbled loud enough for the elderly lady seated next to him to give him an uneasy look. He offered her a quick smile and was pleased to see that at least the old charm still worked on someone. Color flooding her cheeks, the old lady giggled before she turned back to the newspaper she was reading.

Alex glanced over at the washing machine just in time to see the white nightgown drift by again. Fortunately Kate was busy folding a load of towels and didn't see him staring like a fool. He hoped he wasn't drooling.

What was wrong with him anyway? He was acting like a teenager on hormone overdrive.

Alex crossed his arms over his chest and the black muscle shirt with the fishnet midriff he'd chosen to wear, not because it was better than any of his other clothes, but because he didn't care if it got washed. He was planning on tossing it in the garbage as soon as they got back to the house.

Like his clothing, his accommodations, and his first-time-ever visit to a Laundromat, the way he was acting with Kate simply wasn't his style. He was known for his cool sophistication, his urbane wit, his elegant approach to business and pleasure and everything in between. He was known as a playboy, sure, but he'd always prided himself on giving a new, classy spin to the word. No lame pick-up lines for him. No scandals. No messy entanglements with women who were married or unstable. No publicity seekers or gold diggers. No underage bimbos or over-the-hill actresses trying to revive their careers with a fling that was sure to attract lights, cameras, and plenty of action.

Now here he was trying to convince a woman who clearly wasn't interested that he really was the Romeo of the tabloids. That was bad enough. What was worse was that the woman wasn't his type to begin with.

He liked his women long and lean. Kate was a full head shorter than he. She had good hair, pretty eyes, a compact, middle-size body—nice, but not remarkable; a figure that, though it wouldn't stop traffic, had all the right curves in all the right places.

He liked his women sleek and elegant. Comfortable in sequins. Relaxed in silk. Even without the look he'd had at what was in the laundry basket, he knew what kind of woman Kate was: White cotton panties. White cotton socks.

Not his type. Not his type at all.

The thought should have cheered him, or at least relieved him of the burden of thinking he had to try and impress Kate, but Alex was way past being easily amused. Fishnet shirts didn't fit the image he'd worked so long and hard to establish. Laundromats full of ladies in Bermuda shorts and knee-high hose didn't do anything for his sense of the aesthetic. Being bored wasn't something he was used to, and it certainly wasn't anything he enjoyed. Sitting around, idle and unproductive, while his business dealings went to pot and his personal plans were shot to hell was not his idea of a good time.

As if on cue, the lady next to him finished with the newspaper and set it down on the bench between them. The headline across one column of the front page caught Alex's eye: *Martinez Slated for Trial.*

"Damn!" He mumbled the curse and made up his mind. He'd deal with the consequences—and with Special Agent Ellison—when he had to.

As casually as he could, Alex got up and headed toward the back of the Laundromat. He knew there was a pay phone somewhere near the restroom; he'd already heard one woman call for a ride home and another use it to make a call that turned into a knock-down, drag-out fight with a guy named Junior who apparently had more of an appetite for VO and ginger ale than he did for her.

The phone hung half on and half off a plasterboard wall that was covered with penciled phone numbers, rude words, and hieroglyphs that had to be gang symbols. Alex lifted the receiver and stifled an urge to wipe it against his shirt. Since his shirt probably wasn't much more sanitary than the phone, there seemed little point. He dialed Norbert Fielding's private office, waited for the tone, and punched in his credit card number.

Before he was even halfway through, a hand slammed down the hook.

He didn't have to look to figure out whose hand it was.

Alex's own hand tightened around the receiver. He drew in a long, slow breath and then was sorry he did. The place smelled like old socks and fabric softener and humid air. Holding as tight to his anger as he was to the phone, he turned.

Kate's eyes reminded him of storm clouds, lighter gray toward the center and dark as charcoal around the edges. She did her best to keep her voice down, but there was no mistaking the note of exasperation in it. One hand balled into a fist at her side, the other still pressing the phone hook as if to make good and certain the connection had been broken, she glared up at Alex. "What do you think you're doing? Who are you calling?"

"What's this, Twenty Questions?" Alex didn't appreciate being grilled. He didn't bother to tell her. She could figure that out for herself. "I'm making a phone call. Or at least, I'm trying to make a phone call. You have a problem with that?"

"You bet I do. You know you're not allowed to—"

A lady came out of the restroom, and Kate swallowed the rest of what she was going to say and forced a smile.

"I don't blame you, honey." The woman, who was dressed in a pink-and-green housecoat and backless slippers, offered Kate what could only be described as a knowing look. She stopped outside the restroom door, blew a long trail of cigarette smoke out of her nostrils, and gave Alex enough of a once-over to make him squirm. "He's real cute. You keep a close eye on that one. Seen it a thousand times." She took a drag on her cigarette. "First they make up some half-assed excuse for the phone calls, then it's stories about working late, and then they go away for weekends. With the boys, they say." She sent Alex a glare along with a puff of smoke. "Scumbag."

Alex watched the lady shuffle away. By the time she was back over to where she'd left a grocery store shopping cart filled with laundry, he expected that Kate would have given up the fight.

He should have known better.

Kate hadn't moved. And neither had the hand on the phone hook.

"Come on," she said. "We're going."

Alex wasn't about to make things that easy on her. He couldn't hang up the receiver. Not with Kate's hand still on the hook. He made to put it back up to his ear. "You're going, maybe. If you'll give me a little privacy, I'm making a phone call."

"No. You're not." Alex didn't expect her to reach over and pluck the receiver right out of his hand. It was the only reason he surrendered it so easily. "We're leaving," Kate said. She hung up the phone. "Now."

"After I make my phone call."

When Alex reached for the phone, Kate grabbed his arm. Her back to the floor-to-ceiling plate-glass windows at the front of the Laundromat, she stepped to her left so that Alex had a clear shot of the street outside.

"See that green Blazer cruising by?" she asked.

How she knew it was there, Alex couldn't imagine, but

she was right. Just as she spoke, a late-model SUV with tinted windows drove by. It took him a moment of wondering why she was staring deep into his eyes to figure out that she was watching the reflection off the front window in his glasses.

"That's the third time it's been by," she told him.

Alex shrugged. "You've seen one Chevy, you've seen them all."

"They all don't have the same license plates. Ohio. X as in X ray, Y as in yo-yo, Z as in zebra, six one one. It's the same car, all right. And he's driving by here way too slow for my liking."

It was so melodramatic, Alex nearly laughed. Then he remembered the pizza guy and the picture taken of Joe Bartone standing in the shadows right outside the gates of his own Long Island home. He watched the Blazer slow to a crawl, then speed up again as it got past the Laundromat. "What do you want to do?"

Kate nodded, apparently satisfied that for once, he'd made the right decision. "Our car's parked around back. You stay here. I'll get the clothes basket and we'll find a back door." She headed toward where she'd left the laundry, then turned and looked back at Alex. "Don't touch that phone," she said.

It wasn't her suggestion that kept Alex from having another try, it was the realization that she'd be back before he ever got the chance to connect the call. Watching the front windows for any signs of the Blazer, he waited for Kate to return and lead the way down a narrow hallway to a door that opened into the back parking lot. She set down the laundry basket and with a look, signaled Alex to stay back. She ducked out of the building, her back close to the wall.

Too curious not to wonder what was going on, Alex looked through the punched-out screen of the door. He saw Kate go as far as the corner of the building. She darted a look toward the street and apparently satisfied by what she saw—or didn't see—she came back to the door.

"They're gone." Kate glanced toward the street. The neighborhood was a mix of homes and businesses, some retail, some light industrial. It was an old part of the city, and though the streets were tree-lined, they were narrow and congested. There was a steady flow of traffic from both directions—a city bus, a delivery truck, a couple cars and even a bicycle or two—but there was no sign of the Blazer. "There's no use hanging around to see if they'll be back. I'll call the office later and have someone run the plates. Hand me the keys from my purse, then stay inside while I start the car."

"Oh, come on! There hasn't been time to plant a bomb." This time, Alex did laugh out loud. Now that it was filled with wet clothes, the laundry basket was heavier than ever. With a grunt, he hoisted it up into his arms and pushed open the door. "Besides, I'd rather be dead than have anyone find out where I spent my afternoon. If I'm blown to smithereens, so be it. At least I won't have to see the papers when they eulogize me as the Soapsuds Romeo."

"That's not funny."

Kate walked between Alex and the street. She glanced over her shoulder. She checked between the other cars parked in the black-topped lot, and even looked under the beat-up station wagon before she let him go anywhere near it.

Alex wasn't inclined to be overemotional or jumpy, but watching Special Agent Ellison, it was impossible to think of anything but her dire warnings. Even the white nightgown, soaked and soggy at the top of the basket, didn't look nearly as appealing as it had back inside the relative safety of the tumbledown house.

Kate's eyes were steely. Each movement was clean and concise. Each look she darted toward the street, and the sidewalk, and the other cars parked around them told Alex she knew exactly what she was doing. She was looking for the telltale signs that one of the cars parked there had been tampered with, that a car that looked to be empty really wasn't.

"I'm glad I'm not a bad guy."

Checking out the car parked next to them, Kate turned. "What?"

"I said, I'm glad I'm not a bad guy. You can be one tough customer when you have to be, can't you?"

Kate shrugged away the comment. "It's my job."

"No question about that. I'm just saying you do it well."

A rush of color stained Kate's cheeks. Alex couldn't imagine why. As compliments went, it wasn't much of one. Not compared to some of the other things he could have told her.

He could have told her that she looked pretty in pink. The color of her sweatshirt heightened the creamy shade of her skin and contrasted nicely with her eyes. He might have added that pushing her hair away from her face with a hairband was a good idea, too. He liked the way her bangs tickled her forehead, the way a few strands of hair fought free of the band and the way the breeze made it hug her cheek. He could have mentioned that now that they were away from the unappetizing smells that filled the Laundromat, he could just catch a whiff of the perfume she'd splashed on before they left the house. It was the same perfume she'd worn the day before and, though it smelled like it came straight from the shelf at the corner drugstore, he was beginning to like the fragrance. It reminded him of grapefruit. He might even have told her that the way she was looking at him—her eyes wide and her lips parted just enough for him to see the tip of her tongue as it flicked over her teeth—made him feel as if there was something they needed to say to each other.

That was exactly what he was going to say when the silence that hung between them was shattered by a loud *bang!*

4

Even before Kate slammed into Alex, she knew she was probably overreacting. Even before she knocked him to the ground, she suspected she was making something of a scene. Even before she landed on top of him—her nose against his nose and their mouths dangerously close—she knew what she'd heard. And what she'd heard wasn't gunfire. It didn't have the right sharp report. The sound that had cracked the silence between them was nothing more than a car backfiring.

Even before the thought had registered, Kate knew it was too late to pretend nothing had happened. Her legs were tangled with Alex's. Her chest was pressed to his. Her arms were splayed across him, one on each shoulder, and his heavy, dark-rimmed glasses were poking her cheek. It didn't take long for the old fight-or-flight response to kick in, and they were both breathing hard. They were lying flat against the blacktop, or at least Alex was. Kate was pillowed on top of him, simply for protection, she told herself. But protection had nothing to do with the fact that her heart was pounding against his and both his arms were around her.

Even before she saw the gleam in Alex's eyes, she knew he knew everything she knew. And she knew she'd made a colossal mistake.

But by that time, it was too late.

At the same time he shifted his weight, subtly repositioning his hips against hers, Kate felt Alex's lips lift into a smile. His voice dropped to a growl. "Is that a gun in your pants, or are you happy to see me?"

She lifted herself far enough away to offer him a smile that was more wry than the goofy leer he was giving her. "It's a gun," she said. "Tucked into the waistband of my jeans."

"Does that mean you're not happy to see me?"

"It means I'm happy no one was trying to take a potshot at you. I don't have to shoot back, so my gun can stay right where it is."

"Good thing, too." Alex rotated his hips against hers. "It feels so good!"

Kate rolled her eyes. It was a fairly adolescent response to the even more adolescent comment from Alex, but it was better than giving in to the delicious feelings that erupted inside her like Fourth of July fireworks. Rolling her eyes was better than letting them drift closed. Better than allowing the decadent moan caught at the base of her throat to escape. Rolling her eyes was much better than tipping her head back and giving in to the shameless thoughts Alex aroused in her, and since tipping her head back and giving in to the shameless thoughts Alex aroused in her was exactly what she felt like doing, she rolled her eyes again.

"Has anyone ever told you how annoying you are?" she asked.

"Nope." Alex linked his fingers at the small of her back. "As far as I remember, back in the old days—when I still had a life—that's not the way women thought of me. There were actually a few who thought I was pretty special."

"The cigarette-smoking lady in the Laundromat thought you were cute," Kate countered. "You want me to go find her? Maybe she's free tonight."

Alex continued as if she hadn't spoken. "There were even a few who thought I was a nice guy. There were also a couple who said they'd like to jump me. I never really worried about that. I thought they were just kidding." He shifted his hips again, just enough for Kate to realize he was not as cool, calm, and collected as he was pretending to be. He was just as interested as she was. Just as aroused. When he knew that she knew it, a devilish smile touched his lips. "So far, you're the only one who's actually done it."

It wasn't what he said that unnerved Kate. It wasn't the fact that they hardly knew each other and that, like any woman with half a brain, she did her best to avoid even the suggestion of intimacy with men she hardly knew. It wasn't the way the small arced scar at the left corner of his mouth twitched in a cocky sort of way that made her want to slap it. Or kiss it.

It was Alex's smile that worried her.

In spite of the fact that she told herself it was poor form, Kate swallowed hard. She'd seen the effect that smile had on women everywhere. It was what caused them to stand in line to buy issues of magazines that featured Alex on the cover. It was what made them drool over even the most fuzzy pictures of Alex in the most obscure tabloids. She had seen it work its magic on Sophia, the mayor's representative, who'd sat in on the meeting in New York, and on Charlotte, Alex's no-nonsense secretary, who melted beneath it like an ice cube in the hot summer sun.

Up close and personal, the smile packed more punch than any picture. It left Kate feeling a little light-headed, a little short of breath. A whole lot like the world had tipped on its axis, and what had been a fairly ordinary visit to a fairly conventional Laundromat suddenly contained all the kick of a jalapeño pepper.

Crazy. But when he was this close, so was looking into Alex's eyes. Crazy and uncontrolled, like free-falling into the unknown.

Before she could fall too fast, too far, or too hard, Kate repressed her fantasies. She didn't like to think of herself as another statistic, and she knew if she let herself get lost in Alex's smile, that's exactly what she'd be. Nothing but a number, another in the long list of ladies who'd lost their heads and their hearts. She didn't like to think what that would mean to what was left of her pride, or what it would do to the rest of her summer, not to mention her case, her career, and her future.

"I didn't jump you." Kate congratulated herself. She sounded far more sure of herself than she felt. "I was only doing my job."

"Uh-huh." Alex nodded solemnly at the same time he did something with his hips that made heat flash through Kate's bloodstream. "And so you're telling me you're not enjoying this? Just a little?"

"Are you?" The second the words were past her lips, Kate was sorry she asked. Before he could give her an answer she didn't want to hear, she decided to change the subject. "Fooling around in a parking lot with a guy in a fishnet shirt has never been one of my romantic fantasies, if that's what you mean. You think maybe we should get up? I'd hate to make people talk."

"They already are."

Before Kate could ask what he meant, a shadow slipped over Alex's face and a familiar voice called out a greeting. "You two are the cutest things! What are you up to, anyway?"

"Hi, Marge." Adjusting his glasses, Alex beamed a smile up at their across-the-street neighbor. "*We're* not up to anything. It's Missy here." He patted Kate's behind and with a look, dared her to object. "She's a wild woman. She can't keep her hands off me!"

"Oh, yes, I can!" As if to prove it, Kate hoisted herself off Alex and spun around to sit on the pavement. "Just messing around," she said to Marge. "Stan is such a kidder. You know how men can be."

"I know how I'd like Earl to be." With a wistful smile, Marge looked from Kate to Alex. "My Earl's a wonderful man. Don't think he's not. But imagine!" A surge of red stained Marge's neck above her green and purple spandex tube top. "Smooching in the parking lot. That's real romantic."

"Smooching?" The word was enough to make Kate spring to her feet. She managed a laugh that was half bravado, half embarrassment. "I don't want you to get the wrong impression here, Marge. Smooching? In a parking lot? No one's that romantic. Certainly not us. Why, Stan and I are just—"

The words caught in Kate's throat. When she'd thrown Alex to the ground, he'd dropped the laundry basket. For the first time, she noticed that their clothes had spilled.

Marge bent and held up the wisp of white fabric that fluttered near her feet. "Not romantic, huh?" She laughed, apparently pleased at having caught Missy in a lie. "Bet you can't wait to get home, huh, Stan?"

"You bet." Alex stood up and wrapped an arm around Kate's waist, tugging her close against him. "Told you she was a wild woman."

Kate didn't feel wild. When she should have been feeling armed and dangerous, she felt flushed and dizzy instead. It didn't help that Alex's hip was pressed against hers or that he was skimming his thumb up and down her rib cage. She did her best to control a shiver, but it was clear from the start her best wasn't good enough. Alex chuckled, and Kate knew she had to do everything she could to save the situation and what was left of her sanity.

"What a joker!" Kate squirmed out of Alex's embrace and as playfully as she could, gave him a two-handed push that wasn't nearly as forceful as she would have liked it to be. "Always messing around. Come on, Stan." She scooped the rest of the clothes up off the pavement and shoved them into the laundry basket. "We'd better get home and hang these clothes on the line. We wouldn't want them to dry all wrinkled."

"Oh, don't go. Not yet." Marge held on to Kate's arm with one hand. "I was going to stop and see you two this afternoon anyway. Now I don't have to. I thought . . . well . . . seeing as you're new in town and all, I thought you'd like to come out with me and Earl on Friday night."

The suggestion was so completely out of the blue, Kate wasn't sure what to say. She waited for Alex to come up with some sort of half-baked excuse as to why they'd have to pass, and when all he did was look as disconcerted by the invitation as she was, she smiled at Marge. "Out? That's really a very generous invitation, Marge, but we—"

"Oh, no! No excuses." Marge patted Kate's arm. "I know what you're going to say. You're going to say you're newlyweds and you want to spend all your time alone. Well, I can't say I blame you." Her gaze strayed to the laundry basket and the bit of sheer white fabric that hung over the edge. "But you can't spend all your time in the house. Come on. It'll be fun."

"Fun?" Alex found his voice and Kate was sorry he did. Even from behind his glasses, she could see he had the same look in his eyes he'd had back in New York when they'd tried to convince him to leave his plush and privileged life for four months of a world-class reality check. He had the same set to his shoulders, rock-hard and rigid, the same way of looking down his aristocratic nose at everyone and everything, the one that said loud and clear that he not only thought he was better than anyone else, but that he was probably right.

Afraid Marge might notice the change, Kate intervened as quickly as she could. "What Stan means is that it would be fun. Sure. But—"

Marge laughed. "But you want to spend all your time at home in bed together. Is that what you're telling me?"

Alex grinned at the suggestion and fixed Kate with a look, daring her to lie.

Kate groaned. The FBI Academy had never prepared her for situations like this. If she told Marge spending her time in bed with Alex was exactly what she wanted to do, she'd never hear the end of it. If she told her it wasn't at all what she meant, she'd be as good as accepting Marge's invitation.

Weighing her choices and finding them limited, Kate decided on the lesser of two evils. She returned Alex smile for smile, look for look. "We'd love to come out with you and Earl on Friday night," she said. "Sure, Marge. We'll come out with you. Yes."

"No!" Outside the doors of the St. John of Krakow parish hall, Alex planted his feet and crossed his arms over his chest. "I'm not going in there."

Kate wasn't in the mood to argue. They'd been doing that most of the day. Most of the week. Ever since Marge had invited them for a little Friday night fun and frolic. Hoisting her oversize purse up on her shoulder, she stepped aside to let three middle-aged ladies into the building. "I'm no more excited about this than you are," she said, careful to keep her voice down. "But we can't get out of it. Not without looking conspicuous."

"We don't already look conspicuous?" Alex glanced down at his jeans and faded green polo shirt. The jeans were worn smooth over his butt. The shirt strained over his shoulders. "I look like a fish out of water," he said.

It wasn't at all what Kate had been thinking. But then, what she'd been thinking wasn't something she would have admitted anyway.

"And you . . ." He eyed Kate's yellow cotton shorts and her orange T-shirt dotted with yellow flowers closely enough to make Kate squirm inside her scuffed tennis shoes. "You don't look so bad," he announced and he seemed honestly surprised. Alex wrinkled his nose and his glasses wiggled. "Why is that? How could you look like supercop in New York, and in Cleveland like—"

She didn't want to know what she looked like, so she didn't give him a chance to finish. "I shouldn't look like I fit in," she told him. She took a look at the storefronts and bars that lined the street, at the trucks that drove past, and the people out on the sidewalk who ranged from neighborhood regulars to kids on skateboards to the homeless.

"I'm not from anyplace like this. I'm a farm kid from Nebraska." In spite of the fact that they'd spent nearly a week together, it was the first bit of personal information she'd revealed to Alex. No wonder—it was the first time he'd come even close to asking. "The only reason I look like I fit in is because I'm trying to fit in. You'll fit in. . . ."

A group of a dozen or so senior citizens got off a bus and trooped into the building. Kate waited until they'd gone by. "You'll fit in when you stop acting like Little Lord Fauntleroy. Loosen up, Romeo. It's only for one night. Besides, the neighbors are less likely to talk about us if they get to know us. If we hide behind closed doors all the time, they're bound to wonder. And people who wonder are bound to talk. That's the last thing we need."

"No." Alex shook his head, the gesture simple and absolute. "The last thing we need is to go in there. The last thing we need to do . . ." He gulped down his disgust, or at least he tried. Nothing could disguise the acid tones of contempt that laced his voice. "The last thing I need to do in this or any other lifetime is to play bingo."

Kate couldn't help herself. She had to laugh. Now that Friday was finally here and she'd resigned herself to going along with Marge's plans, she realized how much she was actually looking forward to getting out in public. There was only so much of staying at home she could stand, even if it was staying at home with the World's Sexiest Man.

Especially if it was staying at home with the World's Sexiest Man.

Kate twitched aside the thought and all the baggage

that went with it. In the last few days, when she and Alex weren't arguing about bingo, they had settled into a routine of sorts.

She spent her days catching up on paperwork and obsessing about Alex.

He watched TV and paced the living room.

She spent her evenings trying to plow through Ruben Martinez's incomprehensible prose and obsessing about Alex.

He watched TV and paced the living room.

She spent her nights tossing and turning as much as she could in her cramped bed. And oh, yes, obsessing about Alex.

From what she could hear, when he was done pacing the living room and watching TV, he slept like a log.

It was as monotonous as hell, and twice as punishing. Any distraction was a relief. Even if it was spelled B-I-N-G-O.

"Yoo-hoo!" Kate came out of her thoughts to find Marge standing just inside the double doors that led into the church hall. She was wearing purple shorts and a loose purple top with wide sleeves that flapped like wings when she waved at them. "We saved you seats," she said. "But you better hurry. Early bird starts in ten minutes."

"Early bird."

Coming from Alex, the words didn't sound nearly as enthusiastic as they had coming from Marge. Kate watched a muscle jump at the base of his jaw.

She patted his arm and led him inside. "Early bird."

"And that means?"

"I don't have a clue. But we're about to find out."

From the architecture of the buildings, Kate guessed the St. John of Krakow church and school must have been built sometime before the 1920s. One look told her the parish social hall was of the same vintage. The room was massive. What once must have been spacious windows along one wall had been partially bricked in and finished with glass blocks that didn't let in nearly enough light. The linoleum-covered floors had obviously seen their share of church carnivals, afternoon recess jump rope contests, and countless Lenten fish fries. The green tile was coming up in some places, gone in others, and the cement floor showed through. The place had the peculiar smell she'd come to associate with the entire neighborhood, a combination of the chemicals that belched from the local steel mills, the fumes of the cars from the highway that bisected the area, and the passage of time. Though the night was young, there was already a blue haze of cigarette smoke in the air just above their heads.

Never one to be subtle, Alex coughed. "Haven't these people ever heard of secondhand smoke?"

Something told Kate they'd heard of it, all right. The same something that told her they didn't care.

Kate's eyes burned. Her smile wavered. After her brave speech to Alex about getting out in public, unwinding, and having a little fun, she couldn't stand the thought of letting him know she found the whole thing a little intimidating. She had walked smack dab into a world where all the skills she'd learned at the Academy weren't worth jack. Here in a neighborhood of shots and beers, Friday night bingo games, and ladies who actually came out in public with pink plastic rollers in their hair, all that mattered was keeping Alex Romero alive. Back in New York, she'd assured Mark Harrison that she'd do anything to make certain of that, and though she drew the line at pink plastic rollers, she still meant it. To keep him safe, she had to make sure they blended in with the other residents of the neighborhood. And they would, damn it, if it was the last thing she did.

When Alex gave her a look that was misery itself, Kate smiled back brightly.

"This is where you buy your cards." Marge showed them to a table where two elderly ladies were selling paper pads covered with the traditional bingo squares and numbers. "How many sets would you like?"

Quickly Kate scanned the price list on the wall. As

near as she could see, each pad had six bingo game cards. One set was three pads. That was eighteen bingo cards apiece. And that was plenty.

She didn't bother to ask Alex what he thought. She was afraid he might tell her. Instead, she paid for the cards and followed along obediently as Marge led them into the fray.

From wall to wall, the hall was filled with battered wooden tables, wooden folding chairs, and nearly one hundred people who looked to be settling in for the long haul. Most of them had come prepared with chips and pretzels, cans of soda, and tote bags filled with whatever other supplies they needed to make their night on the town complete. Here and there, Kate saw someone with a framed photograph, or a bean bag animal, or a crazy-haired troll set up near their bingo cards. She tugged at Marge's sleeve and pointed.

"Good-luck charms," Marge explained. "Everyone has their own special one. Mostly it's pictures of their kids or grandkids, but sometimes it's something even more special. Take a look at Edna over there." She pointed to a skinny lady with big hair and bright red lipstick. "Brings Wilbur's shoes."

"Shoes." Kate followed Marge's gaze and confirmed the fact. "And Wilbur would be . . ."

Marge chuckled. "Her husband. Dead, of course. Can't see that the shoes brought Wilbur any luck, but Edna thinks they work. You brought something, didn't you?"

Kate looked back at Alex. "Did we bring a good-luck charm?"

"You're my good-luck charm, Missy." Though Alex kept his eyes fixed straight ahead and refused to look around, Kate had no doubt he'd seen enough. He spoke through clenched teeth. "You're all the good luck I'll ever need."

"That's so sweet." Marge found her place and waved Kate and Alex to two seats across from hers. "Isn't that sweet?" she asked the man who was waiting there. "Stan says Missy is his good-luck charm."

Though Kate had never met Marge's better half, dozens of surveillance photos had been taken in the area in the weeks before she and Alex moved in. She recognized Earl instantly as the same middle-aged fellow who'd appeared in so many of the pictures: Five nine, two-forty, brown eyes, sky-high hairline above a fringe of pale, graying hair. She knew he was a line worker at the local Ford assembly plant who liked to fish, listen to Indians baseball games on the radio, and tinker with his car.

"Sweet." Earl didn't sound any more convinced than he looked. He looked like a man on a mission who couldn't be bothered with pleasantries. After they'd settled down, he got his wish. A fellow seated on the stage at the front of the room mumbled something into a scratchy sounding microphone and Earl perked right up. So did Marge.

"This is it!" She patted Earl's arm and slid two slim plastic bottles across the table. The bottles uncapped to reveal spongy tops and Kate realized they were for dabbing their bingo sheets. "You two ready?"

"No." Alex untwisted the cap on his fat blue marker as if he were beheading it.

"Yes." Kate uncapped her red one.

"This will be a double bingo," Marge said, her voice hushed in deference to the reverent silence that descended over the hall. "That's two straight lines any way, or a straight line and a postage stamp, corners, big diamond, or little diamond." Her fingers flew over one of the cards in front of her, drawing out the various winning formations. "It'll probably be a wild ball, too, so you know what that means. Every number that ends the same as the number they call. Get it?"

This time, Alex didn't even try to respond. Kate turned to find him staring at his bingo cards, his dark brows low over his eyes. "What the hell is she talking about?" he grumbled.

Kate clicked her tongue and managed to control her

voice so Earl and Marge wouldn't hear. "It's not that hard if you pay attention. Besides, I thought you were supposed to be some kind of genius."

Even through the haze in the air, Alex's smile was as brittle as a winter sky. "Not supposed to be. Am. I am some kind of genius." He capped his dabber bottle, uncapped it, capped it again, his fingers so tight around it, his knuckles were white. Something written on the plastic bottle caught Alex's eye and he swore and pointed.

Kate read the name of the manufacturer and burst into laughter. "Happy Dabbers, a division of Romero Industries."

"Trust me." Alex hunched his shoulders and sank down in his chair. "As soon as we get back to civilization, I'm selling the company."

The next hour went by in a blur. After a game or two, Kate got the hang of things, and if Alex didn't—if he didn't have fun—it was his own fault. He didn't bat an eyelash as Marge explained each new permutation of the game. He didn't listen when Marge introduced Kate to the wonders of the small cards she called "instants" that cost one dollar and might, if the pictures hidden under the little flaps on them appeared in the right order, mean winnings of up to five hundred dollars. He didn't crack a smile when Marge won a game, and fifty dollars. Kate squealed with delight and applauded, and though she told herself she was only playing along and trying to fit in, she had to admit she was genuinely happy for Marge. She also admitted, at least to herself, that she would be a whole lot happier if she could win a game, too. She poked Alex on the arm.

"I almost won that time. How about you? I only needed B fourteen, O seventy-five, and I twenty-one. What did you need?" She looked over at Alex's cards. Instead of dabbing the numbers that had been called, he'd dabbed out a frowning face. Kate sighed. "I know just how you feel. We're not winning," she told him, "because we don't have a good-luck charm."

"We're not winning," he muttered, "because we don't give a damn."

"Maybe you don't give a damn. I do." There was a momentary lull in the action before the start of the next game and Kate crossed her arms over her chest and sat back in her chair. She looked in one direction down the table to where an old woman had lit a red votive candle near her bingo cards. She looked to the other side of her where a young, shapely lady with platinum blond hair had pictures of her children lined up in front of her.

"We'd win if we had a good-luck charm." Kate didn't even care if she sounded as petulant to Alex as she did to herself. This was serious. Already, nearly half her pad of bingo sheets was gone, and though she'd bought a handful of instants, she hadn't come near to winning anything. "There must be something we could use to bring us some good luck."

Alex stood and patted down his pockets, and if he noticed that the shapely blonde watched every one of his moves, he didn't acknowledge her, or even offer a smart-assed remark. He shrugged. "All out of good-luck charms," he said, dropping back into his chair. "I must have left my stash of shrunken heads in my other suit."

"Very funny." Kate drummed her fingers against the pitted tabletop. "I want a good-luck charm."

"I want my life back. Are we even?"

Kate didn't bother to answer. She didn't know what to say, and besides, the next game was starting and it was the last game before intermission. She'd worry about Alex and his attitude problems later. What mattered now was bingo.

The man with the microphone cleared his throat. "N thirty-three," he called.

"I have N thirty-two," Kate grumbled. "And N thirty-four. And even N thirty-five. Why doesn't he call those numbers?"

"B seven."

"Damn." Kate marked off the number. It was on only

three of her eighteen cards and she knew that wasn't enough. "I'll never win with numbers like that," she grumbled.

"O sixty-six."

"Can you believe it?" Kate shook her head. "Of all the O numbers he could have called. O sixty-six. Who has O sixty-six? Do you have O sixty-six?" She scanned Alex's cards. "You do. You've got it there. And there." She pointed to each O sixty-six she found. "And there. And—"

Her search for O sixty-six stopped when Alex turned in his seat and reached for something under the table. He came up holding an empty gum wrapper and plopped it down in front of her.

"Here," he said. "Here's a good-luck charm. Now will you please be quiet!"

The pink bubble gum wrapper was made of shiny paper that caught the light and made it sparkle against the paper bingo sheets. Kate blinked, genuinely touched by Alex's offering. When the caller yelled "G fifty-seven," she shook away her momentary surprise and got back to business.

Dutifully she dabbed number after number, all the while keeping an eye on the pink wrapper, and when the voice over the microphone called out "B thirteen," and Kate screamed, "Bingo!" she was convinced it was the gum wrapper that had brought her luck.

Her hands shaking with excitement, Kate accepted her winnings from a lady in a housecoat and orthopedic shoes who checked her card, handed her a pile of cash, and went away smiling just because Alex happened to glance her way. "Look!" Kate grabbed Alex's arm. "One hundred dollars. I won one hundred dollars!"

She had to give Alex credit. He tried to muster some enthusiasm. He almost smiled.

"I suppose one hundred dollars is chump change to you," she told him. "Well, it isn't to me." She counted the bills and tucked them into her pocket. "That's a lot of money. Considering we only spent thirty to get in, we've already increased our money by a bigger percentage than most mutual funds pay."

"Most mutual fund investments don't call for the use of an iron lung." Alex coughed and pounded his chest. "Or a good chiropractor." He winced and stretched.

It was a good thing it was time for intermission. Kate's back was sore, too, and her butt had been flattened by the uncomfortable chair. She hardly noticed. Pleased with her winnings and with the way the evening was going, she stood. "Marge and I are going to the snack bar. I'm the big winner." She touched her pocket. "So it's my treat. What can I get you?"

Alex glanced toward the yellow-tiled kitchen at the far end of the room and at the blue-haired lady in a white nylon dress who seemed to be in charge. "I'll have the Mangalore salmon braised with coconut milk," he said. "Curried, I think. A little grilled asparagus on the side touched with balsamic vinegar, and, let's see . . ." He tipped his head back. "A nice crisp white wine. I'll let you choose. Something Chilean would be nice."

Kate made a face at him. It was the only response he deserved.

For once, when Kate walked away, Alex didn't concentrate on the nice, smooth length of her legs or the way her hips swayed just enough to remind him that FBI agent or not, she was all woman. For once, he didn't think about the way her ponytail twitched along her neck, or the fantasy that had been prickling at his self-control all week, the one about trailing his tongue along the same path that ponytail traveled each time Kate took a step. For once, he didn't think about nibbling the flesh just below her ear, or skimming his mouth along the back of her neck. He didn't even consider dipping a kiss inside the neckline of her shirt, just to see if it would make her shiver.

For once, he didn't think of any of those things. At least not too much. He was too busy wondering how he'd found himself inside one of the circles of hell the poet

Dante wrote about. He wasn't sure which circle it was, he only knew it had to be down toward the bottom somewhere. It was a place where women wore flowered housecoats and men had beer bellies. A place of green linoleum and blue bingo dabbers, where even a woman he'd thought of as levelheaded and intelligent could be reduced to lunacy by the numbered squares on a pad of paper.

It was Hell. It had to be. Bingo Hell.

"So how do you do it?"

Alex was so busy wondering what he'd done to earn damnation, he didn't even notice that Earl had come around the table to sit next to him. He shook away his thoughts. "Pardon me?"

"How do you do it?" Earl asked again. "I seen it when Betty brought that money over to your Missy. And again, now. That girl over there, the good-looker with the yellow hair . . ." He tipped his head in the direction of the platinum blonde, who was eyeing Alex while she crushed an empty cigarette pack. "I seen the way she's been looking at you since you walked in."

"Seen what?" Alex cringed at the very thought that his grammar might be influenced by people like Earl. He shook his head and blamed the slip on the amount of smoke. And the lack of oxygen. "What did you see?"

"The way you made them girls all giggly. Like when you told Missy she was your good-luck charm. Hell, couldn't you tell? Marge thought that was just about the most romantic thing she'd heard in a month of freakin' Sundays. How do you think of things like that?"

The notion that he would be having a conversation about romance with a man like Earl in the middle of what had to be one of the worst experiences of his life was nearly enough to make Alex laugh. He might have, if he wasn't afraid to take too deep a breath. He shrugged. "I don't know," he said, and he meant it. "I didn't do anything. Not consciously."

"Looks like you don't have to." Earl shook his head, honest admiration showing on his beefy face. "Some of it's probably your looks. Even with them nerdy glasses. But the rest . . ." He looked down at the floor, then up at the ceiling, then at the floor again before he glanced at Alex briefly and cleared his throat. "Suppose you could teach me?" he asked.

Fortunately Alex didn't have time to answer. He honestly didn't know what to say. Before he had the chance to say anything, Marge and Kate came back and Earl scurried off and disappeared into the cloud of cigarette smoke on the other side of the table.

Kate plunked something down in front of Alex that looked like an overgrown hot dog. It was nestled in a bun and covered with sauerkraut and ketchup. "They were fresh out of Mangalore salmon. Said to try again next week. You'll have to settle for the specialty of the house, a kielbasa sandwich."

"I certainly will not." Alex pushed away the offering with one finger. "I'd rather starve."

"Have it your way." Kate shrugged, unconcerned, and dropped into her seat. She popped open a can of diet cola and reached for Alex's rejected sandwich. "I'll eat it."

There was something about watching other people consume fatty meat products of indeterminate origin that made the short hairs on the back of Alex's neck stand on end. He tried not to pay any attention. Still, he found it impossible to take his eyes off Kate. She was either very good at pretending or she was actually having a good time.

Kate wolfed down bite after bite, washing each one down with a swig of soda straight out of the can. By the time she was finished, there was a spot of sauerkraut juice smack in the center of one of the yellow daisies on her shirt and a blotch of ketchup on her chin.

"Here." Automatically Alex grabbed one of the paper

napkins she'd brought along from the kitchen and wiped her chin.

As personal contact went, it wasn't much. Paper napkin. Ketchup. Chin. Still, Alex felt a tiny current of electricity tingle through his fingertips, as if even that much of a touch of Kate's skin was enough to ignite sparks. It might have been one of those tiny but memorable moments that sometimes sneaks up on a couple, one small step that hurtles them straight over the edge of logic and into a night of passion. It might have been. If Kate had bothered to notice. She didn't.

The lady selling instant cards came by, and Kate jumped up. "How many do you want?" she asked.

Alex crumpled up the paper napkin and tossed it into the brown paper grocery bag where they'd been discarding their used bingo cards. "I don't want any," he told Kate. "And you don't, either."

Kate paid for a handful of instants and ripped them open in record time.

"What a waste of money!" Alex watched her toss losing card after losing card into the brown bag. "You'd be better off going outside and throwing your money—"

"I won!" Kate hopped up and down. "I won. See?" She thrust the card an inch from Alex's nose. "Twenty-five dollars. I won twenty-five dollars!"

She did win, and in some corner of his mind, Alex supposed he should be happy for her. He might have been, if he wasn't worried. He didn't like the fact that Kate's eyes were glassy, or that there were spots of bright color in her cheeks. He really didn't like it when she collected her winnings and promptly spent most of the money on more instant tickets. He'd seen the same sort of behavior everywhere from Vegas to Monte Carlo. Kate had been bitten, all right. The gambling bug had claimed another victim.

Alex tugged at the sleeve of Kate's T-shirt. "You need to sit down and relax. Take a deep breath." He watched the platinum blonde next to them blow out a long trail of cigarette smoke and changed his mind. "No, don't take a deep breath. Settle down. Relax."

Her shoulders squared, Kate sat down. "Can't relax. The next game is about to start." She laid one hand on the pink gum wrapper and grabbed her dabber with the other.

For a moment, Alex actually thought a lecture on superstitions might be in order. He would, he thought, point out that the gum wrapper couldn't possibly be a good-luck charm. He'd found it on the floor. Hell, when he gave it to her, he wasn't trying to bring her luck. He was trying to shut her up. He was all set to remind Kate of that, and he actually might have if she hadn't won the first game and another fifty dollars. By that time, he didn't have to see the gleam in her eyes to know she was way past listening.

"Can you believe this?" Kate tore into another fistful of instants. "I've never been this lucky in my life. Do you suppose that's why we're really here? I mean, do you suppose that it's fate or karma or something? That we're really here not because of you but because of me? So I could find out how lucky I really am? What a great bingo player I really am? They do this every Friday night, don't they? We're not busy next Friday night. I think we should—"

It was all Alex could take, and not just because he couldn't stand the thought of another Friday deep in the Inferno. Before Kate could dab another number or rip open the little door on another instant, he pushed back his chair, got to his feet, and lifted her into his arms.

Kate howled, half in surprise and half in protest. Marge twittered and said something about how romantic the whole thing was. Earl looked up from his bingo cards and, when the next number was called, looked right back down again.

"Wait!" Alex had already gone a step or two when Kate called out. She stretched and grabbed her purse in one hand and the gum wrapper with the other.

If Alex needed any more proof that he'd done the right thing, that was it. Without a care for the stunned expressions on the faces of a few of the bingo players, without a thought about how odd it was that a whole lot more people were too engrossed in the game to even notice, he hauled Kate out of the building.

5

The slap of cool night air against her heated cheeks made Kate wince. She shook her head, and though she knew exactly where she'd been and what she'd done while she was there, she felt as if she were waking from a dream. As far as she could remember, it was a mixed-up sort of dream. It had something to do with breathing too much smoke, buying too many instant bingo cards, and letting herself get too carried away.

Both literally and figuratively.

Kate squeezed her eyes shut and tried to swallow down her embarrassment. It was no use. Closing her eyes didn't make her feel any better, and it sure didn't make her any less aware of the fact that Alex Romero—millionaire playboy, business tycoon, personal friend of everyone who was anyone, and her star witness, damn it—was lugging her down the street like a sack of potatoes.

That in itself was enough to provide humiliation to last a lifetime. Add to it the way Alex's one arm cradled her backside, the way his other arm was wrapped tight across her shoulders, the way his chin nestled on the top of her head, and the way her cheek was pressed against his chest, and she knew one lifetime would never be enough. Not to live this down.

"You can stop now." Kate's voice was no more than a croak, the words rough with embarrassment and the last traces of what had to be the equivalent of the smoke from a triple three-alarm fire. "You can put me down."

"Oh, no!" Alex stopped, but only long enough to let a bus roll by. Once it was out of the way, he crossed a street and kept on walking, his stride long and purposeful. "There's no way I'm putting you down. Not until we're good and far from that place and you're safe from bingo fever."

"Bingo fever." Kate groaned the words. She dared to open her eyes just in time to see Alex glance down at her.

She wasn't sure what sort of expression she expected to see on his face. Or which meant the most trouble. If Alex laughed at her, she was afraid she might take a swing at him. If he didn't, she could only imagine what it might mean. Alex was a powerful and influential man. He wasn't used to incompetence or instability. He didn't tolerate people who were unreliable. He didn't put up with people who were irresponsible.

Bad enough when those people were the folks who worked for him. Worse when those people—that person—was supposed to be keeping him alive.

"Really. You can put me down now. I'm fine." Kate barely got the words past the knot of embarrassment lodged in her throat. When Alex didn't bother to respond, she tried again. "I swear! I swear I won't go running back there to buy any more instants. Please? Please put me down."

This time, Alex stopped. He glanced at her uncertainly, and when Kate lifted her eyebrows in a gesture that told him she meant what she said, he gently lowered her feet to the sidewalk.

"Thanks." Kate set her purse down on the pavement long enough to smooth her shirt and shorts back into place. She wished she could iron out her reputation as easily. She couldn't believe she'd actually been loony enough to bring the good-luck gum wrapper with her, and as if she could as easily distance herself from everything it meant, she balled it up and tossed it into the street. "See?" she asked, holding her empty hands out to Alex. "You're safe. I wouldn't dare go back in there without my good-luck charm."

A minivan sped by and flattened the gum wrapper, and Kate couldn't fail to see the symbolism. Flat as a pancake. Like her career was sure to be when word of this incident got out.

The sight of the squashed pink wrapper was too much to take, and Kate glanced back over Alex's right shoulder toward the church. She looked up at the tall spire and the pigeons whirling around it. She glanced down at the sidewalk where the names of two long-ago lovers were scrawled through the cement. She looked at anything and everything but Alex, because she was afraid if she looked at him, she'd see something in his eyes as disturbing as the sight of her flattened good-luck charm. Something that told her he was disappointed.

She couldn't blame him. She was disappointed, too.

"I can understand if you're upset. Honest, I can." Kate sucked in a long, unsteady breath. She lifted her purse, holding it to her breast like a shield. At the same time, she forced herself to meet Alex's eyes. "I screwed up. Royally. But I hope you'll keep in mind that it wasn't a critical situation. There was no real or implied threat to your person or to your safety. That's not an excuse. If it was, it wouldn't be a very good one. I was just trying to fit in, and I . . ." She searched for words that wouldn't sound as ineffectual as she felt. "I forgot myself."

Kate fished inside her purse. She found her 9mm semi-automatic, a scattering of dollar bills, two used instants, and her cell phone. She pulled out the phone and set the purse back on the sidewalk. "I'm sure you've figured out by now that the phone at the house is a dummy. It doesn't work. The line isn't connected."

If Alex was surprised by the change of subject, he didn't show it. He glanced from Kate to the phone. "Because you don't want me making any phone calls."

"Because we thought you'd be safer if you didn't make any phone calls, yes. Here." She offered the cell phone to Alex. "You can use my phone to call Mark Harrison. You might as well tell him the whole ugly truth. He's bound to find out anyway. Mark's sort of uncanny that way. But he's also one hell of an administrator. I don't want you to think any of this is his fault. I don't have a reputation for being untrustworthy. I never have been before. Mark never would have given me this assignment if I was. Talk to him. He'll know exactly what to do. He'll have another agent here by morning."

Alex didn't bother to look at the phone. He kept his gaze on Kate. His expression was blank, his eyes, unreadable. He didn't look indifferent, he looked guarded, and for the first time, Kate knew exactly what made him so successful. Alex wasn't a man who laid his cards out on the table, not until he knew he had a winning hand.

It made her glad she didn't have to deal with him in business. Or play poker with him. And that made it even harder for her to keep her hands from trembling as she held the phone out to him.

"A replacement Missy, huh?" he asked. "How would I explain that to the neighbors?"

Leave it to Alex to get right down to business. Kate supposed she should thank him for it. If she concentrated on the details, she might be able to forget how awful she felt. At least for a minute or two. "Not to worry. I'm sure the agent assigned to take my place will arrive with all the information you need. A sick parent, a call from an old friend out in L.A. who needs help, emergency surgery." Tired of holding the phone, she shoved it into Alex's hands. "There are plenty of ways to explain away ol' Missy's disappearance. Mark will coach you through it."

Like he'd never seen one before, Alex turned the

phone over and over again. "I'm not sure I remember how to use one of these things."

"It'll come back to you." Kate managed a smile that probably looked as hollow as it felt. "Just flip open the little door over the number keys. It's late and Mark's probably at home by now, but his number is—"

Alex dropped the phone into Kate's purse. "There's no reason for me to call Mark."

"Of course there is!" Kate couldn't believe her own ears. She was actually trying to talk Alex into making a call that would probably result in her spending the rest of her years at the Bureau filing paperwork. Or worse yet, tracking down Smokey cases. She tried not to think about that. Instead, she reminded herself about her duty, and the fact that she owed Alex. After all, he'd put himself on the line. It was the least she could do in return.

"I was out of control," she told him, and she noticed he didn't even make an attempt to contradict her, or to make her try to feel any better. "If I can't control myself, how can I control the situation? I was—"

"You went a little crazy. Big deal." Alex shrugged. "So Stan is married to a crazy woman. Who cares? Who even noticed? You got so caught up, you didn't even realize you were acting as weird as everyone else in that place."

"But I was—"

"You were goofy. Hey, world!" Alex turned toward the street, threw out his arms, and yelled as loud as he could. "Missy Tomashefski is a goofy woman!" The words echoed back from the buildings around them, and it wasn't until after they'd quieted that he turned back to Kate. "See? I told you. No one cares. Besides, there's no crime in getting carried away," he told her.

He was right. But it didn't make her feel much better. "No crime, no," she admitted. "But it shouldn't have happened."

Alex turned up his smile a notch and leaned closer. "Some of the most memorable things I've ever done were things that never should have happened."

Kate didn't like the implication. Or the suggestion that glittered in Alex's smile. "Maybe, but—"

"Will you listen to yourself?" Alex laughed, the sound warm and genuine. When he put a hand on Kate's shoulder, it was clear he meant nothing by it but friendship. "You're trying to talk me into getting you yanked from this assignment. Is that what you really want? Because if you do—"

"No." There were plenty of things Kate didn't know about Alex. But she did know he wasn't a man who played games. He was asking for the truth, and he wouldn't give her another chance to give it to him. "I don't want to be taken off the case. I don't want Mark to know I screwed up. I want to do a good job. You have to believe that."

"Believe it? You think I don't know it?" Alex's hand tightened against her shoulder. The night was warm; his skin was hot. The breeze that ruffled her hair was cool; Kate's temperature was anything but—especially when he skimmed his fingers over her shoulder and up her neck. He tucked a loose curl of hair behind her ear and whisked his thumb across her cheek. His voice was as warm as his touch. "Hey, you saved my life back in New York. That was the bravest thing I've ever seen anybody do, and I'm not about to forget it. The way I figure it, that's a lot more important than the fact that a stupid game of bingo could turn you into some kind of crackpot, goofball, lunatic, maniac—"

"I get the message!" Kate laughed. It was the only thing she could do to keep from shivering beneath Alex's touch. Hoping it looked more casual than it felt, she sidled out of his reach, but even that wasn't enough to break the fragile connection between them. It hummed in the air and vibrated along her skin, and for something to do, Kate reached for her purse and slung it over her shoulder. She glanced back toward the church. "You're sure you don't want to go back and try a couple more instants? I'm on a lucky streak."

"I'm sure." Alex grabbed her elbow and tugged her in

the direction of home. This time, Kate went along without arguing. She knew she should have put up a fuss. She knew it wasn't smart to let herself get carried away. Not a second time. It wasn't wise to waltz through the night with Alex's hand on her arm, and Alex's hip brushing against hers. It wasn't smart to let Alex's voice wrap around her, as soft around the edges as the shadows.

Still, she didn't make any attempt to break the connection. It felt too good.

"Damn it, you broke my connection!"

Alex looked down at the cell phone in his hands. With the early morning light pouring through the kitchen window, it was impossible to see the numbers on the digital display. Not that it mattered. He knew Norbert Fielding's number wasn't there anymore. Kate made sure of that when she snuck up behind him and flipped the phone closed before his call ever went through.

"That's not the only thing I'm going to break." Kate yanked the phone out of his hands. She was wearing a yellow chenille robe and she tucked the phone in one of her pockets and held her hand over it. "You stole my phone. You stole my phone out of my purse. That's pretty low."

Alex crossed his arms over his chest. He wasn't used to being challenged, not by anyone, and the thought that he was being challenged by a barefoot woman whose pink nightgown peeked out from the hem of her knee-length robe didn't help. Neither did the headline on the front page of the morning paper that lay on the kitchen table: *Martinez Trial Opens*.

"I didn't steal it. I borrowed it." Alex lifted his chin, daring her to dispute his logic. "No, I didn't even borrow it. I was using it. That's what phones are for, aren't they? For using?"

"Not by you." In spite of the yellow robe and the pink nightgown and the adolescent-looking blue-and-pink barrettes that held her hair off her face, Kate didn't look a thing like the wacky woman he'd dragged out of Bingo Hell the night before. Though she clearly had just rolled out of bed, she was wide awake, alert as can be, and as determined to keep him out of touch with his life as ever.

"Don't you get it?" Kate's eyes flashed, the color somewhere between thundercloud gray and January ice. "Don't you realize how dangerous it could be for you to contact anyone on the outside?"

"I'm not contacting *anyone*. I'm contacting Norbert. Trying to contact Norbert." Too annoyed to keep still, Alex stuffed his hands into the pockets of his jeans and paced over to the kitchen table and back again. It was a pathetically short distance, and he needed to pace it another three times before he could order his thoughts and control the frustration that threatened to erupt into full-fledged anger.

"There's no danger in contacting Norbert," he told Kate, and he knew it was true. He'd never been more certain of anything, or anyone, in his life. "Norbert and I go back a long way. He's my personal assistant. We play golf together. Hell, I'm his oldest son's godfather! Norbert is not about to sell out to some hit man with my name on his to-do list."

It was apparently too early in the morning for Kate to listen to logic. As if discarding every one of Alex's arguments, she twitched her shoulders. "That doesn't mean a thing. Whether you want to admit it or not, you have to face facts. At this stage of the game we don't know who we can trust."

"We can trust Norbert."

"Maybe." Kate paused long enough to give the word more significance than Alex thought it deserved. "Maybe you're willing to take that chance, but I'll tell you what: I'm not. I told you before, I've worked long and hard on this case. Even if you have a death wish, I'm not going to let anything happen to you. At least not until after you testify."

"Thanks. I think." Alex might have gone right on

arguing the point if another thought hadn't occurred to him. It was his own damned fault, all of it, and the realization gave him a sinking feeling. He didn't have anyone to blame but himself. "I never should have agreed to testify in the first place."

All right, he sounded like a spoiled brat. He sounded like a teenager who'd just been told he couldn't have the keys to the car on Friday night. But that didn't mean Kate had to jump in and try to make him feel any better. Nothing could.

But Kate didn't know that, and she shot forward and put one hand on his arm, her expression so intense, so sincere, so FBI that Alex nearly laughed. "You aren't serious, are you?" She shook her head, immediately dismissing the thought. Of course a woman like Kate couldn't possibly believe he might be serious, not when she was so damned sure about what was right and what was wrong. "Are you forgetting those guys who approached you about laundering money through one of your banks? Damn it, Romero, are you forgetting that they're the scum of the earth? Where do you think they got all that money? Betting at the yacht races and playing baccarat?" She laughed at her own suggestion, but there wasn't a hint of humor in the sound.

"They got it from drugs," Kate said. She let go of his arm and marched to the other side of the table. As if she were clinging to the truth and to her own belief in the right order of things, she clutched the back of one of the chairs. "They got it from gun running. They got it because they have stooges who hang around at bus stations all over the country and sweet-talk teenage runaways and those teenage runaways end up selling their bodies on street corners from L.A. to D.C. just so these guys can buy their mansions and their boats and their time-shares in Cancún. These people are rich. They're powerful. They're ruthless. And you're the only one they've ever attempted to involve in one of their schemes who's been brave enough to come forward and tell us about it. You've obviously made quite an impression. They're afraid of what you're going to say in court. They know you're an impeccable witness and that you have the power to shut them down. Otherwise they never would have hired Bartone to kill you."

"That's supposed to make me feel better?" Alex scraped a hand through his hair. "I'm also not forgetting that they offered me a nice big slice of their profits. I should have cut and run." He glanced at the flaking plaster on the ceiling and at the gold walls that probably hadn't seen a lick of paint since Alex was in prep school. "I'd be in the Canary Islands by now. In some nice, sunny villa overlooking the ocean. Blue skies. Cool waters. Hot babes." He sighed. "I should have turned to a life of crime."

"But you didn't."

There was just enough of a shimmer of admiration in Kate's voice to make it impossible for Alex to look at her. He turned around and walked over to the kitchen sink and stared out the grime-encrusted window to the railroad tracks and the steel mill beyond.

What would she think if she knew he'd hesitated about going to the authorities? Not that he'd ever entertained the thought of accepting a cut of the laundered money that had been offered to him. Not for a minute. But he had thought about ignoring the whole thing. He'd nearly convinced himself that it wasn't as serious as it sounded. What person in his right mind wouldn't at least try to do that? For a few agonizing hours, he'd actually thought about pretending the whole thing had never happened.

And then he'd heard the first news reports about Ruben Martinez's arrest.

That was precisely the reason Alex had taken a special interest in Ruben Martinez. Though Martinez couldn't possibly have known it, he'd served as a reminder to Alex of all that was right. Martinez took a stand. And made a mark. It was rare for a man to have that kind of courage, and if Ruben could do it from a squalid jail cell, Alex knew he could do it from his Manhattan penthouse.

Only at the time, he never considered that the whole thing might end up with him not in his Manhattan penthouse. He never dreamed it would mean he'd end up in a place like this. Frustration swelled into resignation; not used to feeling resigned about anything, Alex let his resignation turn into full-blown anger. His hands curled into fists and his head shot up. Either Kate was a little mixed up when it came to reading body language, or she really didn't know that sometimes it was better to just back down and let a subject drop. Instead of letting things go, she continued her assault.

"Now do you see why you can't contact Norbert or anyone else?" she asked. "Calls can be monitored. Phones can be tapped. People can be bought. As much as you'd like to believe it, you'll never know if Fielding is one-hundred-percent reliable. And if he isn't, by the time we find out, it will be too late."

As resigned as he was, both to his situation and what looked to be his fate, Alex could take only so much. A week of this nonsense was one week too much. A week of being baby-sat and monitored and ordered around was one week more than he could take. "Norbert is as reliable as I am. From what I saw last night, he's a hell of a lot more reliable than you."

It wasn't exactly a mistake to say out loud what they both knew anyway. But it was poorly timed. Alex cursed below his breath. He didn't get where he was in the world with poor timing. He knew when to let people in on what he was thinking, and he knew when to shut up. This was a case of *shut up* if ever there was one. He didn't have to look at Kate's face to know it, but he looked anyway, and what he saw showed him that his words had stung like a slap.

Kate's cheeks were pale, her mouth was pulled tight

into a thin line. Her chin was high and her head was steady. Her arms were straight at her sides. Even as he watched, her hands curled into fists.

"Look . . ." Alex scraped one hand through his hair. He didn't get where he was in life with apologies, either. Aside from the fact that he usually wasn't wrong, apologies were poor form everywhere from the boardroom to the bedroom. They were a sign of weakness, a sign of uncertainty, a clear indication that he should have been thinking when he was talking and he shouldn't have even tried talking until he was done thinking. This time, he'd violated his own cardinal rule. "I didn't mean that," he said.

Kate's gaze snapped to his. "Of course you meant it." She laughed, a brittle little sound. "And to think, for a couple minutes there last night, I actually thought you were human."

"Really?" There was a comeback if he'd ever heard one. A lame comeback. What was it about fighting with Kate that turned his usual eloquence into bumbling? He didn't know. He couldn't explain it. He didn't understand it. It was as perplexing a thought as the fact that for once, Kate might actually be right. He didn't think he'd acted any more human than usual the night before, but he would admit one thing: He'd spent the night wondering what it was about the whole, strange experience that left him feeling a little more alive.

A part of him was willing to write the whole thing off to some weird version of post-traumatic stress disorder. Like people who had lived through a terrorist kidnapping, or made it through a three-day blizzard with nothing but a bag of M&M's and a can of Pepsi, he and Kate had survived bingo. The experience had forged some sort of peculiar bond between them. It was the only thing that could explain how good it felt to walk down the street in the dark with his hand on Kate's arm. It was the only reason it seemed so right to come home with her, even when home wasn't home. It was the only thing that could account for the fact that even after the tacky church hall and the stifling smoke and Kate's bizarre reaction to the whole bingo scene, it had been harder than ever to wish her a simple good night and watch her walk into her room and close the door behind her.

"You had your chance last night."

Kate's words interrupted his thoughts, and for a couple of seconds, Alex wondered if she could read his mind. Then he realized she wasn't talking about what he was thinking about.

"I told you last night, if what I did bothered you, you could just call Mark and—"

"It didn't bother me. It doesn't bother me." He turned and took a step toward Kate, who warned him back with a look fierce enough to make him change his mind. "I meant it when I said I didn't want to see you disciplined for what happened last night. Honest. I shouldn't have brought it up again, only . . ." He stalked over to the table and reached for the front section of the newspaper. There were things he could tell her, if he dared. Things she might or might not understand. If she did understand, she would certainly see the necessity for contacting Norbert. She might even help him.

And if she didn't?

If she didn't understand, if she refused to help, Alex knew Kate would be more vigilant than ever, and he'd be less likely to get a chance to make the call.

Then there was the matter of secrecy, the promise he'd made that no one would ever know what he was doing. And, of course, there was Ruben Martinez's life to worry about.

Alex tossed the newspaper back on the table. "This is hard for me. I hope you'll understand. I've never felt so . . . so helpless." He scoured the knuckles of one hand against his chin. It was stubbly with a night's growth of beard. "I'm not used to not being in control, and I'll tell you something: I don't like it. I don't like it at all. Don't you think that brain trust you work for could have come up with a better way to get me out of New York for a couple months? They could have sent me climbing in the Himalayas or out in the Mediterranean on my yacht."

"You are out in the Mediterranean on your yacht." Her bare feet silent against the burnt orange indoor/outdoor carpet that covered the floor, Kate crossed the room and looked through the stack of old newspapers waiting to be set out on the curb. She chose one section of the previous day's paper and flipped through it, and when she found what she was looking for, she folded the paper over once, then again, and handed it to Alex.

"See?" She pointed to an item in the middle of one of the celebrity gossip columns Alex tried never to read. His own name jumped out at him in bold letters.

" 'Alex Romero, handsomest of handsome hunks, richest of Romeos, and the most eligible bachelor in this or any other world . . .' " Alex cleared his throat. Even he didn't believe that bull. He was afraid if he looked at Kate he'd find her laughing, so he kept reading. " 'Alex Romero . . . blah, blah, blah . . . is spending the summer relaxing after an exhausting schedule that lately has included business mergers, company acquisitions, and being worn to a frazzle by a hot, hot, hot fling with rock star—"

He couldn't take any more. Though Alex avoided reading the scandal sheets and adamantly refused to watch celebrity dish-the-dirt shows on TV, it was impossible to avoid all the gossip. Whether he liked it or not, he generally knew what people were saying. Usually it annoyed him. Sometimes it aggravated him. This time, it embarrassed him. He couldn't say why. He only knew he had to set the record straight.

He offered Kate a half-smile. "I never had an affair, hot, hot, hot or otherwise, with—"

"You don't think I care, do you?" Kate crossed her arms over her chest, the gesture a little too defensive to be completely indifferent. "That's not why I showed you the article. Keep reading."

Alex scanned the item again. "'. . . hot, hot, hot fling with rock star . . .' Well, never mind." He dismissed that part of the story with a grunt. "'. . . is spending the summer cruising the Mediterranean on his ultra-luxury yacht, the *Calypso*—'" His surprise complete, Alex stopped and stared, first at the newspaper, then at Kate. "What do they mean, I'm cruising the Mediterranean?" He looked around at the peeling paint on the kitchen ceiling, and the butcher-block table with its pitted aluminum legs, and the countertops where the avocado-colored Formica was curling at the corners.

"This sure isn't the *Calypso,* and that—" He looked out the window at the snaking train tracks and the steel mill with its belching stacks. "That sure as hell isn't the Mediterranean."

"You don't think we'd put the word out that you were sailing the Mediterranean and then actually let you do it, do you?" Kate shook her head, apparently amazed he would even consider it. "That would put you in a whole bunch of danger, wouldn't it?"

"Which means?"

"Which means, the boat is cruising, all right. You're just not on it."

"But that means someone else is!" Alex's temper soared. "That means the feds highjacked the *Calypso,* and someone else is—"

"Highjacked is a strong word." Kate went to the cupboard and dragged out a box of generic-brand puffed rice cereal. She poured herself a bowl and went to the refrigerator for the milk. "Remember, it's for your own good. We had to make it look real, so yes, there are agents on the boat. Lucky dogs." She splashed milk onto her cereal and grabbed a spoon. "Bet they're not eating Rice Krunchies."

"They'd better not be touching my wine cellar!"

Kate slammed her spoon into her bowl. A splash of milk went up and spots dotted the table. "Did it ever occur to you that maybe staying alive is a little more important than your wine cellar? Or that those guys are sitting ducks? They're putting themselves in the line of fire so you can lay low here, safe and sound."

"Sure. Sure, it occurred to me." Too angry to keep still, Alex stalked out of the kitchen and into the living room. "I'm just not used to having my life hijacked along with my yacht."

Apparently Kate didn't much care. "Don't ever try to use my phone again," she called after him. "From now on, I'm sleeping with it under my pillow."

Alex pulled to a stop. Even in the midst of worrying about his wine cellar and the *Calypso* and Ruben Martinez, it occurred to him that Kate had just presented him with a golden opportunity. If he wanted to use the phone and Kate was sleeping with the phone, that meant if he was sleeping with Kate . . .

The thought was unworthy, even of him. And too enticing even to consider.

Eager to clear his head and cool his fantasies, Alex pushed open the door and walked out to the front porch. He slammed the door closed behind him.

"Trouble in paradise, eh?" a voice called to him from across the street.

Alex stopped at the top of the stairs and looked over to see Earl watering his scrap of lawn. Earl waved, turned off the hose, and headed in Alex's direction. "You and the missus havin' a bit of a knock-down-drag-out?"

The idea was too vulgar to even contemplate and Alex dismissed it instantly. "Of course not. What makes you think that?" He sat down on the top step, his elbows on his knees. A new thought came to him and he looked at Earl in horror. "You didn't hear us, did you?"

"Nah!" Earl lumbered up the steps and dropped down next to Alex. "Seen the way you slammed the door, though. That can only mean one thing. The little lady bein' unreasonable?"

"Unreasonable?" Alex snorted. The word had been coined to describe Kate. "You have no idea."

"Sure I do." Earl was wearing a white sleeveless undershirt and a pair of denim cargo shorts with a huge pocket on either leg. He reached into one of the pockets and pulled out a can of beer. "Want one?" he asked.

Alex watched a drop of condensation trickle down the side of the bright green can. "It's eight o'clock in the morning," he told Earl.

"So?" Earl offered the beer again, and when Alex declined with a shake of his head and a curl of his upper lip, Earl popped open the can and drank it down himself. "Me and Marge have been married thirty-five years. I know all about unreasonable. Only the way I figured it, I mean, watchin' you and the ladies last night, I figured you never had a problem with women."

"Not most women, no." That was true, and Alex wasn't ashamed to admit it. "Most women are like putty in my hands." It was a stupid, macho expression to use, but right about now, Alex didn't care. Stupid and macho were just what he needed. Stupid and macho were better than powerless and vulnerable.

"Well, that's just what I was talkin' about last night. About you showin' me how to do it."

Alex was almost afraid to ask. "Do what?"

Earl elbowed him in the ribs. "You know. Do it. Get the ladies all hot and bothered just by being there, like you was some kind of Romeo or something."

"Well, I . . ." It was on the tip of Alex's tongue to give Earl the same answer he always gave the tabloids: No denials. No admissions. No comment. It was the rational thing to do, the discreet course of action. And if Alex Romero was nothing else, he was rational and discreet.

But sometimes stupid and macho had a way of eclipsing rational and discreet. Alex didn't question the logic or worry about the rationale. He only knew this was one of those times.

He sat up a little straighter. "A Romeo, huh? You think so?"

"Heck, yes." Earl swiped a hand across his mouth.

"Even though you wear them nerdy glasses, women get all . . . I don't know . . . sort of silly, I guess, when you're around. Like their hearts are pumping too fast and they're just itchin' to get their hands on you."

Alex straightened the collar on his short-sleeved plaid shirt and smoothed a hand over his cowlick. "It's true," he said. "Most women find me reasonably attractive."

"Just like I was sayin'." Earl nodded. "So you think you can show me how you do it?"

"I suppose I could give you a few pointers, if that's what you mean. What to say, what to do, how to—"

Across the street, the front door of Earl and Marge's house snapped open and Alex watched Marge walk out on the front porch. She was wearing a purple housecoat, her hair was up in rollers, and she was carrying a plastic pitcher. Marge waved and got to work watering a long row of potted plants. Watching her, Alex felt an uncomfortable little flutter in his stomach. Though he himself had never considered marriage—at least not seriously, anyway—he had an unwavering belief in marital fidelity, no doubt engendered by the long and happy marriages of his parents and his grandparents. He had learned early that a happy home life was the right order of things, and if he'd never found that happiness himself, well, it didn't mean it wasn't or shouldn't be out there for other people. His suspicions aroused, his sympathies suddenly firmly in Marge's corner, Alex narrowed his eyes and glared at Earl. "Hey, you're not thinking of—"

"Hell, no!" Earl's face went as purple as Marge's housecoat. His jaw went stiff. With one hand, he crushed his empty beer can and slammed it onto the porch. "You don't think I'm asking about this so I can go cruisin' to meet some bimbo, do you? Is that how you young guys think these days? Is that how you treat your sweet little wife? Why, you no-good, slimy son of a—"

"No. No. I didn't think that at all." There was something about getting his jaw dislocated by one of Earl's ham-size fists that was as unappealing as helping Earl learn to cheat on his wife, and Alex disassociated himself with it as quickly as he could. "I just wanted to make sure. That was all. I didn't want to help if—"

"Of course not. Sorry, buddy." Earl settled back down. He took a deep breath and clapped a sweaty hand on Alex's shoulder. "I'm glad you asked. Honest. It shows you're a good husband. That's all I'm lookin' to be, too. A good husband. Only, I swear . . ." Watching Marge go from pot to pot, he shook his head. "Sometimes I just don't know what she wants."

"And you want me to help?" It was laughable, or it would have been if Earl didn't look so darned sincere. Alex did his best to keep the cynicism out of his voice. "What do you want me to do?"

"Don't want you to do nothing," Earl replied. "Nothin' different, anyway. Just thought I might . . . you know . . . keep an eye on you and Missy. That way, you could show me the way a woman wants to be treated and I could . . . you know . . . like, copy what you do."

Automatically Alex found himself reaching for the porch railing and holding on tight. Just when it seemed as if things couldn't get any worse, his life took another backslide. From the sublime to the terrible, and from the terrible right down to the really and truly ridiculous. He supposed he must have stared at Earl for some time, because the big man finally stood.

"I knew you'd help," he said, and before Alex could find his voice and point out that he hadn't agreed to help, or even to discuss what surely must be the most ludicrous thing he'd ever heard, Earl went on. "I've been thinkin' about what to do and I've got a plan. You two are going to invite us over for dinner on Saturday."

"We are." It wasn't a question. Alex was way beyond questioning any of the bizarre twists and turns his life had taken.

"Sure." Earl headed down the front walk. "Your Missy can cook, can't she?"

For the last week, they had lived on sandwiches, low-fat

frozen entrées, and Rice Krunchies. Could Kate cook? Alex honestly didn't know. "Dinner." He gave the word an inflection somewhere between this-could-be-the-biggest-disaster-ever and what-a-good-idea. "Next Saturday. You bet."

Looking as pleased as a kid on Christmas morning, Earl gave Alex a wink. "Dinner. That way, I can watch you and your missus sort of up close and personal. You know, like them celebrity couples on TV."

"Celebrity couples." Alex watched Earl walk away. The sublime, the terrible, and the really and truly ridiculous had just taken another outrageous turn. He didn't even want to think about where this one might lead.

6

Even though Kate knew what was supposed to be in the Express Mail package that arrived Saturday afternoon, its contents caught her off guard. She tossed the opened envelope on the kitchen table along with the rest of what was in the package, and held the framed photograph she'd been expecting in both hands, not sure if the knot that twisted somewhere between her heart and her stomach was one of amusement, or amazement, or out-and-out disappointment.

Kate turned the eight-by-ten every which way, looking at it from all angles. The frame was gold, or to be more precise, it was pressed wood painted gold. Inside it, a smiling groom in a tux that looked a little too big and a bride in a gown with too much beading, too much lace, and a bodice cut to expose too much cleavage, stared back at her from the steps of a city park gazebo. The sky was robin's egg blue, and the clouds were fluffy and white; the grass was so green, Kate wondered if the photographer hadn't taken some liberties and touched things up to make the scene look even more perfect than the happy couple undoubtedly already thought it was.

The bride carried a bouquet of white lilies, pink roses,

and white satin streamers that trailed halfway down the front of her gown. She wore white satin gloves that came up past her elbows, a veil that erupted like whipped cream out of a can from the beaded tiara perched atop her head, and Kate's face.

"Incredible." Kate mumbled the word and shook her head in disbelief. It was incredible, all right. Incredible to see her face on someone else's body. Incredible to see Alex standing right beside her, one arm around her waist, his left hand resting at the curve of her hip so the world could see the gold band he wore. Incredible enough to think of the two of them as man and wife, even more incredible to see what looked to be tangible proof that they actually were.

"What's that?"

The question came from right behind her, and Kate couldn't help herself—she jumped. She'd been so lost in her own thoughts, she hadn't heard Alex come into the kitchen.

It had been a quiet and reasonably uninteresting week, thank goodness. After the fiasco of the bingo game, Kate knew she needed to redeem herself, and she'd managed to keep her conduct as by-the-book and strictly professional as was humanly possible. She didn't need to remind herself that the hint of Alex's breath whispering against her neck was almost enough to bring that professionalism crashing down in flames. That was just about as disturbing a thought as the one she'd been having about the photograph—the one in which she wondered what it might be like to actually live out the scene. Kate shook the thought aside at the same time she shook her professionalism firmly back into place.

"It's our wedding picture," she told him.

"Our wedding?" Even though he was behind her, Kate couldn't help but catch the note of doubt in Alex's voice. She turned and held the photo out to him.

"Our wedding." She watched the look on Alex's face

fade from skepticism to amazement, and she had to smile. "Nice couple, huh?"

Alex took the photo from her and stared at it, absently pushing his glasses up on his nose with one finger. "As if I'd ever wear a tux that fit as poorly as that one!" He shook his head in disgust. "And look at the way the guy's standing. He needs to bring his shoulders back a little, make himself look a little taller." He demonstrated, drawing back his shoulders, lifting his chin, and Kate decided it was better to look at the computer-generated photograph than it was to stare at the real, live Alex Romero, whose every movement made his muscles ripple beneath his red polyester golf shirt.

"Where'd they find this guy?" Alex stabbed a finger at the groom, then slid it over to the bride. "And that veil! Talk about living in the past. The eighties are alive and well, huh? And where—?" He ran a finger along the contours of the bride's close-fitting bodice and crinoline-wide skirts and his voice mellowed. Grinning, he glanced at Kate out of the corner of his eye. "You are one hot babe. Who would have thought that perky unicorn shirt of yours hid a body like that!"

"It's not my body and you know it." Kate tugged at the hem of her unicorn shirt, right before she yanked the photo away from Alex and set it on the table. "That body is brought to you by the wonders of computer scanning. Just remember that." She looked at the photo again and wrinkled her nose in distaste. "Where did Mark find that picture of me anyway? I look like I'm in a police lineup."

"You look pretty good to me." Alex lifted his eyebrows, his gaze firmly on the bride's bosom and not on her face.

"My hair looks terrible," Kate grumbled. Part of her wished he'd contradict her. Another part wished he'd agree. At least if he did, it would mean he was looking at her face in the photograph, and not at some nameless bride's cleavage.

"Your hair?" Alex's gaze went from the bride back to

the groom. "What guy in his right mind would get married when his hair looked like that? He should have called off the wedding."

"Don't be ridiculous." Kate crossed her arms over her chest and stepped back for a better look at the photograph. "I'm sure whoever he is, his hair looked better that day than yours does. Anybody's hair looks better than yours does." She couldn't resist the jab and was rewarded for her efforts when Alex ran a defensive hand over his cowlick.

"Besides," she said, "they'd never call off the wedding. Not even for a bad hair day. Can't you see how much in love they are? Look at the way they're standing. He's got his hip right up against hers and she's leaning toward him. His hand is resting on her waist. See? There." She pointed. "Trust me, understanding body language is a big part of my job. These two people—whoever they are—are crazy about each other. You don't think she chose that dress to impress the guests at the wedding, do you? She did it for him, and I'll bet it's driving him crazy. I'd love to see the original of this picture, the real picture with the real faces. I'll bet they're staring into each other's eyes." Before she could stop herself, Kate sighed. "Kind of seems sacrilegious to have our faces intrude on their happily-ever-after, don't you think?"

"If it is a happily-ever-after." Alex didn't sound convinced and something told Kate he was about to pay her back for mentioning his hair. "Pretty soon, he'll find out she can't cook."

Even though Kate suspected he was teasing, she'd had about enough. They'd had this same argument more than once in the days since he'd announced Earl and Marge were coming for dinner that night. She backed away, her hands out as if to disassociate herself from any accountability. "When I applied to get into the Academy, nobody asked if I could cook," she told him. "Nobody told me I'd ever have to. If you hadn't invited the neighbors over—"

"I told you, I didn't exactly invite them. They invited

themselves. And what were you going to feed them, Rice Krunchies?"

"What are *you* going to feed them?" Kate glanced over at the kitchen counter. It was filled with the bags they'd hauled in from the grocery store only a short time before. All four burners on the stove had pots on them, and a couple were merrily boiling away.

Because she firmly refused to let Alex out of her sight, Kate had gone along to the store, but it was Alex who'd insisted on cooking that night, so he was the one who made out their shopping list. A lot of what he'd bought seemed harmless enough, things like orange juice and olive oil and garlic. But there were some exotic-sounding items as well, things they had to search long and hard for and go far afield to find. Things like plantains and black beans and tomatillos. Things no self-respecting girl from Nebraska would know how to eat, much less cook.

"When are you going to tell me what you're making for dinner?"

Alex grinned. "You don't like surprises?"

"Oh, speaking of surprises!" Kate grabbed the batch of photographs she'd left in the envelope. They were smaller than the wedding picture, an odd collection in an odd assortment of cheap frames, pictures of strangers she supposed had been rescued from a variety of Manhattan secondhand stores. She handed the first photo to Alex. It was a picture of a heavyset woman in a bright blue dress that was too tight around the hips and short enough to show her pudgy knees. She had small, dark eyes, coal black hair that looked as if it had come straight from a bottle, and a stubborn chin.

"That's your mother," she told him.

Alex's upper lip curled. "She would not be amused," he said. "And I need a mother . . . why?"

"Why?" Not for the first time, Kate was amazed that a man with Alex's smarts had such a hard time understanding the not-so-amusing game they were playing. "Because you invited the neighbors over, that's why."

"But I didn't invite—"

"I know." She brushed aside his protests. "Either way, they're coming over and we've got to make this house look like we really live in it. That means we need relatives." Kate held up the next photograph in the pile. "This is Frank." She pointed to a thin man wearing jeans, boots, and a plaid shirt. The woman standing next to him was poured into a pair of jeans and had her bleached-blond hair teased out as wide as the shoulders of her satin cowboy shirt. They were posed in front of a wooden dance floor; the sign behind them proclaimed it "Country Hoedown Night."

"This is Cindy," Kate said. "These are my parents."

"Frank and Cindy. My in-laws." Alex's face went noticeably pale. "They aren't line dancing, are they? Please don't tell me I have in-laws who line dance!" He shivered and reached for the next picture. "And this?"

"Your dad. John Tomashefski. He's been dead for six years, so the picture's a little outdated."

Without a comment, Alex set the photos down on the table.

"Oh, and this is our only niece, Christina." She showed him a photo of a curly-haired little girl with a wide smile and a missing front tooth. "She's your brother Ben's child, and we adore her."

"Adore her. Got it." Alex nodded but he didn't look convinced. He gestured toward the pile of phony relatives. "Are you sure this is going to work?"

"No," Kate admitted. "But it's a start. It's one way to make Earl and Marge think we're a real family. The house has to look lived in, and if there's one way a newly married couple makes their house look lived in, it's with pictures of the family."

"You ever been part of a newly married couple?"

Alex's question was so out-of-the-blue, it took Kate a couple moments to answer. Coming from anyone else, she wouldn't have thought a thing of it. Curiosity. Courtesy.

Small talk. Coming from Alex, Kate couldn't help but wonder why he'd asked. Or if he cared.

She sloughed off the question with a lift of her shoulders that made her unicorn buck. "Always too busy," she said, and though she'd told herself a thousand times it was true and she didn't care, that her career came first and that there was plenty of time for her own happily-ever-after, she felt a tiny pang of regret. "After the Academy, I moved around a lot. Omaha, Phoenix, Denver. You?" She knew the answer, of course. She knew everything there was to know about Alex Romero, or at least as much as the FBI could ever find out.

Alex grinned. "Thought about it a couple times," he admitted. "But married?" He lifted the photo of the bride and groom, looked at it briefly and set it down again. "Nah!"

That was it. He set aside the whole idea as easily as he set aside the phony wedding picture. No serious consideration. No explanation. And if the who-gives-a-damn look on his face meant anything, certainly no regrets. But then, what did Kate expect from the most eligible bachelor in the hemisphere?

She reminded herself never to forget it, and watched Alex thumb through the other photos. "Boy, the FBI thinks of everything, don't they? Instant family. Instant proof that we really are who we say we are." Thinking, he rubbed his thumb across his chin. "Have you ever visited friends who are married?" he asked, but he didn't wait for Kate to answer. He went right on. "You can always tell, the minute you walk into their homes, and it's not just because of the pictures on the mantel. The tables are littered with magazines. *Vogue* and *Elle* all mixed in with *National Geographic* and *The New Yorker*. Or you'll go into the bathroom and everything is jumbled together. His shampoo and her shampoo and her cologne and his aftershave and—"

The same thought hit both Alex and Kate at the same

time. Kate's mouth dropped open. Alex looked at the kitchen doorway and the stairway that led upstairs and to the house's only bathroom.

In the time they'd lived there, the bathroom had become, by some unspoken understanding, a sort of neutral zone. It was a place they used as if on schedule; Kate showered first thing in the morning, Alex not until he'd had his coffee and a breakfast that usually consisted of Rice Krunchies and toast. The personal items they needed were strictly that, personal, and they were kept just as strictly separate. Kate's shampoo, her conditioner, razor, deodorant, talc, toothbrush, toothpaste, and facial cleanser were on the dresser in her bedroom. She dragged everything back and forth to the bathroom each morning and again each night. While she never questioned it, she assumed Alex did the same with his personal items. There was never a comb in the bathroom, or a razor. Never a sign of the cheap aftershave he sometimes wore. While what little they had commingled in the living room—a book here, a magazine there—the bathroom had become a shining example of the fact that while they might have been living together, their lives didn't overlap.

Not like a married couple at all.

Kate grabbed a handful of the photographs and was out of the kitchen first. She dropped the pictures here and there around the living room and headed up the stairs. Alex wasn't far behind. While she darted into the bathroom, he hurried into her bedroom. He came back with an armful of personal care products he'd scooped off her dresser.

"Here's shampoo and hair gel and deodorant." He plunked the items down on the sink and Kate grabbed them and tried to distribute them around the room. It wasn't easy. The bathroom was small, and the fact that someone with either a really bad remodeling idea or really narrow hips had added an oversized vanity around the sink didn't help. Even when Kate was in there alone, the room had a walls-closing-in-on-her feel that was compounded by the dark green wallpaper, the shaggy blue-and-green area rug, and a flowered shower curtain that screamed psychedelic in shades of green that didn't match either the wallpaper or the rug. With both Kate and Alex in the room, walls-closing-in took on a whole different meaning. And a whole new level of awareness.

Kate reached around Alex and put her shampoo on the ledge in the shower, and her arm brushed the rock-hard contours of his chest. Alex sidled around Kate and put her hair gel in the white metal medicine cabinet and his leg grazed hers. Kate knew she was lucky there wasn't time to think about the sensations that screamed through her with each brush and every touch. Being in a small room with a guy with a big reputation and a huge ego was not the sort of thing that was good for a woman's equilibrium.

"You should have some stuff in here, too," she told him, and partly because it was true and partly because it meant she could escape for a couple of seconds, she edged between Alex and the sink to get to the door. Once she was in his room and out of sight, she stopped long enough to draw in a long breath, reminded herself that self-control was a law enforcement officer's best friend, and grabbed the first things she could find.

"Here's your deodorant, and here's your aftershave." She handed them to Alex and tried to stand back far enough to give each of them a little breathing room, but the only thanks she got for the effort was the rim of the bathtub pressed into the backs of her calves. She was wearing denim shorts, and the worn porcelain felt smooth and very cold against her bare legs. As far as Kate was concerned, that was a good thing. At this particular juncture, it was better to concentrate on the cold. Better that than thinking about the fact that they'd been in such a hurry when they came in, they hadn't bothered to turn the bathroom light on. There was only one window in the room. The glass was frosted and wavy, a pattern that reminded Kate of a paisley tie. The afternoon sun filtered through, sending odd streaks of light like the flashes off a crystal into the room. The dancing light fell across Alex's chest, and when he grabbed the things Kate brought from his room, turned, and reached over to the vanity, the light caressed his butt in a way she was sure she shouldn't have noticed. Or at least not appreciated.

Yes, Kate decided, redirecting her gaze to the shaggy carpet, cold was a very good thing. Holding tight to the thought, she looked up just in time to see that Alex had set his things down on the back of the vanity in a neat line in front of hers.

"That won't work." Kate reached around Alex. Another mistake. Her arm brushed his. His hip brushed hers. She ignored the jolt that sent a thrill through her bloodstream and rearranged the items, setting Alex's deodorant next to hers, his comb nestling in the bristles of her hairbrush.

"Better?" she asked.

"Not yet." This time, it was Alex who bolted out of the room. Another good thing, Kate decided. When he was gone, the air felt a little less close and a lot more breathable.

Unfortunately he wasn't gone long enough for her to catch her breath. Kate heard him rummaging through her dresser, and before she could voice a protest, he was back with a pair of pantyhose and the white nightgown.

"Oh, no!" Kate made a grab for the nightgown but it was already too late. Alex looped the spaghetti straps over a hanger and hung it on the shower curtain rod.

"Now that's better," he announced. He looked over his shoulder at her and grinned, holding up the hose. "And these—"

"You've got a lot of nerve going through my things." Kate caught one leg of the pantyhose and pulled them out of his hands. They were cheap and she was sure they'd be snagged, but she decided it was a small price to pay to hold on to her pride. She bunched the hose and held them with both hands to her chest. "You don't see me going through your stuff. Not in your dresser drawers. You didn't have to—"

"You have to agree, it will look more genuine."

She did have to agree. But that didn't mean she had to admit it. With a noncommittal *harrumph,* Kate turned toward the sink, ran the water, and soaked the pantyhose. She squeezed them out and tossed them over her shoulder at Alex, who unfortunately had the reflexes of an athlete. He caught them without getting too wet and draped them over the shower curtain rod.

Kate stepped back from the sink to take in the full effect and nodded, satisfied. The bathroom might be small and cramped, but they had accomplished what they'd set out to do. It had a lived-in look. Unfortunately the second Kate realized Alex was watching her carefully, his head cocked to one side, his eyes simmering with a look that told her he wasn't any more oblivious to the muted light and the fleeting touches than she was, lived-in didn't seem as important as how hot Kate suddenly was. And how hot Kate suddenly was wasn't something she wanted Alex to notice.

Heading for the door, she stepped to her right just as he stepped to his left, and Kate found herself with her nose pressed against Alex's red polyester shirt. She decided to offset the error by stepping to her left. Just as Alex moved to his right. This time, her nose was against the button placket front of his shirt, her back was to the pedestal sink, Alex's hands had somehow found their way around her waist, and there was no place to go.

"Good job." Kate couldn't imagine a dumber thing to say. If she had, she probably would have said it. She couldn't imagine a situation as charged with possibilities, either. The problem was, as tempting as those possibilities were, none of them was likely to make her look any more professional, or convince Alex she was as capable of assuring his safety as she knew she was.

Better to think about the job they'd done making the bathroom look like a married couple actually shared it, she decided. Better to concentrate on her self-control.

"It works." Kate was talking about the bathroom, but when Alex nodded and smiled, she had the feeling he was thinking about something else.

"It works, all right." He inched closer. Not that there was much room to move. Still, Alex managed. He shuffled close enough so that his chest was against hers, his thighs exerting just enough pressure to push her back against the vanity.

Kate knew she had a choice. She could keep her arms at her sides with her hands close enough to the front of Alex's jeans to find out what was working, or she could raise her hands to his chest.

She chose to flatten her hands against his polyester shirt, and not to notice the fact that his heartbeat was thumping with all the enthusiasm hers had suddenly developed.

"It's amazing, isn't it?" Kate glanced around the room. It was better than looking up into Alex's eyes and thinking they were a shade of brown as delicious as chocolate, better than noticing the barely controlled smile that flickered at the corners of his mouth. "This room looks so good, somebody might actually think we live together."

"We do live together." His voice was as smooth as the smile that glittered in his eyes.

"Together, yeah, sure." Kate's voice was anything but smooth. It bumped along to the rhythm of her heartbeat. "But not . . . you know . . . together."

How he managed it, she didn't know, but Alex moved even closer. Everything was working, all right. She had no doubt of that at all. Not when the front of his jeans pressed against hers.

Kate sucked in a breath that had nothing to do with surprise and everything to do with a desire as sudden and fierce as any she'd ever felt.

"We could live together." Alex smiled his approval of her reaction. When he bent his knees just a bit and stood up straight again, she felt the full length of his erection against her thigh. "There's really not much to it. We've got the bathroom part down pat." He glanced over his shoulder and back to Kate. "It's the bedroom part that needs some work. Yours or mine?"

Kate pictured the queen-size bed in Alex's room, and though she tried to erase the thought before it even fully formed, she pictured herself in the bed with Alex. She wondered if he'd be as hard inside her as he was now. Would he be a slow and gentle lover or one of those guys who wanted everything fast and furious?

She hated to admit it but at that point, she didn't care. Fast and furious sounded just fine. So did slow and gentle. And everything in between. At that point, she was ready to trade everything she owned for the chance to find out what might happen in the bedroom down the hall: her life savings; her collection of vintage Chicago Cubs baseball cards; even J. Edgar, the goldfish being baby-sat by her neighbor in her Manhattan apartment building.

Given half the chance, she might have done it. If she hadn't remembered the bingo game.

Though it was edged with disappointment, the feeling that twisted through Kate's stomach and cooled the fires of passion that boiled through her blood wasn't exactly regret. It reminded her more of waking up after a night on the town with a dry mouth, a headache and eyes redder than the tail lights of a New York cab. Not remorse exactly. More like an awareness of how incredibly stupid she could be.

Because she knew that of all the things she'd trade for an hour in Alex's bed, her gold badge wasn't one of them.

No illusions or delusions. It was time to put her money where her mouth was. Or at least her actions where her good intentions should have been all along.

With both hands, Kate gave Alex's chest the noncommittal sort of pat she usually reserved for cute but rowdy dogs. "Thanks, but no thanks."

"What?" The seductive glint in Alex's eyes turned to a look of disbelief. "Are you saying—"

"I'm saying no, thanks, Romeo." While he was still too astounded to object, or worse yet, to realize that one more touch of the front of his jeans to the front of hers would make her change her mind, Kate made her move. She slid out from between Alex and the vanity and headed for the door.

"You're saying no?"

Behind her, Alex's voice wavered between amazement and doubt. It was so pitiful a sound, Kate had to stop and turn around.

"Never happened before, huh?" She tipped her head and crossed her arms over her chest, considering the man and the moment and wondering, once the heat of the incident was out of her blood, which she'd decide was more ridiculous. She shrugged away the thought. "At least you'll always remember me as your first."

In typical male fashion, Alex decided to defend himself, even when he wasn't sure what he was defending himself against. "You're not the first," he said, but as soon as he realized he was impugning his ego as well as his reputation, he tried to recover. "I mean, you are the first to say no, of course, but you're not—"

"I get it." It was such a sorry attempt at keeping the old macho image alive and well, Kate couldn't help but take pity on him. "Let's compromise. We'll just say I'm the first woman you've tried to seduce in a bathroom who said no. How's that? Enough to soothe the old ego?"

"No. Yes." Alex shook his head as if ordering his thoughts. "For your information," he said, "I've never tried to seduce a woman in a bathroom. How tacky do you think I am?"

She was tempted not to answer. She was tempted to give him a look that told him he should pay attention to his own questions. She wasn't in the mood to let him off that easily. Turning down what was probably the hottest invitation she'd ever get to an even hotter session of sex with the hottest guy in this or any other universe had a way of doing that to a woman.

"In case you've already forgotten," she told him, "you just did try to seduce a woman in a bathroom. Unless I don't count as a woman."

"Yes. No." This time, Alex raked his fingers through his hair. "Of course you count, but—"

"But I'm just another notch on the ol' six-shooter." She glanced at the fly of his jeans to emphasize her point. "Forget it, Romeo. Like I said, I'm not interested. And if I'm any judge of people, you're not interested, either. Not really."

He didn't jump in to contradict her, and it was that more than anything else that let Kate know she'd made the right decision. Holding tight to the thought, she turned and headed down the stairs.

This time, he followed. "What do you mean I wasn't interested?" he asked. "I proved that, didn't I?"

Kate tossed her reply over her shoulder. "You proved you're as horny as a billy goat. I hate to tell you, but that doesn't come as any big surprise. You can't possibly be interested in me. I'm not a supermodel or a rock star or a princess from one of those goofy little European countries where everybody looks like they just stepped out of a bad operetta. Maybe those women aren't particular about where they get seduced, but I'd like to think I have a little more class."

"Have you stopped to think that maybe I wasn't trying to seduce you? Maybe you were trying to seduce me?"

Kate barked a laugh. At the bottom of the stairs, she turned and faced him, her fists on her hips. "That's classic! Really! Me? Trying to seduce you? Do you really think I'm that hard up?"

"Do you think I am?"

She deserved the comeback and she knew it. She just

hadn't expected it to come with so much sting. Refusing to let the tremor that shuddered through her make her bottom lip tremble or her hands shake, Kate pulled back her shoulders and stuck out her chin. "Well, good. Now that we've got that straight, maybe you'll learn to keep your hands, and other portions of your anatomy . . ."—she gave the front of his jeans a look—"to yourself."

"Gladly."

"Good."

"Good."

"Great!" Kate stomped into the living room. She had fluffed the couch pillows more than once that afternoon, but she fluffed them again and punched one for good measure before she tossed it back down. "You ready to promise that?" she asked him.

"What? That I'll keep my distance? That I'll never touch you again?" Alex laughed. "That shouldn't be too tough."

"Then you promise?"

"Yes."

"Good."

"Great."

"Fine."

"Really fine." Alex stalked the length of the living room. "Really very fine."

"Fine."

It was a good thing the doorbell rang just then, Kate decided. In the great scheme of things, it meant she'd had the last word.

7

Of all the things I've lost, I miss my mind the most.

Alex stared across the living room at the message printed in three-inch-high green letters on Earl's beer-stained T-shirt. If he could get a word in edgewise in a conversation that centered around the fact that Jack Murray at the corner convenience store was adding a shelf of video rentals right next to the corn chips—a conversation Alex was only half listening to—he might have told Earl that he, and his T-shirt, were dead wrong.

Of all the things he'd lost, it wasn't his mind Alex missed the most. It had taken him a while, but through the bad haircut and the worse glasses, the awful clothes and the questionable accommodations, he'd finally figured it out.

Of all the things he'd lost, it wasn't his finely tailored wardrobe he missed the most, or a life of luxury the people in the dingy little living room could never even dream. It wasn't the penthouse apartment in Manhattan or the Long Island estate. It wasn't his Porsche, or the *Calypso,* or the dazzle of the limelight. It wasn't the challenge of running a corporation that could buy and sell

Earl and Marge and the rest of the neighbors ten thousand times over, or even the blood-sizzling exhilaration of playing (and usually winning) high-stakes games that made Wall Street history.

It was the freedom.

Of all the things I've lost, I miss my freedom the most.

In his head, Alex pictured his own special T-shirt, but even as the thought formed, he knew he was being petty and small-minded. In comparison with what people like Ruben Martinez did in the name of what was right, what Alex was doing was small potatoes.

He should have been inspired by the thought. He wasn't. It was hard to be inspired when his world had been reduced to shag carpet and pressed-wood furniture. It was hard for him to be anything but depressed when all he could picture in his head was the image of Alex Romero in his special T-shirt. The picture that was complete with a heavy ball and chain attached to his leg that kept him firmly anchored to this dismal neighborhood, and this dreary house and these dull, dull people.

"John Wayne. That's who I want to see." As if to emphasize everything he was thinking, the old lady seated next to Alex on the couch rapped him on the knee. She was Helen Wysocki, the white-haired lady who lived next door to Marge and Earl. She hadn't been invited to this delightful little soiree, but as Marge put it the moment she stuck her head in the door, "We brought Helen along. She didn't have anything better to do."

It must have been a slow night all around on the neighborhood social scene. Earl and Marge also brought Harold Dills, a middle-aged, quiet fellow with a receding hairline and a weak chin who lived over the butcher shop near the church. Though it was clear from the fact that they kept mentioning someone named Aunt Sophie that there was some familial relationship between Marge and Harold, they didn't bother to explain it, and Alex didn't bother to ask.

He knew better than to expect any answers that would help make sense of the situation. Or of his life.

"Soon as those movies are in that store, I'm gonna get me a John Wayne movie." Apparently because Helen got no response from her first announcement, she assumed Alex hadn't heard. She tugged at his sleeve.

"John Wayne. Great guy." Alex offered her a stiff smile at the same time he slid over just far enough to keep out of reach of the old lady's nicotine-stained fingers. "Big hero."

"Shit." Helen growled the word around a cigarette she hadn't bothered to ask if she could light. "Who cares about all that hero crap? He's the sexiest thing on two feet!"

From across the room, Marge caught wind of the conversation and joined in. "You're not carrying on about John Wayne again, are you, Helen?" Marge laughed and crunched into a handful of the rippled potato chips she and Earl had brought with them. "Helen's living in the past. She needs to get with the program, don't you think? She needs to get a look at some of these cute new movie stars. You know, like that Tom Cruise or that Ford fellow. Or how about that rock star we saw on the *Tonight Show* the other night?" Marge jiggled her shoulders and grinned at Earl, who promptly rolled his eyes. "Or that other fellow. You know the one." Thinking, Marge brushed the salt from her fingers and licked her lips. "The one who's always on the cover of the tabloids. What's-his-name. That rich guy who's a real Romeo."

"I thought Stan was the only Romeo around here." Earl gave Alex a broad wink and, with a sinking feeling, Alex realized the night had just taken a surreal bent. There they sat, comparing Alex to himself. Only the real Alex didn't exist anymore, and the self he was supposed to be . . .

Alex batted the thought away, but it didn't make him feel any better. It only reminded him of the real reason Earl and Marge were supposed to be there that evening.

Lessons in love.

Alex glanced at the kitchen where Kate was getting the dinner he'd cooked onto serving plates. A chill like a Norwegian December night settled in the pit of his stomach.

Earl had asked the wrong guy for help.

As quickly as the idea occurred to him, Alex rejected it. He refused to believe he'd lost his touch with the ladies. No, it wasn't that Alex was the wrong guy. It was that Kate was the wrong woman.

"White cotton panties and white cotton socks."

"What's that?" Helen asked, and Alex realized he'd been mumbling under his breath. He excused himself with a smile and wondered if Helen even saw it through the haze of smoke that surrounded her. Having his freedom taken away did crazy things to a guy's mind, he decided. Apparently it didn't exactly do wonders for his libido, either. That had to be the reason he'd acted like a moron up in the bathroom earlier.

Though he was suspicious of the brand of beer Earl had dropped in the middle of the coffee table when he came in, and though he couldn't remember the last time he'd popped a can and drank right out of it, Alex reached for one of the beers in the six-pack. He took a long gulp, washing down the bad taste left by his encounter with Kate. He wasn't much of a drinker, or at least not as much of one as the tabloids would have people think, but one taste of the beer reminded Alex that he preferred his liquor older than yesterday and strictly single-malt. The beer tasted watery, bitter, and cheap. He took another drink.

He glanced at Earl in his silly T-shirt and Marge in her purple halter top and matching shorts. He looked at Harold, who was smiling amiably, if distractedly, at nothing, and at Helen, lighting up another cigarette even before the first one burned all the way down.

Was it any wonder he was acting crazy?

As if all this wasn't bad enough, he had to get permission for everything he did from Kate, and permission wasn't something she gave easily. As a matter of fact, she never gave it at all. He couldn't make a phone call. He couldn't mail a letter. He couldn't go anywhere or do anything without her following him around and watching his every move. Even in the grocery store, she hadn't let him out of her sight for two seconds. She was unreasonable and hidebound, and he reminded himself that one of these days, he'd have to point it out to her and compliment her on being the perfect bureaucrat. She'd get far with the government.

And he'd never get far with her.

This time, Alex managed to control the grumbled comment he was tempted to make. He consoled himself with the fact that in his real life, he probably never would have given Kate a second look. One day soon, he'd point that out to her, too. He'd be sure to mention that he wasn't in the habit of noticing average women with average bodies, average clothing, and average hair. He'd tell her he was glad he'd agreed never to go near her again. It was the best thing he'd ever done.

He'd remind her that getting close was something he'd never intended to do in the first place. Not really. Not ever. He never would have considered it. Not if he wasn't feeling like a caged animal.

At that moment, Kate came into the room, a serving plate in each hand. The house had no real dining room, just a table with six mismatched chairs tucked into the far corner of the living room. Alex watched Kate sidle around the chairs to place the plates in the center of the table. When she reached over, her unicorn shirt tugged up to reveal a strip of skin above the waistband of her denim shorts, a glimpse of her nicely rounded hips, and a tantalizing view of a backside that was just as appetizing as he remembered it.

Never, huh?

The question echoed through Alex's head in a decidedly cynical voice. Lucky for him he didn't have time to answer it. The moment the food was in the room, Marge popped out of her chair and sucked in a long breath of the tantalizing, spicy aroma that rose off the plates.

"Oh, yum!" she said with a smile of anticipation. "You got Taco Bell!"

Whatever else Alex was thinking suddenly didn't matter. Earlier in the evening, their guests had talked baseball and maligned a West Coast team Alex just happened to own. He ignored it. Then the subject changed to the new VCR Helen had purchased with her latest Social Security check. Though it was clear she didn't have a clue how to use the thing, Helen wasn't happy. She couldn't get the VCR to tape the right channels. She couldn't get it to play tapes. First thing Monday morning, she was going to call the manufacturer and give the folks there a piece of her mind. It was a company for which Alex just happened to sit on the board of directors. But did he point out her errors? Did he explain that most of what consumers perceive as problems come from not reading instruction booklets? Did he mention the company's stellar customer service or its reputation for integrity and reliability? No. He ignored it.

But now things were getting personal. Marge was slandering his cooking skills. And Alex's cooking skills were something he took seriously.

"It's not Taco Bell," he said, his teeth gritted into as passable a smile as he could manage. The rest of them were already milling around the table and Alex followed along. He gestured toward the plates on the table. "It's real food," he said. "Pork roast with black bean sauce. Grilled vegetable tostadas." Kate arrived with two more serving plates and he indicated those with a tip of his head. "Rice and beans. Fried plantains."

"Oh, how exotic!" Marge clapped her hands. She made a move to sit down, then stopped, and poked Earl on the arm. "The hostess gift," she told him in a stage whisper. "You forgot our hostess gift."

For the first time, Alex noticed there was a brown

paper bag on the floor in the living room next to the chair Earl had occupied. Earl retrieved it and brought the bag over.

Kate and Alex exchanged looks. They were the first looks they'd bothered to trade since their guests arrived, Alex realized. He expected to see steely anger in Kate's gunmetal eyes. He even looked forward to it. If Kate was still angry, it meant he had every right to be angry right back. Every right to blame her, and not himself, for the debacle that happened upstairs. But when Kate took the bag from Earl and glanced toward Alex, he was met with a shimmer of humor that only managed to make his temper soar.

She was enjoying this, damn it. Kate was actually enjoying this tacky excuse for an evening at home, and it wasn't because she was unsophisticated or inexperienced or low-class. It was because she knew it was driving Alex crazy.

"Why don't you open the wine," Kate purred, handing him the slightly damp paper bag along with a smile that was as wide and as phony as any he'd ever seen. "I'll get some glasses."

"And a corkscrew." It was an automatic response, but Alex should have known better.

Shaking his head at Alex's naïveté, Earl took the bottle from Alex and peeled the paper bag back from the neck. "Don't need no corkscrew," he said. "It's got one of them new caps. See." He grabbed the cap and turned. "All you got to do is twist it off."

Alex didn't think it was possible for Kate's smile to get any wider. He was wrong. With a look that told him she knew exactly what he was thinking, she headed into the kitchen.

As soon as she was gone, Earl turned away from the table. He made a great show of pulling the wine out of the bag to reveal a label that declared it Lambrusco and the three-dollar-and-fifty-nine-cent price sticker. "When you gonna start?" he asked Alex in a whisper.

Alex was tempted to ask what Earl was talking about. He didn't. He knew exactly what Earl had in mind. He wanted to know when Alex was going to start showing him what it took to be romantic.

Kate marched back into the room with six drinking glasses of various sizes and shapes, and Alex took a good long look at her. At the self-satisfied, crafty smile. At the cocky tilt of her head. At the rock-steady way she held her shoulders, the way that told the world she had everything, and everyone, under control.

When was he going to start showing Earl what it took to be romantic with Kate?

When hell freezes over, Alex promised himself.

Kate was smiling so hard, her mouth hurt. She didn't care. A little pain was worth the satisfaction of knowing Alex was just about as miserable as any person could ever be.

She set the glasses she was carrying on the table and told herself that Alex deserved all the misery one man could get. She lined the glasses up carefully and reminded herself that adding a little more misery to Alex's already miserable existence was the least she could do to pay him back for initiating that little incident up in the bathroom. He was the one who took advantage of the situation, and of the moment, and of a woman who obviously wasn't thinking clearly enough to know disaster when she saw it staring her right in the face. He was the one who knew his personality, his looks, and that smile of his were as potent as a shot of hundred-proof vodka, and yet he'd used it on her like a street fighter who saves a sucker punch for when his opponent least expects it.

When Earl handed Kate the bottle of wine, she accepted it, twisted the cap all the way off, and poured, her mind racing as fast as the unnaturally dark wine flowed from the bottle.

No doubt Alex had used the same methods on her that he used on all those supermodels and rockers, all those starlets and socialites who fell under his spell. No doubt he'd expected the same results. He'd assumed she'd succumb. Because every other woman did, he presumed she'd fall right into his arms and right into his bed without ever questioning his motivations or her sanity.

And damn it, he'd nearly been right.

The realization was enough to make Kate's hands tremble and slop some of the wine over the side of one of the glasses. Fortunately, though Marge noticed—she dabbed at the wet spot on the vinyl tablecloth with a paper napkin—no one but Alex could imagine what was going through her head, and Alex was busy, oddly enough, deep in a whispered conversation with Earl.

She'd been a hairsbreadth away from fulfilling Alex's expectations of her.

The very thought caused a mixture of hot anticipation and cold dread to collide in Kate's stomach like those warm fronts and cold fronts they talked about on the Weather Channel, and with pretty much the same results. Tornadoes that stirred her blood. Thunder that clapped through her brain like the warning bells of doom. A flush that heated her skin and a chill that settled inside her, as deep and durable as permafrost.

She'd been really close to letting it happen.

Even now, the thought seemed incomprehensible. But she knew it was true. Too true. One more wicked little smile from Alex would have pushed her over the edge. One more look that sparked fire would have spelled disaster. One more brush of the front of his jeans would have—

"Watch out, Missy! You'll drown us!"

Marge's shrill, good-natured comment brought Kate hurtling back to reality. She pulled the wine bottle back just in time to keep from filling the last glass over the brim, stammered something about paying better attention, and ignored the smile Alex gave her that made her wonder if he knew exactly what she was thinking.

Kate smiled back. Smiled until it hurt. Her resolve

was firm, and she knew she was right. Alex deserved all the misery she could give him. A plateful of grief along with his rice and beans, and a glassful of hassling to wash it down.

Kate set the wine bottle on the table and handed the glasses all around. She saved the one with the most in it for Alex, and as she gave it to him, she made sure to bat her eyelashes. "I propose a toast!"

She didn't fool him for a moment. She didn't intend to. She could tell he knew exactly what she was up to and one look at the slightly green color that tinted his face when he sniffed the wine told her it was worth it. Since she'd proposed a toast, he'd have to take a drink, and it was clear that giving Alex even a taste of wine as plebeian as the one in his glass was pretty much like giving a glass of garlic juice to a vampire.

Kate raised her own glass and looked at the people gathered around the table. "Let's toast to friendship."

"Friendship?" The very tone of Alex's voice told her he saw right through her plan. What she was doing wasn't anywhere near an act of friendship. He raised his glass and his eyebrows at the same time he lowered his voice. "I say we toast to something more interesting than friendship."

Marge and Helen applauded. They knew exactly what he was talking about, even if Earl and Harold didn't. Harold smiled at nothing in particular. Earl, who was ready to take a swig of the wine, looked at them blankly and waited patiently.

The warm front and the cold front came back at Kate like the backside of a hurricane. The moment she saw the spark of mischief in Alex's eyes, her insides went icy. The ice melted just as fast. The second she heard the suggestive little rumble in his voice.

Kate smiled. Wider. So wide he couldn't possibly guess at the storm playing havoc with her self-control. "What could be more interesting than friendship?" she asked, and she meant it as a rhetorical question. She meant to breeze right on and say something about how nice it was to have friends in the house for dinner. She might have known Alex wouldn't give her the chance.

He sidled up next to her. Close. Not close enough to touch her—he obviously remembered his promise, even if he didn't remember his manners—but close enough to remind her he hadn't forgotten what happened upstairs and he was as ready to get even as she was. "I can think of a couple of things," Alex growled.

Kate refused to be intimidated by Alex Romero's snide innuendos. She set her glass down, and clutching the back of a chair with one hand, she turned to face him. "Really? Would you care to elaborate?"

As if grateful for the opportunity, Alex nodded. He gave Earl a sort of knowing look, though what that was all about, Kate couldn't say. She didn't want to know.

Alex cleared his throat. "What's more interesting than friendship? Missy's forgetting last night. That white nightgown of hers, that's more interesting." He gave the people standing around the table an exaggerated wink and was rewarded by the flush that shot up Marge's neck and into her face, the eager nod he got back from Earl, and the sassy grin Helen managed at the same time she lit another cigarette. Harold smiled at nothing in particular.

Kate sputtered a protest but Alex didn't listen. He turned to her, his eyes glittering with a message as subtle as the neon signs that flashed outside Times Square strip clubs. "And then there's that little ticklish spot of yours. I won't say where, but you remember." He was so convincing, Kate had to stop herself from wondering if something had happened up in the bathroom that she'd forgotten.

"That's real interesting, too," Alex continued before she could recover and offer a protest. "Then there's that little thing you do with your tongue, Missy, honey. You know, when you flick it in and out right up against—"

"That Stan. What a kidder!" Though Alex had promised never to touch Kate, Kate had made no such promise in return. She gave him a whack on the arm that was just sharp enough to let him know she didn't think he was funny. "How about that toast?" she asked no one in particular, and before Alex could take off on another tangent headed straight in the direction of her complete and utter embarrassment, she lifted her glass and took a healthy drink.

Though Kate was a farm girl by background and at heart, she'd lived in the big city long enough to consider herself at least mildly sophisticated. She enjoyed the theater and classical music. She liked to sample the fare at ethnic restaurants. She was sure her taste in wine didn't nearly match Alex's, because her income was nowhere near his. But even she had trouble choking down the Lambrusco.

She did it, though. Jaw clenched, stomach tensed, taste buds screaming at the vinegar kick, she managed a drink and an appreciative smile. She set down her glass, stepped back, and waited for Alex to do the same.

Her actions had all the significance of a thrown gauntlet and Alex had no choice but to accept the challenge, just as she knew he would. Glass raised, he saluted Harold and Helen, Marge and Earl. When he got back to Kate, he raised the glass a little higher, smiled a little wider, and took a drink, and because Kate was closest to him, she was the only one who noticed the shudder that went through him as he did.

Satisfied at even that little bit of revenge, Kate made a move to sit down. As if the gesture was like yelling, "Ready, set, go!" at the start of a game of musical chairs, her guests scrambled. They left two chairs empty. Right next to each other.

Alex smiled. Kate smiled back.

Kate grabbed her chair and nudged it as far to the right as she could. Alex reached for his and moved it as far to the left as he could.

Alex settled himself. Kate sat down. "Shall we eat?"

she asked, and Alex began handing the serving plates around the table.

Marge leaned back in her chair, her purple shorts decidedly tighter across her stomach than when she first sat down. "Are you sure you didn't order in from Taco Bell?" she asked. "It was just as good."

Across the table, Alex swallowed the last of his fried plantains along with the comment he was tempted to make, the one that contained the words *no class* and *low class*. He set down his fork, touched his paper napkin to his lips, and firmly refused to glance over at Kate. He didn't have to. He knew she was grinning. Just like she'd been grinning through the entire, hellishly long meal.

"It's not Taco Bell," he said, and he wasn't surprised that he managed to keep his annoyance out of his voice. After an evening with people who made the Clampetts look like European royalty, he was too numb to do anything else. "I told you earlier. I planned the menu. I cooked the food."

"No kiddin'?" Earl gave Alex what could only be described as an incredulous look. He reached for the last slice of pork, dumped it on his plate, and dug in, talking with his mouth full. "You mean cooking—?"

Earl caught himself just in time. But while the others seated at the table didn't have a clue what he was talking about, Alex knew exactly what he'd been about to say. Earl wondered what cooking had to do with romance.

With a quick lift of his shoulders, Alex signaled Earl. What he signaled, even Alex wasn't sure. If Earl wanted to take this as Lesson One, that was fine with Alex. Though he'd never consciously equated cooking with being romantic, he supposed there was something to it. On the other hand, if Earl didn't get the message, Alex didn't much care. Earl's love life was the least of Alex's problems.

"You two are the cutest couple." Marge's voice broke into Alex's thoughts. He found her staring over his shoulder, back toward the pressed wood abomination that passed for an end table next to the couch and at the phony wedding picture that had arrived that afternoon. She heaved a sigh that did alarming things to her purple halter top. "That must have been the most wonderful day of your lives."

"Of course it was!" Kate jumped in with the comment, probably because she was afraid if she waited for Alex to say anything, it would be something offensive. "It was beautiful! The church service and the reception and the polka band."

"Ah, yes, the polka band!" This time, Alex was the one who heaved a sigh. He dared to look at Kate long enough to give her an angelic smile. "I especially liked the polka band."

"And your dress!" Marge fluttered one thick-fingered hand in front of her face. "Honey, that must have cost a pretty penny."

"Nothing's too good for my Missy." Alex nearly forgot himself and patted Kate on the arm. He pulled back his hand just in time, realizing how lucky he was. From the look she shot him, he suspected he might have self-combusted at the first touch. He recovered in a heartbeat and decided the best revenge was to let their guests know what a fine and noble fellow Stan was. "I worked an extra shift at the mill for three months straight to pay for that dress."

"Really?" Marge propped her elbows on the table and leaned forward. "Now that's true love."

Is it? Earl mouthed the words.

Alex stared at him blankly. How the hell was he supposed to know what true love was? He couldn't even get close to *like* with the woman who was supposed to be his wife.

When Earl looked at him expectantly, Alex nodded, an automatic response. He watched while Earl scrunched his eyes closed, as if making a mental note.

"What did your mother wear?"

It took Alex a moment to realize Marge was talking to

him, and another moment to make him fully aware that with that one question, she had put him in way over his head. What a woman who wasn't really his mother had worn to a wedding that had never really happened was not something the FBI had taken time to instruct him on back in New York.

"Mother?" Alex asked. He told himself it was too soon to panic, but it was hard to listen to his own advice. Though he was the first to admit he appreciated a well-dressed woman, he was just as quick to confess that he didn't pay a lot of attention to the finer points of women's fashion. He scrambled for something to say, and the first thing he remembered was a scrap of a conversation he'd heard from Charlotte, his secretary, after her daughter's wedding the summer before. "Mother wore a two-piece shantung silk suit from Dior's spring collection."

The seconds of absolute silence that greeted his announcement brought home the fact that he'd said the wrong thing.

In spite of the fact that he'd told himself a hundred times over that he didn't need Kate's help—for anything—Alex looked at her, a silent appeal in his eyes.

For what seemed an eternity, she didn't say a thing. As a matter of fact, if Alex had to put words to the look she gave him, he suspected they'd be *You made your own bed, Buster, now fry in it,* or something to that effect. It wasn't until a second before he was going to have to talk his own way out of the mess he'd talked himself into that Kate took pity on him.

She gave him a playful slap and laughed. "Oh, Stan. You're such a cutup! You know what your mother wore to the wedding. We've got all those pictures. It was that dress she bought at the Meadville Mall. The pretty little shirtwaist with the lace collar."

"Of course!" Alex laughed. Heartily he hoped. "The shirtwaist. The one with the lace collar. It was—"

"Blue," Kate said.

At the same time Alex said, "Pink."

Earl and Harold didn't seem to see anything wrong with the discrepancy. Earl stared at Alex intently, apparently waiting for him to impart another pearl of romantic wisdom. Harold smiled at nothing in particular. Marge and Helen were not so easily put off. They looked from Kate to Alex.

"So?" Helen asked. "Was it pink? Or blue? Those colors are hard to mix up."

"Blue," Alex said.

At the same time Kate blurted out, "Pink!"

"Actually it was really sort of grape-colored. Wouldn't you say, honey?" With a look, Alex dared Kate to disagree with him and land them back in the soup of contradictions.

"Grape." Kate smiled, and unless it was Alex's imagination, he actually thought she looked a little grateful at the compromise he'd come up with. "Definitely grape."

"Well, I'll bet she looked gorgeous." Marge nodded enthusiastically. "And I'll bet your mother did, too, Missy. She's such a pretty little thing. Just like you. You've got her eyes."

"I do?" At least Kate had the good sense to sound appalled by the suggestion that she had anything in common with the woman with the cotton-candy hair. She saved herself by recouping in an instant. "I do! You bet I do! I can't tell you how many people have told me I have Cindy's eyes and Frank's smile. It was one of the first things you ever said to me." She looked over at Alex. "Remember, Stan? You said I had my mom's eyes and my dad's smile."

"You bet." Alex smiled for as long as the comment warranted, then smiled a little longer, hoping the smile would encourage his guests to get finished and get out.

But Alex should have known Marge wasn't done. He watched her gaze slide across the rest of the photographs they'd placed around the living room.

"That little girl is so cute," Marge said. "Don't tell me, let me guess." She narrowed her eyes and sucked at her bottom lip, thinking. "She must be related to you, Stan. She looks like you."

Alex couldn't help himself. He had to turn around for another look at the picture. Did the little girl with the curly hair look like him? He didn't think so, but if Marge bought in to the deception, so much the better.

Alex turned back to the table. "That's—"

"Christina," Kate interrupted, apparently worried that he wouldn't remember.

"Yeah. Christina. She's my brother's little girl. My brother—"

"Ben."

Alex gave Kate a sidelong glare. "We adore her," he said, the words precise enough to send Kate the message that this time, he didn't need her help. "Remember the time we took her to the amusement park?" He dared Kate to look smug and superior. He dared her to horn in on a memory he'd just made up. "That little scamp, she just loved the roller coasters."

"And the candy apples." Kate apparently didn't know a good dare when she saw one. Her eyes dreamy, she leaned back in her chair. "She ate two of them after dinner and we warned her she was going to get a tummyache."

"And she did." Alex chuckled. He could almost picture the curly-haired little girl walking between them, one hand in Kate's, the other in his. He could almost hear her begging for that second candy apple and he could almost hear himself finally giving in, too taken by those curls and that cherubic smile to listen to Kate's wise advice that one was enough. He could almost see her holding her tummy and moaning on the way home, and picture how she'd fallen asleep in the car, finally, her head pillowed in Kate's lap. He could imagine getting home and carrying Christina to bed, just like he could imagine Kate bending over her pillow to plant a kiss on the little girl's cheek. In the same way, he could imagine how, once they knew Christina was settled for the night, they would go to their own room and—

Alex shook away from the fantasy before he could get in any deeper. While he'd been in the throes of it, he'd obviously missed something. Helen and Marge were already out of their seats and offering to help clean up, and when Kate said she'd handle it, they headed toward the door. After a wink Alex could only imagine was his way of saying thanks, Earl did the same. Harold lagged slightly behind.

"I've got lawn mowers." It was the first time in at least an hour that Harold had spoken a single word. "Lawn mowers," Harold said again, louder this time, apparently just in case Alex hadn't heard. "I buy them. At garage sales. I fix them up. If you want, you could use one."

Alex didn't bother to ask what he'd do with the thing, or why he'd even want it. "Thanks," he said, moving toward the door with his guests. "I'll keep that in mind."

Marge hugged Kate and then Alex. Harold and Earl shook hands all around. Helen threw some sort of parting comment over her shoulder at the same time she lit another cigarette. When the door finally closed on them, Alex breathed a sigh of relief and headed toward the couch.

"Oh, no, you don't."

Kate's comment brought him up short.

"We've got some cleaning up to do."

"But I—" Alex took one look at the plates piled on the table and his heart sank. "Can't we ask the maid to work late?"

"Maid's night out." Kate grabbed a plate in each hand and led the way into the kitchen. "You want to wash or dry?"

"I don't want to—"

"Let me guess, you've never done either." Kate finished clearing the table, ran water in the sink, and squirted some dishwashing detergent into it. "You might as well dry," she told him, tossing him a cotton dish towel. "It seems as good a place to start as any."

It wasn't any more comfortable working with Kate to clean up the kitchen than it had been sitting next to her through dinner, or at least it shouldn't have been. But by the time they were done a half hour later, Alex felt a little more relaxed and a little less inclined to think she'd snap his head off if he made an attempt at conversation. He was still convinced she'd snap his head off if he broke his promise and touched her, so he was sure to keep his distance.

"We actually did pretty well tonight," he said. He dried the last of the pans and handed it to Kate, then watched while she knelt and stowed it away in a cupboard. "I mean, we almost got into some trouble, but—"

"We?" She glanced at him over her shoulder. There was a glimmer of a smile in her eyes, and though Alex hated to admit it, a smile was probably more than he deserved. "I didn't make that harebrained comment about the Dior spring collection."

"Well, I—" Alex shrugged. It was about as good of an excuse as he could come up with.

"It worked out okay, though, didn't it?" Kate got back to her feet. She motioned to him for the dishcloth and, when he tossed it to her, finished wiping the countertops. "We actually make a pretty good team."

Alex laughed. "You had me going about Christina and the candy apples. I wondered if we really had taken her to the amusement park and she had eaten those candy apples."

"Improvisation." Kate folded the towel, draped it over the side of the sink, and stepped away. "Sometimes a good federal agent has to know when to punt."

"You're a good punter."

"Thanks." Kate's smile came and went quickly. "So are you."

There didn't seem anything left to say, so Alex snapped off the kitchen light and watched as Kate walked into the living room, her unicorn shirt a bright spot in the gloom.

She stopped and turned off the living room lights, turned the single light on at the bottom of the stairs, then stepped back so Alex could go up before her.

"You go up," he told her. "I'm not tired. I thought I'd just watch some TV or something."

"I don't think so." Kate looked toward the coat closet near the front door where the security system was hidden behind a panel of plywood. "I'd rather know the system is activated and everything's shut down tight."

"You'd rather know I'm snug in my bed and not down here doing something illicit like sending messages to New York via carrier pigeon." The words were out of Alex's mouth before he could stop them, and when Kate didn't answer or try to contradict them, he knew he was right.

"Great," he grumbled, and he headed up the stairs.

He and Kate might make a good team, they might be convincing enough to fool the neighbors and compatible enough to clean a kitchen quickly and efficiently, but none of that changed the crux of the problem.

Alex was still a prisoner, and even before he got to his bedroom and closed the door behind him, he'd decided it was time to do something about it.

8

"Of course everything's going okay. Everything's fine. Great. Fantastic." The phone propped between her shoulder and her ear, Kate finished her last spoonful of Rice Krunchies and nodded vigorously, as if Mark could see her all the way from New York. As if saying the words could make them true. "I'm in the kitchen and Romero is . . ." She stopped long enough to listen to the steady, muffled sound of the shower upstairs. "Romero is in the shower," she told her boss. "Has been for the last ten minutes or so."

"And last night?"

"Last night?" The Rice Krunchies turned to bricks in Kate's throat. For one terrifying moment, she was sure Mark was referring to what happened up in the bathroom right before their guests arrived. She batted down the thought as impossible, not to mention downright paranoid, and remembered that Mark was the one who'd arranged for the phony photographs.

"Last night went well." As remarkable as it seemed, Kate knew it was true. Considering all that had happened, and the fact that she felt as jumpy as a June bug all night long, things had gone well. In spite of what had already become indelibly etched in her mind as the Bathroom Incident and the rip-roaring argument that followed it, in spite of the fact that she'd wanted nothing more than to watch Alex squirm and that he'd nearly blown everything with that stupid remark about women's fashion, she and Alex had managed to pull off a little sleight of hand worthy of Houdini himself. "We came across as the perfect family," she told Mark. "The pictures helped. Thanks."

She didn't expect a *you're welcome*, not from Mark, but she didn't expect a grumble of obvious annoyance, either. "What the hell is he up to?" Mark asked. "You're not there to socialize. You're there to lay low. Keep out of the way. That rich, arrogant son of a gun has been a pain in the neck since the moment we started to deal with him, and suddenly, he's inviting the neighbors in? What, he's turned into Mr. Congeniality?"

Kate knew Mark well enough to picture him tugging at his left earlobe, the way he always did when he was baffled or annoyed. She also knew him well enough to catch the subtext of his comment: It was Kate's job to keep Romero under control. Inviting the neighbors for dinner wasn't the worst thing that could have happened, but it was as close to out-of-control as Mark was willing to let her get.

Kate didn't bother to mention that Alex would never, by any stretch of the imagination, be Mr. Congeniality. She also didn't jump at the chance of defending him or herself with the fact that, at least according to Alex, the neighbors had not been invited but had invited themselves. It didn't matter anyway, not after the fact, and no matter what she said, it would sound pathetically like an excuse. Reasons were something Mark begrudgingly accepted. Excuses? Excuses were what got Mark's special agents transferred to places where the sun shone only two months a year and it was cold enough to turn their gold badges to ice.

"I've got everything under control," she assured him,

and suddenly she was grateful Mark couldn't see her. If he could, she was sure he'd see right through the lie.

Control had nothing to do with the Bathroom Incident. *Control* had nothing to do with the perverse sense of pleasure that shot through her veins while she watched Alex with the neighbors. She had enjoyed seeing him uncomfortable and miserable, and she admitted it. She actually thought it was funny to watch him flounder his way through the evening. *Control* certainly had nothing to do with a reaction as childish as that, or with the warm, fuzzy, and unaccountable feelings that had snuck up and blindsided her as they worked together to get the dishes cleaned up.

Control? If she was a betting person, she'd bet *control* was the last word she could have honestly used to describe the evening, especially when she thought about the tingle of regret—and the blast of very real physical need—that had assailed her as she watched Alex go up to bed.

Kate swiped at a trickle of milk on her chin with a paper napkin decorated with blue teddy bears and green giraffes, and decided the best defense was a good offense. Time to change the subject and get her mind back where it belonged—and off the memory of what a perfect view she'd had of Alex's tight butt encased in his blue jeans as she stood at the bottom of the stairway and watched him climb the steps.

"Have you had a chance to check out that SUV I saw circling the Laundromat?" she asked Mark.

At the other end of the phone, Kate heard papers shuffling. She'd worked for Mark Harrison long enough to know he was a facts-at-his-fingertips kind of guy. She waited while he apparently found the report he'd been searching for and looked it over.

"Nothing suspicious," he said, cutting through the details straight to the results. "Belongs to a guy in the neighborhood who seems to be clean enough. He was probably looking to give someone a ride. Or maybe looking to pick up a girl, huh?"

"At the Laundromat?" Kate laughed. "Not the hottest singles spot I've seen." Her smile faded. "You think there's no problem, then?"

On the other end of the phone, she heard Mark's voice sober. "Not from the guy in the SUV," he told her. "But Bartone has dropped out of sight."

"What?" Kate jumped out of her chair and paced the room, just as she would have done if they were meeting face-to-face. "What do you mean, out of sight? You were supposed to have that scumbag under surveillance."

"We did. We caught up with him a couple weeks ago, and he hasn't been out of our sight since. Until last night. He went into a Vietnamese restaurant in Queens and while our guys waited outside, he somehow slipped out the back and right by them. That's what I really called to tell you, Ellison. There's no way he could have any idea where you are, but—"

"But we'll want to be extra careful."

"Right. At least until we can locate Bartone again. It shouldn't be too hard. The way we figure it, he'll go for the yacht. That's where everyone thinks Romero is."

"That's where Romero wishes he was." In a moment of clarity the likes of which had been few and far between since the day she'd met Alex, Kate wished she was on the *Calypso,* too. Facing the most notorious hit man on the East Coast would be a hell of a lot easier on her nerves than playing house with Alex was turning out to be. And less dangerous, too, she suspected.

Her hair was still damp from her own shower, and she combed it through with her fingers while she listened to the steady beat of the water from upstairs. Now that Bartone was out from under the careful surveillance that had rendered him inoperative, the plum job of the guys aboard the *Calypso* didn't look so plum anymore. Kate's stomach did a little jump. "Tell them to be careful, okay?" She didn't have to tell Mark who she was talking about.

"You be careful." He didn't need to remind her of that, either. "Don't let Romero out of your sight."

"Haven't yet," Kate assured him. "Won't."

With a grumbled reply that told her it was the least the federal government expected of her, Mark hung up.

Kate gathered her bowl and spoon from the table and carried them across the room. Just like every morning, she found Alex had left a plate, a coffee cup, and a knife smeared with butter and grape jelly in the sink. Shaking her head, half in disgust and half because she couldn't believe anyone could be so dependent on other people that he didn't know how to clean up after himself, she put the stopper in the sink and ran the hot water.

Only there wasn't any hot water.

"Selfish son of a—" Kate slammed the faucet off and glared up at the ceiling, as if Alex could see the look and know it meant it was time for him to get out of the shower. Not that it would have helped if he could see her, Kate thought.

She put away the box of Rice Krunchies and the carton of milk, wiped off the table, and plunked down, her elbows on the table and her head in her hands.

If Alex knew she was waiting for enough hot water to wash the breakfast dishes, he probably would make some smart-ass comment about letting the butler worry about it. Then just to prove he didn't have to listen, or cooperate, or share anything (not even the hot water), he'd make sure he stayed in the shower twice as long.

Though why anyone would want to stay in the shower once the hot water was gone was beyond Kate.

Too annoyed to care if Alex ended up pruney from head to toe, Kate paged through the morning paper. She skimmed a story about local politics, read her horoscope then promptly forgot it, and checked the baseball scores. There was an article about Ruben Martinez and she read it over and wondered how a man with Martinez's connections had found himself in what looked to be an untenable and very dangerous position. The generalissimo who ran the government in the country where Martinez lived was not a fan of free speech or human rights, and it was obvious Martinez's trial had been stacked against him from the beginning. Kate shook her head, genuinely disappointed. Martinez might not be much of a writer, but he had an effect on people that was undeniable. When he talked, people listened, and what Martinez had to say about bettering the lives of the millions who lived beneath the iron fists of oppressive governments was something the world needed to hear. Good writer or bad, it looked as if Ruben Martinez would be sacrificed to make a political point, and that was a shame.

By the time Kate finished with the paper, folded it up neatly, and pushed it to the corner of the table, the sound of the shower running upstairs had become a sort of background noise, like the hum of the refrigerator and the blast of the train whistles outside. With a jolt, Kate realized the water was still on, and she stood and stared up at the ceiling, her fists on her hips.

"What the hell are you doing up there?" she asked, and because she knew she wouldn't get an answer, at least not while she was standing downstairs in the kitchen, she marched up the stairs and pounded on the bathroom door.

"What the hell are you doing in there?" She yelled over the sounds of the water, and when Alex didn't reply, she pounded again, and yelled again, and pounded some more.

He still didn't answer. Kate's stomach got very hot, then very cold; she reminded herself she couldn't afford to panic. If there was something wrong, she'd handle it. She was trained in first aid, schooled in handling pressure. She'd proved more than once that she could be cool in a crisis. Still, she couldn't help but let her imagination run wild. Maybe he'd slipped in the shower and cracked his head open? Maybe he'd been bleeding to death while she'd been reading the paper? Or maybe Bartone had gotten to Alex? There was a window in the bathroom. It was possible that a marksman who was good enough could have taken aim from one of the houses close by and—

"Alex!" The name escaped Kate on the end of a hiccup of alarm. She tried the doorknob. It turned easily and she pushed the door open and stuck her head into the bathroom.

Though the hot water was long gone, the steam in the room hadn't had a chance to dissipate. The air in the bathroom reminded her of a San Francisco morning, thick with fog and moisture. Kate opened the door wider to let out some of the steam and stepped inside, waving her arms to disperse the cloud. "Alex, are you all right?"

There was no answer from behind the shower curtain, only the noise of the water, and Kate's worries instantly turned to suspicion. It was a little too pat. A little too theatrical. The foggy atmosphere. The hot, sticky air. The return-to-the-scene-of-the-crime scenario no doubt designed to remind her of her indiscretion the afternoon before. She wouldn't put it past Alex to have set it all up just so he could pop out from behind the shower curtain, naked and rarin' to go.

And she wondered what she'd do if he did.

The cold dread in Kate's stomach melted in a rush of supercharged heat, but even she wasn't sure if it was her libido kicking in, or anger. If Alex was waiting behind the curtain, ready to seduce her, would she fall into his arms? Or level him right on the spot?

"Alex?" She tried one more time, eager for an answer because if she got one from Alex, she wouldn't need to get one from herself. "Alex, this isn't funny. If you fell and you're hurt or something that's one thing, but if you're doing this to be cute, well . . . I . . ."

As tired of listening to herself look for excuses not to pull the shower curtain open as she was waiting for Alex to answer, Kate grasped the blue-and-green curtain and yanked.

She saw the stream of water falling from the shower head, and the green bathmat that had been placed at the bottom of the tub. She felt the cool spray of the water.

And she knew it was no wonder she wasn't getting an answer from Alex.

Alex wasn't there.

"Look, I really just want to—"

"I know. I know." Marge kept one hand on her shopping cart while with the other she gave Alex's shoulder the kind of maternal pat he hadn't had since he was a kid and fell down and skinned his knees. "You want to make a long-distance phone call. I know that, Stan. But I'm telling you to be patient. I'll be done in a couple minutes. And then we'll go back home. It's much more economical to make a long-distance call from home than it is from a pay phone."

"I don't care how economical it is. I've got a credit card, and—"

Marge clicked her tongue. "I just don't understand you young folks. What would Missy say if she knew you were squandering money like that? The poor girl. She's such a sweetheart. She deserves better and you know it. And you, not working." At the same time she shook her head to emphasize her disappointment, Marge tossed a pack of toilet paper into a shopping cart already brimming with paper towels, light bulbs, three cans of Spam, and a ceramic lamp shaped like a watering can.

"You don't want to waste the money you do have on silly things, do you?" she asked, and apparently because she saw the look on Alex's face that told her he did, she didn't give him a chance to answer. "Long-distance phone calls from a pay phone are silly," she insisted. "Once we get back, you can use my phone if you want to. We've got one of those special plans. It saves us oodles of money every month because I make so many phone calls. My daughter, Wilma, she lives in Arizona, you know. Then there's Terry, she's the one who moved to Iowa last year. She's not my daughter, but . . ."

Alex braced himself against the sound of Marge's voice grinding out an endless stream of details. He'd never imagined that something as simple as trying to make a phone call could get so complicated. Or so tedious.

He should have known things weren't going to be easy the minute he met Marge coming out of her house at the same time he was coming out of his. He should have been quicker on his feet and made up some sort of reasonable excuse when Marge asked where he was headed. Instead, he'd looked back at the house and pictured Kate in the kitchen, crunching into her Rice Krunchies, and he knew he didn't have long. She might fall for the Alex-is-in-the-shower trick. In fact, he hoped she did. But for how long?

So when Marge said she was going shopping, Alex never questioned it. He went right along. He didn't even object when she told him they'd be walking. There were bound to be phones along the way, he reasoned. There were bound to be opportunities to slip away from Marge so he could call his New York office. But although he'd found a couple pay phones, not one of them worked. He hadn't counted on that, or on a shopping companion who was every bit as tenacious about keeping an eye on him as Kate was.

As if to prove just what a good judge of character he was, Marge chose that particular moment to wind one arm through Alex's and he found himself hauled up yet one more aisle and down another. He hadn't counted on a shopping experience that gave the word *distinctive* a decidedly peculiar twist, either.

But then, never in his wildest dreams had Alex Romero counted on finding himself inside a Kmart.

The very thought was enough to cause a shiver of alarm and something very much like revulsion to snake up Alex's spine. Automatically he glanced over his shoulder, half expecting to see a troop of paparazzi with their cameras poised and ready, salivating over the opportunity to snap photos of him slumming it. Thankfully there wasn't one reporter in sight, but though the realization should have cheered him, it didn't lessen Alex's mortification one bit. He glanced down at the pitted linoleum floor. He looked up at the flickering fluorescent lights. And he groaned.

If Marge thought it was because she rolled the shopping cart around an end-cap display of half-dead geraniums and headed toward the women's clothing department, he figured it was just as well. A person like Marge could never understand what an experience like this could do to Alex's psyche. He might never shake off the memories. He might never be rid of the smells of moth balls and submarine sandwiches and perfume with labels that started with the words *Smells Just Like . . .* Not one of the people Alex had met since his descent into hell could ever understand the trauma of shopping in a place where the fine jewelry department sold toe rings, the clerks wore little red aprons, country music blared over the loudspeakers, and tabloid newspapers were displayed prominently near the registers.

"Wait!" Alex stopped so fast, his sneakers squeaked. Untangling his arm from Marge's, he headed over to the display wedged between the bubble gum and the Doritos. A picture of the *Calypso* took up most of the front page of one of the more notorious tabloids, right under a headline that screamed *Romeo Prowls the High Seas!*

"Can you believe it?" Alex mumbled to himself while he paged through the paper, looking for the story that went with the picture. He found it, along with a series of photographs that was sensational to say the least. And startling to say the most.

The pictures must have been taken from a helicopter. They were grainy and not too clear, but from what he could tell, they showed exactly what they purported to show: Alex Romero in his swim trunks, a champagne flute in one hand, his arm wrapped around a curvaceous blonde wearing a bikini so small it was practically nonexistent.

"Holy—" Alex might have finished the statement if he didn't feel Marge peering over his shoulder.

"That's the fellow," Marge said, pointing to the picture.

"That one I was talking about last night. You know, the rich one who—"

"Yeah. I know." As if it might actually help bring the pictures into focus, Alex adjusted his glasses on his nose. He stared at the pictures, at the yacht that looked odd and unfamiliar with strangers aboard, at the man whose face (at least in the grainy photograph) was enough like his to make even him believe he was looking at Alex Romero.

Though a casual observer would never have noticed, it was clear to Alex that the photographs had been staged by the FBI to further perpetrate the story that he was cruising on the *Calypso*. It was the only explanation for how any photographer could even find the yacht in the middle of the Mediterranean. Back in the days when Alex had a life, he made sure his route was kept strictly confidential simply so he wouldn't be followed and photographed.

Alex closed the paper and shoved it back in place in the rack. It had been bad enough when Kate told him someone else was living out his life on the *Calypso*. It was worse seeing proof. Especially proof that painted him as a party guy with nothing more on his mind than alcohol and scantily clad women.

Is that how the FBI thought of him? Is that what the rest of the world thought? What it expected?

They were questions Alex had never considered before; now that he did, he could understand why. They left him feeling uneasy and uncomfortable—not emotions he was accustomed to feeling. They weren't emotions he liked. He shifted from foot to foot, staring at the photo of the *Calypso*, and the questions gnawed away at his own self-image. He might have found at least the beginnings of answers to them if Marge hadn't poked him in the ribs.

"Uh-oh, Stan. Looks like you're in some kind of trouble."

Alex followed Marge's gaze over to the floor-to-ceiling windows at the front of the store just in time to see Kate storm by. Her hands curled into fists at her sides, her chin high and steady, she headed straight for the automatic doors that led into the store. Marge's assessment looked to be right on. Kate was not a happy camper. What looked to be waiting at the other end of the scowl that creased her forehead and wrinkled her nose wasn't just trouble. It was Trouble. With a capital T. And Alex knew exactly why. A woman as bright as Kate could only be fooled by the shower trick for so long. He was lucky he'd had this much time. And foolish not to have taken full advantage of it.

Alex knew he had to do something, and he had to do it quickly. He wouldn't get the opportunity to sneak away from Kate again. "She hates when I leave the house without telling her where I'm going," he said, whispering to Marge so that it seemed as if he was sharing a confidence. "Missy's a jealous, jealous woman." When Marge looked at him, her face blanched white, he reassured her with a wan smile. "Don't worry. She knows you're a good woman, Marge. She can't possibly think we're carrying on behind her back. Not like she did with that girl back in Erie. Don't you worry about her, either," he added when Marge's mouth dropped open and it looked as if she wanted to ask what he was talking about. He didn't have time to waste on Marge's questions. "She'll be good as new once she finishes physical therapy. No thanks to Missy."

Alex darted a look toward the windows. He could see Kate looking like thunder as she wound her way through the maze of shopping carts outside the doors. "You don't know this, but Missy isn't the most levelheaded girl," he said, nudging Marge in Kate's direction. "She's got a mean streak a mile wide. You head her off at the pass. I'll be right behind you."

Alex had to give Marge credit. She did exactly as she was told. Before Kate was all the way through the doors, Marge was already hurrying over to meet her and Alex heard Marge's voice, tight with an emotion that bordered on panic. ". . . Just shopping, of course . . . your Stan was just helping . . . so nice of him . . . knew you wouldn't mind."

But though he'd bought himself some time, Alex knew it wasn't nearly enough. As much as he hated to take the chance, it was time to play his ace in the hole. He reached into his pocket and pulled out the debit card he'd managed to smuggle out of FBI headquarters in his shoe. He would have preferred making a phone call. It was faster and easier than waiting for the debit card statement to make its way back to Norbert's desk. Since the phone call hadn't worked, Alex knew the next best thing was to make enough purchases with the debit card to leave a paper trail a mile long. Thanks to Marge's dawdling, not to mention her ability to cling like a limpet, now there wasn't time.

There were no lines at the registers, and it took Alex only a minute to head that way. Unfortunately it was one minute too long. When Kate got there, she found him with his debit card still in his hand.

"What the hell do you think you're up to?" Kate's cheeks were a shade of pink that came across as tawny under the fluorescent lights. She did her best to keep her voice down and control her temper, but it was clear from the start, it wasn't easy. Her eyes flashed, and when she reached over and yanked the card out of Alex's hand, her hands shook.

"A debit card? You're using a debit card?" Kate looked from the card to Alex, then back to the card. Something told him if Marge wasn't hovering two aisles over, trying her best to listen to every word (and failing, if the disappointed look on her face meant anything), Kate might have screamed at him. "Let me guess," she said in a rough whisper. "It's a company card. The statement goes to—who? Norbert? Or Charlotte? Either way, it lists where your purchases were made, right? Either way, suddenly someone knows right where you are."

It was too close to the mark for Alex's comfort. But

then, what did he expect? Kate was a professional. She was intelligent. The scheme was so half-baked, she was sure to see right through it.

He smiled, a bold, cocky smile he knew would do little more than send her temperature up a degree or two. It wasn't much. But for now, it was all he had, and he went with it. "What are you?" he asked. "The FBI? How did you find us?"

"That wasn't hard." Kate darted a look past Alex toward Marge. "Earl isn't the most reticent guy in the world. He knew where Marge was going and I suspected you might be with her. What did you tell her anyway? She looks like she swallowed a toad."

"You think so?" Alex glanced over his shoulder at Marge. She was watching the whispered fight with eyes wide, not sure what might happen next. "All I did was tell her what happened to that girl in Erie. You know, Missy. That one you were so jealous of."

Kate pressed her lips together to contain what probably would have been the most rip-roaring tirade Alex ever heard. Fortunately for him, he never got the chance to hear it. With an effort that was almost palpable, she controlled herself. She dragged her gaze back from Marge and gave Alex the kind of look that must have intimidated bad guys from one end of the country to the other. It was steely. That was the only way Alex could describe it. Steely and so full of authority, he might have stepped back if it wasn't for the fact that there was a rack of *TV Guides* poking his spine.

"Looks like I got here just in time," Kate said from between clenched teeth.

"Caught me red-handed." Because he couldn't do anything else, Alex threw his hands up in surrender. He shrugged and chanced a smile he hoped looked less satisfied than it did contrite. "Good thing you got here before I bought anything."

Kate's gaze snapped over to the register. The black conveyor belt that fed merchandise toward the cashier was empty. Just to prove she'd outsmarted him, Alex held his hands up, turned them over.

"I'm clean," he said.

Kate apparently wasn't so sure. She looked him up and down and when she was finally appeased, she snapped his debit card neatly in half and shoved both pieces into the pocket of her jeans.

"Come on, Marge," she said, though she never took her eyes off Alex. "We're going home."

Marge didn't question the decision and Alex didn't blame her. There was a ring of command in Kate's voice he'd never heard before, one that dared anyone within earshot to contradict her. Marge sure didn't, but maybe that was because she was thinking of that fictitious girl back in physical therapy. She unloaded her cart and waited patiently while the wide-eyed clerk whose cheeks were as red as her apron scanned the merchandise.

Alex didn't question Kate's command, either. As each of Marge's items was scanned, he dutifully loaded them into slippery plastic bags. When all the bags were filled, he handed one to Kate, one to Marge, and kept the other three for himself.

He didn't dare meet Kate's eyes. He didn't want her to see the tiny smile that tickled the corners of his mouth.

Just like he didn't want her to see the small, rectangular bulge in the front pocket of his jeans.

The one caused by the small pack of condoms in his pocket.

The pack of condoms he'd managed to buy while Marge distracted Kate. The one he'd paid for with his company debit card.

Kate walked along at Alex's side toward the parking space where she'd left the battered station wagon, her sneakers pounding the pavement, her heart beating hard to the same rhythm. Marge had wisely decided to walk a little way behind them, and that was just fine with Kate. She wasn't in the mood for small talk. She sure wouldn't have been happy to have Marge walking ahead of them, either, taking her good old time. Right now, if even Marge got in her way, Kate was sure she would have bowled her over.

"What the hell is wrong with you?" They were the first coherent words Kate had been able to put together since she stomped out of the store. She shifted the bag of paper towels she was carrying from her right hand into her left and rubbed her right thumb over her fingertips, doing her best to expel the electricity that seemed to have built inside her. "Do you have a death wish or something?"

At her side, Alex chuckled. "Hey, it wasn't Neiman Marcus, but it wasn't that bad. The death of style, maybe. The death of a stellar reputation. Maybe even the death of—"

"Shut up." Looping the handle of the plastic bag over her wrist, Kate reached into her pocket for the car keys at the same time she reached for the handle on the driver's side door.

Alex *tsked* softly. "Hardly the way a federal officer should talk to a—"

Kate yanked open the car door. Fast. Quick enough that Alex nearly slammed right into it. It was enough to stop him in his tracks, and though she suspected nothing would ever make him humble, the threat of bodily harm was at least enough to keep him quiet. When Marge finally caught up, he backed off. He opened the back door for Marge, helped settle her and her packages in the backseat, and climbed in next to Kate without another word.

It was a good thing, too. Kate wasn't sure she could deal with Alex at that moment, at least not with the delicacy the situation—and Marge's presence—demanded.

It took less than five minutes to get back to the house, but they were five tense minutes, five minutes of Kate gripping the steering wheel, grasping for white-knuckled control. Next to her, Alex was wisely silent. In the backseat, Marge was uncharacteristically quiet. When Kate chanced a look at her in the rearview mirror, she saw

Marge chewing her lower lip, no doubt wondering when the bell would ding and Stan and Missy would launch into the next round of the fight.

Fortunately for Marge, for Alex, and for Kate's barely contained self-control, they got home and parked in front of the house without further incident. Before Kate even turned off the ignition, Alex got out of the car, opened the door for Marge, and helped her out with her packages. After a careful look up and down the street and an abrupt nod of permission, Kate watched him carry Marge's bags up to her door. He came back across the street with just the smallest of smiles on his face, and it was that small smile that set Kate off like a California brushfire. What the hell he had to smile about was a mystery to Kate, and just the fact that he could smile after all he'd put her through spoke volumes about the man's lack of character. And brains.

"How many times have we talked about how dangerous it is for you to go out without me?" Kate headed up the front walk to the house, but not before she was sure Alex was headed that way, too. She wouldn't make the same mistake twice. There was no way she was ever going to let him out of her sight again. "You're supposed to be a smart guy. Smart is not taking off without telling me where you were going."

"Smart was getting you to think I was in the shower, though. An old trick, but admit it, you fell for it."

"Not for long." She chanced a look at him out of the corner of her eye. He was grinning and she looked away as quickly as she could, just so he wouldn't think he could get away with spreading his famous charm on thick enough to smother her annoyance. "I found you, didn't I?"

"I knew you would eventually." He kicked at a loose stone lying in the sidewalk and sent it flying into the weeds that made Stan and Missy's front lawn look like the poster yard for Houses Anonymous. "And it looks like I'm alive and well. Maybe that's the moral of the story. Maybe I don't need twenty-four-hour baby-sitting."

"Maybe you're an idiot."

"Maybe I know what I'm doing."

"Right." She jabbed the key in the front door lock, turned it, and pushed the door open. Once she took a quick look around the living room to make sure everything was all right, she stepped back to allow Alex in ahead of her.

"You really made my day. I can tell you that much." Kate threw her oversize purse on the couch and went to punch in the code on the security panel. When she was done, she turned to Alex, her feet braced as if she was ready to fight. "I actually trusted you. Imagine that. Then I go upstairs and find out I've been played for a sucker."

Alex's eyebrows slid up just enough to make him look cocky. "Bet you couldn't wait to take a peek behind the shower curtain."

It was the last straw. Kate slammed the front door shut with enough force to make the house shake. "Yes," she said. "I peeked. And you know what? I wasn't worried about what I was going to see, because in my experience, the guys who talk about it the most are the ones who don't have anything to brag about in the first place."

"Really?" Alex stepped back, his weight on one foot. "So that's why you're mad, huh? Because all this time you've been wanting it, and it suddenly occurred to you that maybe you weren't going to get—"

"Maybe you're not going to get through the summer in one piece." Kate pronounced each word carefully, as if somehow that might make him understand. She refused to be waylaid by his lame shot at humor, or by his half-baked attempt at seduction, if that's what it was supposed to be. She refused to get sidetracked. Not when this hardheaded, arrogant, infuriating bastard's life was on the line. She pulled the pieces of Alex's debit card out of her pocket and broke each half in half again just for good measure. She tossed the remains on the coffee table.

"Do you realize what could have happened if you used that card?" she asked. "If the statement went across someone's desk, someone who was just itching for a chance to find out where you are?"

Defiant to the last, Alex shook his head. "You're wrong. Dead wrong."

"Better dead wrong than dead. You know better than to—"

"I know who I can trust and who I can't trust," Alex shot back. "You seem to have this crazy notion that someone in my office—"

"They've lost Joe Bartone." As soon as she'd heard the bad news from Mark, Kate had decided she would break it to Alex gently. She would preface it with a short but succinct history of the Bureau's successes. She would stress that their failures were few and far between and that even though, right now, this looked to be one of those failures, she was sure things would be set right in a matter of hours. Now instead of delivering the news with all the coolness her profession demanded, she had blurted it out, no preamble, no excuses. She had hit Alex over the head with the bad news and she caught him by surprise.

His eyes widened, then narrowed almost imperceptibly, as if he was taking in the news and analyzing it at lightning speed. Apparently even analyzing it didn't do much toward helping it make any more sense. Not sure he'd heard her right, he leaned nearer.

"That's right," she said. "They lost Bartone. They don't know where he is. He's gone. Disappeared. M-I-A. They haven't seen him in over twelve hours and let me remind you, twelve hours is plenty of time to get from New York to Cleveland."

"But—"

"But nothing." Kate heard the small thread of satisfaction that warmed her words. Maybe he'd finally listen? Maybe he'd finally realize this wasn't some rich boy's game of hide-and-seek? "Stinks, doesn't it? Thousands of dollars in salaries for the federal agents who were watching him. Thousands more in surveillance equipment.

Thousands of hours of hard work just finding the jerk in the first place. And now this. And the worst part is—"

Kate never had a chance to tell him what the worst part was. Just as she was about to, she noticed Marge standing at the front door, her nose pressed to the window.

"Damn." Kate's shoulders sagged. She massaged her temples with the heels of her hands and stalked to the door. She pulled it open, and even as she did, she wasn't sure what words were about to come pouring out of her mouth. She was pretty sure they would be something like "Get lost," but she didn't have a chance to say that, either.

Because Marge was crying.

Kate's anger dissolved in a rush of concern. She took one look at Marge's red nose, her puffy eyes, and the soggy tissue she clutched in one hand, and she decided *crying* was not exactly the right word. If she was writing about the incident in a report, Kate would have used the word *crying;* it was short and sweet and as to-the-point as special agents were supposed to be. But crying was not what Marge was doing.

Marge was blubbering.

Instinctively Kate put a hand on Marge's arm and drew her into the house. "What is it?" she asked. "What's wrong?"

Marge didn't answer right away. Instead, she blew her nose. Swigged. Stuffed her used tissue into her pocket and pulled out a new one. She hiccuped. Whimpered. Glanced from Kate to Alex.

"It's the two of you," she said, her voice rising and falling like the heaving of her bosom. Once the words were out, the dam burst. A fresh set of tears streamed from Marge's eyes and her words flowed just as fast. "And I know it's none of my business or at least you think it's none of my business, but it is. I feel like a mother to you two. You're young and sweet and you've got your whole lives ahead of you. And when I look at the two of you in your wedding picture . . ." She glanced toward the picture.

"I see how much in love you really are, and when we were at Kmart, I remembered that picture. And I thought about that love. And I told myself that it just wasn't right. You two acting like a couple of kids. Fighting with each other when I don't think there's anything to fight about. I bet you two don't even know what you're fighting about. Well, I won't just stand by and not say anything, even though Earl says that's what I should do. I won't stand by and watch you fight. I won't." She stomped her foot, just to prove her point. "I'm not leaving here until you two stop fighting," Marge said. She raised both her chins and managed a look that was nearly a glare.

"Kiss and make up," she ordered. "Right now."

The tenacity with which Marge delivered the edict was surprising enough. What she said left Kate stunned. At her side, even Alex was speechless.

"You heard me." Marge blew noisily into her tissue. "I'm standing right here and I don't care if I have to stand here all day. I won't see two nice kids like you throw away your happiness over nothing." She swung her suddenly determined, red-rimmed gaze around to Alex. "Kiss her," she commanded.

The words sunk in and turned Kate's stomach to ice. She stared at Alex, who, after a moment of confusion that mirrored hers, took a step toward her. Kate took a step back.

"You wouldn't dare," she muttered.

"You heard Marge." Alex managed a sort of shuffle that brought him within a couple inches. Close enough for Kate to have to look up—past the well-muscled chest and the rock-solid jawline and the mouth that launched a thousand fantasies—to see the twin devils of amusement that danced in his dark eyes.

One corner of Alex's mouth twitched into an expression that was almost a smile. "She'll stay here all day."

"All day," Marge echoed.

"I wouldn't be surprised if she stayed here all night."

"All night," Marge repeated.

Alex looked away from Kate, but only long enough to give Marge a quick nod of agreement. "It looks like we don't have a choice, Missy, honey," he said, glancing back to Kate and keeping his gaze fixed on hers. "Marge is one feisty lady. The only thing that's going to make her happy is if we kiss and make up."

Kate stared into Alex's chocolate eyes. She wondered if she looked as terrified as she felt. She hoped not. She refused to let Alex know that something as small as a kiss—and a coerced one at that from a man who didn't mean a thing to her—could make her knees shake and her stomach flop around like a dolphin in a Sea World show.

Not that she'd ever let him know it. Not for the world.

She lifted her chin. "Fine," she said, and she hoped she sounded like she meant it. "We'll kiss and make up." She darted a look at Marge. "Would that make you happy?" she asked.

"It's not me you need to worry about making happy." Marge sniffed. "It's this wonderful man who loves you."

"That's me!" This time, Alex didn't hold back his smile. It hit Kate with all the force of a gale wind, knocking her breath away. But when he took another step closer and made to take her into his arms, she warned him off with a look.

Alex stopped and pulled his hands back to his sides. "I remember," he admitted. "I promised."

"You promised." Kate's own voice sounded too breathy, even to her, and she vowed she wouldn't say another thing until she could get it under control.

"Which means . . ." Alex adjusted his glasses. In keeping with his promise, he didn't touch her. His arms firmly at his sides, he leaned forward, and in a moment of pure panic, Kate was tempted to run. She forced herself to hold her ground, and lifted her mouth to meet his.

Damn him, it wasn't the quick we're-mad-at-each-other-so-let's-get-this-over-with kiss it should have been. It started out innocent enough, a peck on the lips that deepened almost imperceptibly, bit by bit, until his mouth covered hers completely and she was lost. It was a mind-numbing kiss, long and slow, and by the time it was over, Kate was so weak-kneed, she nearly fell over when Alex moved away.

She stopped herself just in time, cleared her throat as if she'd just taken a dose of cough medicine rather than a taste of something sweeter than sin, and dared to raise her gaze to Alex's.

She thought she'd find him looking as satisfied as a cow in a field of clover, grinning the way he'd grinned at the hundreds (maybe even thousands) of other women who'd been caught like bugs in a Venus flytrap by the honey of his lips. She thought the light in his eyes would be brighter than ever, just like it was in the pictures she'd seen of him, when dozens of cameras went off all around him.

Instead, she found Alex looking as if he'd just been hit by a baseball bat.

For a couple of seconds, he stared at her in stunned silence. Finally, like a guy waking from a dream that was full of surprises, he blinked and drew in a long breath. Even before he let it out again, he bolted for the front door.

9

It was Rule #1, and he'd broken it.

Not sure where he was headed, Alex barreled down the front steps and out onto what there was of a front lawn outside the house. His back to the window where, no doubt, Kate was already stationed to make sure he stayed in sight, he leaned against the rusty chassis of the '79 Nova that stood on cinder blocks in the center of the brown and weedy lawn. He hauled in a breath deep enough to tear at his lungs and advised himself to stop acting like an idiot.

He was a man, not a teenaged boy. A man should be smart enough and experienced enough and sophisticated enough not to violate Rule #1. No matter what else he did, how he did it, or whom he did it with, a man should always have Rule #1 foremost in his mind: Never get involved, at least not emotionally.

But Alex had violated Rule #1. Big time. He suspected it was about to happen the second his lips touched Kate's. He knew it for sure when he found it impossible to resist deepening the kiss, even though he was sure it was the wrong thing to do.

Smart, huh? Looked like he was anything but smart.

Experienced? Sure, but what did that matter when he caved in so easily? Sophisticated? It was enough to make Alex laugh, though had he been on the receiving end of it, he would have been surprised at how little humor there was in his laugh.

Annoyed—at himself, the situation, and life in general—he crossed his arms over his chest and grumbled a string of expletives the likes of which he hadn't used since the days he was in college and needed to prove how grown-up he could sound. A weed with jagged leaves and the kind of thick stalk that dared anyone to challenge its right to grow anywhere it wanted poked out from beneath the nearest cinder block. Alex kicked at it with the toe of his sneaker, suddenly convinced as firmly as he'd ever been convinced of anything that if he could just rip it up by its nice, fat roots, he'd feel a whole lot better. When kicking didn't help dislodge either the weed or his sour mood, he bent and wrapped both hands around the stem.

"Ouch!" Alex jerked his hands away. The weed was covered with tiny spikes that jabbed his skin. He sucked at a spot where his right index finger had taken the brunt of the spike's antagonism and glared down at the weed. If it had been a self-respecting weed, it would have shriveled up and died right then and there. Instead, it just glared back at him.

"Oh, yeah?" Alex set his jaw and reached down again. This time, when the spikes dug into him, he was ready for them. He wrapped his hands around the stem tight enough to choke the life out of it, and pulled. The weed gave up the ghost with a minimal fight and before Alex knew it, he was standing with his prize, roots and all, dangling from his hands.

He grinned, but like a junkie eager for his next fix, the satisfied feeling didn't last long. He looked for another weed, and he didn't have to look far. There were dozens of the suckers, everywhere he looked, and with a single-minded obsession he could only attribute to the fact that keeping busy kept him from thinking about how the taste of Kate's lips had nearly turned him upside down and inside out, he mounted the attack.

He snapped the leering yellow flower of a dandelion off its stem, yanked another dozen weeds out by their roots, and managed to rip up a pillow-size portion of the wild, unruly grass that grew around the base of the cinder block. By the time he was done, there was a thin ribbon of sweat on his forehead and his arms ached. That wouldn't have been so bad if it had accomplished his purpose. It didn't. Weeds or no weeds, sweat or no sweat, he still couldn't forget how good it felt to lose himself in the heat of Kate's kiss.

"Damn!" Alex tossed the weeds he'd already pulled onto the hood of the Nova. How anything as simple as a kiss could have gotten so out of control was far beyond him.

Never get involved. At least not emotionally.

The words echoed through his head, and he tried to drown them out with the dying screams of yet another dozen weeds.

Physical involvement was one thing, he reminded himself, tossing an especially fat specimen to join its dead friends up on the Nova hood. Physical involvement was to be expected. When a man and a woman were attracted to each other, when the time was right and neither one of them was betraying the trust of or their duty to someone else, physical involvement was unavoidable. Even desirable. Physical involvement was, after all, what he'd been trying to convince Kate to take a chance on ever since they'd moved into God's little joke of a neighborhood.

Physical involvement, Alex could handle. He'd proven that through a dozen well-publicized liaisons, and though none of them had ever ended in the sort of happily-ever-after the world had set up as the standard against which all relationships were measured, they had all ended in a civilized manner. That's what happened when you kept things strictly physical, when you chose women who were attractive, and fun to be with, and interesting enough (at least for a while) to provide good conversation, dignified companionship, and enough spark to heat up the bedroom.

But what had happened inside the house . . .

All the weeds on one side of the Nova were done for, and Alex moved around to the side that faced the house.

What had happened inside the house was as far beyond physical involvement as the earth was from the nearest black hole. Oh, the thrill was there, all right. There was no denying that. The kiss had all the makings of the prelude to one of those too-rare sessions of lovemaking when the earth really did move, the stars really did shine brighter, and all was right with the world. If that's all there was to it, Alex could have handled that.

Unfortunately this time, all that was right with the world came at a price, namely the hint of vulnerability he couldn't fail to miss in Kate's kiss. If he didn't know the core truth of Kate Ellison before, he sure as hell knew it now. No matter how tough a law enforcement officer she was, no matter how much sophistication had rubbed off on her in her years in the big city, Kate was Nebraska born and bred. She was a woman who still held on to all the traditions he associated with the heartland: unfailing commitment, unwavering loyalty, uncommon devotion. She was a woman who would give her all, and more—in the right situation and with the right man. But she expected the same in return.

"Emotional involvement," Alex grumbled.

"What's that you say?"

Alex whirled around. Earl was standing four feet away, eyeing both Alex and the weeds, uncertainty etched into every inch of his face.

"Emotional involvement," Alex said again, because it felt good to talk about it and because he knew a guy like Earl wouldn't have a clue what he meant anyway. "Like the fat roots of a weed. You know, you can't see them, but they're there. They anchor everything you can see. And when you try to dislodge what you can see . . ." To demonstrate, he yanked at another weed. This one was wedged up under the back fender of the Nova, and it didn't look like it wanted to budge.

"When you try to dislodge what you can see . . ." Alex grunted and pulled again. The weed came out, complete with as complex a root system as he'd ever seen on a plant. ". . . You find things aren't as simple as you thought they would be."

Earl considered both the weed and Alex. He scratched a hand across the place where his belly bulged beneath his white, sleeveless T-shirt. "You mean women," he said.

Alex let go a long breath. Finally he'd found someone who understood! "Yes, I mean women. I mean K—" He realized his near mistake and bought himself some time by tossing the newly dearly departed over on the pile. "I mean Missy," he said. He swung back around and leaned against the Nova. Through the grimy front picture window, he could see Kate watching him. She could be the eagle-eyed federal agent when she wanted to. Alex had known that from day one, when she took on the phony pizza guy without a thought for herself. He could handle all that tough woman stuff. It meant Kate was confident and gutsy and, he admitted, it was a turn-on. What he couldn't handle was the thought that beneath that steely exterior, she was a woman who would take no prisoners, physically or emotionally.

"It's a mystery to me, Earl," he admitted. "*She's* a mystery to me."

Earl ambled over and propped his bulky frame against what was left of the back door of the car. "Supposed to be a mystery," he said, as if everyone in the world knew the secret but Alex. "The way I figure it, that's what keeps us interested for years on end."

"You think so?" When Earl offered a can of his trademark beer—condensation sparkling against the aluminum—Alex took him up on it. It was hot and he was thirsty, from pulling weeds and from dealing with Kate.

It was hot, and a couple minutes ago, when his mouth was on Kate's and the only thought in his head was the desire that screamed through his veins, it had been a whole lot hotter. Cold was just what he needed, even if the cold came in a green can.

He popped the top and swallowed down the beer in a gulp big enough to frost the back of his throat. It wasn't until he looked over at Earl again that he realized his neighbor was looking at the beer longingly. It must have been the only one he'd brought with him across the street. Alex handed the can back to Earl and watched while he smiled his appreciation and took a drink.

"If that's the way it's supposed to be . . ." When Earl handed the beer back to Alex, along with a nod that told him the rest was his, he accepted it gratefully. He held the cold can to the back of his neck and waited for his temperature to drop a degree or two. "If that's the way it's supposed to be, why does she make me feel like I don't know up from down? One minute everything's going just fine, and the next—"

"The next, you feel like you've been dropped smack down on your ass in the middle of some heathen country where nobody speaks English but you."

"That's it!" Earl had described it perfectly, and Alex nodded his understanding. "You said it! I'm speaking English. I'm making sense. And sometimes she makes sense, too. But other times . . ." Shaking his head, he finished the beer. The bitter taste helped wash away the sweetness of Kate's lips; right about now, that was just what he needed. "Sometimes I just don't know. Sometimes I think maybe I'm the one who needs lessons in romance."

"That's a good one!" Earl clapped him on the shoulder so hard, it made Alex wince. "But I'm glad you brought it up, buddy. That's what I came over here to talk to you about. That and to make sure that meddling wife of mine ain't driving you good folks crazy." His arms folded across his belly, Earl watched the window. Alex watched, too, and even as he did, Marge came bustling out of the kitchen with what looked like a cup of tea for Kate. She gave it to her along with a plate of store-bought cookies from the cupboard and settled down across from her, obviously ready for a heart-to-heart chat.

Earl shook his head. "Like I was saying, what I really came to talk to you about was romance. Ain't none in our lives, and by the looks of things, you're running pretty dry yourself. But don't worry. There I was, sitting in church this morning, and I think I figured out something that will help us both." He stood and threw back his shoulders, like a kid called on to recite in front of a classroom. "Dinner," Earl said. "Dinner out."

As much as he hated to admit it, Alex realized that for once, Earl might actually be onto something. "Yeah, dinner. Dinner out." He nodded. Just saying the words convinced him it was the right thing to do. A fabulous dinner at some five-star restaurant might not make him feel any better about his reaction to Kate's kiss, but it would at least show her he remembered what it was to be a gentleman. At least it would remind her that gentlemen were poised, polished, and sophisticated. It would prove—at least to Kate—that he couldn't possibly have been affected by her kiss. Poised, polished, sophisticated gentlemen were beyond that.

Alex tipped back his head. The sun filtering through the haze of rust-colored dust that flew from the stacks of the steel mill heated his skin. "Perfect, Earl," he murmured. "Perfect! Flowers. Candlelight. Maybe some music. Yeah." Feeling better about the world and his place in it, Alex smiled. "That ought to bring her to her senses, make her see that I'm not just some pretty boy with a megalomania complex. I have a sensitive side. A romantic side."

"Just exactly what I was thinking," Earl said, and added, "Only not that megalo-whatever part 'cause I don't know what you're talking about." He gave Alex a knowing wink. "And while you work your magic on Missy, I'll be there watchin' and doin' the same with Marge. Only . . ." Earl scratched a hand behind his ear. "Only what I don't understand, Stan, is about last night. You remember, you were supposed to be showing me what to do to make Marge think I was romantic. But you and Missy, you didn't seem very romantic. Missy avoided you all night long like a dirty dog dodging a bath. And you, all you did was sort of stare at her like you expected her to bite. I figured you was onto something there. You know, like some of the stuff you see in them French movies. But I practiced that stare on Marge when we got home and I'll tell you what, I thought the woman was going to take my head off!"

As much as Alex was tempted to ask about the French movies, he decided it was better not to know. Instead, he nodded his agreement. "It's just like I was saying, isn't it? You never know with women."

"But I do know one thing. . . ." Like a magician drawing a rabbit out of a hat, Earl reached into the pocket of his oil-stained jeans and pulled out four rectangles of paper. "My Marge's eyes will light up when she sees these!" He waved the papers in front of Alex's eyes.

Alex squinted, trying for a better look at the words printed on the papers. "But they look like tickets to—"

"That's right." Earl ruffled his fingers through the tickets and, smiling, tucked them safely back in his pocket. "Tickets to the Knights of Columbus pork-and-sauerkraut dinner at Jan Sobieski Hall. Picked them up at church this morning."

Dreams of candlelight, soft music, and flowers flew out of Alex's head. "But—"

"But nothing. Don't even think about it. This is my treat." Earl patted his pocket. "Next Saturday," he told Alex. "Don't forget, it's a formal occasion. You gotta get all dressed up." He headed back across the street, no doubt to get another beer, but not before he gave the ravaged yard a long look. "You know," he said, "Harold's got lawn mowers."

Alex nodded as if that meant something. As if he cared. He turned toward the street to watch Earl go back into his house, and even with his back to the window, he felt the cold steel of Kate's gaze bore right through him. He squared his shoulders and decided against turning around to return the look. He could take the cold; he didn't want her to think he couldn't. It was the heat he was having trouble with. That, and the uneasy feeling that came with the realization that he wasn't sure if he wanted to see that heat reflected in Kate's eyes. Or if he hoped it wasn't there.

Alex reached for another weed. As he bent, something in his pocket poked his thigh. He patted the pocket, remembered the pack of condoms, and for the first time in what felt like forever, a feeling that was almost hope brightened his mood.

In another couple of weeks, his debit card statement would cross Norbert's desk. Norbert would see a purchase had been made; he'd note the location, and the plan they'd set up years before would be set into motion. It had been Norbert's idea all along and it had all the makings of spy-movie intrigue. That's why Alex had opposed it from the start. Too melodramatic, he remembered telling Norbert. Too hokey. Still, he had finally agreed, mostly because it satisfied Norbert's sense of order and predictability, and Norbert was a friend.

If Alex was ever in danger, he was supposed to use the debit card. That way, when the statement finally made its way to Norbert, he'd have some idea where to find Alex. Then it was Alex's job to start watching the newspapers. There would be a message there from Norbert, somewhere in the personal columns.

Alex had always considered the plan fanciful at best. Now he was grateful for it. The sooner Norbert found him and rescued him, the better off he'd be.

That way, Norbert could save Alex from Kate.

And from himself.

By the time nearly a full week had passed, Kate knew she should have forgotten the kiss. It should have been nothing more than a dim memory of a distant past, like braces and homework and her first day at the Academy when she was so nervous, she'd thought she'd faint. Instead, the memory of the kiss followed her around like a ghost. It nudged at the back of her mind when she was alone and pushed itself to the forefront, leering and as boisterous as a poltergeist, any time Alex was anywhere within twenty feet. Which, considering the size of the house, was just about all the time.

Kate finished towel-drying her hair and made a face at herself in the bathroom mirror. She should have been able to put the whole thing into perspective, she reminded herself, reaching for a comb. She *did* put the whole thing into perspective. When she wasn't busy blowing it out of proportion.

She combed her hair and told herself what she'd been telling herself all week long. The kiss was part of the act. Nothing more than just another piece of the elaborate cover-up designed to make the world think Stan and Missy were husband and wife. Alex never would have kissed her if he hadn't been coerced into it by Marge. Not even for a million dollars—or, in his case, not for *another* million dollars. Oh, he talked a good game. He liked to tease her and he liked to tempt her and he sure as hell liked to talk about how she was missing the opportunity of a lifetime by refusing his generous offer to share his bed.

But though Kate had no doubts that hot sex may have been first and foremost on Alex's mind, something told her the kiss that passed between them had never been part of the equation. It was hot, sure, but it was more than that—a sort of window to Alex's soul, the way his eyes should have been if he wasn't always so careful about guarding his feelings that no one could read them. When it came to the kiss, his guard had been down, way down, and something told Kate that the very fact he'd allowed it to happen surprised Alex even more than it surprised her.

That would explain how he'd been acting all week, too. He'd been avoiding her every chance he got, even going so far as to spend time out in the yard pulling weeds. When they did have to be in the same room, he acted way too friendly. As if nothing had passed between them.

Kate dried her hair. The steady buzz of the blow dryer in her ears helped drown her thoughts, and she was grateful for that. Instead of obsessing about the past, she knew she should have been worrying about the future. The near future. Earl and Marge would be stopping over to pick them up in a little less than an hour, and at least for tonight, she knew she'd have more to be concerned about than the fact that Alex was the best kisser she'd ever had the misfortune to encounter. The Knights of Columbus pork-and-sauerkraut dinner sounded like a disaster just waiting to happen. In a party center filled with hundreds of people, she'd have to be sure to keep a close eye on Alex.

Which was good, Kate decided.

Maybe if she was busy making sure Alex was safe, she wouldn't think about the way her knees had grown weak when he kissed her, and the way her insides had gone into nuclear meltdown. Maybe she wouldn't remember the way his mouth had moved over hers, the way his tongue had flicked across her lips, coaxing her to open her mouth so that he could deepen the kiss.

Maybe.

Kate snapped off the blow dryer, but the buzzing didn't stop. She looked at the dryer, but even before she did, she knew the sound was coming from outside, at the front of the house. She'd left Alex in the living room, and he'd given her a solemn promise—as he had each day since his escape to Kmart—that he wouldn't move an inch while she took her shower. But if it wasn't Alex out in the front yard, who was it? And who in the world would be in Stan and Missy's front yard with a—

"Lawn mower?" Kate spoke the word out loud, trying it on for size and realizing it was exactly right. As quickly as she could, she stepped into her panties and put on her bra. She poked her bare feet into her slippers and shrugged on her yellow robe. She was still tying it by the time she was halfway down the stairs.

One look at the living room told her Alex's definition of not moving an inch was radically different from hers. He was nowhere in sight, and when she called to him and got no answer, Kate's blood pressure shot up to what had to be dangerous heights. She yanked open the door and charged out to the front porch.

She wasn't sure what she thought she'd see. In some corner of her mind, she supposed she expected a getaway car—or more likely a getaway limousine—with squealing tires and Alex smiling and waving good-bye to her out the back window. In another part of her mind, she realized that probably wouldn't have been so bad. At least cars came with license plates, and she had a prodigious memory for license plate numbers. An even worse scenario was the one she thought most likely. The one in which she didn't see Alex at all. The one in which he was long gone.

Instead, what she saw caused her to stop dead in her tracks. She stood at the top of the stairs, vaguely aware that her bathrobe was blowing around her knees and her mouth was hanging open. She managed to snap her mouth shut, but it was the only thing she could do. That, and stare at Alex.

Unaware of her presence, Alex marched back and forth across the tiny front lawn in a convoluted pattern that took him around the Nova chassis. His shirt was off. His jeans were slung low around his hips. There was a thin ribbon of sweat on his chest that made the sprinkling of dark hairs there glisten in the late afternoon light, and an athletic sort of animal energy to every one of his steps. The look in his eyes gave the word *determination* a whole new meaning, one that made her realize, for the first time, that it was the power of his personality and the sheer force of his will that made Alex the success he was.

But it wasn't even that awareness that snatched Kate's breath and turned her to stone. It was the fact that Alex Romero, billionaire playboy, corporate tycoon, and all-around spoiled brat, was mowing the front lawn.

Even as Kate watched, Alex finished the last swipe. He switched off the engine and saw her standing on the porch.

"What do you think?" Like a king surveying his kingdom, he stepped back and swept an arm across the scene. "Pretty nice, huh?"

Kate had grown up on a farm. She'd driven a tractor before she'd driven a car. She knew what green and growing things were supposed to look like, and she knew *pretty nice* had nothing to do with Stan and Missy's front lawn. *Pretty nice* was Marge and Earl's lawn across the street, with its neat edging and a border of flowers that clashed with their ochre house. *Pretty nice* was Helen's lawn next to Marge's, with its chipped and faded statue of the Virgin Mary, its always empty birdbath, and the red and pink plastic flowers poked haphazardly along its perimeter.

Pretty nice was not wall-to-wall weeds, or the clumps of grass that Alex had missed altogether, the ones that stood up here and there, as conspicuous as his cowlick.

"Pretty nice," Kate said. She stared. At Alex. At the lawn. At the rickety lawn mower she was surprised had managed to make even that much of a cut. "Where—"

"It's from Harold. You remember, the guy who lives above the butcher store near the church." Alex pulled a rag out of his back pocket and swiped it over his forehead. He wiped his hands on the rag, stuffed it back in his pocket, and walked over to the porch. "He buys them at garage sales and fixes them up. I gave Earl fifteen dollars of our food money and he picked it up for me. Didn't think you'd mind."

"No . . . I . . ." Kate glanced around again, just to make sure she hadn't imagined the whole thing. Finally she shook her head, ordering her thoughts. "But why?"

Alex shrugged. "Needed it." He plopped down on the bottom step and grinned up at her. "I did a good job, didn't I?"

Kate looked at the place nearest the house, where what grass there was had been cut to within a millimeter of its life. She looked at the tree lawn, where an entire strip had been missed altogether. She glanced toward the Nova, where Alex had apparently tried—and, just as apparently, failed—to cut under the cinder blocks, with questionable results. "Have you ever cut a lawn before?" she asked.

"Heck, no." Like a proud parent beaming at a child who wasn't good-looking, talented, or well-behaved, Alex eyed the lawn. "My groundskeeping staff does all that. Supervised by the head gardener, of course. But I thought, how hard could it be? And it wasn't that hard. And it looks great, doesn't it?"

Kate might have been able to go along with *pretty nice,* but *great* was taking things a little too far. "It's getting late," she said, instead of answering. "You'd better get ready."

This time, Alex was the one who didn't answer. He sat staring up at her, a smile inching up his face. "White cotton panties," he said.

"What are you—" Too late, Kate realized the breeze was still blowing her knee-length robe, and Alex was sitting so that he had a perfect view of what was under it. At the same time she thanked her lucky stars she'd been smart enough to put on at least something before she left the bathroom, she turned and went into the house.

"Marge says it's not too late to plant petunias." Alex was right behind her, all thoughts of underwear apparently gone in the fervor of the agriculture moment. "She says that maybe some marigolds would look good by the steps, and . . ." He was still talking about flowers when he headed up the steps to the shower.

And Kate was still shivering from the combination of scorching heat and icy anxiety that tumbled through her. The one that had started a slow crawl in her stomach the moment she realized Alex was looking at her white cotton panties.

10

It wasn't Kate's idea to sit directly across from Alex at the Knights of Columbus pork-and-sauerkraut dinner. Unfortunately, the second they were in the door, Marge took over, and when Marge was in charge, Kate had learned, her own choices were bound to be limited. Marge waded through the partygoers congregating around the door and headed straight for a table in the far corner. It was already packed cheek-to-jowl with diners, but she found four empty places and slung the strap of her shoulder bag over the wooden folding chair on the end, claiming it as her own. Taking that as his signal, Earl dropped down into the chair across from hers. Kate and Alex had no choice. They took the only seats left: two seats across from each other.

Kate's cop instincts told her that hers was the best seat in the house. In the far corner of the noisy party room, with her back to the wall, she had a perfect view of everyone who came and went. They were near an exit, far enough away from the bar that they wouldn't get jostled by everyone who passed. But while Kate's cop instincts said one thing, her womanly instincts sent a different message—one that warned her that staring at Alex all night would do nothing for her sanity, or her equilibrium. They were the same instincts that reminded her that sometimes, the good guys could be just as dangerous as the bad guys, for all different reasons.

Now here she was, sitting right across from him, with nothing separating them but a white plastic tablecloth, a set of plastic salt and pepper shakers, and a bud vase that contained three pink plastic carnations.

Alex was wearing a seventies throwback blue-and-black iridescent shirt that molded to every one of his various and sundry muscles. She didn't have to remind herself that he was also wearing black trousers that were just a little too tight. He should have looked goofy. He should have looked like an escapee from an old disco movie. He should have at least looked as uncomfortable in his getup as Kate felt in her royal blue polyester dress with its little lace collar and handkerchief hem.

Leave it to Alex not to cooperate. Instead of looking goofy, he looked dark and dangerous. Instead of looking like the king of disco, he looked sleek and sensual. He didn't look classy, not the way he did back in New York. Hell, he didn't even look respectable. He looked like the devil incarnate, from the top of his head to the tips of his pointy-toed shoes. A devil who was born to break hearts.

"You done with those taters?" The man seated next to Kate was resplendent in his white shirt, white slacks, and white shoes. His outfit was topped off with a maroon sport coat. He pointed to the bowl at the center of the table. With a smile and whispered thanks for the distraction, Kate handed over the mashed potatoes. Though Alex had barely touched his meal, it looked as if everyone else around them would give it two thumbs-up. Earl had already had seconds, and thirds. Marge declared the sauerkraut the best she'd ever eaten. Kate had managed half a piece of the greasy pork, a sizable pile of the lumpy potatoes, and two slices of better-than-average bread. Sauerkraut was above and beyond the call of duty.

"Hey! Aren't you gonna eat that?" Finally done cleaning his plate, Earl looked over at Alex's in surprise. "If you don't want that pork . . ."

"Be my guest." Alex passed his plate over. He pushed back his chair and gave Kate a look that could only mean he'd had enough, both of the meal and of the dark-paneled, linoleum-floored basement ambiance of Jan Sobieski Hall. "Well, if dinner's over, we should probably get going," he said.

A waitress in a white dress, a yellow apron, and tennis shoes brought over a plate of pastries, and Marge carefully chose a brownie and passed the plate to Kate. "You are so funny, Stan." Marge laughed and took a big enough bite of the brownie to get chocolate icing all over her lips. "You know you can't leave. Not before the dancing."

Dancing?

Alex mouthed the word and Kate shrugged in reply. Right before she took a triangular-shaped cookie folded around a dollop of raspberry jelly.

"It's Hank Markiewicz and the Polka Dots," Earl informed them with his mouth full. "You'll love these guys. They played at our son Brian's wedding."

On cue and to a smattering of applause, five guys in red-and-white polo shirts and knockoff Dockers trooped onto the stage at the other side of the room. They tuned up for several minutes, and when one of them launched into an accordion riff the likes of which turned the sprinkle of applause into an avalanche, Kate saw Earl lean over and say something in Alex's ear.

Alex's face went as pale as the tablecloth. He glanced at Kate briefly as if looking for assurance, but just as quickly, he looked away. He shook his head.

Curious, Kate leaned forward, but it was impossible to hear. Hank and the Polka Dots swung into a rousing polka, and all around them, chairs scraped against linoleum and couples walked out onto the dance floor, hand in hand.

This time, Kate saw Earl elbow Alex in the ribs. Alex closed his eyes, as if in prayer. He opened them again and raised his voice so he could be heard above the music. "Missy," he asked, "would you like to dance?"

Before Kate even had a chance to get *Are you totally and completely out of your mind?* out of her mouth, Alex was up and waiting for her at the end of the table, Earl was nodding his approval, and Marge was beaming at them like she must have beamed at Brian at his wedding. Kate had no choice. She pushed back her chair and met Alex at the head of the table.

"What's going on?" she asked, and he had to bend to hear her.

"Don't ask." Alex turned toward the dance floor, holding out his hand. When Kate didn't take it, he turned back to her. "Come on," he said. "We have to dance."

Kate glanced from Alex's outstretched hand to the dance floor where couples whirled to the lively beat of the music. Couples who had their hands in each others' hands. Couples who had their arms around each other. The very thought was enough to make Kate's knees weak. There must have been something about weak knees that strengthened her suspicions. She narrowed her eyes and pinned Alex with a look. "How are we going to dance," she asked him, "when you promised not to touch me?"

Alex sighed. It wasn't the kind of sigh she'd been sighing these last days since he kissed her. It was a barely patient sigh, the kind that sounded like the hissing noise of a teakettle right before it erupts into a rolling boil. He lifted his glasses long enough to rub the bridge of his nose with two fingers. He glanced at Marge and Earl, who were watching the proceedings with more than passing interest, and offered them a smile that came and went as quickly as the couples who danced past them in a flash. "Look . . ." he said, getting close so only Kate could hear him. His breath whispered against her ear. "We're going to need to call a truce. At least for a little while. I'll tell you while we're dancing."

The warm brush of his breath against her skin should

have pushed Kate over the edge. It nearly did. It ruffled the hair that hung against her neck and buffeted her resolve along with it. Fortunately Kate was as good as anyone at hanging on by her fingernails. She hung on now, too proud to let him know she was still vibrating like a tuning fork from the white cotton panties comment. Too mortified to admit that if he whispered in her ear again or put his arms around her, she just might succumb to the memory of the kiss that curled her toes.

But then Kate remembered that it was all an act. The night out, the kiss, the marriage. She remembered that Alex had been a whole lot more enthusiastic about mowing the lawn than he'd ever been about kissing her. She glanced briefly at Marge and Earl and prayed they'd found something better to do, but when she realized they were still watching, she knew she had no choice. She sighed, but her sigh didn't sound like Alex's. No simmer of annoyance. No portent of disaster. It sounded pathetically like surrender.

"You'd better have a good reason for this." Kate slapped her hand into Alex's. He closed his fingers around hers and led the way to the dance floor. The first polka ended, but another started right up. As if it were the most natural thing in the world, he braced one hand on her waist and swung her into the dance.

It took a minute for Kate to fall into the one-two-three rhythm of the music and another minute to realize she had nothing at all to do with it. Alex was a skilled dancer, and though the steps were relatively easy, doing them was as difficult as doing anything unfamiliar. It would have been impossible without Alex leading her through every beat and turn.

Finally feeling more comfortable, but no less amazed, Kate dared to look up from her feet only to find Alex looking down at her. "You can dance? The polka?"

Alex gave her the kind of look that must have made the executives who worked for him tremble inside their wing-tips. "College folk-dancing class." He said it with all the enthusiasm of a doctor pronouncing a death sentence. "If you ever tell anyone, I'll use whatever influence I have to make sure you're transferred to someplace where it's one hundred and ten in the shade every day of the year and the cockroaches are a foot long."

In spite of his tone of voice and the fact that he probably did have the connections to do what he said, she knew it wasn't much of a threat. She hop-stepped her way around the room and with every beat, her amazement grew. "I didn't know you could dance."

Alex's grim expression dissolved beneath a smile that tickled the corners of his mouth. "You didn't know I could kiss, either."

Kate rolled her eyes. It was better than confessing that he was wrong. She'd suspected all along that he was a world-class kisser. She'd spent the better part of the summer fantasizing about it, and she'd spent more than enough time the past week reminding herself that the reality was even more tantalizing than her fantasies. "Is that what this is all about?" she asked. "Confession time? Don't tell me, let me guess. After a full week of dodging the issue and pretending it never happened, you've had enough. You asked me to dance just so you can say you're sorry you kissed me and you promise never to do it again."

"Nope." Alex shook his head. A clump of dark hair fell across his forehead.

"Nope, what?"

"Nope, that's not what this is all about. Nope, that's not why I asked you to dance. Nope, I'm not sorry I kissed you and nope, I don't promise it will never happen again."

"Well, that takes care of that, doesn't it?" Kate's heart beat to the bouncy rhythm of the music. But then, she reminded herself, Alex had that effect on women. She was saved from thinking too much about it when she caught a flash of Marge's purple dress out of the corner of her eye.

She turned briefly to watch Marge and Earl tripping the light fantastic with more enthusiasm than skill.

"That's what this is all about," Alex said, watching Earl and Marge over Kate's head.

"You asked me to dance because of Earl and Marge?"

Alex nodded. "Long story," he said, but since they appeared to be going nowhere but around and around, he apparently decided he had time to tell it. "Earl asked me to teach him to be romantic, you see, so—"

"Earl asked you to teach him to be romantic?"

"So I said I would because I really didn't have a choice, you see, so—"

"Earl asked you? To teach him to be romantic?"

"So he's been watching me. Watching us, really. So everything I do with you, he—"

"Earl? Asked you? To teach him to be romantic?"

"Can't you say anything else?" With an impatient click of his tongue, Alex looked down at Kate. The lights that flashed against the mirrored ball that hung from the ceiling reflected in his glasses, creating a crazy pattern that made Kate dizzy.

But then, she reminded herself, Alex had that effect on women.

She forced herself to concentrate. "Earl asked you to teach him to be romantic. But it looked like Earl had to force you to ask me to dance."

"You noticed that, huh?" Alex had the good grace to look at least a little embarrassed. "He was just sort of encouraging me," he said, by way of saving face. "He wanted to see how I danced with you, so he'd know what to do with Marge. He's sort of taking his clues from me. Not that I suggested it or anything, but I suppose there are just some guys who sort of exude this aura of romance." When Kate didn't jump in to pump up a male ego that was already overinflated, he went right on. "He's been watching us and wondering why we don't ever seem very romantic. I figured if we didn't do something, he might get suspicious."

"So you're only dancing with me to keep Marge and Earl from getting suspicious." Kate meant the statement to come out sounding street-smart and cocky. It sounded disappointed instead. That might not have been so bad if it wasn't the same way she was feeling. Maybe it was the buoyant music or the cheerful crowd or just getting out after days of being cooped up in the house, but she had actually started to like the polka. There was a fresh abandon to the dance, an infectious beat to the music. For a couple of minutes, she'd actually been having fun. Maybe that fun had a lot to do with the fact that Alex's fingers were closed over hers, that his other hand rested at the place where her waist curved into her hip.

But fun had nothing to do with obligation, and Alex had asked her to dance only because he felt obligated. She pulled to a stop and watched the startled couples nearby dance their way around a collision. "So you're only dancing with me because you have to."

"I never said that." The song ended and Alex's protest sounded too loud. Kate pulled her hand from his and backed up a step, but before she was out of range, the band started another song. This one wasn't a polka, it was "Smoke Gets in Your Eyes," and it sounded amazingly sweet played on the accordion. Alex reached for her hand and reeled her in, and before Kate knew it, both his arms were around her.

"Dance with me, Kate." She felt the invitation vibrate in Alex's chest and travel through hers. It tickled her ear and wound through her like warm honey.

Kate made one last attempt to save herself. She looked down to where Alex's arms encircled her waist. She looked up and blinked at her own startled face, reflected in Alex's glasses. "But you promised—"

"We called a truce, remember?" Just to remind her, Alex tugged her even closer. He smiled at the same time he braced both his hands against the small of her back.

It might have been the smile. (But then, Kate reminded herself, Alex's smile had that effect on women.)

Or it might have been his touch, the way his fingers traced her spine, up and down, in a pattern as soothing as the song. Whatever the cause, Kate was lost. She was already dancing before she even realized it.

"Not so bad, is it?" Alex asked.

Kate could only murmur a reply. She positioned herself more comfortably, and it seemed the most natural thing in the world for her to loop her arms around Alex's neck.

"I don't think this is the way they usually dance at the Knights of Columbus hall," Alex said and Kate followed his gaze when he took a quick look around. Most of the dancers were older couples, and they danced even slow songs the way they'd been taught. Right and left hands together. Elbows bent. Enough room between them for the Manhattan phone book. "There's a guy over there wearing a bad toupee. He's staring at us."

"Let him stare." For a second, Kate wondered if the pork and potatoes had been drugged. That was the only thing that would explain the giddy feeling in her head, the buzz in her veins that made her feel wound as tight as a yo-yo string at the same time she felt dreamy. Her arms felt too heavy and she leaned a little closer to Alex. Her legs felt as if they were weighted down with lead, and she slowed her steps just enough so that when they moved to the music, her thigh brushed his. She skimmed her fingers over the silky front of Alex's shirt, and when he drew in a long, unsteady breath that proved he was not as disciplined as he pretended to be, she grinned. "We should have tried this dancing stuff weeks ago," she told him. "Maybe we'd be better friends by now."

"Hey, I tried."

Kate wasn't about to accept that bold-faced lie. "You weren't talking about dancing," she reminded him. "At least not this kind of dancing." And dancing wasn't what Kate was thinking about, either. Not when Alex skimmed a thumb from her waist up to her ribs. His touch pulsed over her skin and her breasts ached. She closed her eyes and rested her cheek against his chest, and when she felt another couple shuffle by, and a friendly pat on the back, she knew it was Marge and Earl.

She moved far enough away to look up into Alex's eyes. "You know, this is really a nice thing you're doing for them."

"Oh, no!" Alex's expression went from content to horrified in a split second. "Don't accuse me of being a nice guy. It will ruin my reputation. Besides, it wasn't my idea. It was Earl's. You'll have to give him all the credit."

"Well, whoever thought of it, it seems to be working." She turned to watch Earl and Marge dance by in the other direction. It was obvious Earl was a quick learner. He had both his hands on Marge's waist, just as Alex did on Kate's, and Marge was wearing an ear-to-ear smile.

"Look at them. They look more romantic already. Marge looks so happy!"

"And you're looking pretty good yourself."

The compliment brought Kate up short. She missed a couple of beats and had to find her way back into the dance. "You're kidding, right?" she finally asked, back in sync with the rhythm. "Of course you're kidding. Though you may find it hard to believe, I generally avoid dressing in polyester. Wool suits for work. Khakis and sweaters on my days off. You can't really think this . . ." She plucked at the royal blue skirt. "You can't really think this looks good. I look like I stepped out of a secondhand store where the proprietor has a warped sense of humor." A shiver ran through her. "I look frumpy!"

Alex laughed. "And I look like an extra in a community theater production of *West Side Story*. We're the perfect couple, or we would be, if you'd learn one little thing about me."

It wasn't what he said, it was the way he said it. The way he looked at Kate that made her afraid to ask what he was talking about. The smile deserted Alex's face and his eyes darkened. He captured Kate's gaze with one that wouldn't let go.

"I'm never kidding," Alex said, in that matter-of-fact sort of way that told her he meant it, "when I give a lady a compliment."

"Thank you." She didn't sound as gracious as she'd hoped, but then, Kate wasn't sure she even sounded coherent. It was hard to tell when she was stammering. When her blood was pounding so hard, it sounded like thunder in her ears.

But then, she reminded herself, Alex had that effect on women.

It was the wrong reaction. She knew that from the start. She shouldn't have let one little compliment turn her head. But she did. She shouldn't have been dancing so close to the edge of disaster, either, but Kate didn't care. Alex's arms were around her. His heart beat next to hers, keeping time to the same, crazy rhythm. She would have to be comatose not to notice, and she knew she wasn't that. If she were, she wouldn't feel a prickling like a million jolts of electricity all along her body. She wouldn't be wondering what Alex's touch would feel like if there wasn't a layer of polyester separating his skin from hers.

"This dancing stuff, it's nice." Kate breathed the words and heard Alex murmur his agreement. He rested his chin on her head.

"Could you get used to it?" he asked.

"Used to it?" Kate didn't really need to stop and consider her answer. She knew the answer. She knew she could get used to this and a whole lot more, and for the first time, she admitted that she'd like to try. She backed away because she wanted to see Alex's face when she told him. "I could—"

"Missy! Missy!" Kate was interrupted by a sharp poke on her shoulder. She turned and saw Marge looking flustered. "We just danced by over near our table," Marge said, pointing. "Missy, your purse is ringing!"

It took Kate a moment to decipher the message. "You mean the cell phone in my purse is ringing!" Kate backed out of Alex's arms. Away from his touch, the drugged feeling deserted her, and logic rushed in to fill up all the places that had been brimming with desire only seconds before. "Mark's the only one who has that number," she said. "What could he want?" She headed back across the room even before Alex had a chance to speculate about the answer.

It was a good thing, too, Alex realized. Even he wasn't sure what he might have said. "Tell Mark thanks a lot for interrupting what was turning into the most interesting part of the summer." Alex tried the remark below his breath. Too sulky, he decided. Too honest, too. He wasn't sure he wanted to admit the truth to Kate. Or to himself. He wasn't sure he wanted to face the facts, even though they were staring at him, pounding him on his chest, and shaking him by the collar.

From the moment he'd taken Kate's hand and led her onto the dance floor, he'd wanted her more than he'd ever wanted anything—or anyone—in his life.

There it was, plain and simple. Only it wasn't at all plain. And it was anything but simple.

"Tell Mark I owe him a debt of gratitude for getting me out of something I don't know how I got into." That was more like it. That's what he should have said. Yet as he watched Kate wind her way through the crowd, he wondered if it was true.

Was he glad Mark had interrupted? His head told him yes. The rest of him sent another message. He started after Kate at the same time he shook off the memory of what the touch of her had done, both to his composure and to his better judgment.

Near the bar, a group of guys downing shots and beers stepped aside to let Kate by, and Alex got a good look at her retreating figure. She was right. The blue dress was as frumpy as hell. The color wasn't the right shade to complement her eyes. The skirt wasn't the right length to make the most of her shapely legs. The belt was too wide and too bulky to showcase her waist, and the neck was too high; it didn't show off much of anything. At least not anything interesting.

But if all that was true, why was he enjoying watching her so much?

It wasn't a question Alex wanted to consider. He brushed it aside, and when he caught up to Kate, she was just fishing the still-ringing phone out of her bag. She flipped it open and headed for a door marked by a glowing red exit sign. He wasn't invited, but Alex followed anyway and Kate didn't object.

"I'm here, Mark." Kate's voice was breathless. She covered her ear with one hand, straining to hear above the music. When they got to the exit, Alex pushed the door open and stood aside so she could get through. He slipped in behind her and closed the door, and the final strains of "Smoke Gets in Your Eyes" receded. Alex took a moment to let his eyes adjust to the anemic light of a single bare bulb that hung from an overhead fixture. They were in a hallway wide enough only for the flight of stairs that led up to a back door, and Alex backed up against the door. It was a ridiculous attempt to give Kate some privacy, but it was the best he could do, and she didn't seem to mind.

Kate lowered her voice to a conversational level. "Yes. Yes, Mark. It's me. What was all that?" She repeated the question that had apparently been fired at her from the other end of the line. "Music. Hank and the Polka Dots, to be exact. I'll explain it all in my next report. What's wrong? Why are you calling on a Saturday night?"

After a few seconds of listening to whatever it was Mark was saying, the exhilaration that had brightened Kate's expression out on the dance floor disappeared. Her eyes darkened. She bit her lower lip. By the time the conversation was less than a minute old, there was a V of worry between her eyes.

Alex waited as patiently as anyone could wait while

hearing only one side of a conversation. From what he could hear, the news wasn't good.

"Are you sure?" Kate asked. Apparently Mark was. Kate nodded and asked a couple more questions. She shot a look up the stairway; at the same time, she moved to stand smack in the center of the hallway. She made it look like the most natural thing in the world, but Alex knew exactly what she was up to. She was protecting him, putting herself between Alex and the darkness that lay beyond the back door.

For a second, he thought about nudging her aside and informing her he could take care of himself. It wasn't just the chivalrous thing to do, it was a point of fact, and she could use the reminder. But just as soon as the idea occurred to him, Alex decided not to act on it. Kate was only doing her job, and she was doing it with as much determination as she did everything else, from playing bingo to learning the polka. She was one of those rare women who could be assertive and not lose their femininity, one of those rare people who wasn't afraid to give one hundred and ten percent to a job she believed in.

They were commendable qualities, and the thought should have filled Alex with admiration, both for Kate and for the job she was doing. Instead, it shot him through with some emotion that went too far past admiration for his own comfort. He shifted from foot to foot, shrugging away the idea and the unfamiliar feelings it brought with it. By the time Kate ended her conversation and flipped the phone closed, Alex was ready to talk about anything. Maybe the sound of his own voice would drown out the other voices, the ones that pricked at his conscience. And his heart.

"So?" He didn't budge when Kate moved toward the door. "What's going on? What did Mark want?"

As if she were trying to think of the best way to phrase whatever it was she had to say, Kate tapped the phone against her chin. He knew the exact moment she made up her mind. Her lips pinched just enough for her to look decisive. "They had a line on Bartone," she said.

In spite of the phony pizza guy back in New York who had tried to take a potshot at him, Alex had never completely bought into the idea that a cold-blooded hit man was out to get him. It was too melodramatic. Too movie-of-the-week. He didn't buy into the idea, and not buying into the idea had been easier than thinking the FBI might actually be right. Easier and less frightening. Still, even though he'd never actually believed Joe Bartone was hot on his trail, something about Kate's announcement brought a sweep of relief. He smiled. "That's a good thing, right?"

"It was a good thing. It would have been a good thing. You missed the operative word. I said *had*. They *had* a line on Bartone."

"Which means they don't anymore."

"You got it." Kate drew in a long breath and let it out on the end of a sigh. "We caught up with him in France. Near Cannes. That's where the *Calypso* was docked."

Alex remembered the look on her face as she talked to Mark, and the V of worry between her eyes. "No one was hurt, were they? None of the agents? He didn't—"

"No." Kate rejected the idea with a shake of her head that sent her hair flying. She tucked it behind her ears before she continued. "As far as we can tell, he never even got close to the *Calypso*. That's what's got everyone worried."

Alex didn't need things spelled out in neon letters, but he wasn't a mind reader, either. "Let me get this straight: Everyone's worried because Bartone didn't try anything."

"You got it, Sherlock." Kate crossed her arms over her chest and tapped the phone against her chin again, thinking. "Not only did Bartone not try anything," she told him, "but after spending only about an hour hanging around the dock watching the *Calypso*, he got a phone call."

"And?" Alex couldn't take it anymore. Kate could be as deliberate as every other law enforcement officer he'd ever had occasion to deal with. No doubt, deliberate was an asset in her profession. It was probably just what she needed to be—most of the time. But when there was a story to tell and questions that needed to be answered, deliberate wasn't just annoying, it was unbearable. "And then what happened?"

Kate shrugged, and the gesture answered the question and said something about her frustration level. "Nothing," she said. "Nothing happened. Bartone took the phone call, turned around, and left. According to Mark, the next time anybody saw him was at Kennedy Airport. He's back in the country."

"And we're worried because . . ."

To Kate's credit, she didn't act like it was a stupid question. She explained as patiently as she could, and that might have been reassuring if she hadn't kept darting looks up the stairs and at the back door. "We're worried because it might mean we haven't fooled Bartone." Apparently, she'd waited as long as she was willing to wait. Kate reached around Alex and opened the door into the party room and the *oom-pah-pah* beat of another polka filled the little hallway. She paused on the threshold and darted another look around, as if gauging the distance between where they were standing and where she'd left her purse. Satisfied, she hurried to the table, slung her oversize purse over her shoulder, and grabbed Alex's hand.

"Come on," she said, even though she didn't have to. When Kate made up her mind about something, she could be as bound and determined to get her way as anyone Alex had ever known. She tugged him through the crowd. When they got to the dance floor and Marge and Earl trotted by, she stopped them with one hand on Marge's arm.

"Got to go," she told Marge, her voice loud so it could be heard above the music.

"Go?" For a heartbeat, Marge looked surprised. Then she glanced toward the exit door where, no doubt, she'd seen the two of them disappear together only a short while before. She filled in the blanks with her own imagination, and Marge's imagination must have pretty interesting. Color flushed up her neck and through her cheeks. "Can't wait to get home, huh?" She gave Alex a wink that was so telling, it nearly made him blush.

Though Alex had to admit the suggestion that they might be headed home early so they could jump into bed was enough to set his own imagination on fire, it wasn't enough to deter Kate. She had a death grip on his hand, and she wasn't about to let go. She smiled in response to Marge's suggestion and headed for the door with Alex in tow.

They were across the street, past the gas station, and nearly to the church before either one of them realized they were still holding hands.

It hit Alex just a second before it dawned on Kate, and he waited that second to see what her reaction might be. He was hoping for a blush. Or maybe a smile. He should have known better. While his nerves were standing on end each and every place her skin touched his, hers were obviously occupied with other things. Kate was on duty, and when Kate was on duty, her duty was all that mattered. She let go of Alex's hand and proceeded to lead the way home.

"You're really worried, aren't you?" Stupid question, Alex supposed. But then, after all he'd put up with, he figured he was entitled to a stupid question now and then. "You don't really think Bartone could—"

"Know where you are?" A dog rushed toward the sidewalk, barking at them from the other side of a chain-link fence. Kate didn't spare it a look. She kept walking. "You looking for the honest answer? Or the one that will help you sleep better tonight?" She glanced at him out of the corner of her eye and when he didn't answer, she apparently figured he was man enough to opt for honest.

"I don't think there's any way Bartone can know you're here," Kate said. "That's my honest opinion. But I'd be less than honest if I told you I wasn't worried anyway. That's why I'm not about to take any chances, and a noisy, crowded party with a couple hundred of our closest friends sounds like a chance to me. It's quieter at home. Easier to keep the upper hand."

"And easier to keep an eye on me."

"Damned straight." Kate flashed him a smile that came and went quickly, like the blinking sign that flickered at them as they passed a place called the Little Warsaw Diner. "What's really got me puzzled is why Bartone would go to all the trouble of tracking down the *Calypso* and then walk away."

"It's obvious, right?" A shiver snaked over Alex's shoulders. He got rid of it with a shrug. "The phone call he got. Somebody told him not to bother."

"Right. And if I had to guess, I'd say somebody told him not to bother because that somebody knew you weren't there."

"Except—" Alex caught himself on the brink of an objection.

"Except, you were going to say, no one knows where you are."

"Sure. Right." Alex refused to feel guilty. He had nothing to feel guilty about. Kate had no idea about the pack of condoms. She didn't know he'd used his debit card. That information didn't play into the equation. Besides, if the debit had been processed, the statement had made its way back to New York; if Norbert had seen it, that would have to mean—

"Are you all right?"

Alex hadn't realized he'd stopped stone cold until he heard Kate's question. She'd walked on a few steps ahead of him, and now she turned around and came back. "You're looking a little green. Not the sauerkraut, is it?"

Alex shook his head. "I didn't eat the sauerkraut," he told her, but even while he said it, he wasn't listening to himself. His mind was racing a thousand miles a second. While he was willing to concede that Joe Bartone's sudden arrival back in the States probably had something to do with him, he refused to believe that it also had anything to do with Norbert. The notion that Norbert could somehow be involved in revealing Alex's hiding place was absurd.

Convinced both of the logic of his argument and of Norbert's loyalty and friendship, Alex refused to give it further thought.

There was one thing he did have to consider, though. If Bartone really was on his trail, he couldn't risk getting himself killed. Not before he talked to Norbert.

There was more at stake here than just his own safety. Now more then ever, it was vital that he get in touch with Norbert. If he didn't, if something happened to him, no one would be able to keep Ruben Martinez alive.

11

Alex seldom read what he considered the unnecessary sections of the newspaper. The comics were out. Most of them weren't funny anyway. The Homes section seemed like just another way to make people want what they couldn't afford. Normally he wouldn't be caught dead reading the personal ads. For one thing, he didn't need them. He had all the social life any one man could handle. For another, they seemed a bit pathetic; people advertising for lives when they should have been out living them.

But according to the plan Norbert had devised, there would be a message for Alex somewhere in the personals. Alex spread out the morning edition of the *Cleveland Plain Dealer* on the kitchen table and ran his finger down column after column, just as he did every morning while Kate was up in the shower. Just as he'd done every morning since he'd bought the condoms at Kmart. It was probably too soon to hear from Norbert. At least that's what he told himself each day when he didn't find the message he was looking for. It was probably too soon, and the message would appear the next day, or the day after that.

But for the last week, ever since Kate had told him Joe Bartone had abandoned his hunt of the *Calypso*, he couldn't help but wonder if the debit card statement had already been processed. If it had already made its way back to New York. If it had already gone across Norbert's desk.

His finger on the bold heading for "Alternative Lifestyles," Alex paused and thought through the possibilities. He started with the debit card statement cycle, because if he started anywhere else—like questioning Norbert's friendship—he knew he'd drive himself nuts. If all went well, the statement should be to Norbert by . . .

Alex closed his eyes, thinking. Back in New York, his calendar was full, but Charlotte kept his life running like clockwork: tennis on Tuesday and Thursday mornings, a board meeting every Wednesday evening, a staff meeting first thing Monday, lunch on Fridays with his senior executives. No matter how late his Friday nights, his Saturday mornings invariably included an early run through Central Park, then a visit to the office that he always promised himself would be quick. More times than not, it lasted most of the day.

Once a month, there was the executive board meeting for the Juvenile Diabetes Foundation, then another at the Natural History Museum. There were the charity fund-raisers he attended (and always contributed to), the meetings of the hospital boards on which he sat, and, of course, an endless stream of parties and premieres, concerts and galas. Here in Cleveland, without Charlotte poking him and prodding him and reminding him that he had things to do and a schedule to keep, there were times he wasn't even sure what day it was.

Alex glanced at the date on the top of the newspaper page, just to reassure himself, and scanned the rest of the personal ads, looking for the words Norbert had insisted he memorize:

Not tall. Not good-looking. No money to speak of.

Looking for YOU to share what will probably be a pretty limited future.

He had to give Norbert credit. Once the ad did show up, it would stand out in the crowd of tall, good-looking, professional singles looking for love in all the wrong places.

Today wasn't that day, and as amazing as it seemed, Alex found himself smiling with relief. As much as he wanted to get in touch with Norbert, he was glad the ad wasn't there. It meant that Kate was wrong. The FBI was wrong. Norbert couldn't have betrayed Alex's whereabouts to Joe Bartone or anyone else. Because Norbert didn't know where Alex was. He hadn't gotten the debit card statement yet. He hadn't read that telltale line that showed a two-dollar-and-forty-nine-cent purchase made in Cleveland. If he had, the personal ad would be in the paper by now.

Hearing Kate on the stairs, Alex quickly flipped the newspaper pages. He found himself staring at the front of the Business section, and a photograph of a smiling Bill Gates surrounded by so many well-dressed men, it looked like a Brooks Brothers ad. The headline said something about a business leaders' consortium. Only mildly interested, Alex read through the entire first paragraph before it struck him.

This wasn't just any business leaders' consortium. It was *his* business leaders' consortium.

Alex sat back in his chair, feeling a little like he'd been hit in the solar plexus by an opponent with the punch of Muhammad Ali and the good sportsmanship of Snidley Whiplash.

He wasn't sure what bothered him most. Was it the fact that Gates was acting as front man for a meeting that had taken Alex months of blood, sweat, and tears to plan? Or could it be the awareness that he'd been so tangled up in pork-and-sauerkraut dinners, games of bingo, and the strange feelings for Kate—which suddenly seemed as much a part of his new persona as his glasses and his bad haircut—that he'd forgotten all about it?

"Will you look at this!" When Kate came into the kitchen, her hair still damp from the shower, Alex poked a finger at the photograph. If he concentrated on Bill Gates and the fact that Gates was basking in what should have been Alex's limelight, maybe forgetting the meeting—and all the reasons why he'd forgotten it—wouldn't bother him as much. "Look at this guy. Thirteen hundred people. Thirteen hundred of the most influential business leaders anywhere. Journalists, too. And a handful of politicians. And there he is, acting like it was all his idea."

Kate shuffled past him and left a trail of raspberry-scented shampoo in the air. She barely glanced at the picture in the newspaper. "He's not acting like anything," she said, heading for the coffeemaker. "Give the guy a break. He's smiling. All he's doing is smiling."

"He's smiling too wide."

Kate poured her coffee and added milk and sugar. "He's doing his job."

Alex *harrumph*ed. "He's doing *my* job."

Kate took a sip of coffee. She walked back to the table and set her cup down right on Bill Gates's nose. "You know," she said, "I've been thinking."

Alex thought about moving the coffee cup aside, but decided against it. Gates didn't irritate him nearly as much when he was hidden beneath a coffee cup. Besides, it was obvious Kate had other things on her mind. "Thinking?" he asked, at the same time he scanned the rest of the story, looking for his own name. When he didn't see it, he gave Kate his full attention.

"Thinking about what?"

"About Kmart."

Leave it to Kate. She made it sound like the most innocent thing in the world. But whether she sounded innocent or not was beside the point. She had that look that proved she was anything but. That look that said she was every inch a cop. Her eyes were more gray than blue—steely gray, like the smoke that rose out of the stacks outside the window. Her lips pressed into a thin line, she studied Alex as closely as he studied her—for all different reasons. While he was busy admiring those qualities that made her the woman she was, she was looking for chinks in his armor.

And he was damned if he'd let her find any.

Alex sat back and threw an arm across the back of the chair next to him. "You want to go shopping?" he asked.

Kate went right on as if he hadn't said anything. "I've been trying to figure out this whole thing with Joe Bartone. You know, why he'd go to the trouble of traveling all the way to the Riviera just to turn around and come back again."

"He wanted a tan?"

She didn't even try to humor him with an answer, and she didn't dignify the bad joke by acknowledging it. "How did he know you weren't on that boat? How did he figure out that you were back here somewhere?" She picked up her coffee and took another sip, and when she kept her gaze on him over the rim of the cup, she made it look like the most casual thing in the world. She set the cup down again, smack on top of Bill Gates.

"The way I see it," she said, "there is one thing that could explain the whole thing. That's if you used your debit card that day at Kmart. Before I got there."

This time, it was Alex's turn not to answer. An answer—any answer—would only make him look like he was scrambling to cover his guilty tracks. And he refused to sound guilty. Even if he couldn't help but feel it.

Discarding the notion with a lift of his shoulders, Alex promised himself that someday he'd tell Kate the truth. When this was all over, when he had his life back and when Ruben Martinez was safe, he'd tell her the whole story and she'd have to admit he did the right thing. It would be a triumph of sorts, he supposed, but thinking about it didn't leave him feeling as exultant as it should have. There was something about lying to Kate that sat funny in his stomach.

Over the rim of her coffee cup, Kate watched Alex for any of the telltale signs that he might be lying. He didn't look away or scream his guilt the way so many suspects did, with nervous little habits like twitching muscles and rapping fingers. She wasn't sure if she was disappointed or relieved. She accepted his response for just what it was, not an admission of guilt, but not an exoneration, either.

"Supposed to be the hottest day of the year." She thumbed through the sections of the paper until she found the one that showed a weather map. It was printed with a liberal dose of yellow-and-orange ink, colors that indicated record-breaking heat. "Chance of rain tonight," she said.

She hoped that Alex would take the change of subject as a sign that he was out of the woods. She hoped he might relax noticeably. That in itself would prove something. But if she was looking for easy proof, she was looking for it in the wrong place and from the wrong man.

"You must be one hell of a poker player." Without bothering to explain herself, Kate got up to get the Rice Krunchies and a bowl. As she did, she picked up her coffee cup and glanced down at the wet brown ring that framed Bill Gates's picture. But it wasn't Gates's smiling face that caught her eye. Not this time. It was the face of the man standing just behind him and to his right.

The jolt of recognition that shot through Kate was enough to leave her knees weak. She plopped back down into her chair and grabbed the Business section, turning it around for a better look.

The man was particularly bland-looking, especially in a crowd of the country's most rich and powerful. But then, Kate knew that looking bland was Joe Bartone's stock-in-trade. An ordinary-looking man could easily blend into a crowd. No one would notice him. No one would watch him. Kate might not have noticed him, either, if it hadn't been for one thing.

"He's the only one not smiling." She pointed to the picture and watched Alex's face for any signs of recognition. They came, just as they'd come to her. She wondered if her face went chalky, if her eyes went wide like Alex's did.

"Bartone?" Alex glanced between Kate and the photograph of the man with the ashen hair and colorless eyes, apparently waiting for her to tell him he was wrong. When she didn't, he flipped the newspaper so the picture faced his direction. "It is Bartone. What the hell—"

"Cheeky little bastard, isn't he?" Kate shook her head in amazement. "There he is in living color. Even looks like he belongs."

"But how—"

She shook her head again, this time to send the message that she didn't have the slightest idea how Joe Bartone had managed to penetrate a gathering that added new dimensions to the terms high-powered, high finance, and high-and-mighty. She didn't have any answers. At least not as to how Bartone had managed it. She had the uncomfortable feeling, though, that she knew why.

"He knew you weren't going to be at that meeting. Everyone knew. They announced weeks ago that Gates would be taking your place because of a scheduling conflict."

"So maybe Bartone's not as smart as you give him credit for."

"No." Kate wasn't sure how she knew she was right, she only knew she was. She knew exactly what Joe Bartone was doing in the photograph, and the knowledge was enough to make a fist clench around her heart. It took every ounce of strength she had and every bit of professionalism she possessed to look across the table at Alex and not let her voice break with emotion. "He's sending us a message," she told him. "He's telling us that he can penetrate our security any time he wants. He's letting us know that if you had been at that meeting, you'd be dead by now."

It was the thunder that first woke Alex. It rumbled right outside his window, rattling the old house to the bone and rousing him from a dream that, as near as he could remember, had something to do with Bill Gates, Joe Bartone, and a plate full of pork and sauerkraut.

Not exactly a nightmare in the great scheme of things, but close enough to leave him feeling less than comfortable, especially when he thought about the picture they'd discovered in the newspaper that morning. Alex lay on his back and stared at the ceiling in the next flash of lightning, listening to what sounded like a thousand frantic tap dancers hoofing their little hearts out up on the roof.

The sound of the rain should have been comforting, but for some reason he couldn't put his finger on, Alex couldn't relax. Something tickled at the corners of his mind, and it wasn't just Kate's theory about why Bartone had shown up at the business consortium. As much as he hated to admit it, he knew it was time to face facts. It was no coincidence that Bartone was at the consortium, just as there was no coincidence about his being in all those pictures the FBI had shown him back in New York. Kate was a trained professional who was as levelheaded as she was competent, and she was absolutely right. He would have been a fool not to put credence in her theory just as her superiors had when she called them about the photograph. Joe Bartone knew what he was doing when he posed for that picture, and what he was doing was thumbing his nose at all of them.

But while Alex believed Kate, he knew that though Joe Bartone may have haunted his dreams, it was unlikely that he was anywhere nearby. Sure, he was back in the country. But it was a big country, and Alex was a long way from New York. No, it wasn't the threat of Joe

Bartone that made Alex uneasy. But, he admitted, it was something. Something that just didn't seem to fit with the noise of the downpour and the late-night hour.

He turned over in the queen-size bed and pounded his pillow. He'd never been bothered by storms, so he knew that wasn't what was troubling him. He'd never been afraid of the dark, either, so when he looked over at the digital alarm clock next to his bed and realized it was blank, he didn't really care that the electricity was out.

A gust of wind blew the curtains on the room's only window nearly parallel with the floor and sent a blast of humid air into the room. Still groggy from a sound sleep that had been so rudely interrupted, Alex got up and stumbled across the room to check the window. He inched it down a bit to make sure the rain wouldn't pour in, stumbled back in the other direction, and climbed back into bed, pulling the sheets up to his chin. It was still pitch dark, probably the middle of the night, yet the longer he tried, the more impossible it was for him to get back to sleep. There was something different about the house, he decided, and it wasn't just the symphony of crash-bang thunder and the sizzle of lightning that seemed to be on top of the place. It wasn't something wrong, exactly. Not so much as it was something that wasn't quite right. At least not at that hour. It was something that smelled like—

"Coffee?" Suddenly wide awake, Alex sat up in bed. He sniffed the air, sure he must have dreamed the aroma. But while his other senses might have been tricked by the sound-and-light show going on outside his bedroom window, his sense of smell was just fine. It was coffee all right. Fresh coffee. And it was brewing down in the kitchen.

Too wide awake to ignore the smell, too curious about what it meant, Alex scrambled out of bed and pulled on his black athletic shorts and the first T-shirt he could put his hands on. He paused outside his bedroom door, getting his bearings. It took him a second or two to realize there was a faint glow coming from downstairs. It wasn't an electric light; it wasn't harsh enough. This light was pale and shimmering, and he followed it all the way to the living room.

He paused on the third step from the bottom and looked across the room. Kate was seated on the couch dealing out a hand of solitaire. She had a single, chunky candle lit on the coffee table in front of her. The candle threw inky shadows against the wall at her back, but around her face, the light was as soft as a whisper and as golden as a sunset. The firelight added sandy highlights to her hair and threw a hushed light that softened the determined set of her chin. It brushed against her jeans, turning the color into something as gentle as the undulating shadows and making even her gray shirt and everyday sneakers look as if they'd been touched by the afterglow of the lightning that flashed outside.

Though he'd never considered himself a poetic kind of guy, Alex couldn't help but appreciate the picture. The scene struck him as a wash of subtle color and opalescence, a feathery-edged setting straight out of an Impressionist painting. Or at least it might have been if not for the gun that sat on the table within easy reach of Kate's right hand.

"I didn't wake you, did I?" Kate finished dealing out the cards before she looked up. When she did, the light sparkled in her eyes. Tonight, they didn't look blue or gray, but more like the color of the odd half-light that lingers in the sky right after the sun goes down. When another rumble of thunder rippled through the room, she clutched the deck of cards in one hand as if the thunder might knock them loose, and waited for the echoes to die down. "I was trying to be quiet," she said.

Alex descended the rest of the stairs and stepped into the living room. "It wasn't you. It was the thunder. And the coffee." He yawned and looked at the steaming mug that sat near Kate's cards. "It smells so good, I couldn't help but wake up." Another thought struck him and he cocked his head and looked at Kate in wonder. "If the electricity's out—"

"How did I make the coffee?" Kate picked up the mug and, over the rim, gave him a smile that came and went as quickly as the next flash of lightning. "I found one of those old pecolator pots in the kitchen the other day. Didn't . . ." Another rumble of thunder, and Kate closed her eyes and waited for it to pass. "Didn't think I'd ever need it. But with that and a gas stove, we really don't need the coffeemaker."

Though her smile lasted less than a heartbeat, the one Alex gave her in return lingered longer. He couldn't help himself. There was something about Kate's face in candlelight that made him forget that it was the middle of the night, that the world sounded like it was crashing against their front door, and that the woman he was thinking of as a figure in a Monet painting had a gun close enough to make it—and her—dangerous.

"Always prepared, huh?" he asked, looking at the gun.

Another roll of thunder, this one louder than before. Kate jumped. She darted a glance at him, apparently hoping he hadn't noticed, and when Alex didn't let on he had, she answered. "Always prepared? That's the Boy Scouts, not the FBI," she said. She took another drink of her coffee and he saw that it was black and strong-looking.

Alex stretched. The curtains on the front window were closed, but from what little he could see there didn't seem to be even a bit of daylight peeking through the rain. "What time is it anyway?"

Kate checked her watch. "Two forty-seven."

The reminder was enough to make Alex yawn again. "Two forty-seven? What are you doing up playing cards and drinking coffee? Aren't you afraid it's going to keep you awake?"

"This?" Cradling it in both hands, Kate looked into her coffee mug. "It better." She took another sip and shivered, and when a peal of thunder strong enough to reverberate through Alex's bones growled through the room, she closed her eyes. "I hate my coffee without milk and sugar, I hoped it would have more oomph this way."

"And you're oomphing in the middle of the night because . . . ?"

"Because the power's out." Kate set the mug on the table but she didn't let go. She tightened her fingers around it, her knuckles white against the creaminess of her skin. "The power's out, and so's the security system." She hurried to offer an explanation Alex wasn't even looking for. "I know what you're going to say. You're going to say there's supposed to be a battery backup, and I agree with you one hundred percent. There should be a battery backup. There is a battery backup." She winced as if the very thought was painful. "But it's not working. You have every right to be upset. That's shabby planning and there's no excuse for shabby planning. We've let you down, and I'm sorry." She raised her gaze to his, and for a moment that passed as quickly as the next flash of lightning, he thought he saw some emotion he couldn't identify in her eyes. "You deserve better."

Alex listened to the way she scrambled to save face, not for herself, but for the Bureau. He should have been angry about the slipup. After all, it was his neck on the line. If the government didn't think he was worth the cost of a battery backup, then maybe he was wasting his time. But if all that was true, why was he smiling?

"Once again, Special Agent Ellison, you're wrong." Alex answered his own question at the same time he took two steps closer to the couch. "The security system is out, and you're standing guard." Heck, there was an obvious statement if he'd ever heard one. Yet Alex couldn't help making it, any more than he could help admiring a woman who didn't let anything get in the way of what she saw as her duty, even if it meant weathering a storm alone or drinking her coffee strong and black in the middle of the night. "I couldn't be in better hands."

Kate shrugged off what apparently sounded too much like a compliment for her comfort. "It's my job, remember? And with Bartone on the loose—"

A deafening crack of thunder shook the house to its foundations. Kate waited until its last rumbles died away, and when they did, she took a long, calming breath.

It was the first Alex realized what had been staring him in the face since he'd gotten downstairs. He hurried to the couch and sat down next to Kate. "The power is out, the security system is down for the count, Bartone is on the loose, and you're down here by yourself, even though you're afraid of storms."

He hadn't meant it as a criticism, but Kate didn't know that. She sat up so straight, it looked like she had a broomstick up the back of her shirt. Her jaw hardened into a stubborn line. She glanced at Alex out of the corner of her eye. "I'd deny it in a court of law."

Alex chuckled. "I'm not asking you to testify in court." He ran a hand through his hair, shaking loose the last bits of sleep that clouded his consciousness, and ordered his thoughts. Just like he wasn't poetic, he didn't tend to get all choked up about things like people doing what was expected of them. It was one of the reasons he wasn't the world's most warm and fuzzy boss. Kate's struggle with what she had to know was an irrational fear wasn't the stuff of grand melodrama, and she wasn't about to pretend it was. She was dealing with her fear as she must have dealt with it a thousand times before, by facing it head-on and refusing to give an inch.

In spite of himself and the no-nonsense image he'd done so much to perpetuate, Alex found that he was touched.

He tried a smile aimed at making Kate relax, but she was too busy staring at the deck of cards she had squeezed in one hand to notice. "You should have woken me up."

"Yeah. Right." She shook her head, obviously disgusted with herself. "That would look great on my service record, wouldn't it? 'Wakes witnesses in the event of storms.' " She gave him a grim smile. "There's a recommendation if I ever heard one."

Alex sat back and put his arm on the couch behind Kate. "Yeah, if I was just a witness. But you could have woken me up. As a friend."

Another rumble of thunder shook the room, but this time, Kate didn't go pale. She shot Alex a look, apparently checking to see if he was serious. When she saw he was, she smiled her gratitude. "I made it through a tornado when I was a kid," she explained. "One of the disadvantages of growing up in Nebraska."

"Anybody hurt?"

She shook her head. "Everyone was fine, thank goodness. But every time there's a storm . . ." She shivered and hugged herself and for the first time, Alex realized there were tears of frustration in her eyes. "It's so damned annoying! I'm supposed to be tough enough to take on the bad guys, and here I am, shaking because of a stupid storm."

She was shaking, and though Alex knew the smart thing to do was to ignore it and keep his distance, he had one arm around her before he could stop himself. He pulled her close and the shaking didn't stop. He supposed he should have been offended. He would have liked to think his touch was enough to calm any woman's worst fears. But in a weird sort of way, he knew Kate's continued trembling was a good sign. It meant she was so upset by the storm and by the fact that he'd discovered a secret she obviously wanted to keep buried, she didn't even bother to remind him about their truce. Or wonder if he might have gathered her into his arms simply because he had ulterior motives.

Did he?

The question hit Alex like a two-pound sledgehammer.

He liked to think he wasn't as shallow as all that. After all, he'd offered the hug for comfort. But with Kate close enough for him to feel the bedtime warmth that still clung to her skin, with her close enough so that each tiny tremor that cascaded through her body was echoed in his, even he had to question his own motives.

Alex suppressed a sound that, had he given it permission, would have come out as a groan. While his motives may have been in question, his desires were shouting themselves through his bloodstream loud and clear. Just holding Kate made his pulse pound. Just feeling the silken texture of her hair against his neck made him feel like he was about to jump right out of his skin.

Swallowing down the sweet taste of longing that coated his throat and blocked his breathing, Alex forced himself to get a grip. He didn't earn his Romeo reputation by ignoring his libido, but he didn't take advantage of women in their weaker moments, either. His mind made up, even if his body wasn't convinced, he moved back far enough to look into Kate's eyes.

"I'll tell you what," he said. "You worry about the bad guys. I'll worry about the storms. Deal?"

"You don't have to be so nice about it." Kate's voice teetered on the edge of tears. She looked away, and even the candlelight couldn't soften the misery etched into every inch of her expression. "Face it. Your bodyguard is a wimp."

"My bodyguard is the bravest and most dedicated woman I've ever met." Because he didn't know what else to do with his hands, and because he had to do something before he cupped Kate's chin and turned her face to his for a kiss, Alex smoothed a strand of hair behind her ear. "While I was upstairs sound asleep, you were down here alone, facing the storm and whatever else might have come your way." Just putting the thought into words made him feel like a heartless SOB. He scrambled for a way to make it up to her. "I'm scared to death of frogs," he said.

Kate gave a watery laugh. "You are not."

He wasn't, but she didn't have to know it. "Scout's honor." He crossed his heart and held three fingers in the air, Boy Scout style. "Came across one on the golf course one day and ended up missing a birdie shot because of it."

"Because of a frog?" She gave him a look that was skepticism itself.

"Big frog." Alex slipped his arm from around Kate's shoulders and held his hands a foot apart. When she raised her eyebrows in disbelief, he narrowed the distance once, then again. He honestly didn't have a clue how big frogs were, and he put his hands down before Kate could catch on. "Well, it was scary, no matter how big it was. Besides, it might have had a bigger brother waiting around somewhere."

By this time, Kate's smile was genuine. "Thanks."

She sniffed delicately and slid back where she came from, and for some reason Alex wasn't sure he wanted to think about, the darkness seemed colder and blacker with the space of a couch cushion between them. Whether Kate realized it yet or not, something had changed between them. It was subtle, sure, but it was there, just like the lightning and the thunder and the rain on the roof. He wondered what he'd done, and what it meant, and where the hell it meant they were headed.

He turned the thought over in his head, examining it as a scientist might study some new species. He was used to wanting women. Hell, he was used to wanting this woman. All summer long, it had been impossible for him to forget that Kate was pretty and smart and as sexy as hell. But while he might have been used to the pangs of desire, he wasn't used to wanting a woman simply so he could comfort and protect her.

Protect?

Alex glanced to where the candlelight glinted against the cold barrel of Kate's gun.

The last thing Kate needed was protection. He knew that. But even as the thought occurred to him, he decided the fact that she didn't need protecting was what made wanting to protect her more appealing than ever.

The thought was as foreign as the emotions it conjured and, not as uncomfortable with it as he was unsure what to do about it, he waited for Kate to make the next move. He wasn't sure if he was disappointed or relieved when that move consisted of her shifting a red eight onto a black nine in one of the solitaire piles on the table.

"I'm fine now," she said, and as if to prove it, a rumble of thunder shook the house, but not Kate's composure. "I guarantee you, you've got nothing to worry about. I've got my coffee and my deck of cards. That will keep me awake. So you can go back to bed and—"

"I could." Alex knew she was right. There wasn't a thing he had to worry about. Not as long as Kate was on duty. But that didn't mean he had to make her stand the long watch alone. "What do you say we play a couple hands?"

"Really?" Kate laughed, surprised. "You want to play cards? In the middle of the night? Aren't you tired?"

"Not anymore." Before he could remember he was plenty tired, Alex hopped up and headed toward the kitchen. It wasn't easy finding his way around in the dark, but he managed to find a cup and the coffee. By the time he was headed back into the living room, Kate had the solitaire game cleaned up and was shuffling the cards.

"What game?" she asked.

Alex grinned. No matter how chivalrous he might have been feeling, there were some opportunities too good to pass up. "Actually I was thinking of strip poker."

Kate's heartbeat staggered and her blood caught fire. Standing just where the circle of light melted into the darker shadows behind him, Alex looked like the embodiment of every fantasy she'd ever entertained. His dark hair blended with the night. His eyes sparkled with the glint of candlelight and the suggestion of something hotter. His lips twitched into a smile that looked all the more wicked because of the stubble of beard that shadowed his jaw. His body . . .

Kate took a deep breath and hoped it looked as if she were bracing herself against the latest crash of thunder, rather than against the thrill that shot through her and left her weak. She should have known that asking Alex an open-ended question meant setting herself up to walk right into a trap. She promised herself that sometime later, when her breathing slowed to something near normal and her body stopped vibrating, she'd kick herself for it. For now, she allowed herself the fantasy. She had to. She was absolutely helpless against it.

She let her gaze glide from Alex's smile to Alex's inside-out T-shirt to Alex's exercise shorts. The ones with the worn elastic waistband. The ones that hung low on his hips. The ones that, at the moment, looked too tight across the front.

Memories of the Bathroom Incident rose up, unwanted, and the fantasy pitched in another direction, one that found Kate scrambling for the first thing that might be able to save her from another humiliation. "Strip poker?" Her laugh sounded as hollow as her words. She hurried on before Alex could notice. "I don't think so. I got dressed really fast." She waved one hand at her shirt. "There isn't as much under here as there's supposed to be, and—" What she was saying registered at the same time as her embarrassment. Kate clamped a hand over her mouth before she could talk herself into any more trouble.

Fortunately Alex just laughed. "Oh, that's a great excuse! You've got nothing on under that shirt of yours. That really ought to talk me out of wanting to play strip poker!"

If he hadn't laughed, Kate wasn't sure what she might have done. As it was, there was something about Alex's laughter inside the sanctuary of candlelight that chased her embarrassment away, just as there was something about his company in the dark that had eliminated her fear of the storm.

She recovered in a heartbeat and threw him a smile, along with a look that grazed his body, head to toe. "You don't look like you're in much better shape in the amount-of-clothing department."

Alex looked down at his shorts and T-shirt. He shrugged. "You win two hands and I'm down and out."

Two hands. Two winning hands. And he didn't know that back at the FBI Academy, she was known by some of her fellow trainees—whom she'd left sadder, wiser, and in possession of a little less of their paychecks—as Old Poker Face.

Temptation had never been greater. Or as appealing. Or as arousing.

Kate shifted in her seat. She wasn't lying when she told

Alex she'd gotten dressed too fast to put on everything she usually did. The electricity had gone out soon after the first rumbles of thunder woke her and as soon as it had, Kate grabbed her clothes. She hadn't bothered with a bra; right now, her nipples were rigid against the inside of her shirt. The sensation should have warned her that things had already gone too far. Instead, it only made her more aware that in this case, too far wasn't nearly far enough.

Too bad she thought of the security system, and Joe Bartone, at the same time.

She tried to talk herself out of being sensible. She told herself that while she would have preferred a nighttime in Alex's bed, she would settle for a half hour or so. She reminded herself that it was unlikely anything was going to happen in that half hour. At least anything she might need her gun and her badge for. She fought to hang on to the delectable sensations that tingled through her with all the delicacy of the storm that crashed outside.

But it was no use.

Her last look at Alex had pushed her over the edge from caution to out-and-out, no-holds-barred, can't-deny-it-anymore lust. But it also served to remind her that Alex Romero was way too delicious for the world to lose. And that was exactly what might happen if she hopped into bed with him. She couldn't forget that she was supposed to be keeping him safe. If that meant Kate had to pass on taking a taste of the temptations he offered, then so be it. She was on duty.

As if to reassure herself, Kate's hand moved toward her weapon.

Alex caught the movement and flinched. "Hey, I was just kidding!" He hurried over to stand in front of her. "You didn't think I really meant it about that strip poker stuff, did you?"

He obviously didn't think Kate would ever shoot him, or even threaten him with the weapon, yet he abandoned the Romeo persona in a heartbeat. He went from studly to boy-next-door-friendly so fast, Kate wondered who he was trying to talk out of the seduction. Her? Or himself?

"I was thinking of poker," he said, dropping down on the couch next to her. "Regular old poker. You do play poker, don't you?"

Before she could answer, he took the cards right out of her hands. He shuffled them quickly and sat up so he could deal them onto the coffee table. As he did, Kate could have sworn he mumbled something under his breath. Something that, amazingly enough, sounded a whole lot like "damned chivalry."

If Kate had never realized it before, by the time her watch showed that it was close to four o'clock, she knew why Alex was so successful when it came to business. He was as much of a poker face as she was. He must have been formidable across a board table, unbeatable when it came to contract negotiations. He wasn't afraid to bluff and feint and dodge his way to victory, even when all the victory entailed was a game of cards and the bogus bets Kate scrawled on the back cover of an old *National Geographic* that lay on the coffee table.

It should have been easy to resent a guy who didn't flinch even when all he was holding was a pair of twos. It should have been a piece of cake to dislike a person who won far more often than her fellow trainees back at the Academy ever had.

She might actually have felt at least some mix of those emotions if not for the fact that Alex was so damned charming.

Kate took a sip of the coffee he'd just refilled for her. After four mugs of coffee and a rush of Alex-induced adrenaline pumping through her veins, she probably wouldn't sleep for a week. At that point, she was beyond caring. She'd managed to work her way past feeling as if she were going to go up like a bottle rocket every time Alex so much as looked her way.

Since he'd sat down next to her and they'd settled in for some serious poker playing, something amazing had happened. Poker had done the trick that living together for the last two months had not been able to accomplish. It made them comfortable with each other.

The storm had passed, and a soft, steady rain beat on the roof. It made a nice backdrop to the quiet shuffling of cards and a conversation that, despite the fact that they were alone and could scream at the top of their lungs if they wanted to, was as hushed as the glowing candlelight.

The darkness invited confidences, and though they weren't about to share their deepest, darkest secrets, they had managed to keep up a conversation that, for once, was more pleasant than adversarial.

It was nice knowing they could actually get along. Or maybe it was all just some sort of caffeine-laden fantasy. Maybe her brain was just a little addled from lack of sleep. Or cycling from the combination of nerves and extra-strong Maxwell House. Whichever it was, it felt too good to question. Kate yawned and stretched, and when she realized her stretch caused her shirt to ride up and expose a portion of her bare tummy, she didn't even blush and stammer and pull down the shirt like some red-faced adolescent. Alex slanted her midriff an admiring look, and Kate gave him a smile of thanks at the same time she grabbed the tally sheet.

"Looks like . . ." Kate chewed the end of a Bic pen while she went over her figures. "Looks like you owe me three million four hundred and thirty-seven dollars." Her smile brightened. "You're the only one I've ever known who might actually be able to pay up."

With a good-natured snort, Alex tossed his losing hand onto the table. "I only owe so much because of that last hand. If you hadn't upped the ante to two million—"

"If you hadn't met it and raised it another million—"

"We'd be dead even."

He hadn't counted on the fact that she was as good at

numbers as she was at cards. She did another quick set of calculations. "Not quite." She jabbed the pen at the figures, just so he wouldn't miss them. "Even without that last hand, I'd be winning by exactly eighteen dollars."

"Which means if this was strip poker, I'd be buck naked by now."

"Unfair!" It must have been the caffeine. Kate couldn't imagine what else could have possessed her to blatantly discuss what she'd spent the last couple hours trying to forget. "You're trying to distract me and make me forget you owe me three million four hundred—"

"And thirty-seven dollars. Yeah, yeah. I know." Alex waved his hand in the air, as if that alone could make the mind-boggling amount disappear. For all she knew, it was exactly the way he did business back in New York. "That's not the real question, though, is it? The real question is, would it distract you?" He turned enough so that his knee brushed hers. "If I was buck naked?"

"You're expecting me to bluff." Too late, Kate realized she was clutching her cards tight enough to make the edges curl. She tossed them down on the table and mixed them in with the rest of the cards before Alex could notice and read it like a neon sign going off directly above her head. "You know what?" she asked, scooping up the cards. "I'm tired of bluffing. The answer is yes." She looked right into Alex's eyes as she said it and was glad to see she'd caught him off guard. He sat as still as a stone and she knew it was because he couldn't imagine what she might do next.

"It would distract the hell out of me," she admitted. She tapped the cards into a neat pile. "There. Happy to hear it?"

"Real happy."

"Because it means you win after all? Or because it means I've finally come to grips with the fact that I'm nothing but another weak female who melts at your feet with the slightest encouragement?"

Alex leaned forward. He was within inches of her, but

he didn't touch her. He didn't raise his voice, either. It was as quiet as the whisper of light that caressed his jaw and defined the stubble on his chin so that Kate was sure she could count each little whisker.

"Because it means I'd really like to distract you while I was buck naked." He ran one finger up her left arm all the way to her shoulder and let it slide down again, across the front of her shirt. "Because it means it would be a lot more distracting, and a whole lot more fun, if you were buck naked, too."

"Don't I know it!" Kate sucked in a breath. Alex's touch was feather-light, even when it trailed across her breast, but she had no doubt he knew exactly what he was doing, and what he was doing was driving her wild. He let his hand drift up again and this time, he paused where her nipple showed beneath the fabric and brushed his flattened palm against it.

She closed her eyes and swallowed around the sensations that rocketed through her. "Fun or no fun, it doesn't change a thing." She opened her eyes to find that Alex had moved a hairsbreadth closer, close enough to hook one arm around her waist. He pulled even closer and his hand stole under her shirt.

His fingers were cool against her too-hot skin. He skimmed them up her ribs and found her breast. He cupped it, trying the feel of it in his hand while he rolled her nipple between his thumb and forefinger.

"That changes something." She felt Alex's words more than she heard them, felt the way his smile tugged his lips and his cheek grazed hers. It was sandpaper rough and she rubbed hers against it at the same time she put both her arms around his neck. "What else do you want to change?"

She wanted to change everything. She wanted to change a world where a man could be in danger because he was honorable and honest. She wanted to change a world where a man's fortune automatically set him apart from the people around him, where it made him different.

Better, at least in his eyes. She wanted to change herself into a woman who thought of passion before she thought of duty, one who gave in to the sensations streaking through her. Because she knew she couldn't do any of it, she settled for raising her mouth to Alex's and kissing him.

That in itself was enough to cause some changes. She felt Alex's muscles bunch beneath her hands, and she heard him pull in a breath right before he deepened the kiss.

She already knew he was a good kisser. How could she forget? She already knew that when his mouth slanted over hers, he'd taste like coffee and white-hot sex and the promise of so many incredible intimacies, she couldn't even begin to imagine them all. But it didn't take her long to put two and two together and realize that what she'd experienced before was Alex Romero, the public kisser. After all, the first and only time he'd kissed her, Marge was right there in the room.

Now they were alone, and Alex Romero, the capable, talented, knock-your-socks-off public kisser, turned into Alex Romero, the private kisser. All alone, surrounded by darkness and the pattering rain and the staccato tempo of their own rough breathing, his kiss deepened to a new level of intimacy that went beyond showmanship. Beyond even the rockets'-red-glare kiss he'd used before to brand her lips and make an assortment of fantasies that were already pretty explicit more graphic than ever.

One of which was happening even as she thought about it.

When Alex trailed a series of shimmering kisses down her neck, Kate tipped her head back and moaned.

"Nice, huh?" His voice was as dreamy as his kiss.

"Real nice. But then, I always thought it would be." It was the truth, and Kate decided there was no use denying it. Of course, *real nice* didn't even begin to describe the sensations that pounded through her, or the tendrils of heat that twitched and vibrated over every inch of her body. But *real nice* would have to do. For now. Maybe for always.

As if Alex could sense exactly what she was thinking, he trailed his hand down over her ribs and slipped it out from under her shirt. He moved back far enough to give her a close look. "So it's real nice and you always thought it would be, and so we're stopping because . . . ?"

Kate took the opportunity to move back, too. Further from temptation, and the invitation that still glimmered in Alex's eyes. "We're stopping because I'm still me and you're still you."

"Which means?"

If he was so smart, why didn't he see this as clearly as she did? Kate grabbed for her coffee and wrapped her fingers around the mug, but even the warmth of the cup wasn't enough to replace the heat of Alex's body next to hers. "Which means I'm not Cinderella." She shot him a look, and when it seemed as if he still didn't understand, she tried again. "Which means when the ball is over, you'll still be Prince Charming and I'll still be a pumpkin."

He skimmed a hand over her thigh. "So who says the prince and the pumpkin can't dance to their own music?" His fingers moved up and down, drifting closer and closer to her crotch. "A woman from your world and a guy from mine—"

"Exactly!" Kate scooted even farther away, before she could convince herself that the here and now was more important than the combined total of the rest of her tomorrows. "That's how you think of it. Us and them. Only I'm not an *us*, I'm a *them*. I'll never be an *us*. Limousines and chauffeurs and—"

"And you're saying I'm an elitist?" Alex was stunned. He sat back and cocked his head, waiting for an answer.

"I'm not saying . . . well, I am saying . . ." It wasn't Kate talking, it was the caffeine. The lack of sleep. The nerve endings that were still jangling like the bells on the entire team of Santa's reindeer. She gave up with a sigh. "What I'm saying is that we can't. The electricity is off and so is the security system. Joe Bartone is out there somewhere." She gave a pointed look toward the front door. "And I'm on duty and . . . hell . . ." With a groan, Kate gave up trying to dance around the subject. "All right, I'll admit it. I'm on duty and I'm going to do my duty. And my duty is to protect you. And I'm going to protect you because, damn it, Alex, you're just too darned gorgeous! I can't stand the thought of you splattered all over the place thanks to Joe Bartone. Besides, if you were gone, who would every woman in America swoon over?"

She didn't honestly think he'd answer, but Alex looked thoughtful. "You'd give up the chance of the two of us going to bed together, just to make sure I was safe? You'd do that? For me?"

There was so much honest amazement in Alex's voice, Kate couldn't help the fact that he suddenly tugged at her heartstrings. She didn't exactly feel sorry for him, but she did regret what they both had to sacrifice. "Which isn't to say that it wouldn't be great," she said, hoping to make them both feel better.

"Better than great." Alex sighed his surrender, and something told her it was as close as he'd ever come to admitting she was absolutely right. "At least we admit that much. At least we admit it would be great."

"Better than great."

"Another time, another place . . ."

"Another universe!" Kate laughed. "Of course we could even the playing field a bit if you'd pay me the three million bucks you owe me."

Alex's eyes twinkled and his lips twitched into a smile that tangled around Kate's heart. Damn him, even when she was trying to talk herself out of something she would have liked nothing better than to talk herself into, he had to look like the heart-stopping, mind-numbing hero right out of a romance novel.

"That's as close as anyone's ever come," he said, "to making me want to give away three million dollars."

The soil was muddy, the grass was soaked, and though the rain had finally stopped somewhere around six in the morning, the neighborhood was still slick with water and dotted with puddles that reflected the patchwork quilt of fat gray clouds on a high blue background. The knees of Alex's jeans were waterlogged as soon as he knelt down.

He looked over at the flowers lined up against the porch and shook his head, surprised at the mess. The flats of marigolds and petunias Marge had picked up at his request hadn't made it through the storm in very good shape. The heavy rain had caused the soil in the flats to spatter, and the brassy petals of the marigolds were freckled with mud. The delicate petals of the red and white petunias didn't look any better. The flowers were torn from the force of the wind. Their leaves were flattened as if they'd been stomped on by heavy boots. The roots of each of the plants were swimming in a sea of rainwater that had all but washed the soil out of the little plastic containers.

But then, what did Alex expect?

He wasn't sure he'd weathered the storm any better.

Alex sat back on his heels. In the hours since the storm had passed and the electricity had finally snapped back on, neither he nor Kate had slept. He suspected she was too wired on caffeine to think about giving sleep a try. And while he'd been smarter and hadn't gulped down half the coffee she'd managed to consume, he knew better than to go up to bed, close his eyes and empty his mind. As soon as he did, he knew he'd be a goner, and he was pretty sure, in this instance, that wouldn't mean falling asleep.

It was the first time he'd been able to appreciate the

old saying: Idle hands are the devil's workshop. Only in this case, it was his idle mind he was worried about. And the devil was the devilish tickle of temptation that still tingled through his fingers. The one that had started the second he touched Kate's bare skin. The one that still swept through him like a Santa Ana wind.

Alex fought against the sudden, fierce tightening of his body. There was no use torturing himself; just the thought of how Kate's nipples had turned pebble-hard in his fingers was torture enough. There was no use adding to the agony by reliving the taste of her tongue against his, or the mind-numbing, mind-blowing, mind-boggling possibility that what they'd started down on the couch might have finished up in his bed. There was no use doing anything but trying to save himself. Before it was too late.

"Steady, boy." He mumbled the advice at the same time he stabbed his trowel into the muddy soil. He yanked one of the beaten marigolds from its place in the six-pack, shoved the roots of the plant down into the soggy soil, and mounded mud up around the toothpick-thin stem. He made a second indentation in the soil about six inches away and reached for another plant before the hole could fill with water.

He reminded himself that this was exactly the reason he was out in the mud at this ungodly hour. He was keeping his idle hands busy. And he was supposed to be keeping his idle mind occupied, too. He was supposed to be thinking about marigolds, not about Kate. Not about the moist feel of her lips beneath his, or the way her breasts filled his hands. He was supposed to be keeping himself busy, involved with the garden so that he didn't think about getting involved with a woman who was as tempting as any, and smarter, braver, and more determined than any person—man or woman—he'd ever met. Instead, here he was, soul-searching, his brain filling with thoughts he never would have dreamed possible at the beginning of this little masquerade. He shook his head, amazed, disgusted, and confused all at the same time. While Kate might have been worried about keeping her star witness from losing his life this summer, her star witness was more worried about losing his mind. And his heart.

Fortunately for Alex, his thoughts were interrupted when a kid on a bike flew by and tossed a morning newspaper down on the sidewalk right next to him. He knew a sign from above when he saw one. This sign said, *Do something to get your mind off Kate!* as surely as if it were written in bold letters across the front page. Alex scooped up the newspaper and took it over to the front porch.

He glanced at the headlines. The banner across the top of the page talked about some dust-up between a couple prominent local politicians. The headline closest to it concerned the opening of a new exhibit at the Rock and Roll Hall of Fame. Uninterested, Alex flipped the paper over.

Martinez Found Guilty.

The headline in the right corner of the front page made the air rush from his lungs. He dropped onto the second stair from the bottom, pulled in a breath, and let it out again along with a curse.

"Damn." Alex scanned the story. ". . . verdict reached . . . unanimous decision . . ." He read the words below his breath, speeding through the story. It was continued on the inside, and he flipped the pages, looking for the rest. Unfortunately there was nothing in it that offered any more hope than did the headline.

". . . found guilty of crimes against the state by a jury that from all reports, seemed more interested in returning a speedy verdict than it did a fair one . . . Martinez's sentencing is scheduled in two weeks and while no member of the government will comment on what his fate might be, sources say there are only two possibilities: Martinez will either spend his life in prison at hard labor or he'll face a firing squad."

"Damn." Alex tossed the newspaper aside, then grabbed it up again, as if looking at the article a second time might change anything. He knew it wouldn't, and he flipped it back down on the step next to him. "Damn."

He had only two weeks, and absolutely no hope of accomplishing anything in that time. Not if he didn't hear from Norbert. Fast.

The thought crashed into Alex along with the sound of a shrill train whistle from the tracks behind the house. He didn't know what was wrong with him. He didn't know why his brain was reacting as if it were stuck in the mud like the marigolds. He supposed he could attribute the whole thing to going without sleep, and he decided to settle on that. It was better than admitting that it was just about impossible to think about anything else, when all he could think about was Kate.

Batting the thought aside, he snatched up the newspaper again and flipped through page after page until he found the personal adds.

"Sexy lady with a taste for naughty pleasures . . ." "Single, professional, no children, no smoking . . ." He read through the ads as quickly as he could, grumbling the words below his breath. "Looking for a Jewish doctor . . ." "Not tall. Not good-looking. No money to speak of. Looking for YOU to share what will probably be a pretty limited future."

Alex's heart stopped, then started again with enough of a jolt to make him sit up straight.

"Not tall. Not good-looking." He read the words again, slower this time, as if he might have misinterpreted them. "No money to speak of. Looking for YOU to share what will probably be a pretty limited future."

Alex's face lit with what he supposed was probably a pretty silly smile. The words matched the message Norbert promised, and Alex nodded, confirming that to himself. Eagerly, he read through the rest of the ad to the part where Norbert indicated where and when he wanted to meet. "August 7. 8 P.M. Gund Arena."

Alex had read the *Cleveland Plain Dealer* enough to know that Gund Arena was one of the area's premier sports and concert venues. Silently he congratulated Norbert. It was a brilliant plan. A very public, very crowded place. A place where the two of them could easily slip out from under Kate's watchful gaze. They'd meet on the sly, and it wouldn't take long. Just long enough for Alex to give Norbert the information that would save Ruben Martinez's life.

August 7. It wouldn't give Norbert much time to do everything he had to do. But Norbert was efficient as well as resourceful. Alex knew he could count on him to get the job done.

Feeling better already, Alex sat back and willed the tension to drain out of his muscles. Idly, he wondered what was happening at Gund Arena that night and how he'd convince Kate they needed to be there. Would he tell her there was a sports team in town he couldn't wait to see? He shook his head, discarding the thought before it fully formed. It was summer, and as far as he knew, the city's basketball, soccer, and hockey teams didn't play in the summer. The Cleveland Indians played in the stadium next to the arena, so baseball wouldn't work as an excuse, either.

Maybe Norbert had a rock concert in mind? Alex nodded, satisfied. He was no fan of overly loud music, but he did see that a night of ear-splitting guitars, psychedelic lights, and screaming fans might provide a great cover.

Eager to check out his theory, he paged through the newspaper, looking for the Entertainment section. In between the movie reviews and a story about a sitcom star who had just confessed to the world that she was really a he, he found a listing of upcoming events.

"August seven." Alex mumbled the words below his breath and skimmed his thumb down the listing. "August two. August four. August five. August seven." His finger poised above the column of newsprint, he paused and stared at the words printed there. His excitement melted.

His confidence in Norbert's judgment wavered. Hell, it just about disintegrated. If this was Norbert's idea of a joke . . .

Alex flipped back to the personal ads, just to make sure his eyes hadn't been playing tricks on him. He turned back to Entertainment and checked the listings again. His shoulders slumped and the excitement that had been buzzing through him ever since he recognized the words of the message dwindled. Right along with the projected size of Norbert Fielding's Christmas bonus.

"Damn," Alex mumbled.

"Ain't fightin' with the missus again, are you?"

With a guilty start, Alex jumped. Earl was standing on the front sidewalk watching him and Alex closed the newspaper in a hurry. "Fighting? With Missy?" He laughed. If only Earl knew. Maybe fighting would have been a better option than what he and Kate had been up to lately. Back in the days when all they did was fight, at least he didn't spend hours on end thinking about the silky feel of her skin, and the heat of her mouth, and the—

"No." Alex answered quickly, before he could get even more carried away or Earl could guess that anything was wrong. "No way. We haven't had a fight in weeks."

"I didn't think so." With a broad wink, Earl closed in. "I mean, what with that candle burnin' last night and all."

"Candle?" It took Alex a moment to put two and two together. When he did, he wasn't sure it equaled four. "But the curtains were closed. How did you—"

"Couldn't see nothin'. I promise you that." Earl waved away Alex's concerns with one oil-stained hand. "Woke up during the storm is all. Saw that little bit of light peeking out from between your curtains and knew it wasn't a flashlight. You devil." He winked again, and this time, added a broad and very satisfied-looking smile to the mix. "Who would have thought that a storm like that could provide a fellow another opportunity to be romantic. You're always thinking, aren't you?"

Alex wasn't sure he liked the direction in which the

conversation was headed, but he didn't know how to get out of it. "Are you telling me, after you woke up and saw our candle, you—"

"I figured I better do the same." Earl nodded vigorously. "Had a heck of a time finding a candle, but finally remembered the one Marge always keeps in the bathroom. Smells like vanilla or something. She's had it wrapped up in that plastic it came in since the day she brought it home from the store, and that had to be three years ago. I thought she might mind that I unwrapped it and lit it, but when I woke her up . . ." As amazing as it seemed, Earl's face actually turned bright red. He cleared away his embarrassment with a cough. "Well, I can only say I hope you and Missy was having as much fun by candlelight as me and Marge!"

Alex opened his mouth, but nothing came out. He snapped it shut again and blinked at Earl in amazement. Whatever fates controlled his life must have been having a laugh-filled riot of a time in whatever place it was the fates lived. So far this morning, his mood had veered from perplexed to horny to panicked. A panic that had been eliminated when he found Norbert's message. From hope, his spirits had tumbled to disbelief. And now, this. Though Kate had certainly had her reasons for breaking off their encounter the night before, and while those reasons were sound, and good, and even admirable, the results were the same.

The bone-chilling, stomach-churning, ice-in-the-bloodstream realization was too much to take. While the world's most eligible bachelor was getting shot down, the beer-bellied, balding grease monkey across the street was having wild, passionate sex.

Alex offered Earl a noncommittal smile and left it up to his neighbor to interpret whether it meant Stan and Missy did, or didn't, do what Earl and Marge obviously did do.

"So what you up to here?" Earl changed the subject as easily as he changed the oil in his beater of a car.

"Just getting these flowers planted." Alex pointed with the hand that still held the newspaper. And a great idea occurred to him.

He eyed Earl carefully, but if Earl knew Alex was considering using him as a patsy to put the wheels of his plan in motion, he didn't show it. Lost in thought, the big man stuck his hands in the pockets of his jeans and rolled back on his heels, his head cocked to one side. Even as Alex watched, a twinkle kindled in Earl's eyes and his face split in a wide grin of remembrance.

Hell. Alex shook away his misgivings along with the prickles of jealousy he couldn't help but feel. It was obvious what had happened at Earl's house wasn't a friendly game of poker and an innocent kiss or two. The way he figured it, Earl owed him. Big time.

"Hey, Earl . . ." Alex unfolded the entertainment section and smoothed it out. "What are you and Marge doing on August seventh?"

13

"Is this excitin', or what?"

Grinning, Earl tightened one arm around Marge's waist at the same time he tipped his head back and gazed at the massive facade of Gund Arena. It was seven-thirty at night, the temperature had to be at least ninety degrees, and the sidewalk in front of the building was packed with more black leather and tattooed skin than Kate had seen since the night she'd been in on the raid of a biker hangout on the outskirts of Phoenix.

Exciting wasn't exactly the word she had in mind.

Instinctively she tightened her hold on her oversize fake leather purse. Silly to feel she needed the assurance of the 9mm semi-automatic tucked inside. Silly to feel exposed and vulnerable. Yet silly or not, Kate was grateful for the courage the weapon offered. Though the crowd was probably not nearly as rough as it looked, she couldn't be too careful. She didn't need to remind herself that she'd already made the ultimate sacrifice in the name of Alex's safety. The possibilities of all she'd refused on the night of the storm continued to supply her dreams with enough erotic images to fill the shelves of any self-respecting porn shop. Abstinence made her grouchy, and being grouchy made her more determined than ever that she was not about to risk Alex's neck. Not after what she'd given up for the cause.

With a practiced eye, Kate glanced around. The raucous crowd outside the arena gave new meaning to the words "wrong side of the tracks." They'd parked the car less than fifteen minutes before, and already Kate had seen muscle-bound fellows in skimpy shorts and tiny shirts, women who looked tough enough to bite through nails, and enough people with missing teeth to make an orthodontist dream of Ivy League schools for his kids.

The lady in front of Kate had a beehive hairdo and a midriff top that exposed way too much flesh for decency or civilized taste. She had a tattoo on her left shoulder that proclaimed her "Bubba's Bitch." The man at the woman's side, who Kate could only presume was Bubba himself, had a series of earrings and a ponytail that hung to the middle of his back. He also had a tattoo of a snake on his arm that wound all the way from his shoulder down to his wrist. The serpent's head—fangs bared, of course—covered the entire top of his hand. The couple they were with was a little more sentimental. They wore matching outfits: black leather slacks, black leather vests, spiked dog collars.

To Kate's right, Earl and Marge looked positively dull amid the colorful crowd, even though they'd both pulled out new blue jeans and plaid shirts in honor of the occasion. She didn't need to remind herself how Alex looked. In spite of her urgings that he might want to blend into the crowd as much as possible, he'd insisted on blue jeans and a fire-engine-red golf shirt, the kind with the button placket front, the little collar, and some embroidered symbol over the heart that was a poor copy of a famous designer's.

He looked like a social worker or, worse yet, a cop. Kate glanced at him, then glanced away again as quickly as she could, fearing if she looked too long, it might send a message to the crowd that it was time to point and stare. It was the first time she was actually glad they were jammed into the line slowly waiting to file inside. At least the possibility of Alex's being noticed was slim.

Though anyone with half a brain could see that it was already too late to extricate herself from the throng moving ever closer to the yawning doors of the arena, Kate knew she had to try. One more time. She inched to her left, closing the already impossibly small space between her and Alex.

"You sure about this?" she asked him.

"Sure?" Alex had the advantage. He was taller than Kate, and he craned his neck, looking over the crowd toward the doors. "Why wouldn't I be sure?"

It was the same thing she'd been hearing from him ever since Earl had announced this outing, a sort of mantra that, by now, Kate could repeat in her sleep. She sighed, but before she had a chance to either argue the point or resign herself to the experience, she got jostled from behind. It was enough of a bump to jar her back to reality. Her hand automatically going to her purse, she whirled—and found her nose pressed against what looked to be a solid wall of tattooed flesh.

The owner of the flesh and of all those tattoos was well over six feet tall and wearing leather biker pants and a black leather vest that didn't make it across the span of his bare chest. He must have been an old hand at the let's-intimidate-everyone-in-the-crowd game. He stepped back just a fraction of an inch and glared down at Kate. "What are you lookin' at?" he demanded.

At her side, she felt Alex bristle and step forward. Considerate of him in a 1950s sort of way, Kate supposed, but she did have a job to do. Part of that job was making sure he didn't get his head cracked against the sidewalk, or his arms snapped like twigs, or any of his other delectable parts—parts she didn't want to think about at the moment—mangled beyond repair. And this guy looked like he could do it.

With the movement of one hand and a half-smile, she

let Alex know that the only way to handle punks was to play their game. She pulled herself up to her full height, which was just about enough to bring her up to the gold ring hanging from the guy's left nipple. Kate tilted her head to look up into dull, red-rimmed eyes that were textbook-perfect examples of what too little common sense and too much pot smoking could do to a man.

"I'm sure not looking at you," she snarled. She dismissed him with a toss of her head and an unmistakable hand gesture.

The big guy flinched. He apparently wasn't expecting to get dissed by a woman in a T-shirt that had lime green teddy bears all over it. Satisfied, Kate turned back toward the doors and prayed that the line would move nice and fast, before he came to his drug-smothered senses and decided what to do next.

"Are you sure that's the best way to handle these people?" Alex leaned close and mumbled the question in her ear.

She brushed off his worries with a wave of her hand, but she couldn't quite set her own mind at ease. She'd seen the way Alex's upper lip curled while he watched her deal with the rude guy behind her. She'd seen the way he moved through the crowd, his arms close to his sides and his shoulders rock steady, and she was reminded of the game she used to play with her brother and sister when they were kids: Cootie. Alex looked like he was afraid he was going to get cooties, and to be honest, Kate couldn't blame him. In this crowd, he'd be lucky if that's all he got.

So why had he agreed to come? Every time she even mentioned the Laundromat, he shuddered, and when they'd gone to play bingo, he'd acted like he was stepping in front of a speeding train. So why was he Mr. Agreeable about this?

Kate went over every possible answer she could think of, but she was no closer to a solution than she had been the day Earl asked them to come and Alex accepted. That's when she'd put the question directly to him.

"Why not go?" Alex had told her. "After all, Earl and Marge were nice enough to invite us."

"Yeah, invite us to hell." Pulling herself back to the present, Kate mumbled the words. She didn't worry about anyone hearing. Two guys over on her left yelled insults at each other, right before they traded punches. The crowd shouted encouragement, then hissed their disappointment when two of Cleveland's finest, already looking harried this early in the evening, waded in to break things up.

By the time it was all over, they were close enough to the doors of the arena to feel the blast of the air-conditioning.

"All set, you two?" Earl looked over and flashed them the sort of smile Kate thought guys reserved for each other before they stepped into the neighborhood massage parlor. "It's going to be a rock 'em, sock 'em night."

"Great." The single word Alex ground from between clenched teeth told Kate more than his *Why wouldn't I be sure?* mantra had revealed in a week. Curious, she turned to take a close look at him, but he acted as if he hadn't spoken a word, and Kate wondered if she'd imagined the whole thing.

She knew she wasn't imagining anything the next minute when she stepped inside the building. Cold air settled against her heated skin and sent a wave of goose bumps up her arms and across her shoulders. Kate drew in a deep breath. It was the air-conditioning, she reminded herself. The air-conditioning was making her shiver. But as she looked around, she realized she'd been right when she compared the experience to hell. This *was* hell, at least for a law enforcement officer intent on protecting her witness. A sea of people fanned out before them, moving faster now that they'd made it through the turnstiles. They shouted and laughed and a couple of them screamed rude words at each other. From inside the auditorium, she heard the heavy bass rhythm of music that, even out by the concession stands, was way too loud. A mishmash of vendors selling everything from foot-long hot dogs to programs for the night's event called out to them. She saw T-shirts and rubber snakes for sale, posters, and plenty more beer than the already overexcited crowd needed.

Every nerve in Kate's body tingled, and for once, it had nothing to do with the fact that Alex was close enough to reach out and touch. The hairs on the back of her neck stood on end, and her instincts called out a warning.

"This is no good." Kate pulled to a stop and grabbed on to Alex's arm, hauling him to her side. "We've got to get you out of here."

"We've been through this before." When he saw that Earl and Marge had stopped to see what the problem was, he waved them on ahead, and Kate found herself wishing he wasn't such a good actor. She wished she could read what was going on behind the guarded expression on Alex's face. "We're here, we'll stay here. Otherwise Earl and Marge will get suspicious."

"Let them get suspicious." Kate stepped out of the way of a college-age guy who lurched unsteadily by. "There's too much going on, Alex. Too many people." She looked around at the dozens of concession stands and the dozens more doors that led into everything from the restrooms to first-aid stations. "Too many places Bartone could be hiding."

"Bartone isn't hiding anywhere." Even as Alex said it, she saw him glance around. So if he didn't think Bartone was lurking around the arena, who was he looking for?

Alex looked back toward the main entrance and the hordes of people still streaming in. "There's no way the guy can know we're in Cleveland, right?" he asked, but he didn't wait for her to answer. He looked in the other direction, toward where Earl was buying four beers. "And even if he closed his eyes and eeny-meeny-minymoed at a map, and ended up picking Cleveland as the place we were most likely to be, there's no way he could know we were coming here tonight." His glance returned to hers. His voice was infinitely patient. At the same time it aggravated the hell out of Kate, she couldn't blame him. They'd been through this a dozen times before. "Right?"

"Right." Kate puffed out a breath of annoyance. "Right. Right. Right. But that doesn't change a thing. It's dangerous."

"Chicken?" Alex shot her the question along with one of his trademark smiles and a look that made his eyebrows slide up behind the heavy rims of his glasses. "Afraid the crowd might be a little tough for you?"

"I'm not even going to answer that." Kate refused to participate in adolescent sparring. He knew she couldn't stand to have her courage questioned, and rather than admit it, or get drawn into a fight in a place that was way too public, she headed over to where Earl and Marge waited for them. At her side, she knew Alex was smiling with triumph.

"So what do you think?" Earl asked. "Is this excitin', or what?"

Oh, it was exciting, all right.

Kate followed Earl and Marge to their seats. As she did, she glanced at Alex. She was eager to find something in his expression that might explain what the hell they were doing there in the first place. But eager or not, it didn't matter. He was as inscrutable as the sphinx, and just as crusty.

None of it computed. Not the place or the event or Alex's sudden urge to show Earl and Marge he was nothing but a good ol' boy after all. None of it made any sense.

They wound their way through the arena and down flight after flight of steps that led to the main floor, and Kate realized that if she was looking for things that made sense, she'd come to the wrong place. Inside the main part of the auditorium where the night's events would take place, the real world seemed a million miles away. Lights pulsed overhead and arced across the restless, screaming crowd, blinding Kate one second and plunging her into darkness the next. The music was loud enough to vibrate through her bones. It made the beer in her plastic cup quiver.

She willed herself to hang on tight, both to her beer and to her sense of perspective. But in spite of the fact that she knew Alex was probably right, in spite of the fact that she knew there was little chance they were in any real danger, Kate couldn't help but think of lambs being led to the slaughter.

"Great." She grumbled the word, and even she wasn't sure if it was because of the uncomfortable images of bleating lambs that rose in her mind. Or the fact that once they stopped, she realized they had front-row seats. She tried to position herself on the aisle, but just as she was about to suggest Alex switch spots with her, the lights went out completely and the crowd went wild.

"Just great." Before she could get batted around by the row of guys behind her who were jumping up and down and screaming for all they were worth, Kate dropped into the nearest seat. She sighed and resigned herself to her first-time-ever, all-out, no-holds-barred professional wrestling match.

Alex hadn't counted on sitting close enough to the action to see every one of the wrestlers' hokey moves. Even as he watched, some guy dressed all in green with an ugly scar across one eye jumped with both feet on top of another muscle-bound guy with waves of long hair and a face that looked as if it were chiseled from stone. Sitting this close, Alex couldn't fail to notice that the green guy missed by a mile. Maybe the rest of the crowd didn't see that. Maybe they just didn't care. The place erupted. People screamed and waved homemade signs that proclaimed everything from the prowess of their favorite wrestlers to the advice of their favorite Bible passages. They chanted and threw empty plastic beer cups and wadded-up hot dog wrappers. They stomped their feet and pounded the arms of their chairs until the building itself felt as if it were rocking all around Alex.

Through it all, Kate sat next to him looking as politely interested as anyone could with four hundred pounds or more of sweat, oiled muscle, and very bad attitude writhing around only a couple feet away. Not that she was paying much attention to the wrestling. Every time Alex looked at Kate, he found her scanning the crowd. He wasn't sure what she was looking for, but he knew why. The place was a nightmare, especially for a law enforcement officer like Kate, who took her job very seriously. He could feel the tension vibrating through her, humming like a harp string.

He appreciated the fact that she was watching out for him. Honest. And someday, he hoped, he would have a chance to tell her. But that someday seemed a long way off. The only way he was going to be able to do what he had to do was to shake away from Kate's watchful eye. Once before intermission and once after, Alex had tried excusing himself to go to the men's room and twice, Kate had followed and waited for him right outside the door. Once before intermission and once after, Earl had reached in his pocket for beer money and Alex had snatched the bills out of his hand and offered to go out to the concession stands and twice, Kate had trotted along at his side.

At this rate, Alex would never have a chance to talk to Norbert.

If he could ever even find Norbert.

The thought settled in Alex's stomach along with the lukewarm hot dog he'd eaten for dinner. It had about the same effect. His stomach clenched, disappointment and fear settling in beside the hot dog, adding to his misery. He'd thought bingo was one of the circles of hell, and he was still pretty sure he was right about that. But if bingo was a little slice of demonic real estate, it was at the top of the list, a place for people who did things in their earthly lives like jaywalk and cut off those funny little tags on their mattresses that warned against just such action. Pro wrestling was way lower when it came to the circles-of-hell department, right down there where the flames were the hottest, the damnation was more eternal, and the devils wore everything from leather pants and biker jackets to the male equivalent of g-strings.

Wondering when Norbert's tastes had gone from impeccable to downright lousy, Alex took another look around the arena. Good taste or bad, he trusted Norbert like he trusted none of the other executives who worked for him—trusted him with his life—and in spite of the fact that his logic told him it was unlikely, he still hoped to find Norbert somewhere in the crowd.

A winner was declared between the wrestler in green and the guy with the long hair, though if Alex saw who it was, he forgot it again the next instant. A couple of cameras flashed somewhere nearby and Kate looked over her shoulder, checking out the photographers. Apparently she didn't think they were suspicious. He had a feeling if she had, she would have been up and over the back of her seat and at their throats in an instant.

"This isn't on TV, is it?" Kate asked the question and looked around quickly, as if the idea had suddenly occurred to her.

"Lord, I hope not!" Alex sank into his seat and dropped his head into his hands. The very idea of being seen at a wrestling match was atrocious. The thought of being seen—and possibly recognized—conjured images of what the fellows at the country club might say, and the field day the tabloids would make of the story. He could see the headlines now: *Wrestling Romeo! Romeo of the Ring! A Walk on the Wrestling Wild Side with America's Sexiest Hunk!*

His stomach did another slow churn. But even before it stopped churning, another thought occurred to him. Wasn't being seen exactly what he was hoping to accomplish?

The question caused a stab of guilt to prickle at Alex's conscience. Weren't there some things more important than what the tabloids thought of him? Isn't that what he'd been telling himself all summer? Isn't it what he'd learned from Ruben Martinez? Weren't there things worth risking ridicule—and even bodily harm—to accomplish?

He wasn't into touchy-feely pop philosophy, so he didn't bother answering the questions. He did sit up, though, and take another look around. There were no TV cameras and that, at least, was one saving grace in an evening filled with blood, sweat, and jeers. But there was no Norbert to be seen, either, and as another set of contenders was introduced, Alex took the opportunity to stand up so he could take a better look. As he suspected, Kate didn't like that at all. She jumped up beside him, grabbed him by the arm, and pushed him back into his seat.

She leaned over him and gave him what the people around them probably mistook for a smile. "You're a target when you're standing," she said from between clenched teeth.

"Yeah. I know. Sorry." Alex managed a sheepish grin in return, and he hoped it looked apologetic rather than ecstatic. That way, Kate wouldn't suspect what had just happened. She wouldn't know that just for an instant, between when he got up and when she sat him down again, Alex had looked across the auditorium and caught the eye of Norbert Fielding.

It took Alex a second or two to place Norbert. Even so familiar a face looked different in an unconventional setting. And this was about as unconventional as any setting could get.

Where he'd gotten it, Alex didn't know, but Norbert was dressed in a yellow T-shirt with "Event Staff" emblazoned across the front of it. It looked just like the T-shirts worn by the bouncers stationed up and down the aisles. Norbert even looked like a bouncer, or at least as much as a middle-size balding guy with glasses could look like a bouncer. He stood at the end of one of the aisles, his feet apart, his arms crossed over his chest.

Norbert saw Alex at the same time Alex saw him. His eyes brightened with recognition and something so much like relief that Alex knew he'd made the right decision in contacting Norbert. Norbert nearly waved. He caught himself at the last second and tipped his head in greeting. Apparently that was as much of the tough-guy bouncer persona as he could handle. He also smiled.

Just before Kate pushed Alex back down in his seat, he saw Norbert look over his shoulder. Alex knew what that meant. There was a sign directly behind Norbert. One that read, "Section 545." That was where Norbert wanted to meet.

Now all Alex had to figure out was how he was going to get there without Kate tagging along.

They never warned her about this at the Academy.

Kate sat back in her seat, scanning the crowd. No one had ever told her she might find herself just three feet away from muscle-bound, broad-shouldered, over-testosteroned brutes beating the crap out of each other. Or at least if they had, she'd assumed they'd be muscle-bound, broad-shouldered, over-testosteroned brutes beating the crap out of each other who she could at least arrest.

She wondered what the screaming fans saw in what they charitably called a sport, and speculated about the possibility that she might find at least some redeeming social value in the whole experience if not for the fact that she was wound as tight as a watch spring.

It didn't help that when the next two wrestlers were introduced, the place went wild. Apparently it was some sort of grudge match, and the noise level rose to reflect all the action the fans expected. Kate's anxiety level shot up right along with the decibels. In a place like this, Alex could get murdered ten times over and no one would even notice.

"That's just what I need, a little pep talk." Kate grumbled the words, though it wouldn't have made a bit of difference if she had screamed them out loud. No one would have heard. Though he was sitting right next to her, Alex didn't even notice. He was watching the action in the ring—action that, at the moment, consisted of a big guy in black waling on a bigger guy in black with a metal folding chair—and Kate couldn't for the life of her figure out why. From all she knew about Alex, she would have thought he'd be long gone by now, maybe not on his way home (not until Earl and Marge were ready to leave), but at least out buying rubber snakes or cups of watery coffee, anything to get away from the carnage that was so phony it was laughable, and so mean-spirited it was frightening.

The very idea started the questions pounding through her head. Kate stopped them with a word of warning to herself. There was no use going over it all again. It wouldn't get her anywhere.

"Is this excitin', or what?" Earl was sitting on Kate's left, and he leaned closer, yelling above the noise of the crowd. "I hope you two are having a swell time."

"Swell." Kate darted a glance at Alex. At the moment, he wasn't looking swell. He was looking like she was feeling. Like he wanted to pop out of his seat and get the hell out of Dodge. Earl noticed it, too, and his face clouded with confusion.

"Stan gets a little antsy when he has to sit still this long," Kate told him. "You know, an attention-span problem. That's why I was a little surprised he accepted your invitation to come tonight."

"My invitation?" One of the wrestlers climbed up on the ropes that surrounded the ring and leapt on top of the other guy. Earl leapt up, too, hollering for all he was worth. Kate wasn't sure which of the wrestlers he was cheering for, but whichever it was, he was apparently satisfied by the outcome. Grinning, he plunked back down.

"That Stan! He's a crafty, devil, ain't he?" Earl couldn't help but shake his head in admiration. He leaned across Kate and looked over at Alex, but Alex wasn't paying the least bit of attention. "Probably wanted to surprise you," Earl said, turning his attention back to Kate. "Coming here tonight was his idea all along."

Bells rang in Kate's head, and she didn't think they were the bells that signaled the end of the round. She sat back, feeling like the guy in the ring, who was being swung around by one arm and bounced against the ropes. "You mean he—? Are you telling me he—?" Her brain bounced around, too, from one possibility to the next. And she didn't like any one of them.

"This was your idea!" She turned to Alex and screamed the question at him almost before she could stop and consider that a level, reasonable approach might have been more effective.

Not that it mattered.

He didn't have a chance to answer.

Just as Alex turned to her, the crowd let out a deafening cheer, and one of the wrestlers flew out of the ring and landed at their feet.

Kate might have been able to hang on to both her control and what little handle she had on the situation if not for the fact that the other wrestler was close on the first one's heels. He jumped out of the ring and on top of the first guy and they continued their smashing and grunting in a puddle of sweat not two feet away. A couple of the fans in the row behind Kate couldn't control their excitement. They scrambled over the seats to join the fray. Not to be outdone, six burly bouncers appeared out of nowhere and started swinging their fists.

One of the bouncers picked up a fan and tossed him aside. Airborne, he headed right for Alex and Kate, and at the same time she grabbed Alex's arm to yank him out of his seat, he did the same for her. They both bailed, and the next second, she found herself with her butt stinging against the concrete floor, her hair in her eyes, and the way-too-sweaty body of one of the wrestlers right against hers.

"Are you all right?" Alex's voice called to her over the commotion. His hand shot through the knot of writhing bodies and she latched on to it. He pulled her to her feet.

It was the second time Alex had offered her a hand up. In a flash, Kate remembered the day she'd tussled with the would-be assassin in Alex's office. He had helped her to her feet that day, too, and she would never forget the look on his face when he did. He was amazed, both by the fact that someone had tried to kill him and by Kate's quick response to the threat. He was insulted that anyone could think so little of his precious self that they might actually try to hurt him. He was annoyed that his well-ordered world had been invaded by a force that couldn't help but change his life.

The expression that darkened his chocolatey eyes now was full of all those same things, but there was one essential ingredient missing: Alex. He didn't spare a second thinking about himself. His concern was all for Kate.

The realization stopped her cold. Right before it sent a thread of warmth blossoming through her.

"Thanks." Still hanging on to Alex's hand, she smiled. He didn't have a chance to smile back. Somebody threw a punch and Kate pushed Alex out of the way at the same time she ducked. One of the wrestlers slammed into her. Another younger wrestler tried to help. She felt muscled arms close around her. Her feet left the floor, and she found herself getting turned around.

"Put me down!" Kate screamed, pounding her fists against the strong-as-steel-bands arms that held her like a vise. "Put me down!" But no one could hear her. The crowd must have thought it was all part of the act. The place went wild.

It took a well-placed elbow to the gut to get the guy to

listen. By the time he deposited Kate on the floor, she was at the far end of the aisle. She was safely out of harm's way, sure, but she was also so far away from the action, there was nothing she could do when she saw Alex scramble up the stairs and head out of the auditorium.

"Hey!" Kate reacted instinctively. She yelled for Alex and darted back the way she came, but it was impossible to get past the snarl of wrestlers, bouncers, and fans that was just starting to get untangled. Not that it would have made any difference. Even as Kate struggled forward, Alex kept right on going. The last she saw of him was his bright red shirt in the pulsing, overhead lights.

"Damn!" Kate stomped her foot and tried to sidestep the brawl. She moved to her left and came up against the wrestlers, each now throwing insults at the other. She tried going right and ran up against a solid wall of bouncer flesh.

"Excuse me!" Kate raised her voice. The two guys standing shoulder-to-shoulder in front of her must have been from the equivalent of the bouncer SWAT team. Biggest. Baddest. Least likely to move when they didn't want to.

Kate tried again. "Excuse me!" When they still didn't pay any attention to her, she jumped up and down and waved her arms. That worked, or maybe they just weren't used to anyone in a crowd like this being so polite. One of the burly bouncers spared her a look.

Kate sighed with relief. "Excuse me," she said, trying to move past the guy. "I've got to get up there." She pointed to the exit where she'd seen Alex headed.

"No, ma'am." The bouncer shook his head. His diamond stud earring winked at Kate in the spotlights. "You'll have to wait until security has the area secured."

"No, but see, I can't wait." Kate tried a smile. That didn't have any effect on the stony-faced bouncer, either. He crossed his arms over his chest.

"This is nuts!" With a look that told Earl and Marge

she had everything under control, Kate scrambled under the chair where she had spent most of the evening watching the action instead of taking part in it. Her purse had fallen to the floor in the ruckus and she grabbed it and slung it over her shoulder. If worse came to worst, she could always show the guy her badge. "Look," she said, "I've got to get by. If you'll just listen to me for one second."

"No!" The bouncer barked the word with all the warmth of a marine drill instructor. He glared at her and, as crazy as it seemed, Kate realized why they were waiting for security. This guy actually thought she was a part of the melee. He actually thought she was a willing participant rather than a innocent bystander. They were waiting for security because security was going to turn them over to the cops and the cops were going to escort her out of the building. And once she was out of the building, she'd never get back inside to find Alex.

Kate made a move to dart around the bouncer, but he anticipated it. He made a grab for her arm.

She reminded herself he was only doing his job. But she was only doing her job, too, and she didn't have time to explain. She grabbed the bouncer's arm before he could get ahold of her, stepped forward, braced her foot against his, and twisted with all her might. The guy was at least a hundred pounds heavier than she was, but just like they always promised her at the Academy, she had the element of surprise to back her up. His feet went right out from under him and while he was still flat on the floor, too stunned to do anything but blink up at the overhead strobe lights, Kate leapt over him and raced up the stairs.

She didn't know if any of the other bouncers followed. She didn't stop and look. She took the steps two at a time, speeding in the direction where she'd seen Alex disappear. At the top of the steps, she bulldozed open the double doors that led out to the wide hallway where the concession stands were located. Her brain pumping pure, high-test adrenaline, her heart pounding, she pulled to a stop and looked up and down the nearly empty corridor.

"Shit!" Too much to expect she'd find Alex just standing there waiting for her. Kate took off at a run. She stopped at the first concession stand she came to.

"Seen a guy in a red shirt?" she asked. "Dark hair, glasses?"

The startled woman behind the counter shook her head. Kate tried the next concession stand and the one after. Everyone gave her the same answer. Apparently, with as many as twenty thousand people in the building, it was hard to remember one face, even if it was the face that had launched twenty million fantasies.

Kate rounded a bend in the hallway and saw a security station not thirty feet ahead. She slowed her steps and turned to look at a rack of everything from disposable cameras to T-shirts and drink bottles that featured a picture of somebody named the Malagasi Cobra, a guy with so many muscles, she wondered how he was able to move.

"You a fan of the Malagasi Cobra?" the vendor asked.

"Yeah. Sure." When a pair of uniformed security guards jogged by, apparently on their way to take the mess inside in hand, she turned her back and gave them plenty of time to walk away. When they had, she reached into her pocket, pulled out a twenty, and handed it to the vendor. She slipped a T-shirt over her head. The Malagasi Cobra might have a face only a mother could love, but his T-shirt did a lot to hide the lime green teddy bears she knew the cops would be looking for.

When the vendor offered her change, Kate told him to keep it with a wave. "Say, you haven't seen a good-looking guy with glasses, have you?" she asked, and she hoped four dollars and ninety-five cents was enough of a tip to get the guy to talk. If he had anything to say. "He's wearing a bright red shirt."

"Just saw him."

Kate punched the air with one fist in the universal *all right!* sign. "Which way did he go?"

The man pointed to a door ten feet or so down the corridor, and Kate took off at a trot. She yanked the door open and darted inside, and it wasn't until she saw the wall lined with urinals that she bothered to think where she might be headed.

Kate recovered in an instant. There was no one in the men's room, so no one would care that a woman had made a foray into so private a male domain.

She stepped farther into the men's room and looked around. There was a second door across the room, one that led back out into the corridor. With a sinking feeling, she immediately saw the possibilities of all that had probably happened. Still, now that she was there, she knew she had to at least give finding Alex a try. "Alex?" she called. "Alex, are you in here?"

There was no answer. She didn't need one. She knew that even if Alex had gone in there, he was gone by now. Just as the thought occurred to her, Kate heard the door behind her open and close.

"Well, lookee who's here!"

Kate groaned. She knew the voice, and even if she didn't, it wouldn't have taken her long to realize who'd come into the men's restroom. She turned and ran up against a solid wall of tattooed flesh. Of course that didn't mean much of anything. Tattoos at a wrestling match were sort of like candles at church. They were everywhere. Still, there was no mistaking the hefty shoulders, the belligerent stance, or the smart-assed tone of voice. And if that still wasn't enough, she knew she'd recognize that nipple ring anywhere.

14

Alex supposed he must have read too many Tom Clancy novels. Not that he didn't like Clancy. The guy was a genius, and he sure knew how to keep a reader on the edge of his seat. But there was no way a levelheaded business executive should have been thinking like some sort of master spy. Not unless he had too many old book plots roiling around inside his head. And in spite of the fact that he was embarrassed to even admit it, old book plots full of spies and counterspies, good guys and bad guys, evil geniuses, and heroes willing to give all in the name of world freedom must have been exactly what were going through Alex's mind.

Otherwise, he never would have thought to throw anyone who might be following him off his track by entering the men's rest room by one door and leaving it again as quickly as he could be the other. Otherwise, he wouldn't have kept glancing over his shoulder looking for the telltale signs of pursuit as he made his way toward Section 545 and his rendezvous with Norbert.

Alex rounded a bend in the wide corridor that ringed the arena and wondered if master spies ever felt as guilty as he did at the moment. He doubted it. Master spies were supposed to be cool in the face of adversity. They were supposed to care about their missions more than they cared about themselves. More than they cared about any other person.

So much for his chances of ever being a master spy.

Alex twitched away the uneasy feeling that twisted along his shoulders. No matter how many times he reminded himself that Kate was a professional and that professionals could take care of themselves, he couldn't help but feel guilty about leaving her in the arms of that overgrown, muscle-bound goon who'd picked her up and moved her out of the way of the ruckus. Not that he didn't appreciate the fellow's intentions, or the results. In spite of their image as hard-assed big-mouths, he knew the wrestler who'd scooped Kate up off her feet was only trying to keep a fan safe. In the process, he'd also provided Alex with the perfect avenue of escape. Still, the idea of abandoning Kate didn't sit well with Alex's conscience, or his heart. Not when all he'd really wanted to do was fold her into his arms and keep her safe forever.

Forever?

The single word brought Alex up short. He stopped in the middle of the corridor. A middle-aged woman with a black eye patch and a tattoo of a spider on her arm nearly walked up his back. She growled an obscenity Alex only half heard. A smile was enough to soothe the spider lady's temper, and the near collision was enough to bring Alex to his senses.

Forever was a long time.

He reminded himself of the fact as he took off again, headed toward Section 545. Forever was too much to think about, because he didn't have forever. He had only a few minutes to find Norbert and tell him everything he needed to know. For now, that was more than enough to worry about.

Ahead, Alex saw the familiar neon yellow of a bouncer's shirt flash through a crowd of vendors relaxing together before the rush that was bound to occur when the show was over. He quickened his pace, ticking off the section numbers posted above the doorways that led into the arena. "Five forty-two, five forty-three, five forty-four."

Directly across from Section 545, there was an orange metal door marked "Utilities." Even as Alex read the sign, the door snapped open, and Norbert peeked out. "Alex!" He called and waved. "Over here!"

Relief swept over Alex, washing away his guilt. Like a master spy, he had a mission, too, and right now, that mission was all that mattered. With one more look over his shoulder to make sure Kate was nowhere around, he ducked inside the utility room and closed the door behind him.

When he walked into the men's restroom, the guy with the nipple ring had been in the process of lighting the joint that hung out of the left side of his mouth. He froze for a moment when he recognized Kate, then—priorities firmly in place—he touched his lighter to the joint, inhaled deeply, and grinned.

"Well, if it ain't Teddy Bear Lady!" He sucked in another long breath and held the smoke deep in his lungs. "What are you doing, Teddy Bear Lady?" He exhaled along with the question. "What are you doin' hidin' those cute green teddy bears of yours under a wrestling T-shirt? Afraid I might find you too easy, huh?"

"Yeah, right. There's something to be afraid of." Kate rolled her eyes to emphasize her point. Not that she thought the guy noticed. He was way too blurry-eyed to pay attention to details. He might even have been too high to see the big picture. Trading him look for look, Kate considered her lousy luck. The last thing she needed to do was waste time with this lowlife. Firmly holding her purse, she made a move to get past him.

She moved to her right. And the guy stepped to his left. She stepped to her left. And he moved to his right. It might have been easier to find a way around him if he wasn't a wall of black leather, tattoos, and muscle. He was at least a head and a half taller than Kate, and two times wider than she was even on her most bloated PMS days.

She clenched her jaw. Sensing her frustration, he chuckled so hard, the red-and-blue dragon on his belly shook. Leaning back against the door, he took another drag on his joint. "Not so fast. You don't think you can just walk out on me, do you? Not the way you treated me outside when we was waiting to get in. You was rude, Teddy Bear Lady. That ain't the friendly way to be at all." He studied Kate carefully, his look gliding over the front of her Malagasi Cobra T-shirt thoroughly enough that it should have sent Kate's temper soaring. It might have, if she'd had time to care. The way it was, all she wanted to do was get back out into the arena and search for Alex.

Grumbling her impatience, Kate turned on her heels and headed for the other door.

Before she was halfway there, the big guy scrambled around her. Smiling, he blocked the exit. Maybe the light was better than on the other side of the men's room. Maybe the dash to get around her was the fastest he'd moved in days, and maybe moving fast did something to clear his brain. Whatever the reason, the guy took another close look at Kate and his eyes went wide.

"Hey, you had something to do with that trouble inside the arena a couple minutes ago, didn't you?" He gave her a cat-that-ate-the-canary look. "It was you! That's why you're wearing that shirt with that scumbag Malagasi Cobra on it. That's why you're hiding here in the men's room. You don't want security to find you and throw your cute little ass out of the building."

There was no use arguing, especially with a dopehead who saw right through her disguise and her plan. There was no winning, so Kate didn't try. "And what are you hiding in here for?" she asked. "So you can smoke a joint?"

"Hell, yes!" The big guy grinned. He held the joint at

eye level and looked at it lovingly, then offered it to Kate. "You got balls, that's for sure, Teddy Bear Lady. Wanna party?"

She declined. "What I want to do," she told him, "is get out of here. I'm looking for someone and I have to find him fast. So if you'll just excuse me . . ."

Kate moved to step around the guy, but again, he mirrored her every move, stepping left when she moved right, moving right when she stepped left. He was having so much fun harassing her, he chuckled the whole time. Kate put up with it, but only because the last thing she needed was a scene. But when she made one more attempt to get around him and he grabbed her arm, she'd had enough.

"All right. You want to play games?" Kate shook off his hand and stepped back, beyond his reach. She braced her arms at her sides and planted her feet. Without taking her eyes off her leather-clad mountain of a tormentor, she reached into her purse. She felt around until she found the wallet that contained her gold badge, and in one liquid movement, she yanked it out of her purse and flashed it in front of his eyes.

"Special Agent Kathleen Ellison," she snapped. "FBI."

The big guy's mouth opened far enough for the joint to fall out from between his lips. It hit the floor, and he didn't stoop to retrieve it. He stared at Kate, his face going from flushed to pale in the blink of an eye. "Holy shit!" It was too bad the element of surprise wasn't considered a scientific cure for being high. It worked every time. The guy sobered up right in front of Kate's eyes. The swagger went out of his shoulders. The bluster disappeared from his voice. Fear settled in his eyes and panic followed close behind. "Holy shit! You're not really—? You are, aren't you? You're not . . . You're not going to arrest me for—"

"Drug trafficking? Assaulting a federal officer? Obstruction of justice?" Kate ticked off as many offenses as sprang to mind. Not one of the charges would ever stick;

she knew that. But this guy didn't have to know it. She had to take advantage of him while she still had the upper hand. "What's your name?" she asked.

The guy swallowed hard. "Timothy, ma'am." He snapped to attention. "Timothy Sedgewick the Third."

"Timothy Sedgewick the Third?" The name didn't fit with the skintight biker pants, the grinning skull that covered most of one bulging bicep, or the attitude. But then, Kate wasn't sure standing in a public men's room in a Malagasi Cobra T-shirt with a guy who was blasted and a burning joint on the floor between them fit with her usual persona, either. "Timothy." She tried for the right tone of voice and the kind of smile she was taught to use back at the Academy. The one that was supposed to inspire confidence and trust. The one that was supposed to make even the most belligerent of witnesses think of her as a friend.

"Timothy, I'll tell you what. I can help you. But only if you help me."

"I ain't a snitch." Timothy's words might have sounded noble, but they didn't carry a whole lot of conviction. It was hard to take a guy too seriously when he was shaking in his knee-high black leather boots. "I might have made some mistakes in my life, but that doesn't mean I'm gonna tell you—"

Kate held up one hand, cutting Timothy off in midsentence. She didn't have time to listen to the guy's life story. "You don't have to tell me anything. All you have to do is move so I can get out of here and back to what I was doing. Can you do that for me, Timothy?"

He nodded but he didn't move.

Kate reminded herself that Timothy obviously wasn't the brightest guy. And he was as high as a kite. That was about the only thing that enabled her to hold tight to what was left of her patience. "I'll tell you what, Timothy, I'll pretend I never saw that joint and I'll pretend you never grabbed my arm. But if I do that, you've got to do something for me."

"Okay." Timothy nodded.

Now they were getting somewhere. Kate felt some of the tension ease out of her shoulders. "You have to move." She tried to urge him along with the wave of one hand. "I'm looking for somebody, you see, and—"

"Is he dangerous?" Timothy's eyes got wide.

"Dangerous?" It wasn't a word she usually associated with Alex, but the more Kate thought about it, the more she realized how well it fit. "He's dangerous, all right," she told Timothy, but she didn't bother to mention the biggest danger was to her, to her equilibrium and her desires and her heart. There was only so much confessing she wanted to do to a stoned biker.

"Then I'd better help."

Timothy's offer brought her up short. Kate leaned nearer, as if she wasn't sure she'd heard him right. "Pardon me?"

Timothy stood up straight and pulled back his shoulders. "I'd be proud to help, ma'am," he said. "Can't send a little thing like you into danger all alone. Tell me who you want me to take out for you, and I'll—"

"Whoa! Whoa, Timothy. Hold on there." Kate stopped him before he could say another word. She didn't want to even think about where his train of thought was headed. "All I'm trying to do is find somebody. I'm not looking to arrest him and I'm sure not looking to have anybody take him out. It's a man. The guy I was standing with outside in line."

Thinking very hard, Timothy narrowed his eyes. "You mean the guy in the red shirt?" he asked. "The geeky one with the glasses?"

If Kate had more time, she would have liked to stop and savor what Alex's reaction might have been to that description. She promised herself she'd laugh about it later. "That's the guy," she said. "Seen him?"

Timothy actually thought about it for a long moment. "No." He shook his head. "But I can help you, ma'am. I can help you find him if you want."

Kate knew it was a bad idea. It was never smart to involve civilians in anything, no matter how insignificant that involvement appeared to be. But Gund Arena was a big place, and Alex had already been out of sight for too long. They could cover more ground if two of them were looking. "I just want you to find him. Do you understand that, Timothy?" She stared at Timothy long and hard, hoping she was making herself clear. "No rough stuff. You got that?"

When Timothy nodded his understanding, Kate moved toward the door. "You check the other men's rooms and ask anybody you see. I'll talk to the people at the concession stands. We'll meet back here in fifteen minutes."

"Yes, ma'am."

Kate had the distinct feeling that Timothy would have snapped her a salute if she'd stood still long enough to let him. She didn't. She moved toward the door and Timothy stepped aside to allow her by. "And get rid of that joint," she told him.

"Yes, ma'am." Timothy stomped on the joint, picked it up, and tossed it into the nearest trash can.

"Now let's get going." Kate stepped aside and let Timothy leave first. She waited a couple of seconds before she followed. She'd rather not have to explain to anyone what she was doing in a public men's room with a guy like Timothy.

Outside the door, she paused only long enough to draw in a deep, calming breath. She was ready to get down to work. Kate hadn't walked three steps down the concourse when she heard Marge's startled voice behind her.

"Missy? Missy, what on earth were you doing in the men's room with that . . . that man?"

"So that's the story. That's what I need you to do."

Norbert nodded and closed the small leather-bound notebook in which he'd written copious comments while

Alex talked. He didn't ask questions, and though Alex couldn't help but catch the gleam in his eyes when he realized what Alex was up to, he didn't waste any time putting his admiration into words. It was typical of Norbert. He was as bright as any man Alex had ever met, but he was content to stay in the background, putting the wheels into motion without making a lot of noise about the process.

It was just what Alex expected, and he was grateful for it. They didn't have time for small talk.

"I can take care of it tonight, right from my hotel room," Norbert said. "I'll call Switzerland. Max Dunant will, no doubt, be only too pleased to help." Norbert smiled, and Alex knew exactly what that smile meant. Thanks to the hefty commissions he earned for dealing with only a small portion of Alex's fortune, Max lived well. He would cooperate. Alex was sure of it. Even if it was some ungodly hour of the early morning in Zurich.

"Thanks, Norbert. I appreciate it. I appreciate everything you've done." Alex clapped his friend on the back. They were squeezed into a room that contained a huge air-conditioning unit, a rack of brooms, dust mops, and slop buckets, and an assortment of fuse boxes and telephone cables that patterned the walls. There wasn't much room to move around. Norbert was seated on an industrial-size trash can while Alex stood with his back to the door. "I never thought we'd need that goofy plan of yours," he admitted. "I'm glad you talked me into it."

"Doesn't sound so goofy anymore, does it?" Norbert waved away what had almost sounded like an apology from Alex. "I'm only glad it's the good guys who've got a hold of you, not the bad guys. I've been worried, Alex. We've all been worried. One minute you're there in the office and that phony pizza guy is being dragged out the door. The next minute—" He shook his head, amazed. "Just like that. You're gone. I can't tell you how relieved I was when that debit card statement finally crossed my desk. I'd been haunting the mail room. Kept asking them if they'd seen anything come through with my name on it. They must have thought I'd gone insane. Then one day, there it was. Like magic!"

Alex glanced over his shoulder. Through the thick metal door, he could hear the muffled sounds of voices and footsteps. The show was probably just about over, and that meant he didn't have much time. He had to get Norbert out of there before Kate found either one of them. He didn't need her asking questions. Not now, when he was this close to arranging everything.

"Damn, but I wish we had more time!" Alex scraped a hand through his hair. It had been a long time since his last haircut, at the FBI office in New York. In the back, his hair brushed the top of his collar. In front, it kept falling across his forehead. He pushed it back with one hand. "I want to know all about that North Sea project. And the acquisition of Megatron. I want to hear all about the symposium, too. I can't believe Gates had the nerve to stand up there in front of everybody and—"

Norbert's laugh cut him short. "I'm glad nothing has changed. You're the same old Alex you always were. I'm glad you're all right."

"Depends on your definition of all right." The moment he'd closed the door behind him, Alex had removed his ridiculous, uncomfortable glasses. He rubbed the bridge of his nose with two fingers. "Christ, Norbert, they've got us living in the kind of neighborhood I never even knew existed. I've got a house with a panoramic view of the steel mills, and—"

Alex stopped himself before he could go any further. He wasn't sure what was niggling at the back of his mind, preventing him from saying another word. Maybe it had something to do with the way Norbert sat up and watched him carefully the second Alex gave even the slightest hint about where he was living. Norbert was hanging on every word, interested, sure. But was he more than interested?

As soon as the thought crossed his mind, Alex rejected it. He was getting as bad as Kate, seeing bogeymen in the shadows when all he should have seen was Norbert, a friend who'd gone above and beyond to help him when he needed it most.

Guilt spread through his veins like ice water and Alex laughed, hoping to cover what felt like a gaping chasm in the conversation before Norbert could realize what it meant. "—and the chassis of a seventy-nine Chevy in my front yard."

Norbert stopped himself just short of laughing. "Sorry, boss." He took one look at Alex and tried his best to wipe every last vestige of a smile off his face. Apparently even Norbert's best wasn't good enough. In spite of the fact that he tried to take the whole thing seriously, he chuckled. Genuine amusement sparkled in his eyes, and Alex relaxed. Damn Kate, anyway. She was the one who had him looking for danger when there wasn't any. She was the one who caused him to question the man who'd been his best friend for years.

"If you think that's bad, you ought to see the rest of the neighborhood." There was something about pushing the envelope that made Alex feel powerful and in control. The hell with being careful. The hell with tiptoeing around the subject. Norbert was his friend, and he could tell Norbert anything. He would tell him everything, just to prove to Kate that Norbert couldn't possibly betray him. "The house across the street is the most god-awful shade of yellow you've ever seen, and—"

Norbert couldn't take any more. He laughed out loud. "Sorry." He held up one hand, begging Alex to hold off until he'd composed himself. "Sorry, but the whole thing is just so hard to imagine. When I saw you across the auditorium, I wasn't even sure it was you. The tacky shirt, and those glasses . . ." He shook his head in amazement. "Are they nuts, making you live like that?"

It felt good to finally find someone who understood all he'd been going through. Alex smiled his appreciation. "I'm telling you, Norbert, it hasn't been easy. When this is over, we'll celebrate. We'll go up to the lodge in Canada. You can bring Allison and the kids and—"

"And who are you going to bring?"

Norbert's question brought Alex up short. He glanced at his friend. Norbert's eyes were bright, and there was a half-smile on his lips. But Alex knew him well enough to know Norbert's contemplative look. Norbert was being insightful, the way he was insightful about handling business. For a guy who was as honest as the day was long and as open as a book, Norbert sure knew how to fish for information.

Alex sighed. "How did you know?"

Norbert hopped off the garbage can, tucked his notebook into his back pocket, and straightened his neon yellow T-shirt. "Doesn't take a genius. I saw you try to help her when things got out of control inside the auditorium. The way you looked at her . . . well, I've known you for a long time. Seen you with plenty of women. I don't think I've ever seen you look at any one of them like that."

Alex shrugged. It wasn't much of an answer, and not one Norbert was willing to accept. He stood, patiently waiting for Alex to say more, and Alex wondered what he'd gotten himself into. He'd just convinced himself he could tell Norbert anything. But could he tell him this? Could he tell him about Kate?

For some reason, he felt more vulnerable about doing that than he did about revealing where he was living. But he owed Norbert. He owed him for years of work done well. And he owed him for going out of his way to come there tonight. He owed him, because he'd questioned Norbert's loyalty, and he felt like hell about it.

"She's an incredible woman," Alex said. "Smart and stubborn and brave and—"

"And have you been to bed with her?"

Alex wasn't used to admitting defeat, especially when it came to women. "Would you believe me if I told you no?" he asked.

"Hell, no!" Norbert laughed. "But I do believe you when you say she's smart. That means I'd better hightail it out of here before she finds either one of us." He headed for the door. "Only, Alex . . ." Norbert hesitated, his hand on the doorknob. "Are you sure about this woman?"

"I'm not sure about anything." It was as close as he was willing to come to letting Norbert know that for a second, Alex hadn't been sure of him, either. Alex twitched his shoulders, discarding any remaining doubts. "I'm not even sure if I'm me"—he put his glasses back on—"or Stanley Tomashefski. About the only thing I am sure about at this point is that I appreciate your help. Thanks, Norbert." Alex stuck out his hand.

It took Norbert longer than it should have to take Alex's hand. But then, Alex told himself, maybe he was imagining it. Norbert shook Alex's hand, but he didn't meet Alex's eyes. Or maybe he was imagining that, too. "Take care of yourself, okay?" Norbert mumbled, and he headed around Alex and out the door.

By the time Alex followed him into the corridor, all he could see of Norbert was the flash of his yellow shirt as he headed out the main doors and into the sultry Cleveland night.

Had he made a mistake in trusting Norbert? Alex shook off the question. It was too late to second-guess himself. Too late to worry. The only thing that mattered now was if he was in time to save Ruben Martinez. That, and what the hell he was going to tell Kate when she found him.

"Imagine, running into my cousin Timothy like that!"

Kate gave as much of a laugh as she could possibly muster, all the while scanning the crowd over Marge and Earl's shoulders. It wasn't that she was embarrassed about lying to the two people who were the closest thing she had to family in a city where her marriage, her background, and even her identity were a sham. Hell, at this point, she was pretty sure she could look straight into the saintly eyes of Sister Mary Helene, the teacher who had ruled Kate's eighth-grade classroom with an iron fist, and lie without missing a beat. But she was afraid if she stopped watching the crowd, she'd miss something that might help her find Alex, so she stood with her back to the wall and refused to meet Earl and Marge's eyes.

"But you were in the men's restroom!"

Kate didn't have to see Marge's face to know it must have been ashen with horror. Her voice was enough to convey the message loud and clear.

A twinge of conscience pricked at Kate, not because she'd ventured into what was apparently sacrosanct male territory, but because by venturing into what was apparently sacrosanct male territory, she'd upset Marge.

She suspended her search of the crowd long enough to give Marge a smile and a reassuring pat on the arm. "I wish there was another way, but I couldn't let Uncle Joe and Aunt Eleanor down. I saw Timothy head into the restroom with a joint in his hand—"

"That's a marijuana cigarette." Earl supplied the explanation for Marge's benefit.

"I know what it is." Marge gave him a withering look and returned her attention to Kate. "And?"

"And I just couldn't let him get busted. Not again. I had to try to stop him. Lucky thing I did, too." Kate leaned forward and lowered her voice, sharing the confidence. "The security cops came by not a minute later. They would have had Timothy like that." She snapped her fingers.

"Thank goodness." Hanging on every word of the story, Marge clung to Kate's arm with both hands. "Were you able to help the poor boy?"

"Oh, I think so." It was the first time since Earl and Marge found her that Kate knew she was being absolutely honest with them. "I think I talked some sense into ol' Timothy."

"And you're all right?" Earl was apparently ready to forget the whole Kate-in-the-men's-room incident, and that was just fine with her. "I mean after that fight in there—and then both you and Stan disappeared. We was worried."

"I'm a little worried myself." Kate mumbled the words under her breath. The show must have just ended. Fans were starting to stream out of the doors that led from the auditorium. Already there were knots of people around the concession stand across the way, and other people gathered in groups of three and four who were meandering toward the main doors.

After a three-hour diet of bash 'em and mash 'em, the crowd was about as pumped as any crowd could get. They hooted and yelled. They blustered and strutted. She saw a couple of punches get thrown, and she watched as the cops stationed here and there along the concourse hurried over to get things under control.

It had been hard enough trying to find Alex when the outside corridor was nearly empty. Trying to find him in a sea of overexcited wrestling fans looked to be close to impossible. She searched the crowd again before she turned her attention back to Earl and Marge. "You haven't seen Stan?" she asked.

They shook their heads in unison.

"Damn." Kate grumbled the word and continued looking.

"Don't worry." This time, it was Earl who patted her arm. "Stan's a smart fella, even if he doesn't always act it. He'll figure out how to find us. He's bound to head back to the seats now that the show is over. He'll know that's the only logical place to meet us—we're his ride home. If we stay right here, we're bound to see him come by."

Earl was right. Waiting was the most logical plan, much more logical than running through the building, looking she didn't know where for she wasn't sure what. She might actually have felt better about the whole thing if only she could be certain Alex was able to get back to the seats.

But what if he wasn't?

The questioned gnawed at what was left of Kate's self-control. It crawled over her skin like icy fingers, freezing her through to the bone.

What if they weren't the only ones who'd been watching that wrestling match? What if Joe Bartone was somewhere in the crowd, keeping an eye on Alex's every move? What if he'd seen Alex leave? What if he'd been faster and smarter than Kate, and had been able to follow Alex? What if even now—

Kate pulled herself back from the brink right before she was set to go over the edge. It wouldn't do any good to panic. She knew that. She caught sight of a Cleveland police officer across the concourse, and she decided it might do some good to get help. At this point, blowing Alex's cover, and her own, was less important than finding him alive.

She excused herself without bothering to explain to Marge and Earl where she was going, and headed over to where the young uniformed officer was standing. Before she got there, she heard Marge's voice behind her.

"There he is, Missy! There's Stanley. And isn't that nice? He's with your cousin, Timothy!"

Kate turned just in time to see Timothy Sedgewick striding through the crowd like some sort of latter-day Paul Bunyan. His mouth set in a grim line, his shoulders rock steady, Timothy had one hand twisted firmly around the back of Alex's collar. Alex wasn't a small guy, but Timothy had the advantage of a lifetime of eating fast food, about six inches, and a look in his eyes that said he definitely considered himself to be on a mission from God. Half leading him, half dragging him, he hauled Alex over to Kate and deposited him next to her.

"Good work." Kate couldn't help but smile and give Timothy a thumbs-up. Not only was Alex alive, but he was looking embarrassed enough to make her wish she'd bought one of those disposal cameras that sported a picture of the Malagasi Cobra. This was a Kodak moment if there ever was one.

Alex wasn't so sure. He smoothed the wrinkles out of his shirt, straightened his collar, and ran a hand through his hair. He glared at Timothy, then turned an equally friendly look on Kate. "I could have gotten away from him easily," he grumbled. "I just didn't want to create a scene."

The relief that swept through Kate at the first sight of Alex settled deep inside her, warming her inside out. The heat lasted just about long enough for her to realize what he'd put her through. "What a typical male thing to say!" She discarded her warm and fuzzy feelings in favor of the healthy dose of anger that shot through her like lightning. She knew if she said another word to Alex, she'd end up screaming like a banshee, so she turned to Timothy. "Where'd you find him?"

"Just walking along. Over there." Timothy pointed.

"Alone?"

"Yeah. All by himself."

"Did you see him talk to anyone?"

The last question was apparently more than Alex could take. "Hello!" He waved a hand in front of Kate's face. "I'm right here. Why don't you just ask me?"

"Oh, you are right here." She packed the sentence with as much sarcasm as she could and hoped he didn't miss the point. "Funny, last time I looked for you, I saw you heading out of the auditorium. What a typical thing for you to do. You just walk away. Just like that. What the hell do you think you're—"

"So, are you going to introduce us?" Smiling a greeting, Marge squeezed between Alex and Timothy. Earl was right behind her. "Isn't it wild that in a place as crowded as this, you should run into Missy's cousin?"

"Cousin?" Alex asked.

"Cousin?" Timothy echoed. "And who's Missy, anyway?"

It was time to stop thinking and start taking quick action. Kate grabbed Timothy's arm and dragged him out of earshot of the others. "Thanks, Timothy." She pumped his hand. It was the most effective way she could think to give him the not-so-subtle hint that the game was no longer afoot. "I couldn't have done it without you."

"Yeah, but—"

"No buts." Kate gave him her best I-am-a-federal-agent look. "You've done your country a service. Don't ask any questions. I've got everything under control, so if you'll just vacate the premises . . ."

Apparently the look worked, and Kate made a mental note to try it again some time. Timothy gave her a "Yes, ma'am," and headed for the door.

"He had to get going," Kate told the others when she joined them. "The boy's had a busy day."

"We all have." Earl heaved a sigh and headed toward the nearest exit. "What with all the excitement of coming down here, then that fight. I haven't had this much fun since I can remember. Was this excitin', or what?" He laughed long and hard. "I'm gonna sleep like a log tonight."

"I'll bet Missy and Stan won't." Marge turned and gave Alex a wink. "This girl just can't stand to have you out of her sight."

"Is that so?"

She hated it when Alex sounded so smug. She hated it when he looked smug, too, and now that she thought about it, Kate realized he looked very smug, indeed. While she wondered where he'd been and what he'd been up to, she knew there was no use asking. She'd never get a straight answer out of him. When Alex's footsteps slowed, Kate twined an arm through his and tugged him along.

"As a matter of fact, that is so." She gave him the sweetest smile she could call up from beneath the depths of an anger that was growing by the second. "And I'm going to make you a promise here and now, Stan. I'm never going to let it happen again. I'm going to keep an eye on you if I have to handcuff you to your bed."

Alex's smile was as wicked as the sparkle that brightened his eyes. "Is that a promise?"

15

“Still icy, huh?”

Alex followed Earl’s gaze across the yard and over to the front porch where Kate had been sitting and pretending to read the morning paper ever since Alex came outside to water his flowers.

Icy? The very word sent a shiver up his spine and across his shoulders. Icy was an understatement.

It had been five days since the night they went downtown to see the wrestling match, five days since he’d slipped away and talked to Norbert. And in those five days, Kate had kept her word. She hadn’t let him out of her sight. When he came outside to mess with his flowers, she came outside with him. When he stayed inside and watched some mindless, brainless, witless TV show, she sat on the couch right beside him. A couple of days earlier he’d forgotten his shaving kit when he went to take a shower, and when he left the bathroom to get it, he’d found her sitting on the floor right outside the bathroom door.

He’d only been half kidding when he told her he liked the idea of being handcuffed to his bed. Even now, the thought had certain fantasy possibilities that played through his mind and sent tingles like champagne bubbles dancing through him as if they had Saturday night fever. He'd been so grateful to finally see Norbert, so happy to talk to him and set him on the road to solving the problem of Ruben Martinez, that he had been giddy with relief. It was tough holding that kind of happiness inside. He should have known better than to respond to the handcuff comment at all. He knew Kate was angry, and he knew she had reason to be. But he'd been in such a damned good mood, he couldn't help himself. He should have known that at a time like that, even a comment that would normally make a woman swoon would only make things worse.

And it had.

Now not only was Kate watching him twenty-four seven, she was still angry. On the chilly scale, the iceberg that sank the *Titanic* was a "one." Kate's anger when he disappeared at the wrestling match could safely be classified as something like a "ten." But the minute he'd given her that smart-assed reply to her handcuff threat, her anger had zoomed off the scale, all the way to the when-hell-freezes-over stage. She'd barely spoken a word to him since.

"Brrrrr." Alex answered Earl's question with a shiver. He chafed his hands up and down his arms. From Kate's vantage point up on the porch, he must have looked like some kind of lunatic. The sun was shining, the sky was a bright blue beyond the haze of steel mill pollution, and the temperature was in the high eighties. "The woman's got a memory like an elephant," he told Earl, and even though he knew Kate couldn't hear them from where she sat, he kept his voice down.

Earl nodded. "They all do, Stan. They all do. Wouldn't be surprised if you're not still hearing about this on your twenty-fifth wedding anniversary. Oh, she'll pretend she's forgotten. They're all for that forgive-and-forget stuff when it suits their purposes. Then when the time's right, she'll pull it out on you. Zap! You're dead meat before you even know what's happening."

Kate's cell phone rang, the sound cutting into their conversation. Alex heard her answer, then lower her voice, and he knew the call must be from Mark at the FBI office in New York.

Earl took the interruption as a signal to change the subject. He turned his back on the house. They were standing on the front sidewalk and Alex turned toward the street, too. At least with his back to Kate's watchful eyes, he could pretend he had some small vestiges of privacy left in his life.

"So," Earl asked, "what are you going to do about it?"

"Do?"

In the days since the start of this monumental Cold War, Alex had been angry to match Kate's anger. He'd been aloof to show her he really didn't care how she wanted to act. He'd been smug. He admitted it. He'd been smug plenty of times, because he was still so proud of himself for contacting Norbert without Kate ever finding out about it. But he hadn't really *done* anything about trying to thaw the permafrost that glazed their relationship. He didn't know what to do. He shrugged, and he didn't have to explain a thing. It was enough of an answer to give Earl a pretty clear picture.

"Just what I thought." Earl rocked back on his heels. "Seems to me it's time for you to do some soul-searching, Stan. You can spend the best years of your life trying to read Missy's mind, or you can take control of the situation."

"I can?" Even to his own ears, the question sounded ridiculous. Alex was a leader, not a follower. He made quick decisions and took quicker action. He never had to worry about taking control, because he was always already in control.

Until now.

Alex's shoulders slumped. He gave Earl a sidelong look. "Any suggestions?"

"Now you're talkin'!" Earl thumped him on the back. "The way I see it, Stan, you've got to take a dose of your own medicine. You know, put a little of that romance magic of yours to serious work for yourself, just the way you did for me."

"On her?" Alex glanced over his shoulder long enough to see that even though Kate was still on the phone, she was watching him carefully. The look she gave him was cold enough to make him shiver. He turned back to Earl. "What do I have to do?"

"Listen to you!" Earl chuckled. "You sound just like I did a couple months ago."

He did. Alex squeezed his eyes shut and hoped when he opened them again, he'd find out it was all a bad dream. No such luck. When he opened his eyes again, he found Earl grinning from ear to ear. "What you're telling me . . ." Alex danced around the subject. There was something too incredibly unbelievable about coming right out and saying it. "What you're saying is that I should take romance lessons? Me?"

"You got it, son." Earl's grin got wider. "You're good at givin' instructions. Now it's time for you to start listenin' to some of your own advice."

"Romance lessons?" Alex groaned. He prayed the paparazzi would never find out about this. He prayed he'd never be subjected to headlines that said things like *Romero on the Rocks* or *Romeo Requires Remedial Romance*. He glanced at Earl. "From you?"

"Hell, yes!" Earl laughed. "If I do say so myself, I've turned into a regular Don Juan, at least where Marge is concerned. Sure am keepin' her happy." He winked and elbowed Alex in the ribs. "Don't see why it can't work the same for you."

Alex saw about a hundred reasons, but he didn't bother to point them out.

"You gotta woo the girl, like you did when you first met her. You did woo her when you first met her, didn't you?" Of course, Earl assumed he had. He waved away the question without expecting an answer. "The first thing you're going to need to do is ask her out on a date."

"That won't work." Alex shook his head. His hair fell over his forehead and he pushed it back with one hand. "What good would a date do? She won't let me out of her sight the way it is."

"Jealous. I know the type." Earl nodded sagely. "But that ain't what we're talking about here. We ain't talkin' about watchin' TV together, or her sittin' there like a regular Doberman watchin' you while you work outside. We're talkin' about a date, boy."

The implications of all Earl meant hit Alex. He couldn't believe he'd been soft-headed enough to almost buy into the concept. "Oh, no!" He took a step away from Earl, distancing himself from the whole idea. "The last time you talked to me like this, I ended up eating pork and sauerkraut." Just the thought sent a wave of pure terror right through him. "No." He tried for the same decisive tone he used from the head of the board table. "I'm not doing that again."

"I ain't askin' you to do that again." All this debate was apparently more than Earl could take, at least without quenching his thirst. He yelled for Marge and when she came to the door across the street, he asked her to bring him a beer. "And them two shirts of Milly and Lester's," he added.

Marge obliged and within a couple minutes, both Earl and Alex had beers in their hands. When Marge saw Kate on the phone, she didn't stay. She waved and headed back home. Earl had the top popped off his beer before Marge had the front door closed behind her. The two sky blue shirts Marge had brought with her were looped over his arm. Alex didn't bother to ask what that was all about. He was pretty sure he didn't want to know.

"Now, as I was sayin' . . ." Earl took a long drink and urged Alex to do the same. He hesitated, remembering the bitter taste of Earl's favorite beer and the metallic *ting* of the aluminum can against his lips, then decided he might as well. Earl waited for Alex to take the first, long sip before he started in on him again.

"We ain't talkin' about pork dinner and we ain't talkin' about bingo. Hell, I don't like bingo, neither. It's a sissified girls' game. I'm talkin' about a man's pastime now."

Something like hope bubbled through Alex along with the swallow of cheap beer. "Polo?"

Earl snickered. "I said a man's game, not somethin' those spoiled rich boys do on the weekend. Besides, polo ain't romantic and don't forget, romance is what we're after here. You want to take her someplace with a little atmosphere. Someplace where you can sit together and do a little cuddlin'. You'll have dinner, a couple drinks. You'll have a whole lot of fun so's by the end of the evening, she'll be in a real good mood. That ought to thaw her out a bit. What you've got to remember is that the whole time, you've got to act like the most romantic guy in the world."

Alex knew better than to open his mouth. He knew better than to ask a question he really didn't want to hear the answer to. But there was something so macabre about the situation, he couldn't help himself. "And that pastime would be . . . ?"

Earl's eyebrows slid up. His eyes lit. He set his beer can down on the sidewalk and like a conjurer waving a magic silk handkerchief, he held up the shirts.

Alex took in the picture in an instant. He looked at the two matching shirts, light blue with a row of dark blue buttons marching up the front, and dark blue piping around the collars and sleeves. He looked at the little names embroidered over the hearts. One said "Milly" and the other "Lester." When Earl flipped the shirts over for him to see the backs, he gaped in horror at the words. "Stosh's Bowl-O-Matic Lanes."

"Oh, no!" By now, Alex knew better than to let the element of surprise rob him of his voice. He'd equivocated before, and equivocating had gotten him nowhere but Bingo Hell. This time, he was all set to stand his ground. "Not a chance."

Earl was not so easily put off. He flipped the shirts around the other way, as if showing them off in all their polyester splendor might actually get Alex to change his mind. "Come on, Stan. Get real! Here's a chance to show Missy what you're made of. What woman could resist? You can flex your muscles in front of the little lady, do some showin' off, have a few laughs. By the time you get home . . ." As if the temperature had just shot up a dozen degrees, Earl waved a hand in front of his face. "She'll be ready for anything!"

Alex honestly couldn't remember the last time he'd been wrong about anything. An unerring sense of what to do and when to do it had gone a long way toward making him a success. So did survival instincts that were as sharp as a well-honed knife. As much as he hated to admit it, though, he knew he'd been off base with Kate from day one. If not, he wouldn't be sleeping alone every night. And she wouldn't be Miss Ice Queen.

Could there actually be something to Earl's theory?

"No." Alex shook his head, driving out the thought before it had a chance to lodge itself further. "There's no way bowling is romantic," he told Earl and himself.

"Sure as hell is." Earl pointed at the shirts. "Where do you think Milly and Lester are that they can't bowl with the league tonight? Met at bowling just two months ago, her an old-maid teacher and him a lifelong bachelor. Right from the start, they couldn't keep their hands off each other. They're down in the Bahamas even as we speak, and I guarantee you, they ain't bowling!"

"Bowling?" Alex looked at the shirts. He had to admit, Kate would look mighty fine in sky blue. It would bring out the color in her eyes. And those little buttons . . .

Alex let his mind wander. He pictured himself undoing each of those buttons, one by one. He'd start at the top, and as each button slid from its hole, he'd kiss the bit of Kate's skin that was exposed. Then when all the buttons were undone . . .

Swallowing hard, Alex glanced at Kate. She was off the phone and her eyes looked anything but sky blue. They were as hard and icy as diamonds. What was it Earl had called her, a Doberman?

Dobermans were more cuddly than Kate.

"Couldn't hurt." Earl leaned nearer. "Especially if you follow my lead. Take your cues from me. Do what I do. A few pointers and in no time, you'll be a regular Romeo." Earl gave him a little nudge in the direction of the front porch. "Now go get her. And don't forget, this is a date."

Before he could talk himself out of the whole absurd notion, Alex took another swallow of beer and traded Earl his half-full beer can for the bowling shirts. He headed over to where Kate was sitting.

"That was Mark on the phone."

It had been so long since she'd spoken an entire sentence to him, the sound of Kate's voice brought Alex up short. He paused at the bottom of the steps and looked up at her. This close, she didn't look any friendlier than she had since the night of the wrestling match, but he noticed there was something more than just anger in her eyes. She looked as if she was holding tight to some emotion; when she spoke, her voice was carefully controlled, as if she refused to allow her feelings—or anything else—to get in the way of her professional duties.

"You'll be happy to know the trial is scheduled for next month." She folded her hands on her knees and Alex wondered if she was as relieved by the news as he was. One more month! One more month before he could get back to the life Kate and her cohorts had taken from him. One more month, and he'd celebrate with champagne and caviar. One more month and he'd do ten extra laps in the pool every morning, just to make up for all the days he'd spent doing nothing at all. One more month . . .

A smile cracked Alex's expression. He was tempted to

punch one fist into the air. He stopped himself just in time.

One more month?

He glanced around. The flowers he'd planted weren't nearly as lush as those that edged Marge's neatly trimmed front lawn. But they were growing. And there was plenty more of the growing season left, even here in Cleveland where he heard the frost came early and annuals didn't last much past the middle of October. If he was back in New York, he wouldn't see if the beds filled in. He wouldn't see if the potted plants he'd positioned in each of the busted-out windows of the Chevy chassis would ever bloom the way he'd pictured they could.

One more month?

Alex glanced down at the bowling shirts he carried, then up at Kate. One more month and he'd never get another chance to make up to Kate for all he'd put her through. She deserved something for the aggravation, the bug-out to Kmart, the disappearance at the wrestling match. He couldn't promise her any fun. Hell, how could anybody have fun bowling? But romance . . .

Romance was something else. Romance was something he could guarantee.

"Look, I was thinking. . . ." Alex pulled in a breath that felt too tight for his lungs. He looked up at the roof, and the shingles that needed replacing. "Earl and Marge are kind of desperate to—"

That was the wrong approach. He tried again.

"Since you probably weren't planning anything but following me around all evening anyway, I thought—"

Another bad foray into the world of dating. Alex pushed a hand through his hair and tried to remember how this was supposed to be done. Back in the days when he had a life, this kind of thing had been second nature to him. He'd never had to search for words. He'd never felt silly and embarrassed. He'd never had to chop his way through an impenetrable forest of words to get around to asking a woman out, because the second he paid even a little attention to a woman, she knew exactly what he wanted and was only too eager to oblige.

Kate was not in an obliging mood. Come to think of it, he was pretty sure she never had been in an obliging mood. Not when it came to him.

The icy sensation filled him again, and Alex shivered. He shook away the thought and reminded himself that he only had one month. If he didn't get in a little practice, he'd never be ready for real life when it was finally his again.

He had to remember that he wasn't Stanley Tomashefski. He was Alex Romero, the Romeo of the tabloids. And women were putty in his hands.

The very thought shot Alex through with a little of the old adrenaline he used to feel when he was on the hunt. He raised his chin, allowed one corner of his mouth to lift into the tiniest of smiles, and took the steps two at a time.

It wasn't at all what Kate expected. He saw her back away, unsure of what he might be up to. That was fine with him. Always good to catch them off guard.

Before she could recover, he dropped down on the top step beside her, took her hand and wound his fingers through hers. He turned up his smile a notch.

"Come out with me," he said. "Tonight." When Kate opened her mouth, probably to ask if he'd lost his mind, he pressed one finger to her lips. He watched her eyes darken, her breath catch. He noticed the brush of color in her cheeks, and like magic, it all came back to him. He *was* the Romeo of the tabloids, and he hadn't lost his touch.

Alex scooted closer and lowered his voice to a rumble. "Don't say a word," he purred, his breath close enough to ruffle Kate's hair. "Not unless that word is yes."

Kate stared at herself in the mirror above her dresser and reminded herself—again—that Alex was a master charmer. She reminded herself—again—that she was un-charmable. She asked herself—again and again—why, if all that was true, if she knew what he was and if she was supposed to be immune to it, was she standing there dressed in a bowling shirt?

Good question. No answers. At least not any she wanted to seriously consider. She knew if she did, the words *shallow* and *self-centered* would pop into her head. Along with the ever-popular *horny as hell*.

If she wasn't shallow and self-centered, she wouldn't have been swayed by what was obviously a ploy on Alex's part to smooth over her anger. And though she liked to think she hadn't started out as horny as hell, she was willing to admit that's exactly what those couple minutes on the front porch with Alex had reduced her to. Otherwise, she wouldn't have let those chocolatey eyes of his persuade her. She wouldn't have listened to the way his voice vibrated in the air like pure sin. She wouldn't have noticed that the entire time he was holding her hand, he traced lazy circles across her palm with his thumb. She wouldn't have been affected by it. Any of it. And she wouldn't still be quivering like a teenager getting ready for her first date.

Now here she was, dressed in her best blue jeans and somebody named Millie's bowling shirt that was a little too short for her and a little too tight across the bust. Kate tugged the shirt into place and swung her right arm back, just to make sure the buttons wouldn't pop when she went to throw the bowling ball. Confident of that, at least, she grabbed her purse and headed to the door.

Before she got there, she heard Alex knock.

"You ready to leave?" he called. "I saw Earl and Marge getting into their car across the street. They'll be here in a second."

"Yeah." Kate took one last look at herself in the mirror. "As ready as I'll ever be." She opened the door and sucked in a breath of surprise.

Lester, it seemed, was as small a person as Millie. His

shirt wasn't nearly big enough to cover Alex's broad chest. He wore the bowling shirt open over a white T-shirt. The look probably wouldn't pass muster with the bowling league, but something told her Alex wouldn't care. Besides, it wasn't Alex's bold fashion statement that surprised Kate. It wasn't even the tentative sort of half-smile that played its way across his lips. It was the straggly bouquet of flowers he held in one hand.

"These"—he held the flowers out toward her—"are for you."

Kate stared down at the bunch of marigolds and petunias, their colors muted in the dusky light of the hallway: gold that looked as if the shine had been rubbed off it, and red that was too brown, and white as yellowed as antique linen. The flowers had to be from the little plot of rocky ground Alex generously referred to as his garden. It was clear from the first day he'd gone out there that he didn't have a clue what gardening was all about, and the fruits of his labors were living (almost) proof.

In spite of the inordinate amount of time he spent messing with them, the marigolds were stunted and mud-spattered. The petunias were windblown and misshapen. One look at the bouquet, and it was obvious to Kate that the man had been followed around for years by an army of clothing consultants, interior designers, and personal shoppers who made him, his home, and everything he touched look like a million bucks. If he'd been making fashion decisions on his own, he would have been able to arrange the bouquet with a little more panache. As it was, all the fat, round marigolds were on one side and all the trumpet-shaped petunias were on the other.

It was another blatant attempt to smooth over the troubled waters between them, and not a very artistic one. It was a pathetic little bouquet, if Kate did say so herself, and it was one of the sweetest things she'd ever seen.

A knot of emotion suddenly wedged in her throat, and Kate cleared it away with a cough at the same time she cleared her mind by reminding herself Alex was a pro.

"Oh, you're good!" she told him. "You're really good!" She took the flowers from him because she couldn't stand watching him holding them out to her a minute longer. "You think a bowling date and a few flowers are going to make me feel better about what happened last week? Have you lost your mind?"

"No." Alex grinned. "On both counts. Look . . ." He poked his hands into the pockets of his jeans. Kate refused to notice the way his jeans drooped just enough over one hip to make him look delectable and dangerous. She refused to be affected by the little-boy grin or the sparkle in his eyes that fizzed like fireworks in the dim light of the hallway. She refused to remember the way his thumb had traced an invisible pattern over her palm because when she did, it made her palm—and other parts of her—itch for more, and she refused to give that much away to a man who was nothing more than a spoiled brat.

"Look, I know I screwed up at the wrestling match. And I know how pissed you are. You have every right to be. You've been trying your best to keep me safe, and I've been tempting danger since day one." Alex ventured a step or two over her threshold, close enough to skim a finger over the bouquet she had clutched in front of her like some sort of shield. He plucked a single petal from one of the marigolds and, holding it between his thumb and forefinger, he skimmed it over Kate's cheek. His touch was feather-light and the petal was smooth. Its spicy fragrance filled Kate's head, and though she knew it was a bad strategic move, she closed her eyes.

"We've only got another month together." Alex's voice resonated through her like the racy fragrance and his tingling touch. "And I promise . . ." He leaned nearer and lowered his voice and, like it or not, Kate had to open her eyes. She had to see what he was up to. She found him just a hairsbreadth away. He wasn't smiling now. He was perfectly serious. It was a side of him she'd never seen, or maybe just a side of him she'd never noticed.

"I can't promise I'll be perfect," Alex told her. "But I can promise I won't leave your sight again. I can't promise it will be the best month of your life, but I can promise I won't annoy you or cause you to worry that I'm gambling with my life. I can't promise I'll make you happy, Kate, but I can try. I owe you. For all you've done."

For a spoiled brat, he sure knew how to apologize.

Kate hadn't even realized she'd been holding her breath until she discovered there was no air left in her lungs. She gasped and pulled in a sharp breath, instinctively taking a step back, putting some distance between Alex and all the sensations he caused to erupt inside her.

Apparently Alex didn't look on her retreat as an insult to his Romeo skills. He gave her a smile that packed enough wattage to light up the Big Apple on New Year's Eve. "You ready to go bowling?" he asked. He offered her his arm and Kate accepted it.

Even though something told her that by doing so, she was accepting a whole lot more.

16

The way Kate had it figured, she should have been able to make some sort of sense out of what was going on. She was an experienced investigator, and though she couldn't remember one at the moment, she knew she'd come up against more baffling situations than this. She should have been able to figure out the pattern of the evening: why when Earl opened a door for Marge, Alex opened a door for her. She should have been able to clear up the puzzle of why when Earl jumped up to get Marge a second beer and a bag of her favorite cheese puffs, Alex did the same thing, even though Kate hadn't finished her first beer and she didn't like cheese puffs. She knew—somewhere deep inside her where her brain was still working and her nerves weren't in a jumble and her imagination wasn't speeding over possibilities, probabilities, and incredibilities—she knew she should have been able to unscramble the code, to unriddle the riddle.

But she couldn't.

Because across one of the red Formica tables that gave Stosh's Bowl-O-Matic Lounge (located inside Stosh's Bowl-O-Matic Lanes) its unique ambiance, Earl looped one arm around Marge's shoulders and pulled her just a little closer. And Kate wondered if Alex was about to do the same to her. And that meant she was too busy tingling with anticipation to try to figure out what the hell was going on.

Just as she expected, just as she hoped, and just as she feared, Alex didn't miss a beat. From the corner of her eye, she saw him stretch one arm across the back of the red not-even-good-enough-to-qualify-as-fake leather booth; a second later, he slipped it around her shoulders and tugged her just a little closer.

Kate's heart stopped. She knew it was a physical impossibility, but she swore it was true. Her heart stopped, then started again with such a thud, she wondered if everyone in Stosh's Bowl-O-Matic could hear it above the thunk of falling pins and the thunder of bowling balls making their way down the polished wooden lanes. Alex's arm settled around her shoulders. The sprinkling of dark hair along his forearm tickled her neck. His palm cupped her shoulder. His fingers drubbed a playful *rat-a-tat* against her arm.

And in that one moment, she knew there was no use trying to make sense of anything. Because she knew she couldn't, and every one of her nerve endings—all those little fellas standing at attention and jumping up and down and screaming their surrender—sent a clear message. She didn't really care what Alex was up to or why, as long as he didn't stop.

"So that's the story." Earl ended whatever it was he'd been talking about with a laugh, and because Marge and Alex laughed, too, Kate followed right along. She didn't have any idea what they were laughing about. She hadn't been listening.

Marge leaned over the table and looked at Kate eagerly. "Now it's your turn," she said. "Tell us how you two met."

It took a couple of seconds for Kate's brain to kick-start. When it finally did, she gave Alex a look that told him she had everything under control. The same someone back in

New York who thought up their identities and their backgrounds had anticipated that someday, somebody might ask this very question. That same someone had come up with an answer, one Kate had down pat before she ever left Manhattan.

"We met at work." She smiled at Marge and Earl, and when she saw them still staring, her smile faded. "At work," she said again, certain they must not have heard. If they had, they wouldn't be waiting for more. "We worked together. At the factory."

"I think Marge and Earl have figured that part out." Alex gave her shoulder a squeeze. "I think what they're looking for is the real story."

"The real story." Kate ripped open her bag of cheese puffs, hoping to buy enough time to come up with a real story. "There really isn't much to it," she said. She scooped up a handful of puffs and popped them in her mouth and stalled a little more while she chewed. "Stan and I just . . . well, we just met."

"That's my girl. Too shy to admit the truth!" Alex laughed and, as he leaned forward just a little, he pulled Kate along with him, until she was caught in the crook of his arm. He settled himself more comfortably in the corner of the booth, turning so that if Kate had had the slightest inclination, she could have easily slid onto his lap.

The thought sent a sizzle of awareness through her, and for a second, she was tempted to call his bluff. Not that Earl or Marge would have cared. For all they knew, Missy and Stan were a young, newly married couple, and those were the kinds of small, loving things young, newly married couples did when they were out together. But calling Alex's bluff would mean calling her own, too, and Kate wasn't ready for that. She wasn't about to admit that sitting so close to Alex gave her not only the kinds of impure thoughts Sister Mary Helene had always warned them against, but a couple ol' Sister Helene had probably never even imagined. That was the last thing she wanted to think about in the middle of Stosh's Bowl-O-Matic.

Kate was stuck. There was nothing she could do but sit there with Alex's arm around her, and Alex's thigh pressed against hers, and Alex's mouth so close that when he turned to look at her, his breath brushed her cheek. That might have been a problem if she didn't decide she liked it—a lot. She might as well make the most of it.

With a sigh, she leaned her head back against Alex's shoulder. He smelled like Old Spice. The scent combined with the heat of his skin and the distinctive aromas of Stosh's Bowl-O-Matic: the hot dogs slowly revolving in the glass heating case on the counter across the aisle, the beer in clear plastic cups on the table, the rented bowling shoes. It made Kate's head whirl, until she was as ready as Marge and Earl apparently were to buy into whatever fantasy Alex had decided to spin.

"I worked on the floor of the factory," Alex said, and in spite of the fact that she was as ready as Earl and Marge to listen, Kate wondered if Alex had ever been on a factory floor. She suspected if he had, it was in a golf cart driven by some gopher who was eager to please the boss. "And Missy worked in the office. I'll tell you what, from the very first time I saw her . . ." He laughed, and Kate tilted her head back to get a look at him. She was just in time to see him shake his head, as if he was trying to get his memories in some kind of order. He didn't look at her; he looked over Earl and Marge's heads, past the bar and the wall-mounted TV broadcasting the Indians game, over to where their bowling team was just getting ready to start playing again now that break was almost over. His expression was as dreamy as his voice.

"The very first time I saw her, I thought I must have been hallucinating or something. She's such a pretty thing, but there she was, hiding inside one of those suits. You know, the sort with the long skirts and the jacket that hides everything a beautiful woman should never hide.

And one of those shirts," he added. "The kind with the button-down collars. She was all dressed up that day because she was doing her job, trying to talk somebody into something, and that somebody didn't want to be talked into it, because he was hardheaded and stupid and just plain so sure of himself, he didn't think he needed anybody's help to do anything. And she did her job, and she did it well."

Alex pulled himself back from whatever place his memories had taken him. He smiled down into Kate's eyes and she felt her heartbeat falter in response. "She saved the guy's life, and he never even bothered to tell her how much he appreciated it."

"Saved his life?" The sound of Marge's voice broke the spell that had somehow made Kate forget they weren't alone.

As if he'd just realized it, too, Alex laughed. "Saved his life. Figuratively speaking, of course," he added quickly for Marge and Earl's benefit. "Only, well, I worked the floor, remember." Alex shrugged, and when he did, his arm rubbed Kate's back. She ignored the tremor that vibrated along her spine and grabbed another cheese puff. "I knew even if I got up the nerve to talk to her, it would never work. I knew what she'd say if I asked her out. She'd tell me we were from two different worlds, and she'd be right."

Kate might have been able to pretend she hadn't caught on to the thread of truth in the first part of his story. She couldn't pretend this time. She knew exactly what he was talking about. She swallowed hard and nearly choked, and washed down the cheese puffs with a drink of beer. Even after all that, when she turned, she found Alex watching her carefully.

There was an unmistakable message in his eyes and in the tiny smile that tickled the left corner of his mouth and made it look as if the crescent-shaped scar there was winking at her. The only question was, what was that message?

Apparently Alex wasn't bothered by such questions. He went right on with his story. "I didn't let that stop me," he told Earl and Marge. "I didn't care what Missy might say. Every day, I made some excuse to go to the office for something and pretty soon, my supervisor caught on. So he played along. He sent me to the office on little errands. You know, dropping off the time sheets, or getting the mail. And every time I went in, I'd just stare at Missy." He crooked a finger under Kate's chin and turned her face to his, and even though she knew the story and the loving looks that went along with it were a lot of hooey, she felt her heartbeat speed up and her insides heat up. It was all made up, she reminded herself. It was all ridiculous. It was all part of an elaborate lie to fool the two people across the table into believing something that was so far out of the realm of possibilities, it wasn't even funny.

"And once . . ." Alex pulled in a long breath and let it out again on the end of a sigh that brushed Kate's lips. "Once, I noticed the way the sun stroked down through these windows in the office that were high up on the wall. And when it did, Missy's hair looked like honey and her lips looked like roses and her eyes looked as blue as that little bit of sky I could see out the window. And I knew right then and there that I was going to marry her."

Hooey.

The word ricocheted through Kate's head.

Hooey, hooey, hooey.

Hooey that sounded so right. And felt so good. Hooey that was turning her insides to mush and her outsides into one gigantic radio receiver that was getting Alex's message loud and clear and turning it into electronic impulses that jangled along every inch of her skin.

"That is so romantic!" Marge couldn't have been nearly as excited as Kate. At least not the same kind of excitement. Or for the same reasons. But she wiggled in her seat, impatient and anxious to hear more. "So you asked her to marry you? Right then and there?"

"Heck, no!" Alex laughed. "I never even said a word to her. It was a couple of weeks later that I finally got up enough nerve to ask her out on a date."

"And?" Marge leaned forward.

"And when I got there, I found out she quit. She didn't work there anymore."

Like balloons that had their air slowly released, both Earl and Marge deflated right before Kate's eyes. She couldn't blame them. Wherever Alex was getting this story from, it was a good one. She couldn't wait to find out how he'd get Missy and Stan together in the end.

Earl took a long gulp of beer; apparently the suspense was too much even for him. "So then what did you do?" he asked.

"Yeah." Kate couldn't help herself. The whole thing was amazing. She gave Alex a look that told him that now that he'd built up the story, he'd better have a rousing conclusion. "Then what did you do?"

He poked her arm playfully. "You know what I did. I asked for your address. And you know they wouldn't give it to me. Said it was confidential. You know, they couldn't share it because it was part of an employee's file."

"That's so sad!" Marge sniffed and popped another cheese puff into her mouth. "It's a good thing I know there's a happy ending to this story, or I couldn't stand it. How did you find Missy after that?"

"I asked around. Turns out she kept to herself a lot. No one knew much about her. But then I remembered that one day after work, I saw her get on the bus that stopped right in front of the factory. So I rode the bus."

"You did?" Kate and Marge asked the question at the same time.

"Sure, I did." Alex smiled. "I rode that bus every day for two weeks. I didn't even know what I was looking for, but I looked out the windows and one day, well . . . there she was, walking up to her apartment building."

"And you—"

"Jumped off the bus." Alex finished the sentence for

Marge. "Ran up the walk. Told her she was the prettiest girl I'd ever seen. I was all set to ask her to marry me right then and there, but . . . well, I waited until our first date."

"He asked you to marry him on your first date?" Marge pressed a hand to her heart and turned to Kate. "That is so romantic! And you said yes?"

"How could I resist?" Kate tried for a laugh that never quite made it. It got smothered under the sudden knot of emotion in her throat. Beginning to end, the story was a lot of bull. Kate reminded herself that she knew that, and told herself that she'd better not forget it. But there was a certain thread of tenderness, a certain element of *what if* in it that reminded her that their lives could have been a lot different—if Alex wasn't Alex, and she wasn't who she was.

She'd never thought about it before. The possibilities. The potential. She'd never admitted to herself that though she was doing her job—and doing it damned well in spite of the fact that Alex was uncooperative—she was also doing something else. She was keeping Alex alive because she had to, sure. She was keeping him alive because next month in New York, he'd blow the whistle on some powerful people who needed to be shut down before they could do any more damage. But there was more to it than just that—more to worrying about him, and going after him when he was missing. If Alex was killed, it would hurt her case, but it would also hurt her, way down deep inside. If Alex wasn't a part of her life anymore, she'd miss him.

A month from then, when he wasn't a part of her life anymore, she would miss him.

The thought caught Kate off guard, and she sat up and blinked away her surprise, moving away from Alex because she was afraid if she didn't, he'd see the truth there on her face. No illusions or delusions. She knew there was no use wasting the truth on a cause that was built on hooey and impossible dreams.

"Hey, time for us to get started again!" Earl popped out of his seat. "We've got three more games to bowl, so don't you worry, Stan." He leaned across the table and gave Alex a thump on the shoulder. "You'll do better this time, buddy."

Kate doubted that, and from the expression on Alex's face that hovered somewhere between abject surrender and utter pain when he looked over at the lanes, she knew he did, too. She had to give him credit; though his bowling skills were nonexistent, at least he was out there trying, and at least the rest of the team didn't resent his futile attempts at throwing anything but a gutter ball. At least not too much.

"Ready?" Kate slid out of the booth and got ready to follow Earl and Marge, who were already on their way over to lane number seven, where the rest of the team waited. Before she could stand up, Alex grabbed her hand and tugged her back down.

"What did you think about my story?" he asked.

"Improbable." Kate dismissed the whole thing with a lift of one shoulder and a roll of her eyes. "Unlikely. Too far-fetched to even begin to believe."

"Which means you don't think—"

"That you've ever been on a bus in your life? Not likely, buster." Kate slid all the way out of the booth, unwinding her fingers from Alex's as she did. She hoped to make a clean break and get over to lane number seven before he could catch up, but if there was one thing she should have learned about Alex, it was that he was persistent. In an instant, he was right behind her. He spun her around and cinched both hands around her waist.

The least he could have done was fight with her. About something. About anything. The least he could have done is ask why she was running away, so she could get all defensive and they could trade insults and they could finish bowling and go home with nothing in the air between them but some of the good old-fashioned resentment that had colored their relationship from the first day they met. But the second Alex tugged her closer, Kate knew that fighting was the last thing on his mind. He gave her a smile that dissolved in searing heat.

"So I never did tell you how much I appreciate all you've done for me."

"It's my job, remember?" Kate ran her tongue over her lips. In spite of the beer, her mouth was suddenly dry.

"You do your job well." Alex's laugh rumbled through his chest and vibrated in Kate's bones. "And if there's one thing I've learned from running a company, it's that people should always be thanked for doing their jobs well."

Something told Kate if he was talking about putting in a good word for her in Washington, or offering a big, fat bonus in her next paycheck, she'd lose it right then and there. "What did you have in mind?"

"This late-breaking news just in."

Leave it to the real world to interrupt.

Alex must have heard the voice just as Kate did. He lifted his head and backed away, glancing over his shoulder toward the TV mounted over the bar.

Kate looked that way, too, just in time to see a good-looking guy in a pin-striped suit and wire-rimmed glasses fade away to a live shot of an airport terminal.

"We're here in Los Angeles," a woman's voice reported, "just as Ruben Martinez, author, poet, and human rights activist, is disembarking from the plane that has brought him to freedom."

"Hey, did you hear that?" The news was so amazing, Kate couldn't believe it. As hard as she tried, she'd never made it past the third page of the second chapter of *Strange Freedoms*, but that didn't make her relief any less real. No one deserved the railroading Martinez had gotten at his trial. And everyone deserved to be free. She grabbed Alex's sleeve with both hands and gave him a little shake. "Did you hear that?" she asked Alex. "Martinez is free." She watched Martinez walk down the airplane steps and toward the cameras.

He looked thinner than he did in the picture on the back of Kate's book jacket, thinner and haggard and just about as happy as anyone Kate had ever seen. He walked up to a bank of microphones, said a few words in Spanish, and immediately got hustled away by a troop of guys in suits and sunglasses.

"Wow!" Kate breathed the word in awe. It was nice to know there were still happy endings out there in the world—at least sometimes. And it wasn't until the live shot was over, and they were back to the good-looking guy in the pin-striped suit, that she realized Alex hadn't said anything at all. She glanced his way and found him grinning from ear to ear, and she realized he didn't have to say a thing. Something told her he was thinking about happy endings, too.

"Incredible, yes?" She smiled up at Alex.

He didn't answer. Instead, he pulled her into his arms and planted the kind of kiss on her lips that Kate had always imagined lovers saved for each other on New Year's Eve. It had just as much sparkle. Just as much pizzazz. It was a celebration, and an indulgence, and if this was what partying with Alex was like, she felt as if she should be flinging back her head and screaming, "Let the party begin!"

Alex let go of her as suddenly as he'd grabbed her, and Kate found herself fighting for breath.

"Just a small token of my appreciation." Alex's face was lit with a grin that carried out the party theme to perfection.

"All right, you lovebirds!"

This time, it was Marge who interrupted them. They turned to see her and the rest of the team waiting for them at lane seven.

"No time for messing around," Marge called. "Save it for when you get home. Now it's time to get down to some serious bowling!"

"Is that what *you* feel like getting down to?" Alex threw back his head and laughed. "Bowling?"

"Bowling?" Kate laughed, too. She felt so good, it was the only thing she could do. "We're supposed to be bowling?"

"Afraid so."

When Alex slung an arm over Kate's shoulders and steered her toward the rest of the team, she gave him a sidelong look. "You're in an awfully good mood for a guy who's the absolute worst bowler I've ever seen in my life."

"Think so?"

"I know so. Face it, Romeo, as a bowler, you stink."

"Yes, I do." A light kindled in Alex's eyes. "But you know, suddenly I don't care much about bowling."

"You don't?"

"Nope." When they got to their lane, Alex escorted Kate to one of the high-backed hard booths where she could sit and wait her turn. He went over and found the bowling ball he'd chosen, the one stamped with a Romero Industries logo. He weighed it carefully in his hands. Right before he moved into position to throw what would surely be his umpteenth gutter ball of the night, he glanced back at Kate. He stopped and turned around, and even when the other team members grumbled in good-natured protest, he headed right for Kate.

With a devilish grin and a smile that was just as wicked, he leaned over and whispered in her ear. "I don't care about bowling," he said, "because bowling will definitely not be the high point of this night." He stood up and gave her a wink. "Who cares about bowling after what Marge said?"

"Marge?" Kate asked the question of herself. Alex had already turned around and gone back to stand at the head of the lane. He rolled the ball. It faltered, spun, turned, and clunked into the gutter. Their teammates applauded, and Alex turned and gave them all a bow of royal proportions.

Kate started to applaud, too. But then her hands froze in midair at the same time her cheeks flamed. Because she'd just figured out what Alex was talking about. She'd just remembered what Marge said:

Save it for when you get home.

By the time they got home, Alex was the proud owner of a Worst Bowler of the Night trophy that looked particularly suited to the pressed-wood end table where he displayed it, and Kate felt as if she were plugged into a two-twenty line. Anticipation hummed through her, until she felt as jumpy as a Slinky that had just been given the old heave-ho down a long flight of stairs. That might not have been so bad if jumpy wasn't accompanied by a tingling way down deep inside that got more heated every time Alex looked her way.

And he'd spent a lot of the evening looking her way.

Her hands poised above the numbers on the lighted panel of the security system, Kate let the thought come and go, and enjoyed the burn of desire that came along with it. All night, Alex had been charming and funny and as attentive as any date could ever be. All night, he'd upped the ante on the message he'd first sent her way when he came up with that fantastic and sweetly romantic story of how Missy and Stan met. He'd done it subtly, with that reference to Marge's comment, and a look now and then meant only for Kate. He'd done it not-so-subtly with the outrageous kiss they'd shared right there in front of God and everybody at the bar. He'd kept up the barrage on the way home when he trailed a hand over her thigh as they sat in the backseat of Marge and Earl's car.

Kate had stopped wondering why. She'd decided she didn't give a damn. She knew a gift horse when she looked one in the mouth, and this one was calling her name. She decided to enjoy it, at least for as long as it lasted.

Thankfully Earl and Marge had headed right home after they'd dropped Kate and Alex off, and hadn't expected to come in for a beer and a rehash of the night's less than stellar bowling results. Now that she was finally alone with Alex, Kate's hands shook as she punched in the numbers on the security panel. She closed the door of the closet where the panel was hidden, and turned to find Alex standing right behind her.

"So what do you think?"

"Think? About what?" Kate hated to sound coy, or worse yet, like some airhead teenager who didn't have a clue what a guy was after. But she didn't want to jump to conclusions, either. After all, Alex was a pro. Especially when it came to women. For all she knew, the way he'd acted at the bowling alley was nothing more than second nature kicking in. For all she knew, it didn't mean a thing.

Only she knew it did. She could tell by the way his eyes sparked when he looked at her. By the way he wound a finger around a strand of her hair and pulled her imperceptibly closer. "You need a written invitation?"

"No." Kate shook her head, and Alex grazed his thumb over her cheek while he tunneled his other fingers through her hair. "Not a written invitation. Just a demonstration. I'm a cop, you know. We don't like to deal in shades of gray. We like everything in black and white."

"Fair enough." Alex moved closer, but he didn't kiss her, and Kate didn't understand why. It was what she was waiting for, what she'd been waiting for since that amazing moment in the bar when he'd grabbed her and kissed her like there was no tomorrow. She tipped her head back, just to make things a little easier for him, and found him eyeing the row of dark blue buttons along the front of her bowling shirt.

"Kisses be damned!" Kate mumbled the words and it was just as well Alex didn't hear, or at least pretended he didn't. It was a tough concept to explain. What wasn't so tough was knowing exactly what to do.

They were standing on the landing at the bottom of the stairs, and there wasn't much room to maneuver. Still, Kate managed to take a small step back, far enough away so that Alex could watch her every move. They left a single lamp lit in the living room and its light seeped across the green shag carpet, brushing the room and everything in it with streaks of light and shadow.

Kate undid the top button on her shirt and watched Alex's eyes darken in appreciation. She slid the second button from its hole and saw him skim his tongue over his lips. After that, she didn't bother counting the buttons. She undid the rest of them and shrugged out of the ugly bowling shirt.

"Are we still talking about the same thing?" she asked.

"Oh, yeah." Alex sucked in a long, unsteady breath and let it out again. With one finger, her traced the lacy edge of her bra across her breasts and up to her shoulder. This time, it was Kate's turn to suck in a ragged breath. She wasn't sure why she bothered. She couldn't catch her breath. She couldn't stop her heart from beating a wild rhythm. She closed her eyes, drinking in the electrical sensation that tingled over her skin everywhere Alex touched her. When he dipped a finger inside her bra to massage her swollen nipple, her knees went weak.

"We've done this before." Alex caught her gaze and held it, his eyes hot chocolate. "Last time, this is the part where you made me stop."

"I didn't. . . ." A tremor of pure pleasure rippled up Kate's spine and she braced herself against it and tried again. "I didn't want you to stop. Only I knew you had to."

"And tonight?"

It was her last chance to pull herself from the edge, her last shot at keeping herself from tumbling over into the vast who-knows-what that lay like the shadows all around them.

"Tonight isn't like that other night, is it?" When Alex moved his hand to her other breast, Kate swayed and leaned into the touch. "Tonight is like . . ." She arched her back and rested against the wall, allowing him to cup her breast in his hand, and her words were punctuated by her rough breaths. "Tonight you're like someone else. Someone warm and funny and considerate and—" Kate couldn't stifle the groan that rose from her throat. She would have liked nothing better than to go on feeling without rationalizing, to go on enjoying the remarkable sensations that tingled over her skin and made her blood feel as if it had been shot through with carbonation. But she knew before she could do that, she had to let Alex know what she was thinking.

She stood and skimmed her hands up Alex's chest and to his shoulders. "I think this is the real you, Alex," she told him. "And I like the real you. I'd like to go to bed with the real you."

"Thank goodness! We are talking about the same thing." Alex's laughter rumbled in the air between them. Still smiling, he glided his hands across her back and unhooked her bra. He slipped it off her arms and dropped it on the stairs and backed far enough away to allow a smear of light to caress her breasts.

Kate watched him yank off his silly glasses and toss them down on the stairs along with the bra. She watched him watching her, and the heat between her legs shot up a dozen degrees. After he'd looked his fill, she saw him inch closer and dip his head. His hair was soft against her bare skin and when he took one of her nipples into his mouth, she was grateful for the wall behind her. Without it to hold her up, she was sure she would have collapsed right onto the floor. Of course, collapsing onto the floor wouldn't be all that bad. As long as Alex was down there with her.

She thought she might actually tell him about the idea and see if he'd care to take her up on it. She might have done it, too, if she could get a coherent thought formed in her head, or a coherent word out of her mouth. Instead, she tipped her head back and enjoyed the feel of Alex's mouth against her skin. He kissed the soft place between her breasts and the hollow at the base of her throat. He skimmed his tongue up her neck and kissed his way to her ear and when Kate reached for his belt and unfastened it, the kiss turned into a nibble.

"Your bed or mine?" he whispered in her ear.

"Yours is bigger." So were other parts of him. Kate skimmed her hands along the front of Alex's jeans, unzipping them as she did. She knew better than to start slipping them off. She knew if she did, they'd never get up the stairs and into the bedroom. Instead, she skimmed her hand inside and tested the length of him, and the width of him, and the hardness of his erection against her palm.

And then she knew for sure that they'd better get upstairs. Fast.

In one fluid movement, Kate grabbed her bowling shirt from where it had fluttered to the floor and raced up the stairs. Alex was right behind her, and when they got to the bedroom, he grabbed her by the waist and spun her around. His mouth was on hers before Kate even had a chance to catch her breath.

Kate wasn't really sure what happened after that. Sensation flowed into sensation and touch and taste mingled and overlapped, and she couldn't say if Alex removed her clothes, or if she removed his. She was, however, really sure about what she felt. And what she felt was incredible. Incredible enough to make her forget every word of warning she'd ever given herself. Incredible enough to erase her doubts, and every single one of her worries. Incredible enough to make her smile when she slid her hands across Alex's broad chest and remembered the days she'd stood in line at the grocery store, and drooled over Romeo's abs.

"What?" Alex had been busy trailing a line of soft kisses along her neck. Feeling Kate's smile, he backed away. "What's so funny?"

"Nothing's funny. Really." But Kate couldn't help but smile, and she knew Alex wouldn't be satisfied until she told him what she was smiling about, and she wanted him to be satisfied, so he could get back to what he'd been doing. "I was just thinking . . . you know, about the tabloids and the whole Romeo thing and—"

She didn't expect Alex to take her words so seriously. They hadn't bothered with the lights in the room, and the square of light coming from the window and the streetlight beyond was just enough to show her the shot of anger that streaked across his face. He turned away from her and Kate felt her heartbeat falter. Without the heat of his hands against her skin and the heat of his body next to hers, the room felt suddenly cold.

Just as quickly, Alex turned back to her. He locked his hands around her waist and pulled her against him. "This isn't like that," he said, his voice husky. He loosened his hold on her long enough to cup her chin with one hand and turn her face up to his. "You have to know that, Kate. Here and now. This isn't like that at all." Now that he had her attention, he slipped his hands to her shoulders. He smiled down into her eyes.

"I've never been here before," he whispered. "Not like this. Not with you. I never realized . . ." He pulled in a breath and let it out again, and it ruffled the wisps of hair around Kate's face. "I never realized I could want more from a woman than just her body. But it's true. Can you give me more, Kate? Will you?"

She answered him with a kiss that was meant to be as tender as the feelings that squeezed around her heart, but it didn't take long for the kiss to deepen until it seared her soul and made her ache to have him inside her. Apparently Alex was thinking the same thing. Like a ballroom dancer, her swooped Kate into his arms and dipped her until she was lying on the bed.

And it wasn't until that very moment that the thought of protection ever occurred to her.

"Oh, hell!" Kate sat up before her head had a chance to make a dent in the pillow.

Even in the darkness, she could see the excitement

fade from Alex's face. He sat down on the bed next to her. " 'Oh, hell' as in 'Oh, hell this is fun'? Or 'oh, hell' as in 'Oh, hell, something's wrong'?"

"Oh, hell as in oh, hell, who would have thought to bring condoms along." Kate buried her face in her hands and did a few quick mental calculations. This late at night, Kmart would be closed, but there was a twenty-four-hour drugstore a couple of blocks away, and if they drove fast, they might—

Her thoughts were interrupted when she heard Alex get up and cross the room. She lifted her head just in time to see him grin and pull something out of the top drawer of his dresser. She was never so happy to see a little foil-wrapped package in her life.

Kate sat up. "How did you—" She stopped herself before something she knew she'd regret could come spilling out of her mouth. "Never mind. I don't want to know. And I don't want to wait any longer. Alex—"

She held out her arms to him and he hurried back to the bed. Kate supposed that some wacky research lab somewhere must have done a study on how long it took to get the average condom on the bigger than average guy. Statistics or no statistics, she figured they broke the record.

And probably the bed springs, too.

And the sound barrier.

Because when he finally buried himself inside her, Kate let out a moan of pure pleasure, and a little later, when he brought her into a full-blown, head-over-heels, mind-popping, body-numbing, electrical-charge orgasm and she did the same for him, she knew they must have made enough noise to wake up the neighborhood.

And the best part about it was that she didn't even care.

17

Kate wasn't sure what woke her up, but when she opened her eyes, she realized it must have been close to dawn. It was still dark out, but she heard the hum of traffic out on the freeway and it sounded pretty steady, like the very beginnings of rush hour. She yawned, and she might have stretched if she wasn't lying on her stomach and if Alex didn't have his arm thrown across her shoulders. She didn't want to move too much. She didn't want to wake him.

Or maybe she did.

The second the thought crossed Kate's mind, she smiled. After hours of the most incredible sex ever, she knew Alex must be just as exhausted as she was. Which meant she shouldn't even think about waking him up. Which meant she should keep still and keep quiet and let the poor boy rest. After all, being the world's greatest lover probably took a lot out of a guy. Which meant she should just close her eyes and go back to sleep. Which meant she'd have to wait at least a couple more hours to make love to him again.

Kate yawned and stretched and when Alex hardly moved, she flipped over and gave him a little shake.

When that didn't work, either, she sat up and poked his shoulder.

That's when she saw the time on the clock radio. Or more accurately, when she didn't see the time on the clock radio.

"Shit!" Kate scrambled out of bed. Though it promised to be a warm day, it had cooled off considerably during the night. Out from under the blankets and away from the heat she and Alex generated, the cold air scraped her bare skin. She reached for her jeans and pulled them on and grabbed the first shirt she could find. It turned out to be Lester's bowling shirt; buttoning it, she headed for the door.

"What's wrong?" His eyes still closed, his voice husky from sleep and the last whispers of passion, Alex groped under the blankets, searching for Kate. When he realized she wasn't there, he flipped from his stomach to his back and propped himself up on his elbows. "Where are you going?"

He looked delectable with his hair flopped over his forehead and his eyes half focused and his bare chest gleaming in the dim light. Delectable enough to make Kate think about not going anywhere. About hopping right back into bed, right on top of Alex. That would wake him up for sure.

But then she looked at the clock radio again and she knew that any bone-hopping she had in mind would have to wait. "Downstairs." Kate wasn't sure why she bothered to keep her voice down. Maybe it had something to do with the cool gray shadows, or the fact that the few hearty birds that lived in the neighborhood weren't even up and chattering yet. "The electricity's off again," she explained. "I'll try the battery backup on the security system."

"I'll make the coffee."

It was a simple enough offer, but the idea that Alex would rather sit downstairs with her than sleep had a curious effect on Kate. It brought a lump of emotion to her throat, and as she watched him slip out of bed and into his black exercise shorts, she realized her eyes were misty. She dashed away the thought—and the tears—and wondered briefly how bad she looked with her hair uncombed. She reached for the doorknob.

Just as she did, three things happened. They couldn't have happened all at once, but they happened so fast, Kate wasn't sure which came first. The door crashed open and a flash blinded her. The sharp crack of automatic weapon fire blasted through the room.

"Alex! Get down!" Instinctively Kate dropped and rolled. She sprang to her feet on the other side of the doorway and assessed the situation as quickly as she could. In the dark, she could see Alex facedown on the floor next to the bed. She couldn't tell if he was hit. She couldn't take the time to find out. And she couldn't give the assassin a second chance, not when they were trapped like fish in a bowl, in an upstairs room with no way out.

No way except the doorway.

Kate gathered her wits and her courage. She told herself to count to five, and made it as far as three before she charged out into the hallway. It was a reckless, stupid maneuver, and just impulsive enough to catch the man who stood outside the door ready to fire again off guard. With a yell she hoped sounded vicious enough to scare the bejesus out of him, she caught the figure dressed all in black with a left hook that snapped back his head and knocked the gun out of his hand. She made a grab for the gun and missed and it slid into the shadows in the corner of the hallway. Before she could decide if she should try for the hit man's gun or make a run for wherever she'd left her purse with her own gun in it, Kate felt a blow to the back of her head. She staggered and recovered, whirled and kicked. She connected. The guy doubled over and growled a curse, and while she still had the advantage, Kate grabbed his left arm and twisted it back.

A garden-variety bad guy would have been incapacitated, or at least slowed down. But even before the killer raised his head and glared at her, and she saw that his eyes were nearly colorless and his skin was just as pale, she knew this was no garden-variety bad guy. The best didn't give up so easily. The gunman brought his right arm around his body and clamped his hand on Kate's shoulder, twisting and throwing her at the same time. She flew across the landing and smashed into the window at the top of the stairs. The glass shattered but the window frame held. Kate's head hit the wooden frame and snapped back. She would have crumpled and gone right out the window if she hadn't made a blind grab for something to hold on to.

That something turned out to be her assailant. Instinctively he stepped back. Before he had a chance to settle himself, Kate braced one foot behind both of his and shoved. Just as she expected, he went down. Just as she hoped, they were near enough to the steps that he couldn't regain his footing. He rolled backward and went over the edge.

Unfortunately he had the presence of mind to grab hold of Kate and take her with him.

The world spun, and for what seemed like a very long time, Kate hovered in midair. After that, everything happened in fast forward. She slammed onto the steps. The carpet was cheap and thin and didn't provide nearly enough protection. As she tumbled down, with her arms and legs tangled with the assassin's, she felt each and every hard wooden edge that lurked beneath the shaggy green carpet. Her spine got poked. Her head got banged. Somehow, in the confusion, the killer managed to get his hands around Kate's throat and she felt his fingers press into her flesh, crushing her windpipe and cutting off her air.

They landed at the bottom of the stairs with Kate flat against the landing, the hit man on top of her. Instinctively she fought against the thread of panic that threatened to give the killer the upper hand. Though it seemed to take a lifetime, she managed to unpin her arms, and she tried to pry his fingers loose. When that didn't work, she kicked her feet and bucked to wiggle out from under him. From somewhere very far away, she heard Alex call her name. She thanked the guardian angels in charge of billionaire playboys that he was apparently alive and well, at the same time she hoped he had the good sense to get out of the house as fast as he could and to stay as far away as he could possibly get.

He didn't. She heard Alex barrel out of the bedroom and head for the steps, and she knew she had to do something and do it fast. An explosion of bright stars burst somewhere behind Kate's eyes and she felt herself flash out of consciousness. Not an option. She forced herself back to reality and groped for anything she could use as a weapon. The only thing she found was the bra she'd discarded on the steps.

Beggars couldn't be choosers. Especially beggars whose windpipes were about to pop. Fumbling through the dark, Kate snapped the strap around the assassin's ear and stretched the bra across his eyes.

It wasn't much of a plan, but then, she didn't have a big enough cup size to make it much of a weapon, either. The important thing was that it caught the guy off guard just as Alex came up behind him and jumped on his back. The killer's hold on her throat loosened, and Kate made her move. She twisted out from under him and rolled off the landing and onto the living room floor. She pulled herself to her knees just in time to see Alex go flying back against the stairs.

It was dark and even after only a couple seconds without enough oxygen, Kate's brain was in a whirl. Still, when she saw the assassin reach into the pocket of his black jacket, she realized she wasn't going to like whatever it was he had hidden there. Before she had a chance to find out for sure, she lunged forward and grabbed the guy around the knees; he toppled over her and off the landing. He came down hard on both knees and she linked her hands and clubbed him on the back of the neck with both fists. It wasn't enough to immobilize the guy, but it bought Kate enough time to look over and see if Alex was all right.

He was just pulling himself up off the stairs, and if looks could kill, they wouldn't have had to worry about the hit man. Alex would have incinerated the guy right on the spot.

But looks were one thing; actions were something else. Especially hotheaded actions. And when Alex made a move toward the killer, Kate knew she had to do whatever it took to keep them apart. She charged forward and threw the front door open; at the same time, she grabbed Alex's arm and swung him that way.

"Get out," she told him. "Now." And he actually might have listened if the killer hadn't grabbed his ankle. Alex kicked the guy away and headed for the door, his hand clutched on Kate's arm. She wasn't about to argue. For once, she was only too happy to let him take the lead and to follow him right outside. She was almost to the door when the hit man grasped her around both legs and pulled her back into the house.

Kate hit the carpet face first. Her head rang. Her ears popped. Blood trickled from her nose.

"Get to a phone," she yelled to Alex, and even in her own ears, her voice sounded like it came from very far away. Not that she allowed herself the luxury of listening. At least not for long. With an effort that made pain shoot through her shoulder and pound through her head, she jumped to her feet, whirled, and brought her fists up.

Only to find herself completely alone.

"Damn." Kate stumbled for the open door. Out on the sidewalk, she looked up and down the street. Though the light wasn't much better than it had been in the house, she was pretty sure neither Alex nor the killer had taken off down the sidewalk. She would have seen them if they had. Telling herself she was operating from experience and knowing it was, instead, nothing but pure instinct and a gut reaction, she headed toward the back of the house.

Across the snaking train track, the mill was pouring steel. The orange glow of the furnace brightened the sky and sent the world into a relief of stark black shadows and fiery spots of undulating light. It took her a few seconds to make out the figures struggling on what there was of a back lawn. She had just broken into a trot when she saw the killer raise his arm. When he brought it down again, the garish yellow light glinted off the blade of a knife.

Kate accelerated into a full-fledged run. She grabbed the guy, and just as she did, Alex made a slick move of his own. As if they'd practiced the maneuver a hundred times, he pushed at the same time Kate pulled. Before he hit the ground, the hit man got off one jab. It was enough to slice into Kate's arm, but she ignored the pain and the blood and went after him.

He coiled and sprang, but he never had a chance to make another rush at her. Just as he was about to, Kate heard a voice that was high and tight with excitement. It was coming from the front yard.

"Missy? Stan? What on earth is going on here?"

A professional hit man couldn't afford to take any chances, and an audience of nosy neighbors was definitely a chance. With a sound that rumbled through the air like a growl, he kicked and slammed his steel-toed boots into Kate's ribs. He whirled toward the rickety fence that separated their scrap of a lawn from the steep hill that led to the railroad tracks. She watched him slide to the bottom, kicking up a shower of gravel and dirt as he went. He hit with a thud and rolled. He was up and running before she had a chance to move.

Kate grasped the fence post and fought to catch her breath. It wasn't the smartest thing to do. With each ragged breath, her throat burned, her ribs ached, and her head pounded. The little stars came back, this time in

Technicolor. They popped through her head in perfect time to the wild thumping of her heart. Her stomach clutched in protest, but she refused to be sick. She didn't have time. With a grunt, she turned and offered Alex a hand up.

"Are you okay?" Kate's voice was little more than a croak, and every word felt like it was edged with fire. "Did you get hit?"

"Hit by a truck." Alex grimaced. "That guy made those hulky wrestlers look like amateurs. What the hell did he hit me with?"

Kate wasn't worried about details. All that mattered was that Alex was all right. That he hadn't been shot. That he hadn't been killed. She did a quick assessment, running her hands over his arms and legs, checking for wounds or broken bones, and when she didn't find any, relief washed over her like warm water and her knees turned to rubber. Before she had a chance to give in to the sensation and collapse on the spot, one of Alex's arms went around her. Holding each other up, they limped toward the front of the house.

Halfway there, they met Marge and Earl.

"What's going on here?"

"What happened?"

"Missy, are you all right?"

"Stan, are you hurt?"

"We're fine." Kate answered before Alex could. As if to prove her point, she pulled away from Alex and stood up as tall as her protesting ribs would allow. Heading back into the house, she waved away her neighbors' concern. "Honest, we're fine. It was just a—"

"Burglar. It was a burglar." Once they were inside, Alex slumped against the wall. "We chased him away."

"But we heard shots!" Marge clung to Earl's arm with both hands. "And Missy dear, you have blood on your face! And your arm—"

"It's nothing. Really." Kate wiped her face against her sleeve, and then realized Lester probably wouldn't appreciate it. She glanced around, looking for her purse, and when she realized she'd been too hot for Alex when they got home to care what she did with it, she turned back to Earl. "Earl, go home and call nine-one-one," she said, each word scraping like barbed wire inside her bruised throat. There was a stack of paper napkins on what served as their dining room table and she reached for it and pressed it to the wound on her arm. "Tell them to send a patrol car. Tell them to watch for . . ." She scrunched her eyes shut and tried to recall as many details as she could. "Tell them a white male, five-nine, five-ten maybe. Hundred and seventy-five pounds. On foot, but that doesn't mean anything—probably has a car parked nearby. Tell them—"

"What's she talking about?" Marge peered into Kate's face and placed one hand on her forehead as if she was checking for a fever.

Earl grabbed Kate's right hand, checking for a pulse. He glanced at Alex over his shoulder. "Is she okay?"

Alex came over, and when Marge pulled a tissue out of the pocket of her purple satin robe, he took it and held it to Kate's forehead, and even before he pulled it away, she knew he was sopping up more blood. "She's fine," he told Earl and Marge. His eyes were shadowed, but it didn't take a genius to see he didn't think Kate looked fine. There was a crease of worry between his eyes, and a muscle jumped at the base of his throat. "Or at least she will be. When you call, Earl, tell them to send an ambulance. We'll get her to the hospital and—"

"Stop it!" Kate shoved Alex's hands away and stalked to the other side of the living room, even though when she did, the room spun and her stomach lurched. She braced herself against the wall. "Stop babying me. I do not need babying. And I really don't need to go to the hospital. I don't have time for that. What I need—" She shot Earl a look. "What I need is a black-and-white. A patrol car." Earl finally got the message. He scrambled out the door and on toward home and satisfied that at least that much was taken care of, Kate glanced around the room. "And I need my cell phone." Kate whirled the other way and saw her purse next to the end table where Alex's trophy was displayed.

Unfortunately Marge anticipated her move, and Marge was a nice lady. A nice lady who was only trying to help. She got to the purse before Kate did and reached inside. Marge's eyes went wide. Her mouth dropped open.

"Missy?" Marge's hand came up holding Kate's gun with two fingers. "Missy, is this yours?"

The last thing they needed right now was Marge in a state of either shock or panic, and Kate could tell that she was headed fast in that direction. She made a careful move toward her. "You can give me the gun, Marge. It's mine. And it's loaded, so you'll want to be careful."

"Loaded?" Marge gulped.

Kate held out her hand. When Marge didn't respond, she gently reached for the gun and took it out of her hands. She made sure the safety was on, tucked the gun into the pocket of her jeans, and breathed a sigh of relief. She motioned Marge to hand over her purse, and when she did, Kate reached inside and pulled out her badge.

"There's no use lying to you any longer," she said. She held up the badge so Marge could see it. "I'm an FBI agent. My name is Kate Ellison."

Marge couldn't have looked more stunned if Kate introduced herself as one of the Roswell aliens. "And this isn't Stan. This is Alex Romero," Kate said, glancing over at Alex. "You've heard of him, right?"

"Alex Romero!" Marge's eyes went as wide as saucers. Her voice rose to nearly the same pitch as the squealing police car siren Kate heard pulsing in the distance. "Alex—!" Marge scrambled over to Alex, grabbed one of his hands in both of hers, and pumped it. "It's such a pleasure to meet you. I'm a fan. A big fan. That's why you always looked so familiar to me!"

In spite of all that had happened to him in the last few

minutes, Alex was, after all, still Alex. Kate watched him throw back his shoulders and give Marge the kind of smile that could melt camera lenses at fifty feet. "You've probably seen me in the newspapers." He tried to sound humble, but for Alex, that was going some. "Maybe in an article about one of my charities or at some party or—"

"No. No. That's not it." Marge motioned him to be quiet while she spent a few seconds thinking really hard. "I know!" She grinned. "That TV show. You know, the one where you ask people to spell words and that nice girl who has all those pretty dresses turns the letters over for you."

Alex's smile melted. "No. No, Marge. You've got it all wrong. That's not me, that's—"

"Wait until I tell the girls at the beauty parlor." Marge clasped her hands to her heart. "They are going to be so impressed. Imagine. A game show host. Right here in our neighborhood."

"But I'm not—"

"You are going to give me your autograph." Marge backed Alex up against the banister. "Burglar or no burglar, you've got to find time to give me your autograph."

If it didn't hurt so much, Kate might have laughed. But then, when she thought about it, none of it was really funny. And it hurt way too much.

A wave of exhaustion hit her and Kate closed her eyes and listened to the frantic sounds of a police car siren as it made its way down the street. It was almost loud enough to block out the two little voices that warred inside her head. One of them tried to talk her out of doing what she knew she had to do. The other one reminded her she had a duty, and she had to follow through on it, no matter what the consequences.

"Damn." Kate fished her cell phone out of her purse and punched in Mark's number. She tried to take a deep breath. The way she figured, she was going to need it. She was going to need a lot of breath and a lot of words to explain to her boss how Joe Bartone had nearly killed Alex tonight. And what she was doing in Alex's bed when it happened.

"What the hell just happened here?"

Kate didn't bother to excuse herself around the couple of forensics guys who were just walking out of Alex's bedroom. She charged right past them as they were pulling out their yellow crime scene tape, and one look told them that if they were smart, they'd make themselves scarce for a few minutes. Fortunately they were both pretty smart. They disappeared downstairs, and Kate stalked into the room and slammed the door shut behind her.

It was the first time in two hours that she'd allowed herself to stop moving, the first time in two hours that she wasn't dealing with Mark on the other end of the phone, or the uniformed officers who'd arrived in each of three patrol cars, or the guys from the crime lab who weren't far behind. It was the first time in two hours that she didn't have to tell and retell her version of all that had happened to the detectives who showed up in an unmarked car, or the four agents from the local FBI office who had set up a sort of mini–command post down in the kitchen. It was the first time in two hours that she'd been able to avoid the cute but determined EMS techs who insisted that she needed to go to the ER.

It was the first time since the attempt on his life that she was alone with Alex, and face-to-face with her own anger. It was an anger that hadn't made sense until just a couple minutes before. Until then, it had been a vague sort of thing, a sense of uneasiness, a slow boil that she'd attributed to adrenaline rush. But now that the excitement was dying down and she had a chance to think about it, her anger was starting to make sense. And she didn't like what that sense was telling her.

Kate dragged in a breath that scraped her throat and burned her lungs. She promised herself she wouldn't get emotional, but it was tough not to, especially when she looked over at the bed. Not that she was sentimental. She wasn't feeling the least bit sappy about the bed where she'd spent the most incredible hours of her life. If that's all there was to the knot that suddenly tied up her stomach like a Boy Scout's latest project, she could have dealt with it. But that wasn't it at all.

The pillow where Alex's head had rested only a couple of hours before was completely blown away. There were puffs of polyester fiberfill in clumps all over the room, and the mattress was painted with a series of little circles, each one marking a spot where a bullet had slammed into it. If Alex had been lying there instead of pulling on his exercise shorts . . .

"Yeah." Alex was standing on the other side of the room near the dresser. Apparently he hadn't spent the last couple hours being badgered. He'd had time to change his clothes, he was dressed in blue jeans and his red polo shirt. He had his hands poked into the pockets of his jeans, and he was looking at the bed, too. He shook his head. "I was just thinking the same thing. That could be my brains splattered all over this room."

Kate shook the thought away and swallowed the lump in her throat. Not an easy task considering it felt as if her throat were made of rusty scouring pads. She dragged her gaze from the bed and reminded herself she wasn't there to trade war stories or pillow talk. She was there to find out the truth.

"Impossible!" She snorted. "Something tells me you don't have any brains."

"What's that supposed to mean?" Alex bent and tied his sneakers, but he didn't look at Kate. It was that more than anything else that told her she was on the right track.

"I want some answers. And I want them now." Kate crossed her arms over her chest and tried not to wince when a stab of pain shot through her ribs. She apparently didn't succeed. Alex was up in an instant. He hurried over to where Kate stood just inside the door and let his gaze flicker over her, from the torn knee of her jeans to her bloodstained bowling shirt and the bandage the paramedics had put on her arm. Anger flashed in his eyes. He smothered it under a sympathetic smile and nudged back the collar of Lester's shirt, and when he took a look at Kate's neck, he flinched. "You look like hell," he said.

Kate didn't have to ask what he was talking about. She'd taken a quick look in the mirror. Her neck was bruised and abraded. There was dried blood crusted under her nose and in her hair. She hadn't had a goddamned moment to brush her goddamned teeth. And she didn't need him to stand there with his hair freshly combed and his shoes neatly tied and tell her she looked like hell.

She also didn't need to be reminded how good it felt when he touched her. Kate sidestepped out of his reach and pretended not to notice the flicker of disappointment that hurried across his face. "We're not here to talk about me," she said. "We're here to talk about you."

"I'm fine." Alex shrugged. He wasn't completely fine. He had a small cut on one cheek that had been cleaned and bandaged by the EMS crew, and it was clear from the way he moved it that his right arm was sore. "I wouldn't be fine if it wasn't for you, though. I'd be . . ." He glanced over at the bed and at the demolished pillow and a shiver snaked its way across his shoulders. "Looks like you did it again. You saved my life."

"Spare me the crap." All right, Kate wasn't being gracious. But she wasn't in the mood to be gracious. She wasn't in the mood for anything but some answers. "I wouldn't have had to save your life—"

She was interrupted by a knock at the door.

Kate yanked the door open and glared at the crime scene guys.

"Sorry, Special Agent Ellison." The older of the two men stepped into the room. "We've got to wrap things up. If you could just—"

She didn't wait to hear any more. She couldn't keep still that long. Without another word, Kate left the room and went into her own bedroom. When Alex followed her, she waited until he was inside and shut the door.

She scraped a hand through her hair. Her head felt as if there were an army of elephants stomping around in there, and she squeezed her temples with two fingers, hoping to ease the pain. When she felt Alex come up behind her and reach to stroke her forehead, she hurried to the other side of the room.

"I wouldn't have had to save your life," she said, "if Joe Bartone didn't know exactly where you were."

If he heard the challenge in her words or saw it in her eyes, he didn't respond. Kate curled her fingers into her palms and wrapped her thumbs across her fists. "Would you care to start explaining?" It wasn't a request. It was an order and even before it was out of her mouth, she knew Alex wasn't going to obey it. If there was one thing she should have learned about Alex over the past months, it was that he didn't like getting ordered around.

His shoulders went stiff and he clenched his jaw. "What are you saying? Are you saying you—"

"I'm saying you know more about this than you've let on. I'm right, yes? Someone knew we were here, Alex, and I sure as hell didn't tell anybody. But you did. You told someone. And that someone turned right around and sent Joe Bartone an engraved invitation with our address on it."

"No." Alex laughed, but it was the kind of laugh that didn't carry much conviction. "No," he said again, and this time, it was clear he was answering some question of his own, not anything Kate had asked.

It was all the proof she needed. "Who did you talk to, Alex? Who knew you were here?"

"Here?" It was a sunny morning but in the tiny, airless bedroom, the light wasn't good. Still, she couldn't fail to miss the look of surprise that crossed his face. Or the instant denial that came fast on its heels. "Impossible!" He slashed the air with one hand. "No. That's impossible. I won't even discuss it, it's so impossible."

"So somebody did know." The ugly truth stared Kate right in the face. This was something she should have known about. Something she should have prevented. She'd lost control—of the situation and of herself—and it had nearly cost Alex his life.

Kate wasn't sure what was worse, the feeling that a knife had just been twisted through her gut or the tears of anger and frustration that sprang to her eyes. Because she refused to cave in to the emotion, she wiped away the tears with the back of her hand. She didn't do anything about the stabbing pain in her gut. She couldn't. And besides, something told her the pain was the only thing that was going to get her through the next few minutes. She waited, until the silence that stretched between them felt as if it would break and shatter into a million dangerous pieces.

Finally Alex nodded. "Norbert." He pushed a hand through his hair. "I talked to Norbert at the wrestling match."

"Shit." Kate turned around and kicked the bottom dresser drawer. It might have been a more effective and less painful demonstration of her anger if she had happened to be wearing shoes. She swore again, this time because her toes hurt. "How the hell did Norbert—"

"Will you listen to me? Just for a second?"

Alex paced to the other side of the room and back again. It didn't take long; her bedroom was considerably smaller than his. "I used the debit card," he said. "I didn't have any choice. That day at Kmart. I bought . . ." He cleared his throat and glanced away. "I bought the condoms."

Kate hadn't thought she could get any angrier. She'd been wrong. She choked on her words, and not because her throat hurt. "Because you knew I'd fall into bed with you?"

"Because I needed to use my debit card."

Might as well shoot down her ego as well as her career. Kate braced herself against the truth and forced herself to focus on the career and not the ego. "So you used the card and the statement went to Norbert."

Alex nodded. "He had this plan. It doesn't matter how it was all arranged. He set it up years ago. Once he got the statement and saw what city I was in, he got in touch with me through the local personal column. We met at the wrestling match."

"And the reason you were so anxious to see Norbert was what?" It was Kate's turn to pace. She refused to get too close to Alex, so she stalked the width of the room. It took her six steps to get to one wall, six steps to get back. She swallowed the taste of anger in her throat, winced against the pain, and got even angrier because it hurt so damned much. "What did you have to do, check your social calendar? Make sure your next hair appointment was scheduled? Shit, Alex, what could possibly be so important that you'd risk your own life for it?"

Alex turned to the nightstand beside Kate's bed. He opened the drawer and pulled out her copy of *Strange Freedoms,* the book she'd barely touched since they'd arrived in Cleveland.

"Ruben Martinez," he said.

Kate leaned forward. "Excuse me. Martinez? And he has what to do with this?"

Alex drew in a breath. "He doesn't have anything to do with this. Not really. But I . . ." He glanced up at the ceiling as if he might find the words he was looking for in the chipped plaster. "I've admired the man for years," he said. "I've admired his courage and his willingness to speak the truth even when the truth was something no one else wanted to hear. I've admired his talent. His astonishing writing talent."

Kate offered her opinion of that subject with a grunt of disbelief, but Alex didn't notice. He went right on.

"When I realized what was happening to Martinez, I knew I had to do something. I mean, here was this man who could have been sipping champagne in Paris or being wined and dined in New York and instead, he was back in his own country, back where they needed him most. And instead of kowtowing to the powers-that-be so they'd leave him alone, he was spitting right in their eyes. He was telling them everything they didn't want to hear. Everything they needed to hear about free speech and human rights and—" He gave a tiny laugh and glanced at Kate out of the corner of his eye.

"I sound like an ad for Amnesty International, don't I? I don't mean to, but, well, corny or not, it's the truth. Everything Martinez has ever done has really touched me. And the fact that he was willing to stand up to his government is what inspired me to come forward when I did. I told myself that if he was brave enough to face down the guys who would probably put him in front of a firing squad, the least I could do was make a phone call to the FBI."

He was obviously hoping the confession would soften Kate's stance. He glanced her way again and when he did, he offered her a smile. When she didn't respond, either to the smile or to the look, Alex cleared his throat and turned toward the window. One hand braced against the frame, he drummed his fingers. "When I realized things were only getting worse for Martinez, I knew I had to do something. Before I left New York, I got in touch with his government. We . . ." He turned back to Kate. "We negotiated. And they agreed to free Martinez in exchange for twenty million dollars in cash." He didn't give her a chance to ask one of the dozens of questions that was clambering through her head.

"They insisted that no one could know about the deal. If word got out, Martinez would be killed, no questions asked. They demanded the money before his sentencing, and they weren't about to take 'But honest, I'm busy bowling' for an answer. The more you tried to stop me, the more I knew I needed to do something. Here I was . . ." Alex threw his arms out, taking in the shabby room with its shabby furnishings. "Here I was, hiding like a scared little sheep, and there Martinez was, putting his life on the line. I knew I couldn't do that, Kate. I knew I had to get in touch with Norbert. He was the only one who had access to the right bank accounts."

"So you laid yourself out on a silver platter. You contacted Norbert, and Norbert gave our old friend Joe Bartone a call. And he was only too happy to pay us a visit. Even cut the electric lines so he could surprise us."

"No." Alex tossed the book down onto the bed. He bunched his hands into fists and held his arms tight at his side. "No. It isn't possible."

"It is possible." Kate stalked to the other side of the room. Though she had promised herself she wouldn't get close enough to touch Alex, she found herself not two feet from him before she even realized where she was headed.

Like metal to a magnet.

She refused to let it happen. Not this time. This time, she had a job to do, and what was left of her career to salvage. "Did you take a good look at that bed in the other room?" she asked him. "That could be you lying there, with a couple dozen bullet holes in you. And probably me, too, right there next to you. Joe Bartone knew exactly where you were, and if there's only one person you told that to, there's only one person who could have given him the information. It had to have been Norbert Fielding."

"But . . ." Alex looked the way Kate probably did when Bartone booted her in the ribs. Like it was hard to take a breath. Like it was hard to figure out if his heart was still beating. Like she must have looked when she realized Alex been setting her up for a tumble in his bed since day one. Great, so they both understood all about betrayal. They finally had something in common.

"We'll pick him up." She spun toward the door. "When we can find Norbert and talk to him, he might be able to lead us to Bartone."

"You're wrong, Kate." Behind her, she heard Alex's voice grate over the words. "Norbert would never—"

"But he did." At the door, Kate spun to face him. Her gaze traveled to the copy of *Strange Freedoms* that lay on her bed. She thought about the few minutes of live coverage they'd seen of Ruben Martinez's release, and the way he looked drawn and thin and so happy to finally reach freedom. And she thought about the kiss Alex had given her and about how it felt like Christmas and Fourth of July all rolled into one.

"That was an incredible thing you did for Martinez," she said, and the words choked her. Before he could notice, she pulled open the door and marched out of the room. "Incredible, but really, really stupid."

18

The investigation went on most of the day, and by the time things had finally quieted down, Alex had taken refuge in Kate's bedroom. It was the only room in the house that wasn't crawling with cops. He had no intention of falling asleep, but he supposed stress did strange things to people. He lay down on Kate's bed and closed his eyes, breathing in the faint scent of her that still clung to the sheets, and the next thing he knew, the light crawling in through the room's only window told him it was nearly evening.

The house was quiet. Alex sat up and scrubbed his hands over his face. He looked at himself in the mirror, decided even a comb wouldn't help his hair, and stepped out into the hallway. The window that looked out over the front yard was broken and he shuddered, remembering the muffled thump of Kate's body hitting it and the wrenching noise of crashing glass. Beyond the spider-veined window, he saw two black-and-white patrol cars parked in front of the house, and a third police car in Earl and Marge's driveway. Both Earl and Marge were on the front porch, craning their necks and staring over at the house as if that would help them make sense out of everything that was happening.

He heard men's voices coming from the kitchen, and he remembered the makeshift command post. From the fact that the agents were debating between Chinese and Mexican, he assumed they were discussing dinner plans. The living room was empty except for a tall man in a gray suit who stood with his back to the stairway. When Alex got to the bottom of the stairs, Mark Harrison turned around. He was holding Stan and Missy's wedding picture.

"Nice couple." Mark replaced the photograph on the table next to the couch. He turned and looked at Alex. "Too bad there's no happily-ever-after in this story, huh?"

Alex didn't feel like making small talk. Or trying to guess the answers to riddles. He strode into the living room. "Where's Kate?" he asked.

Mark lifted his shoulders in a gesture that wasn't quite a full-fledged shrug. "Gone," he said simply. "The paramedics insisted she go to the hospital to—"

"She's all right, isn't she?" Though he was reasonably certain the cops weren't about to let him go anywhere, Alex couldn't help himself. At the mention of the hospital, a wave of something very much like panic broke over him. He moved toward the door. "If she's still there, I'd like to find out what's going on. Is she really hurt?"

"Physically? Emotionally? Or are we just talking about her career?"

Mark didn't strike Alex as the kind of guy who liked to play games. That was good. Because Alex wasn't in the mood for games, either. He pulled himself to a stop and felt a muscle bunch at the base of his jaw. "We're both adults," he told Mark. "Consenting adults. Don't give me that crap about the poor innocent woman and the big bad playboy. I've had a rough day, and stereotypes don't cut it."

"Good. Because I've had a rough day, too." Mark didn't look like he'd had a rough day. In spite of the fact that he must have just gotten off a plane and trekked over here to the wrong side of the railroad tracks, he looked crisp and professional. He wasn't a flashy dresser but then, he didn't need to be. Mark Harrison exuded the kind of aura that reminded people he was in charge. He strolled over to the couch, sat down, and straightened a black-and-gray tie that, while it matched his mid-price suit, was hardly inspired. He flicked a piece of lint from his trousers and leaned forward, his elbows on his knees. "You want to explain?" he asked.

"Explain?" It was on the tip of Alex's tongue to tell Mark he didn't owe anyone an explanation. Anyone but Kate. For some reason, the words wouldn't come. They were lost behind the memories that crowded around him: the sounds of the gunfire and the crashing glass and the sickening clump of bodies rolling down the stairs, and the realization that through it all, Alex had never once worried about getting shot or getting killed. He'd thought only of Kate.

"No explanation," he said, and because he wasn't used to looking ignorant or spineless, he turned away. "You wouldn't understand anyway."

"Try me."

Alex looked over his shoulder at the older man. Mark Harrison was nearing retirement age, and it was clear at a glance that he'd seen more in his years with the FBI than Alex could even imagine. His face was a map of lines and well-worn furrows that, no doubt, had come more from frowning than smiling. His eyes were as impenetrable as his expression.

Alex watched him adjust the cuffs of his crisp, white shirt and something caught his eye. "You're wearing a wedding ring." It was something Alex hadn't noticed the first time he'd met Mark. But then, he'd been a little preoccupied that time, first with trying to talk Mark and his entourage out of shanghaiing him, then with trying to keep himself alive. "You been married a long time?"

"Thirty-six years tomorrow." It must have been a trick

of the late afternoon light. For a moment, Mark looked almost wistful. "Three kids. Five grandkids, and another one on the way. I hope to God it's a girl. Five boys, and Grandpa never gets a moment's peace."

"Thirty-six years. Wow." It sounded banal. Like the kind of conversation Alex was used to trading at cocktail parties. But he meant it. Thirty-six years was a long time. And he was impressed. "Thirty-six years. And the same woman, all that time?"

Mark nodded, and for a second, his steely exterior faded enough for Alex to see the man behind it. A man who, after thirty-six years, was still very much in love with his wife.

"Then you do understand, don't you?" Alex asked him. "You know I'd never do anything to hurt Kate."

What there was of a dreamy expression on Mark's face closed down as if steel doors had slammed on it. He didn't have to move a muscle for Alex to know he was angry. "You almost got her killed," he said.

It was the same thought that had been tormenting Alex since the commotion had quieted down enough to allow him to think. The same thought that had pounded through his dreams during his nap and followed him around even now, mirroring his steps and mocking him. If they had been sleeping soundly, if Kate hadn't woken up and realized the power was off, he and Kate would both be dead.

"I'm willing to accept part of the fault," Alex said. "But not the blame. In spite of what you and Kate think, it wasn't Norbert who betrayed me. It couldn't have been."

"Yet, you talked to him." Mark picked up a file from the pile of folders on the couch next to him and flipped through some papers inside. "Just about a week ago. You met with him and talked to him. And before that, he knew you were in Cleveland because of a bank statement."

"Yes." There was no use denying the obvious, and nothing to feel guilty about. Alex raised his chin.

"And my guess is that when that statement crossed

Mr. Fielding's desk is just about when our friend Joe Bartone decided to cut short his trip to the Riviera."

"We don't know that for sure. Besides—"

"And was that a personal statement?" Mark looked Alex right in the eye. "You know what I mean, Mr. Romero. Was that a company account, or was it just your personal account?"

There was something about the FBI nosing into his business that didn't sit well with him, something about Mark questioning Norbert's loyalty and Alex's judgment that made him talk from between clenched teeth. "It was a personal account."

"And were your personal bank statements routinely seen by other folks in your company? Accountants? Bookkeepers? Mail clerks?"

"No. Not that particular account. That statement was for Norbert's eyes only. But—"

"So Mr. Fielding received the statement personally? He was the only one who saw it?"

"Yes. But—" It was instinct to try and defend Norbert. Instinct that made Alex shoot forward. And common sense that told him what Mark said was true. But coincidence didn't automatically mean guilt. He dropped into the chair across from Mark.

"Glad you're finally seeing the sense of this," Mark commented. Lucky for him, he didn't look any happier about the situation than Alex felt. He was pretty sure he wouldn't be able to control himself if Mark decided to gloat. Not a good idea, considering that assaulting a federal officer was probably some kind of offense that would have him in a jail cell with even less ambiance than the little house overlooking the steel mills.

"Looks like your friend Fielding contacted Bartone and told him he was on the wrong track; you weren't on the *Calypso*. So Bartone came back to the States and waited for more information. You apparently gave Fielding all he needed when you talked to him at that—" Again,

Mark flipped through the pages of the report. He looked over at Alex uncertainly. "Wrestling match?"

There was no way he could ever explain, so Alex didn't even try. He thought back to his meeting with Norbert in the little utility room at the arena. As Alex had already admitted—first to the FBI agents who'd questioned him about it and later to the Cleveland detectives who'd asked all the same questions—he'd all but presented Norbert with an engraved business card that included his address and phone number. He'd told Norbert about the house and the neighborhood. He'd even mentioned his alias. But hell, that didn't mean anything. Norbert was his friend. Norbert never would have betrayed him.

"I'm not buying it." Too on-edge to keep still, Alex got up and stalked to the other side of the room. He got as far as the stairway before he turned and paced back the other way. "Theories are great. Especially when they make everything fall into nice, neat boxes. But I'm just not buying it. The way I remember all those cop shows on TV, you'd need to prove both motive and opportunity. All right, I admit it. I gave him the opportunity. But what about the motive? Why would Norbert possibly want to get me killed?"

"The oldest motive in the book. And I don't mean love." Good thing Mark wasn't trying to be funny. His joke fell flat against the feeling that twisted through Alex's gut.

This time Mark reached into another folder. He came out holding a single sheet of paper covered with numbers. Alex didn't have to take a close look at them to know what they showed. He swallowed hard, and braced himself against what he knew was coming.

"At just about the time you were watching the personals for word from Mr. Fielding, he was depositing a rather sizable amount in one of his bank accounts."

"Thirty pieces of silver?" Alex snorted a laugh. He didn't know why. It wasn't funny.

Mark didn't think so, either. "More like four million," he said. "All in cash."

"Four—" Again, the sheer impossibility of the whole thing overwhelmed Alex. He grappled with everything Mark said, and one last time, tried to talk himself out of believing what looked like the truth. "Has anyone even talked to Norbert about this? I guarantee you he'll have an explanation. He's a good and honest man, and I won't see him railroaded. Not for something he couldn't possibly have done."

"I'd love to talk to Mr. Fielding." Tugging on his left earlobe, Mark rose from the couch. "Problem is, we can't find him. He's missing."

"No." Alex shook his head. "That's impossible. People like Norbert just don't go missing. Norbert plays miniature golf with his kids. He grows tomatoes. He's not the kind of guy who disappears. He was just in Central America. You knew that, didn't you?"

"Now that Special Agent Ellison told us about your connection to Ruben Martinez, we do. Fielding landed in New York fourteen hours after delivering the money for Martinez's release." Again, Mark paged through the report. He snapped the folder closed. "That's the last anyone's seen of him."

"But there's Allison and the kids." Alex scraped a hand through his hair. "They must be gone, too. Which proves they're just on vacation or something. Norbert would never—"

"Mrs. Fielding and the children are in Connecticut where they've always been. She hasn't seen her husband, or heard from him. Has no idea what might have happened to him."

"An accident. A kidnapping." Even to his own ears, Alex's voice sounded a little too desperate. He couldn't help himself. Every word Mark spoke was another chink in a wall of trust and friendship Alex had always assumed was strong and solid. "You guys are the FBI. You're supposed to be on top of these things. Have you checked the hospitals?"

"We've checked. Everywhere." Mark looked away and

Alex knew, whatever he was going to say, it was going to be the final break that would make the wall come tumbling down. "The same day Fielding got back from Central America, he withdrew that four million from his bank account. That's when he disappeared."

"So he left, and took the money with him." The words settled inside Alex like ice, and he knew suddenly what it would have felt like if Joe Bartone had succeeded. If he was dead. He felt the cold settle inside him. "And when he finds out Bartone wasn't successful?" he asked.

Mark shrugged. "My guess is that Mr. Fielding is already out of the country. As for Bartone . . ." He hauled in a long breath and let it out again. "I have no doubt that he'll be back for another try. Which is why you're leaving."

"Leaving?" Alex tried to understand the enormity of the word. It was no use. After months of what felt like solitary confinement, it was impossible to make any sense of the concept. He understood suddenly why Ruben Martinez had looked so stunned when he stood before the cameras at the Los Angeles airport. Freedom was a glowing ideal. But it was also a tough idea to grasp, especially when it was so unexpected.

"You're going back to New York, Mr. Romero. And you're leaving—" Mark glanced at the slim black watch on his right wrist. "You're leaving in exactly forty-five minutes. Between us, the NYPD, and your own security people, we feel you'll be safer there. Certainly safer than you would be here."

"And Kate?"

Mark turned and collected the folders from the couch. He tapped them into a neat pile. "I told you, she's gone," he said, and he didn't bother to turn around and look at Alex.

The truth of what Mark was saying hit, and suddenly Alex didn't feel so cold anymore. "You can't do that." He tried to measure his words, to make himself sound reasonable instead of like some lunatic who didn't stop to think before he spoke. But that was easier said than done. He didn't feel logical and reasonable. Not when it came to Kate.

"You can't take her off this case. It's hers, and she's done a damned good job of it. She's put everything she had into this case." Fortunately Mark wasn't crass enough to point out that double entendres did not become Alex. He ignored the comment and Alex went right on. "She kept me safe. Plenty of times. At the Laundromat, and when I was dumb enough to go out to Kmart on my own. She came after me. She did everything she could to do her duty. You can't blame her for this mess. Not when it's all my fault."

One of the men in the kitchen answered a ringing phone and called for Mark. He headed that way but not before he turned back to Alex. "You've got me all wrong, Mr. Romero. I know Special Agent Ellison's value to this investigation and to this organization. There are . . . problems with what happened here. I'll admit that. But there are ways around problems. Kate is a good agent. I'd never take her off this case. No." He shook his head. "She did that herself. Requested administrative leave, and I had no choice but to give it to her. Last I saw her, she was getting into a cab, heading for the airport."

The agent in the kitchen called for Mark again. Before he opened the door, he glanced back at Alex. "If you're smart, you'll just forget the whole thing. Let her go. It would be the best thing for both of you."

When the phone rang, Kate didn't even bother to glance over at it. She supposed in the great scheme of things, that was a good sign. It meant she was doing better. Better than what, of course, was the question.

Since she'd left Cleveland and come home to her Manhattan co-op to drown her troubles in pints of Ben & Jerry's, bags of double-buttered microwave popcorn, and every sad love song she could find in the oldies collections at the local music store, she had gone from jumping when the phone rang to pretty much ignoring it. Not bad in a week's time. Especially considering the phone had been ringing a lot. In another month or two, she might actually progress all the way to unplugging her answering machine.

She hadn't made it that far yet, and she heard her own voice repeat some inane message about not being able to pick up the phone, and the beep that followed.

"Kate? It's me, Alex." The familiar voice filled Kate's living room and tunneled straight through to her heart. She ignored that, too. Just the way she'd ignored it the last time Alex called. And the time before that. And the time before that. The times before that, the way she remembered things, she wasn't as immune to the smoky undertone of his words, or the way her skin tingled when he said her name. She'd gotten better and that, at least, was a good thing.

It was like Pavlov's dogs. Only in reverse. Little by little, she was learning not to salivate at the sound of the bell.

"Kate, you haven't returned my call. Any of my calls. I wish you would. I really need to talk to you."

"You do not." She had just finished her lunch, a bag of theater-style, extra-salty, extra-greasy popcorn, and she wadded the empty bag into a tight ball and tossed it at the answering machine. She missed by a mile. "You don't need to talk to somebody who almost got you killed."

Alex hung up, and the tape in the answering machine clicked to a stop. Kate watched the little red light on the side of the machine blink.

On. Off. On. Off.

It was enough to make her crazy.

She pulled herself off the couch and went over to the machine. She hit the delete button without bothering to listen to the message again.

"Besides, how did you even get my number?" Kate listened to the whir of the tape as it rewound. She glared at the machine, as if somehow she could see Alex through it. "My number is unlisted," she said. "Un-listed. That means you shouldn't even be calling me. That means you shouldn't even have it. But then, I suppose when you have enough money, you can buy anything you want."

The thought did little to comfort her, and she wandered from the living room into the kitchen and put the kettle on to boil. Chunky Monkey for breakfast and popcorn for lunch. Her stomach was not amused. She rattled through the cupboards until she found the box of peppermint tea she kept for just such emergencies, and plopped a tea bag into a mug. When the water boiled, she steeped the tea, loaded it with sugar, and went back to the couch.

Just as she sat, the phone rang again.

Kate glanced at the antique kitchen clock that sat next to J. Edgar the goldfish on a bookshelf on the other side of the room. Ten minutes. A record, even for Alex.

"Go away, Alex. I'm not listening!" She grabbed the remote and snapped on the TV and turned up the volume until the televangelist on the screen was talking loud enough to drown out the voice on the answering machine. Which is why she never even realized it was Mark Harrison on the phone until she heard the final words of his message.

". . . certainly changes things," Mark was saying, and Kate punched the volume button on the remote over and over until the little graphic that popped up on the TV screen showed it was as low as it could get.

"I know you're technically still on leave," Mark said, "but I thought you'd like to know. Looks like things aren't as cut-and-dried as we thought. I don't know if this means Mr. Romero is in more danger than we thought, but . . . well . . . We'll talk when you call."

"Talk? About what?" Kate leapt off the couch and hurried to the phone. Her curiosity was piqued; the hair on the back of her neck was standing on end at the apprehension in Mark's voice and the mention that Alex might be in danger. She picked up the receiver.

"I'm here," she said. "I'm here, Mark. What are you—"

She was answered by the sound of a dial tone.

Frustration boiled through Kate, and she punched in Mark's private number. She was talking even before he'd identified himself.

"It's me," Kate said. "I didn't hear your message. What's going on?"

"It probably doesn't mean anything," Mark began, and Kate felt her frustration level kick up a notch. She heard him shuffle through some papers. "We found Norbert Fielding," he told her. "In New Jersey, of all places. Shot through the back of the head. He's dead."

It wasn't something she expected to hear, and it took Kate a long moment to process the information. "Dead?" Even after a long moment, the news didn't make any sense. "Why would he be—"

"I know. It doesn't fit. He betrays Romero, collects his money, and skips town. The only thing I can figure is that Bartone was pissed that after all that effort, he didn't get the chance to kill Romero when he paid you that little visit. Before you shoot that theory full of holes, let me tell you not to bother. I've already done that myself. It doesn't make a lot of sense, does it? Bartone is a professional. He wouldn't waste time on this kind of revenge killing. Not when he still had Romero to take care of."

"Unless Alex was right all along." The magnitude of what she was saying hit Kate even as the words left her mouth. Her knees crumpled, and she dropped into the chair next to the phone. "Mark, what if Alex was right? What if it wasn't Fielding? What if he didn't betray Alex? Or collect the money? Or skip town?"

"It had to be him." Even without seeing him, she knew Mark was tugging at his left earlobe. "All the evidence points to Fielding. He knew Romero's location, even before he talked to Romero at the wrestling match. He got the debit statement, remember? He knew you were in Cleveland, and—"

"What if someone else saw that statement?"

"Someone like—?"

Kate leaned down and grabbed her tennis shoes. She slipped them on and had them tied before Mark could even continue. "There's no time for theories," she told him. "Where's Alex? Who's with him?"

She heard Mark shuffle through papers. "He's working at home," he said.

"Manhattan or Long Island?"

Again, she heard the papers. "Long Island," he answered. "But honestly, I really didn't want you to worry. I just thought you should know what was going on. Romero's as snug as the old proverbial bug. There's a squad car stationed outside, and we've got agents close by. His own security people have been with him round the clock since we brought him back. I'll give them a call. Let them know they need to be careful. You think—"

It was drizzling, and Kate grabbed her jacket from the peg near the door and slipped it on. She reached for her sleek black leather purse, made sure her gun was inside it and loaded, and slung the shoulder strap over her arm. "I don't know what to think," she said. "But I do know one thing. If Norbert didn't double-cross Alex, someone else did. And if Alex doesn't suspect that someone, he could be in a lot of trouble."

"You're probably right. I'll get right on it. Only, Kate . . ." She heard the hesitation in Mark's voice. It was unusual for Mark to let doubts creep into his thoughts, and even more unusual for him to let them play out in his words. That was the only thing that kept her from rushing out the door.

"What?"

"I hear you charging around, Kate. I know what you're doing. Do you think it's a good idea to go out there?" Mark asked. "Do you think it's a good idea for you to see him?"

"No." There was no hesitation in Kate's answer. She

was certain that seeing Alex again was a big mistake. "I don't think it's a good idea at all."

She headed for the door anyway.

By the time Kate got to Alex's Long Island home, it was raining in earnest. The front door was protected by a roof held up by giant stone pillars, but the wind was blowing and rain pounded against the front door. She hunched down into her jacket and turned her back on the sweep of lawn and the spectacular view of the ocean beyond. She stamped her feet against the cold and wet that made its way clear through her, the one that had nothing to do with the temperature and everything to do with the fact that she didn't like what was going on even one little bit.

She didn't like that no matter how many times she'd called from the car, Alex didn't answer the phone. She didn't like that when she called Mark, she learned he hadn't been able to get hold of anyone at the house, either. She didn't like that when she pulled up to the impressive, curving and very long driveway, the gatehouse was empty but the iron gates that swung across the drive were open. She didn't like that the police who Mark had assured her were on duty were nowhere in sight, or that the FBI agents he'd told her were "close" obviously weren't close enough to stop her when she drove in, parked her car, and marched up to the front door, unnoticed and unchallenged.

She thought about ringing the bell and decided it probably wasn't the wisest course of action. If something was wrong . . .

Kate remembered the debacle back in Cleveland, the terrifying *rat-a-tat* of the automatic gunfire and the way Alex dropped to the floor next to the bed. She thought about the panic that overwhelmed her when she didn't know if he was dead or alive, and a chill caromed through her. She forced it down. She didn't have the luxury of allowing personal feelings to get in the way of her duty. Not this time. Especially since even after a lifetime's supply of Ben & Jerry's, a truckload of popcorn, and more sad songs than she ever knew had ever been written, she still wasn't sure what those personal feelings were.

Instead of the bell, she reached for the front door. She wiped her wet hands against her wetter jeans. The knob turned easily in her hand.

"Probable cause," she reminded herself in a whisper. "You've got to have probable cause or you can't search without a warrant. You can't just walk in." But then she told herself to shut up. When the time came, she'd figure out a probable cause. If she had to. She'd work it through and find some probable cause. Right after she worked through the part about her personal feelings.

Moving quietly in her sneakers, Kate stepped into the front entryway and paused long enough to swipe her wet hair away from her face. Any self-respecting billionaire should have had a security system that announced her arrival loud and clear before she ever got this far. The fact that Alex didn't—or that it wasn't working—only served to further her misgivings. She took her gun out of her purse and carefully made her way through the house.

The place gave the words "stately mansion" new meaning, from the rooms that were big enough to hold her entire apartment to the stained glass windows, polished marble floors, and sweeping vistas from the floor-to-ceiling windows. She looked into a library, a formal parlor, a music room, and a dining room set with a silver service that took her breath away. But she didn't find Alex. She didn't find anyone.

Back at the entryway, Kate glanced up the winding staircase that dominated the foyer. She would search the upstairs, room by room if she had to. She was already on the bottom step and headed up when she thought she heard Alex's voice.

Kate paused and listened. It was Alex, all right, and the voice was coming from somewhere beyond the rooms she'd searched.

Relief overcame caution. Or at least it almost overcame

caution. Though she was tempted to run, toward the voice and toward Alex, Kate pulled back. Carefully she made her way down a long hallway lined with paintings. Her back to the wall, her gun clutched in both hands, she stopped outside a door that was partway open and listened.

"Have you tried Norbert's house yet this afternoon? I just can't believe he hasn't called Allison with some kind of message."

Alex sounded fine. Perfectly fine. Perfectly normal. And Kate breathed a sigh of relief. From the little she could see through the open doorway, it looked like this was Alex's office away from his office. The walls were lined with bookcases and a desk covered with files dominated the far side of the room. He'd even brought Charlotte along. She was seated in the chair across from the desk, pen in hand and a notepad poised on her knee. Kate stepped around the door and into the room.

Alex wondered if he'd been wasting his time all these years. He should have abandoned his business career and become a magician. He thought about Kate and, poof! Like magic, there she was. He narrowed his eyes and stared across the room at the vision that had interrupted the letter he was dictating.

Of course, he'd thought about Kate a lot in the last weeks, and she'd never appeared before.

The thought intruded on his brief moment of glory, as did its logical conclusion: If she had never appeared before, it meant she hadn't appeared this time, either. Not really. He was hallucinating. She was a figment of his imagination. Only when he imagined Kate, he imagined her as he'd seen her that last night in Cleveland, naked and eager. He thought about the silky feel of her beneath him, and the heat of her body as it surrounded his. He thought of her hair touched with silver in the moonlight, and her skin glowing warm with passion.

He didn't think of her in a navy blue windbreaker so soaked with rainwater, it stuck to her skin. Or with her hair plastered to her head and cheeks. He didn't picture her in jeans and sneakers that were so wet, they were leaving a puddle on his tongue-and-groove floor.

"Kate?" Alex popped out of his chair and shook away his fantasies. She wasn't an illusion, she was real, and his surprise melted into relief. And his relief turned into a grin. All this time he'd been calling and she hadn't been calling back. And now here she was—

Alex's smile wilted. Most women didn't make social calls carrying a gun.

"What are you doing here? How—?" He looked beyond Kate, out to the empty hallway. "How did you get in here?" he asked. "I didn't hear the bell. No one announced you."

"That's the problem, isn't it?" Kate stepped farther into the room, glancing around as she did, assessing everything in sight. Whatever she saw—or didn't see—she apparently approved. She tucked the gun into the purse she had slung over her shoulder. "We need to talk."

She came to talk?

Alex swallowed the taste of disappointment in his mouth. All this time, he'd been dreaming about Kate, and thinking about Kate and making bargains with God and the devil and anybody else who would listen. He'd trade anything and everything he had for one more night with Kate. And she came to talk?

Hanging out his emotions where his employees could see them wasn't Alex's style. If Charlotte hadn't been there, he might have given in to the temptation to race across the room and take Kate into his arms and kiss her until he convinced her that talking was the last thing they needed to do. But Charlotte was there. And Kate didn't look like she wanted to be kissed.

"We need to talk," she said again, her look as steely as her voice. She glanced at Charlotte before she swung her gaze back to Alex. "In private."

"We are in private." Alex wasn't about to be railroaded, either by his own emotions or by Kate. He checked the cuffs of his light blue oxford shirt, smoothed a wrinkle from his khakis, and went around to the front of his desk. "I assume you're here on business." He let his gaze flicker to the bag where Kate had stashed her gun and back again to her face, but he didn't give her time to answer. He didn't need to hear the words out loud. Of course she was there on business. What else would she be there for? "Anything you have to say, you can certainly say in front of Charlotte."

"All right." Kate drew in a long breath. "It's about Norbert. They found him. I'm sorry. . . ." Her gaze wavered, her voice faltered. She composed herself again in a heartbeat and went on. "I'm sorry, but he's dead."

Alex realized he had expected the news all along. He must have. It didn't surprise him. It didn't even make him angry. All he felt was a grief that tore through him like a knife. It was only the tip of the pain he'd feel for a long time to come. He knew that, too, and he set it aside until he could struggle with it in private. There were other things to worry about before he could indulge himself: Norbert's wife, his children, his reputation.

"So, I was right about Norbert all along. I knew he would never betray me." Alex was so relieved, he almost felt guilty. Neither emotion had time to take root. Another thought occurred to him, and his heart bumped against his chest. "But if it wasn't Norbert . . . Someone else?"

Kate nodded, and Alex knew exactly what she meant. If someone else had betrayed him, the danger might be closer than either of them had ever imagined. He knew what he had to do, and he reached for the phone.

"I wouldn't move too quickly, Mr. R." It was Charlotte who stopped him. Even before he looked at his secretary, he heard the malice in her voice. While he and Kate had been busy talking, Charlotte had come up behind Kate. She raised a gun to Kate's head.

Alex looked at his secretary, at her soft, wrinkled skin and her perfectly combed silver hair, at her pretty pink suit and her choker of tiny pearls. At her matching shoes and her pearl earrings and the touch of pink blush she wore on her cheeks. And he couldn't help himself; he had to laugh.

"This is some kind of joke, right?" His laugh fell flat against the desperation that shone in Charlotte's blue eyes. "You're not serious. You can't be. You can't be—"

"Quiet." Charlotte's voice shook. So did the gun. "Don't make this any harder for me than it already is. I like you, Mr. R. You know I do. You've been kind to me and to my family, but . . ." Her voice cracked and she swallowed hard and raised her chin. "The money's more important, I'm afraid."

"The four million." Alex had the feeling Kate would have liked to let out a groan along with the words. She controlled the show of weakness and kept herself perfectly calm and perfectly steady. "You got the four million from Bartone. You were the one who deposited it in Norbert's account, then took it out again. You knew we were in Cleveland all along."

"Not all along. Not until that statement showed up. Took you long enough," Charlotte said, glancing at Alex. "I thought we'd never find you. Of course, I saw the statement long before Norbert knew it had arrived. But I had to wait for him to go to Cleveland to meet you. Once he did, it was easy to have someone follow him. And you."

"And then they killed him." Alex stepped forward, and it took every ounce of self-control he had to keep himself from going head-to-head with Charlotte. He would have done it if the gun was pointed at him. He would have done it no matter what, except that it might endanger Kate. "Think about Norbert. Think about his kids. Doesn't that tell you what kind of people these are? They killed him, Charlotte," he said. "How can you live with yourself knowing that?"

"I'm sorry for that, too. But there are times . . ." This time, it was Charlotte's turn to laugh. There was no humor in the sound. A single tear rolled down her wrinkled cheek. "Junk bonds, bad stocks, poor investments. I've been trading on-line, Mr. R., and I've lost everything. I didn't know what to do. I didn't know where to turn. I—"

"You could have asked me. You know I would have helped, Charlotte."

"Oh, you would have helped, all right." Charlotte shook her head, dismissing the thought in much the same way she must have dismissed it when it first occurred to her. "But you would have known and every time you looked at me, you would have thought of it. You would have remembered how weak I am, and how I let things get out of hand. You'd never admit it. Mr. R. You aren't that small-minded. But somewhere in the back of your head, you would have remembered. And you would have thought less of me because of it. That's why when they called . . ."

"They." Alex nodded, finally understanding. "The guys who offered me a cut of the money laundering pie. The ones I'm scheduled to testify against."

Charlotte gave him a watery smile and sniffed back tears. "That's right. They knew the FBI would never make the mistake of letting anyone know where you were. But they thought I might be able to help. Just watch and listen. That's what they told me. Just watch and listen, and if I heard anything . . ." She shrugged. "Well, it was a godsend, that's what it was, Mr. R. They offered me four million just when I needed it most, and I couldn't say no, could I? Once you're out of the way and I get the money they promised, I can pay off my debts and no one will ever know how foolish I've been."

"So you're going to hand Alex over to them on a silver platter?" Kate looked from Alex to the fireplace across the room on his right. "You know it will never work, Charlotte." She did it again, slid her gaze toward Alex's right and finally, Alex got the message. She was planning something, and whatever it was, she wanted him to head in that direction when it happened. "What did you do, Charlotte? Give the staff the day off? Tell the cops they could leave because the FBI was here? Tell the FBI you didn't need them because the cops had everything under control? You've turned off the security system and left the front door unlocked. What are you planning?"

Kate's question was answered, and not by Charlotte. A car pulled up in the driveway and parked in front of the house, and by this time, even Alex recognized the man who got out of it. It was Joe Bartone, and he headed straight for the front door.

19

There wasn't time to think. There wasn't time to do anything but save Alex.

Once she was sure Alex knew what to do, Kate made her move. As fast as she could and with as much power as she could pack, she jammed her elbow into Charlotte's stomach. As if all the air had been let out of her, the older woman let out a muffled *oomph.* She lost her balance and her feet went out from under her. Just as Kate feared, she got one shot off. Just as Kate expected, it went to Charlotte's right, wide of its mark and far from where she'd instructed Alex to take cover.

Thank God. For once, he'd listened.

While Charlotte was still off balance, Kate snatched the gun out of her hands. She didn't need any more trouble from Charlotte, so just for good measure, she clunked her on the back of the head with the butt of the gun. Charlotte groaned. She was unconscious before she ever hit the floor.

By the time Kate turned around, Alex was staring at her.

"What?" Kate refused to feel guilty. She needed Charlotte out of the way and Charlotte was definitely out of the way. Her methods apparently made Alex uneasy. He looked from Charlotte to Kate.

"Glad you never got that mad at me."

"I did," Kate told him. She'd let him think about it. They didn't have time for chitchat. She pocketed Charlotte's gun, grabbed Alex's hand, and tugged him toward the door.

"No." Alex stood his ground. But only for the space of a heartbeat. He pulled her in the opposite direction. "Not that way. He's bound to find us. This way."

There was another door on the wall opposite the one Kate had come in. Alex pushed it open and before he could dart into the hallway beyond or get all John Wayne on her and insist on going first, she sidestepped her way around him and led the way. With Alex's hand on her shoulder guiding her, they twisted and turned their way through what seemed like miles of hallways and finally found themselves in the kitchen.

The place was a chef's dream of counter space, cooking islands, and stainless steel appliances. Kate didn't care about any one of them but the phone. It was on the wall next to the refrigerator and she hurried over to it, picked it up, then slammed it down again.

"Dead," she said. "Charlotte must have cut the lines. No wonder I couldn't get ahold of you earlier."

Alex took hold of her arm. "You tried to get ahold of me?" She didn't know why the question was so important, but it obviously was. He stared at her as if his life depended on the answer. "You called me back?"

A sizzle snaked its way right from his hand and through Kate's rain-soaked windbreaker. It crawled through her T-shirt and way down deep into her skin. Too bad she didn't have time to enjoy the way it made her insides feel as if they were made of molten wax. She heard a noise from the hall. "I called you back," she said in a harsh whisper. "I tried to warn you."

"You called me back to warn me?" Alex whispered back.

"Look . . ." Kate glanced toward the kitchen door. "I don't think we have time for this right now. We'll talk about our relationship problems later."

"But he's—"

"In the hall. Yeah. I know. He must have heard the shot and gone to the office first. But don't forget . . ." She looked down at her soaked clothing and her dripping tennis shoes. "I'm leaving a trail. It won't take him long to find us."

There was only one thing to do. Kate gave Alex a shove in the direction of a door that led outside. "We've got to split up, and you'll be safer out of the house."

Alex didn't budge. "But you—"

"Don't worry about me." Kate had both her gun and Charlotte's, and enough ammunition to last long enough for Alex to get away. "Get out of here. My car's parked up front. There's a phone in. Hit redial and you'll get Mark. He's the last one I called." There was another noise from the hallway. This one sounded closer than the last. She fished her keys out of her pocket and tossed them to him. "Then get the hell out of here."

Alex nodded, but he didn't move. Not right away. He skimmed a finger along Kate's jaw. "I'm sorry, Kate. About Cleveland."

The last thing she needed was a confession that would make her regret what had happened back in the little house overlooking the steel mill. Kate backed away from his touch. "Get out of here," she said. "That's an order."

Alex didn't look happy about it, but surprisingly he listened. Quickly and quietly, he made his way to the door. He opened it and ducked outside and Kate breathed a sigh of relief. Now to create a diversion.

It wasn't hard to do. She was standing behind a broad island with wide counters and numerous drawers. She yanked open the drawer closest to her and found it chock-full of silverware. She reached for a handful of spoons, lobbed them across the room and listened to them crash against the ceramic-tiled floor. That done, she positioned herself behind the island, prayed Alex would make it to the car to call for reinforcements, and prepared to make her stand.

Just as she expected, Bartone came in with guns blazing. Kate ducked behind the island and got off a couple shots of her own. Her aim was perfect, but Bartone was wearing a bullet-proof vest. The shots slowed him down, but they didn't stop him.

Kate pressed her advantage. She popped up from behind the island to squeeze off another shot. Or at least she would have squeezed off another shot. If her gun hadn't jammed.

Panic rippled through Kate, but she knew she didn't have the luxury to worry about it. She grabbed Charlotte's gun out of her pocket and used that. But Charlotte had intended her gun to be an intimidator, not a killer. Kate managed five more shots, and then her ammunition was gone.

She ducked back behind the island while she gathered the courage to run. She might actually have made a start if, the next thing she knew, she didn't feel the barrel of Joe Bartone's gun pressed to her head.

"Nice to see you again, Special Agent Ellison." With a curt movement of his head, Bartone ordered her to stand. Kate had no choice but to obey. She raised her hands and eyed him warily.

"Don't worry," Bartone said. "You know I didn't come here for you. You've been damned inconvenient, though. If you'll just tell me where Romero is—"

"You've got to be kidding." Kate wasn't sure what made her decide to argue with the guy. It was not right up there on the list of smart things to do when a hired hit man had a gun to your head. "Romero's not even here," she told him. "He's long gone. I knew about Charlotte and I warned him. Once I got here, he was already on his way back to the city."

"Wrong." Bartone nudged her with the gun, forcing her to turn her back to him. In spite of the fact that she told herself not to panic and reminded herself that she'd done all she could and that Alex was safe and that was really all that mattered, Kate couldn't help but think of poor Norbert Fielding and how he'd been shot in the back of the head. She gulped down the thought and the fear that came with it. At least her obituary wouldn't say she'd died while investigating a Smokey the Bear case. At least she knew she'd given her life for a good cause. At least she could go thinking about Alex and that one magical night they'd shared.

And die with a smile on her face.

She closed her eyes, as prepared as she ever would be to hear the final click that would tell her Bartone had pulled the trigger. But instead of a click, she heard a sickening thump. Behind her, Joe Bartone went limp.

Kate whirled around to find Bartone crumpled at her feet. Standing over him was Alex, with a death grip on the thing he'd used to knock Bartone out cold—his Worst Bowler of the Night trophy.

Kate blinked at him in wonder. Right before she snapped back to reality.

"I told you to get the hell out of here," she yelled.

Alex plunked the trophy down on the countertop and yelled right back. "That's a fine way to thank the guy who just saved your life."

"All right. Fine." Kate kicked Bartone's gun away from his hand and across the room and bent to retrieve it. She should feel relieved. Elated. Ecstatic. Yet all she felt was angry. Didn't the man ever listen? Didn't he know he could be dead right now? "Thank you," she growled.

"You're welcome," Alex barked right back.

The wail of a police siren coming up the drive punctuated their words, and Kate knew Alex had made the phone call that brought in the cavalry. She supposed she should thank him for that, too, and maybe someday she would. Right after she beat some sense into that gorgeous head of his.

"What kind of lunatic comes back to a house where a

hit man is trying to kill him?" She wouldn't have had to scream if there weren't so many police cars making so much racket outside, if she didn't have to make herself heard over the front door crashing in and the thunderous arrival of what sounded like half the population of Long Island.

"The kind of lunatic who was trying to save you," Alex screamed back. No doubt, he wanted to make himself heard, too.

"Great. You saved me." She pointed to where she'd dropped her purse on the floor near Alex's feet. "My handcuffs are in there," she told him. "Get them out, will you?"

She expected him to yell back. Or at least to resist. Instead, Alex scooped up her purse, reached inside, and grabbed the handcuffs. When he held them out to her, his face split with a heart-stopping grin. "Is that all you can think of at a time like this?" he asked.

Heat flooded Kate's face. And other portions of her anatomy. This time, it had nothing to do with anger. "It wasn't," she admitted. "At least not until you mentioned it." She glanced at the handcuffs dangling from Alex's hand, and the smile on his face, and the look of pure devilment that brightened his eyes. "But since you brought it up—"

She never had a chance to finish. The back door flew open and a SWAT team rushed in. The door from the hallway opened, too, and Mark and a couple of agents Kate knew from the office hurried into the kitchen. Right on their heels was a brigade of burly guys in dark suits; from the deferential way they approached Alex, she had no doubt they were his private security team.

"Get him out of here!" Mark called over the general chaos, pointing to Alex. The security guys surrounded him and hustled him out the door.

"Wait!" Kate called after him but this time, she knew Alex wouldn't hear her even if she yelled. There were more security guys out in the hallway. And cops. One of them had Charlotte in handcuffs and was leading her out to a waiting car. Kate darted her way in and out of the crowd, but the harder she tried, the harder it was to catch up with Alex.

By the time she got to the front door, there was an army of reporters and TV cameras outside waiting. They had, no doubt, gotten wind of the fact that the local police were waiting for something big to go down and they were ready to roll when it happened. They had their cameras rolling and their microphones out. She pulled to a stop outside the limits of the cameras' eyes and watched Alex extricate himself from the grip of the biggest and burliest security guy. He smoothed his shirt into place, ran a hand through his perfectly styled hair, and beamed a smile that Kate recognized. One that made her heart stop and her blood run cold.

It was the old smile, the Romeo smile, and she had no doubt it would be on the cover of every magazine in the checkout line at the grocery store in record time.

"Everything's under control," Alex said. He was as smooth as newly Zambonied ice. As calm as a mill pond. He glanced around; in spite of the crowd, and the rain, and the fact that he'd just escaped a killer, he was clearly in charge. "Thanks to the quick work of the FBI and the local police, everything's fine. I can't thank them enough, and for now, I can't comment any further."

A black limousine pulled up to the front of the house and the security guys hurried Alex over to it. They opened the back door, but before Alex got inside, he looked around.

Was he looking for Kate?

She stood on tiptoe behind the phalanx of reporters and cameramen and cops that blanketed the front steps, but it was impossible to tell if he saw her through the chaos.

Until she saw him smile.

Alex's smile lit up the rainy afternoon, and Kate felt an answering smile well up inside her.

Then she saw the camera. The one Alex had intended his smile for.

Kate dropped back down to the soles of her sneakers and moved away from the doorway. She'd forgotten. After a summer of pretending he was someone else—and a night of believing it could actually be true—she'd forgotten who and what Alex Romero really was.

Cameras flashed and reporters screamed questions, and through it all, Alex looked as if he was born to play the starring role in this little drama. He was the old Alex Romero.

By the time the security team finally got Alex into the limo and drove away, Kate realized she was going to be sick.

This time, it wasn't from the popcorn.

After the trial was finally over and all the guilty verdicts were in, Kate waited inside the courthouse a full hour. She congratulated the prosecutors and talked to Mark and the New York cops who had testified. She dawdled getting her raincoat on and grabbing her briefcase because she hoped if she waited long enough, all the cameras and reporters would be gone and all the hoopla would be over.

She was right.

By the time she stepped out into the gathering gray twilight and felt the December wind whip her raincoat around her knees, the steps of the federal courthouse were deserted.

A chill stole down the neck of her raincoat and she shivered. In spite of the cold and a sky that promised the snow the local forecasters predicted, she thought she might walk home. She knew it was pathetic in a romantic comedy movie sort of way, but pathetic was pretty much in line with how she was feeling.

"Congratulations."

The sound of Alex's voice startled Kate out of her grim thoughts. She turned and found him standing on the sidewalk, his hands in the pockets of his dark cashmere coat.

"You won your case. Congratulations."

Kate forced a smile. "We couldn't have done it without you," she said. It was true, and it was the least she could tell him. "You did a great job testifying. You had all the facts and all the figures."

"Hey, I've got a great staff. They take care of stuff like that." Alex's smile came and went. "So . . ." He shuffled from foot to foot and looked down the street toward the sleek limo that was obviously waiting for him.

"So . . ." Kate shifted her briefcase from her right hand into her left. "Congratulations to you, too. On the Ruben Martinez thing." Her gaze drifted briefly to the newspaper box on the sidewalk nearby and to the picture on the front page that showed Ruben Martinez in Oslo accepting the year's Nobel Peace Prize.

Alex shrugged, as if the fact that he had saved the life of a man who was quickly becoming a cultural icon and a symbol of free speech was no big deal. "We haven't talked," he said.

It was the understatement of the year. They'd barely spoken a word since the day late in the summer when Joe Bartone paid a house call in Long Island. "You've been avoiding me."

Kate looked over Alex's shoulder toward the waiting limo. "I've been busy."

"You've been avoiding me."

"Look . . ." Kate drew in a long breath and let it out again, and it puffed around her in a frigid little cloud. She didn't want to lay her failures out for all the world to see right there on a Manhattan street corner, but something told her she didn't have any choice. If she didn't get the words out now, they'd haunt her for the rest of her life. And she'd probably never have a chance to tell Alex again.

"Yes, I have been avoiding you." She bit down on her lower lip, composing herself. "I appreciated the flowers.

All of them." She thought back to the dozens of roses that had arrived in the days right after the incident on Long Island. "And I appreciate that you tried to call. I don't even know how many times because I unplugged my answering machine."

"A lot of times."

"A lot of times." That didn't make her feel much better. "I didn't talk to you . . . I couldn't . . . I won't. . . ." She whirled away, though why she hoped to find the words she was looking for somewhere in the gray landscape of streets and skyscrapers, she didn't know. She turned around again. "You said it yourself, Alex. You said you were sorry for what happened in Cleveland."

Alex looked at her in wonder, obviously struggling to remember what the hell she was talking about. It dawned on him in an instant and he took a quick step forward, his hand out. He stopped himself before he touched the sleeve of Kate's raincoat and she was glad. She didn't need the heat of Alex's hand to remind her how cold she was feeling.

"I said I was sorry, and you thought . . ." He shook his head. "I meant I was sorry because I almost got you killed."

Wasn't it just like him to hog the spotlight?

"No. I almost got you killed."

Alex pulled one hand out of his pocket and scraped it across his chin. "No," he said. "I almost got me killed. And I almost got you killed, too. And that's what I was sorry about. Can you ever forgive me for that, Kate?"

"Forgive? You?" He had to be kidding. Even now, with their professional relationship at an end and what there was of a personal relationship in a shambles, the man had no sense of how to behave. "Why would I need to forgive you? I'm the one who lost control of the situation. Hell, I even lost control of me."

"I like it when you lose control."

Alex gave her a little half-smile and Kate's heart crashed against her ribs. She had to cut and run—fast.

Before she convinced herself there was anything more to the twinkle in his eyes than the usual Romeo charisma.

"I was unprofessional," she said, and he didn't contradict her. How could he? "I was out of line. I'm glad it ended well. I'm glad you're all right. Now you can go back to your world, and I'll—"

"Go sleep in the ashes by the fireplace?" Alex chuckled. But though it looked as if he would have liked to say more, he glanced at his watch instead, and at the waiting limousine. "Look, I've got to go. I promised Norbert's wife I'd stop over there today, and I'm going to be late."

"Oh, God!" Kate groaned. So much for the sad finish to their star-crossed relationship. There were other things they had to talk about, things that were more important than the fact that her heart was broken in about a zillion pieces. "I've been so tacky. I heard what you did. For the kids. I heard about the trust funds you set up for them—"

Alex stopped her, one hand in the air. "It's the least I can do," he said. "Norbert was a good friend, and I owe him big time." He stopped and cleared his throat. "Look, I've got an invitation to a movie premiere and—"

"I don't think so." There was no use fooling herself. Movies weren't what Kate wanted from Alex. She wasn't looking for the lights and the cameras, even if she did admit she was looking for the action. She wasn't looking for the glitz and glamor. She wanted to share a lifetime with Alex, not a headline. She wanted his mornings, noons, and nights. She wanted to open Christmas gifts with him, and cry at their children's weddings and grow old talking about how they'd shared a remarkable summer. "I've got to go."

Kate turned and walked away, and for what seemed like too long a time, Alex watched her go. He watched the familiar swing of her hips, and the confident way she carried herself, and instead of seeing a highly trained professional who'd saved his life, he saw a woman. And his future.

And they were both getting farther away from him by the second.

Alex pulled himself out of the trance that held him and hurried after Kate. She stopped at a cross street and he closed the distance between them. He was almost all the way to her when something lying on the sidewalk caught his eye. He stopped, smiled, and bent to retrieve it.

Kate stopped to wait for traffic at the next cross street and blinked away a tear. She refused to turn around and watch Alex's limousine pull away. She knew she was a coward, but she couldn't do it. Even though she knew they had just said good-bye forever, there was something about watching him drive away that would have made it official.

The light changed, and she was just about to cross the street when somebody thrust something over her shoulder.

Startled, Kate turned around. Alex was right behind her. He was holding out a pink gum wrapper.

"Look. I just found it. It's our good-luck charm, remember? From bingo."

Kate looked from the gum wrapper up into the tiny flicker of hope that flashed in Alex's eyes. A smile blossomed on her face. "And what do you think that good-luck charm is all about?"

"Can't say." Alex tucked the gum wrapper into his pocket and patted it. "But I know an omen when I see one, and the way I see this one, it's a pretty good omen. I'll tell you what, let's skip the movie premiere. How about a date, Special Agent Ellison? A real date."

It was tempting. But so was keeping her sanity. Kate's smile faded and she shook her head. "What's the use?" she asked. "You're you and I'm me, and—"

"And we hardly know each other. Not really. All right, we lived together all summer." The logic of Alex's argument dissolved around him and his shoulders dropped. He recovered his legendary aplomb in a heartbeat and attacked the problem from a new angle. "But that wasn't us. That was Stan and Missy. Let's give Kate and Alex a try and see what develops."

It seemed a safe enough compromise.

"Just a try, right?"

"A try." Alex wound his arm through Kate's and turned her in the direction of the waiting limousine. "I've still got to make that stop to see Allison Fielding. But after that, what do you say to a game of bowling?"

Six Months Later

According to the guests who packed the church to the rafters, it was the most beautiful wedding ever.

The bride wore a gown with too much beading, too much lace, and a bodice that was cut low enough to expose too much cleavage. She carried a bouquet of white lilies, pink roses, and white satin streamers that trailed halfway down the front of her gown, and wore white satin gloves that came up past her elbows. In a move some of the more traditional ladies in attendance didn't quite understand but forgave nonetheless, she passed on both a veil and a beaded tiara and opted instead for a single tiny white rose in her hair. It was agreed all around that though the effect was less showy, it did look elegant, and the groom seemed to approve.

As was expected, he looked particularly handsome in his tux. He stammered his way through the exchange of vows and his hands shook as he placed a simple gold band on the bride's finger and she did the same for him. That seemed to surprise a number of those in attendance who had assumed he would be as cool, calm, and collected as usual, but it apparently charmed the bride. Her smile could be seen all the way from the back of the church.

After the ceremony, the happy couple paused briefly on the church steps for photographs. The groom looped an arm around the bride's waist and looked down into her eyes, and there was so much love in that look and in the lingering kiss he pressed to her lips, even the lone, purple-clad bridesmaid (who was used to crying over happy endings) couldn't keep from clutching the arm of the best man, who happened to be her husband, and sobbing her approval.

In a move that thrilled the paparazzi and confounded the security team who watched the proceedings from behind their Ray-Bans, the bride and groom decided to walk to their wedding reception. They led a parade of the rich, the powerful, and the commonplace through the streets, and when cars horns blared, the crowd waved.

When they got to the reception, the bride and groom stopped outside to allow their guests to go in ahead of them.

Alex watched the last of the guests disappear inside. He swooped Kate into his arms and held her close against him, and his gaze flickered briefly to where the swell of her breasts showed above the low-cut bodice of her gown. "Alone, at last!" he growled.

"If you call this being alone." Kate glanced up to where a helicopter from one of the TV networks hovered just above the treetops. "What do you say, Romeo?" She gave her husband a smile that promised all the love they'd vowed in church only a short time before. "You want to give the folks in the checkout lines at the grocery stores something to talk about?"

"Oh, yeah!" Alex grinned. He slanted his mouth down on Kate's and she put her arms around his neck, and if at the start they intended the kiss as nothing but showmanship, they forgot about the cameras and the crowds and the whirring helicopter soon enough.

"Ready to go inside?" Alex's smile brushed Kate's lips. He didn't sound any more ready than she felt. As much as she wanted to celebrate with her family and friends, she just as soon would have skipped the reception and gone right on to the honeymoon. She had packed the white nightgown, and the *Calypso* was waiting in Cannes. Kate was anxious to get Alex aboard—and have him all to herself.

But then she remembered her duty.

"Ready," she said. She twined her fingers through Alex's and he opened the door. The music of Hank Markiewicz and the Polka Dots greeted them as side by side, they walked into the reception and the warm welcome of their guests.

The doors to Stosh's Bowl-O-Matic swished closed behind them.

ABOUT THE AUTHOR

Connie Lane was born and raised in Cleveland, Ohio. She has worked as a journalist, editor, and creative writing teacher. Under the name Constance Laux, she has written a number of highly acclaimed historical romances. She has been nominated for the prestigious RITA award by Romance Writers of America and has received the KISS award from *Romantic Times* magazine as well as a nomination from *RT* for historical romance of the year in the Love & Laughter category. She now lives in a suburb of Cleveland with her husband and two children.